SALT
HOUSE
PLACE

SALT HOUSE PLACE

A NOVEL

JAMIE LEE SOGN

Published by Lake Union Publishing, Seattle

www.apub.com

Amazon, the Amazon logo, and Lake Union Publishing are trademarks of Amazon.com, Inc., or its affiliates.

ISBN-13: 9781662510861 (hardcover)
ISBN-13: 9781662510854 (paperback)
ISBN-13: 9781662510878 (digital)

Cover design by Laywan Kwan
Cover image: © Edalin Photography / Shutterstock;
© Jon Feingersh Photography Inc / Getty; © bradleyhebdon / Getty;
© Kniel Synnatzschke / plainpicture

Printed in the United States of America
First edition

PRAISE FOR JAMIE LEE SOGN

"A masterful tale of lost and toxic friendships, *Salthouse Place* is full of twists you won't see coming and will have you racing to the end in one more explosive, heart-pounding revelation."

—Lyn Liao Butler, author of *Someone Else's Life*

"This slow-burn tale of friendship, grief, and the seductive allure of cults ratchets up in intensity as the pages turn, culminating in twist after shocking twist. Fans of *Nine Perfect Strangers* will devour *Salthouse Place* and root for Delia, the appealing heroine."

—Sarah Pekkanen, *New York Times* bestselling author of *The Golden Couple* and the upcoming novel *Gone Tonight*

To my parents, who taught me to love words.
And to David, who gave me the courage to share my own.

CHAPTER 1

Then

The same summer I lost my virginity to my best friend's brother, I lost my other best friend to the waves and depths of Blythe Lake. In the morning, before the full brunt of the July heat hit us, we piled stolen beers and wine coolers onto our inflatable pool float and set sail to our destination, a wooden platform in the middle of the lake. Cara swam out in front, the float's rope tied around her torso as she cut through the water's mirrored surface. Zee and I followed on either side of the float, righting it in the wake lest our precious supply fall. At one point, we stopped paying attention and a lone can of PBR tilted and rolled off. I saw it out of the corner of my eye before it vanished into the water.

"No!" I wailed and dunked my head below, grasping for it. It sank fast, and I lost sight of it in the murky silt far below.

When I surfaced, Zee tattled on me. "Delia lost one!"

Cara tossed her blonde hair over her shoulder and looked back, laughing. "Delia, you bitch! Tom would kill you if he knew you were wasting his stash!"

It wouldn't be a month later that Tom Snyder, already enrolled in the local community college, would take me in his arms and whisper into my flesh how beautifully sad I was. Even then, the thought of him ignited something in me: a heat that warmed my body in the cool water. That morning, his blue eyes, which always looked a bit sleepy, had followed us with suspicion as we tumbled out of the Snyder house in bikini tops and cutoff denim shorts.

"Looks like trouble," Gary Snyder, Cara's dad, commented while flipping a pancake. "You girls won't even stay for breakfast?"

Zee picked up a stack of pancakes in her bare hands. "We'll take it to go."

"Sorry, Mr. Snyder," I apologized for Zee. "They look delicious."

"Delia, come on," Cara called to me from the door.

Tom sipped his coffee and turned his attention back to his phone, where I imagined he must be messaging dozens of girls prettier than me. Little did he know our backpacks contained booze we had pilfered from under his bed, where Mrs. Snyder didn't clean. "The best part is he can't say anything." Cara had laughed as she reached and pushed aside dirty magazines to get to the last six-pack in the very back, against the wall.

Zee handed out pancakes, and we ate while walking down the Snyder driveway, a long and winding unpaved road connecting to the lakeside boulevard, where the biggest houses stood.

Our floatie of contraband made it the rest of the way with no further casualties. We carefully transported the load to the safety of the platform, its wooden planks smoothed over from a decade of sun and water, the underside lined with algae, which extended down the long chain connected to the concrete anchor somewhere down deep. In busier times, boys would hold contests to see who could dive the farthest and try to touch the anchor. Nobody ever could. It was a Tuesday, or maybe a Wednesday, and though the lake had been full the weekend before for the Fourth of July, it was quiet now. We were the only ones as far as we could see. It was the summer before our junior year in high school, and the only thing greater than the endless blue skies above us was the possibilities.

We slipped out of our shorts and laid out our long limbs on the bobbing raft. Zee handed out drinks, and we cheered for nothing in particular. My shoulders and Zee's were brown and freckled with summer; our dark hair glinted with streaks of orange from Sun-In hair formula.

Cara, already pink from our swim over, applied SPF 60 sunblock she produced from her bag; her ice-blonde hair didn't need any lightening. Our teenage bodies stretched against the raft, stretched across the hours of the day itself, as we lost ourselves in drinking and gossip. We played Fuck, Marry, Kill and Would You Rather.

By midday we were drunk, but I didn't know if it was more from the beer or the sun. I slipped into the water to cool off.

"We forgot to bring food." Zee opened another beer with a metallic crack. "We should walk to Matt's Burgers soon. I'm starving."

"I thought we were drinking our calories today." Cara watched me circle around them.

"Burgers sound so good," I said. Now that Zee mentioned it, my stomach was growling, asking for more than alcohol to fill it.

"You always take her side." Cara flipped over onto her stomach, the outline of her white shoulder blades sharp and rising along her upper back. "Besides, we all know the real reason Zee wants to go to Matt's Burgers is to see her lover boy." She puckered her rosy lips and made a prolonged kissing noise. "Oh, Jason. Oh yeah, Jason." The noises transformed into breathy groans, and Cara ran her fingers along her breasts, touching her visible nipples through the thin blue fabric of her bikini top. A rosy heat flushed across my cheeks.

An empty beer can hit Cara square on the head, and we all burst out laughing. "I wish," admitted Zee. "Besides, he's not even working today. I already texted him."

"So, who is it?" asked Cara.

"Who what?"

"Who's working at Matt's?"

"Nobody. I want some french fries."

I chimed in, emboldened by the booze, "If by french fries, you mean dick."

"Ooh, Delia for the win!" yelped Cara. We high-fived across the float.

"You guys are such jerks." Zee lay back, turning away. For a moment, Cara and I exchanged glances, like maybe we had gone too far. I opened my mouth to apologize. "It's Keene," murmured Zee.

"I knew it!" Cara thrust her beer into the sky and took a swig.

"Okay, he's pretty hot," I admitted of our longtime friend.

"I mean," said Zee, tilting her sunglasses down to look at me. "He's no Tom Snyder."

A burning flashed through me, and I looked at Cara, panicked. She only laughed. "Oh my God, such a gross joke."

"Yeah, gross," I echoed.

Zee pushed her sunnies back up onto her nose. "He totally checked out your ass as we were leaving. You should go for it, Delia."

"Um, ew! My brother is off limits. Just so we're clear." Cara said it with a smile, but her tone had turned stern.

The mood soured. I climbed onto the float and lay with my eyes closed. I let the gentle waves pull me out and in again. Soon, the warmth and my drunkenness rocked me to sleep.

I don't know how long it was until I woke up again. Zee was shouting, "Let's get out of here, I'm burning to a crisp."

I pulled myself back, hand over hand, on the rope. When I reached the raft, a red-faced and woozy Cara handed me our bags. "You keep those on the floatie. Zee and I can swim back."

"Are you sure?" I asked, making room for them to hang on.

"Yeah, we're fine." Zee threw her shorts and sunglasses onto the float and dove into the water. She doggie-paddled to where the float looped onto the raft and loosed it. I lay down and began kicking our load back to shore. Zee stayed steady with me, one hand on the float. We paddled silently. I looked back in time to see Cara leap from the raft. I waited for her to break. The seconds ticked by as I spun my head for her. Where was she? I had opened my mouth to yell when she exploded from the water underneath the float, nearly tipping the whole thing over.

"Cara!" I yelled, trying to steady the bags from falling. "Don't scare us!"

Cara splashed Zee right in the face. "Race you! Ready, set—" Then she was off before she even finished.

"Bitch," choked Zee, wiping her eyes.

"Let her go," I said. It was too late. Zee was already chasing Cara, cutting through the water. I sighed with annoyance and slowed my paddling to enjoy my buzz, letting the current carry me to the beach.

I glanced up to see the splashes from Zee, who had caught up to Cara. They were neck and neck. My back rested on the hot plastic, and my legs hung off the end of the float. I stretched out and thought of Tom.

Before my feet touched the bottom of the shallows, I heard Cara. Her scream was shrill and skipped across the water like a flat stone. I stepped off the float into waist-high water.

Cara was running toward me from the beach. "Did you see her?"

"Who?"

"Zee! She's gone!"

I looked around at the placid water. There was nothing. "What do you mean, gone?"

"She never made it to shore. She caught up to me, and I thought she passed me. Then when I got here . . ." Her wild eyes did another sweep of the beach. "Zee!"

"She probably already ran up to the road as a joke," I reasoned. Trying not to think the worst, I handed Cara her backpack while I carried both mine and Zee's. "Come on, you'll see. She's up at the trailhead laughing at us."

We left the float and walked the trail up to the road, back and forth ten times. There was no sign of Zee. Was Cara right? Had she not made it to shore? Impossible. The lake was so calm. Zee was a strong swimmer. There was no way.

"She drowned!" Cara wailed in despair. "Delia, what do we do?"

We returned to the beach. I looked across to the raft, where minutes before we had all been together and alive.

"Zee!" I screamed. My voice echoed off the water and dispersed among the stoic evergreens. "Zelda!" I called again.

Cara joined me. Our cacophony of despair rattled the air without answer in return. The lush evergreen walls simply absorbed our screams and redistributed them as mocking birdsong. I dropped to my knees in the shallows and reached out through the water, perhaps to will her into my grasp.

We refused to give up. By the time we called our parents and they called the police, it was evening, and our legs were labyrinths of red bloody scratches where we had fought through the branches and brush: looking, looking. It was lucky, said the police chief. The divers could work later than normal with the summer sun, which was as reluctant as us to look away.

"The divers?" I asked. I told them Zee was a good swimmer and she couldn't have drowned. They needed to check the roads. Cars driving by—maybe someone had picked her up.

"She wouldn't leave without her bag and phone," Cara said, correctly.

The trooper nodded stiffly. "We'll look at all possible angles."

My mom dropped Cara off at her house while I waited in the car as the mothers whispered in the porch light. The night descended around us on the drive home. My mom turned on the headlights, then reached over and squeezed my knee. "They'll find her, honey. Zee will be okay. She's a strong girl." She, not my father, asked me about the alcohol on my breath.

I showered and scrubbed the lake and the sun from my skin. I brushed my teeth until my gums bled. In my towel, I carried the telephone handset from the hallway, its long spiraling cord stretching across my bedroom, and took it under the covers with me. My pillow was soaking; I hadn't bothered drying my hair. I dialed Cara. "Have you heard anything?"

"No. You?"

"No."

"My parents say not to use the phone, in case they try to call."

"Yeah, smart." Neither of us hung up. If we did, we would lose the last connection we had to Zee: each other.

"Did your parents call her parents?" I asked Cara.

"I think the cops did."

"What did they tell them?"

"I don't know." Her voice broke, and she stifled a cry.

"She's okay. She's somewhere. They'll find her," I repeated.

"I don't know . . ."

"What don't you know?" I snapped. "If you two weren't acting like idiots in the first place—"

"What?" Her voice dared me to say it.

"Maybe she wouldn't have run off." My cheeks turned hot.

"Maybe she didn't run off. Don't you get it?" Her voice was sharp.

"No, I don't."

"Maybe something happened in the water."

"Like *what*?" I almost shouted.

"I don't know!" The line hummed with silence. "Will you promise me something?"

I sighed. "Anything."

"Promise we'll get through this together. No matter what I tell you, you'll stay by me?"

I paused for a beat. "No matter what."

"Okay." A breath in. "It was because of me. I felt her swimming up on me, so I started swimming harder, really kicking. And I—I didn't mean to! I kicked her. Hard, even. I remember feeling her under my heel. How her skull hurt my foot . . ." She trailed off, the end of the sentence lost.

"Sounds like it was an accident. And I don't think a small kick would have knocked her unconscious or anything—"

A rap at my door. "Delia?" My mom cracked open the door. I peered out from underneath my covers. She shook her head and made a telephone with her thumb and pinkie. "You can't tie up the line. Just in case."

"I have to go," I told Cara and hung up before she could answer.

The call didn't come that night. It didn't come the next day either. They wouldn't find a body in the lake—a fact that, in my mind, ended any silly speculation a wayward kick from Cara had caused Zee to drown.

Eventually, I didn't see the police dogs go by on the trails surrounding Blythe Lake anymore. The volunteer search parties that trawled along the coast and piers of the town grew smaller and smaller until they stopped altogether. One day, Zee was declared dead. One night we went to sleep and Zee still existed, somewhere. The next morning, we woke up, and she didn't. She became an apparition, slipping through my fingers when I tried to grasp her in the corners of those dark places I visited all too often in those times.

For weeks, I went to the beaches of Blythe Lake, watching and waiting. I would come home sunburned and starving, having feasted on nothing but thoughts of her. "You can't spend the rest of your life waiting on the beach," Mom warned me. I went back the next morning and the morning after. Time moved forward; people forgot. Even I stopped looking sideways at the glimmering water when driving along the winding roads around the lake. She was no longer the flesh and blood teenage girl with whom I snuggled and ate popcorn and took astrology quizzes under the covers. She was merely a thought, an idea keeping us all awake with the nagging persistence of a girl that *used to be*.

CHAPTER 2

I could still taste it—the old beer and lake water dried on my lips. The sunlight reflected off the water's surface like a mirror ball. Waves and currents threatened as the collapsing silence pushed against my lungs. I was underwater, clutching at the sky above. The water rushed in.

"Delia?"

I jumped in my seat.

Nothing but deadlines and city shadows loomed over me. I sat at my desk, staring out the east-facing windows of my apartment.

"Delia? You there?" Renata's voice came through the phone.

"Sorry, Ren, I'm here. Got sidetracked."

"More like zoned out." A pause. "Everything all right?"

I stood and pressed my hand onto the window, feeling the cold through the glass. The stark Seattle cityscape peeked through gray linen clouds before me. On a clear day, if I held my cheek against the glass and peered down the street, I could make out the Space Needle. "Winter blues, I think. The letdown after the holidays, you know." I took my hand away and left spaces of warmth for condensation to fill.

"Is it winter blues? Or birthday blues? I have access to a calendar, you know."

"No," I asserted, even though she was right. My birthday was tomorrow. What she didn't know was it wasn't my own birthday I dreaded each January. We would both be turning twenty-five this week.

"I wish you would let me take you out, even for one drink to celebrate. I hope you're letting your man treat you, at least. Who hates their birthday?"

A ding announced a new email in my inbox, and I sat back at my computer. "I don't hate my birthday. Just wish it didn't come around so often." Without looking at who'd sent it, I clicked to hide the notification. "Rain check on the drink? I'm buried in work right now."

"I am too. That's why I was hoping you would say yes." Her voice lowered. "If I don't come up with some kind of excuse to get out of the office soon, I might end up prosecuting myself for murdering one of these former-frat-boy lawyers." I stifled a laugh.

Renata Figueroa was an assistant United States attorney for the Western District of Washington, one of the few female-identifying lawyers in a boys' club. If anyone could survive, even thrive, under the pressure cooker of the job, it was Ren. We'd met on our first day of law school, and I understood her. While most people might label Ren a ballbuster, I knew she was simply willing to outwork anyone else.

I understood her like she understood I wasn't snobby or stuck up; I valued my space. She was one of the few who'd supported me when I had to leave law school only two semesters in.

"I hope you're taking the night off. Tell Teddy hi for me. Oh, and Delia?"

"Huh?"

"Happy birthday."

"Thanks." I looked up at the heavy rain beginning to rap on my window.

When I was a child, a teenager even, *my twenties* had seemed like such a magical aspiration. Now I was here, right in the middle of them, and I was certain I had missed an invitation to the actual party where the roaring twenties were happening for my peers.

In all my Capricorn stoicism, I'd told my boyfriend not to fuss over anything special for my birthday night. "Why celebrate getting older?" I asked, chewing on a fingernail.

"Jesus, Delia, you're not turning fifty." Teddy laughed. "You're twenty-five! Don't you want to go out to a club or see a show?"

I groaned. "Sounds like a nightmare. I did a twenty-one run in college and still have flashbacks to . . . well, nothing, because I can't remember anything from it. I hate losing control. Why is that anyone's idea of fun?"

"What if I cook you a romantic candlelight birthday dinner for two?"

I relented with a sigh. "Perfect." *Poor lovable Teddy,* I'd thought. Sometimes I wondered if he knew me at all.

—⚊—

When my birthday came around, there was a storm and a record-breaking dump of rain. Impressive, even for Seattle. I was more than happy to spend the blustery day alone. It was my normal state of being, after all, save for a couple of attachments, namely Ren and Teddy. I kept my circles small, in the vein of ships passing around a single isle, rocky and impenetrable. Alone meant freedom.

Alone meant security; that was to say, no disappointments.

Around lunchtime, my phone rang. The word *MOM*, punctuated with the heart eyes emoji, appeared on my phone, the contact name she inputted herself. I answered and couldn't even get out a hello before she broke into the "Happy Birthday" song, the Stevie Wonder version, which was the preferred version in the Albio household.

"Thanks, Mom."

"So, what are you doing to celebrate?"

"I think Teddy's cooking for me."

"How chivalrous! Are you busy this weekend? Or the next? Since you didn't come home for Thanksgiving or Christmas, maybe you could visit home for a small birthday celebration?" She sensed my hesitation. "What if I promise to make pork adobo and pancit? Your favorite."

"I'll think about it, Mom. I will." She continued on with general Mom updates until I told her my inbox was waiting for me. "Love you lots," I told her.

I felt guilty. Teddy's family lived in Seattle, and somehow he had convinced me to spend the past holidays with them. Like many of my white friends' families, his parents were overly sweet and welcoming to me, and his siblings were easy to get along with. His younger brother and two older sisters couldn't fathom not having a sibling, so I, as an only child, was something of an oddity.

"So, who did you play with as a kid?" they had asked.

"I had friends." Grinning tightly, I defended myself over gravy and mashed potatoes. "Actually, I had two friends who were like my sisters. We were inseparable."

"Siblings help to keep you in check, so you don't get too confident with yourself. Friends are great at giving you emotional support, but siblings are great at tearing you down from your pedestal once those friends go home," Teddy observed.

"You've never been a teenage girl." One of his sisters rolled her eyes, giggling.

After dinner, the family played games. They recruited me for the girls' team. We shared wine and jokes, and by the time both holiday weekends were over, they had even let me in on some inside jokes. I hadn't had girlfriends in a long time. As we drove away, I turned and waved goodbye and wished I was waving goodbye to Teddy and driving home with his sisters instead.

—∞—

Birthday dinner was nice, as everything with Teddy was—*just nice*. Pasta with homemade pesto sauce and a well-chosen bottle of young Chianti. True to his word, he even added a few mismatched candles to the table-top. We were in bed and licking cake off each other before midnight.

In the morning, the storm had passed on; I woke to his nuzzles against my neck. I smiled and brushed him away.

He stretched out his arms over his head and rubbed his eyes. "I forgot to ask, what are you doing next Saturday?"

"Nothing planned. Why?"

"Want to do a polar plunge with my friends and me? We're thinking of making it a new New Year's tradition."

"What on earth is a polar plunge?"

"We're going to jump into Lake Washington. Scandinavians do it all the time. It's good for your health, revitalizes the system."

"What system?" I asked in horror. "Will you be in a wet suit?"

"A wet suit would defeat the purpose. We were thinking of getting matching Speedos—"

"It sounds awful," I confessed. "What's the point?"

"Because it's fun! Luke's already got a bunch of guys in on it."

I gave him side-eye. Of course, this had Luke written all over it. Teddy's coworker and generally annoying sidekick. "It's stupid. People die of hypothermia, you know."

"People also die of boredom." He wrinkled his nose.

"I'm pretty sure that's a lie." I threw a pillow at him at the exact moment our morning alarms went off in tandem. Rolling off the bed, I narrowly avoided his reach.

"No, hit the snooze for once, Delia."

"I can't. I have to go."

"You know," he said. "You wouldn't have to go if you moved in." I summoned all my strength to hide my panic. I put on my bra and buttoned up my shirt, watching as Teddy leaned out of the bed and searched for his own garments strewed about the floor. By the time he pulled on his pants, I was ready to go.

"Does this mean you're not joining?" he asked.

"Joining what?" I combed my hair with my fingers.

"Are you kidding me?" His nostrils flared.

"The polar bear thing?"

"I didn't mention any bears, but yes."

I walked into the hallway and found my shoes. "Are there other girls doing it?" I called back to the bedroom. "Or is it a guys' thing? Actually, don't answer, because it doesn't matter. I'm not jumping into Lake Washington in January. Sorry, I'll let you and your boys have this one all on your own. It will be more fun without me whining, anyway."

"Will you come watch at least?"

Having gathered my things, I went back in and sat down on the bed next to him. "Sure. I'll even wear a mini keg of brandy for when you lose feeling in your fingers."

"My amazing puppy." He leaned in for a kiss. I pushed him back under the guise of playfulness.

"I'm late." I left, letting his apartment door close behind me, barely hearing his objection.

"How can you be late? You work from home!" he called.

On the bus, I checked my emails. It was looking to be a light Friday morning. So, I let myself drift a bit. Teddy. Last night, before we tumbled into bed after too much wine, he'd informed me we were coming up on our one-year anniversary. "Already?" He was becoming an issue, I thought.

I lived my life a specific way, by design. I lived alone, worked alone as a freelance legal copywriter, and socialized with a small, select group of friends from college. As a rule, I didn't entertain long-term relationships. In fact, Teddy was the longest-term proper boyfriend I'd ever had until this point in my life. I was feeling the domestic walls closing in. This wasn't the first mention he'd made of moving in together. My normal strategy was to ignore his not-so-subtle hints. So far, it had been successful. Unfortunately, he was getting more straightforward. At some point, I would have to tell him things weren't working anymore.

I dreaded it. Teddy was nice. He was great. The best guy I'd ever been with. I should be happy, by all accounts. At least that's what Ren and Mom said. I wasn't happy. I didn't have an answer for why.

—᙮᙮᙮—

At home, I showered and washed him away, changing into black yoga pants and a cheeky sweatshirt with the word *YAWN* emblazoned on the heather-gray fabric. I checked my emails again and reviewed my deadlines before diving into my deliverables for the day. I wrote website and marketing copy for several law firms. It was boring, solitary work. I loved my job.

At lunch, I warmed up some teriyaki-chicken leftovers and ate on my couch. My phone dinged, and I glanced down. An email notification, but from my personal email. I stared at the sender name and subject line. I opened it.

> From: Cara Snyder
> To: Delia Albio
> Subject: We need to talk
>
> Hi friend!
>
> I know it's been a long time! Like everyone, life got in the way and you should know that despite busy days, I've been thinking of you! I know we haven't talked in a while, but I wanted to connect. I've appreciated your support through the years and wanted to get your thoughts on something... maybe you'll think me dramatic, but I have to say... it's something life changing.
>
> Email isn't the place to get into it all. Let me know if you're interested in knowing more. I hope we can find some time soon.
>
> -Cara

My heart stopped. Cara. I read it again.

I know we haven't talked in a while. The understatement of the year. A decade had passed since I'd last spoken with Cara Snyder.

Of course, the memory of Cara was inseparable from the memory of Zee. A chill passed through me, like an unexpected wave sweeping me off my feet and submerging me in a thousand childhood memories.

I wanted to get your thoughts on something. Something "life changing," she'd written.

It had to be about Zee. What else could it be?

Was there an update on the case? I googled my hometown and "Zelda Harris," but there were only the old articles I knew by heart. Nothing new.

I let work emails go unanswered for the rest of the day, while Cara's stayed open on the screen. I looked up Cara's Instagram, and her latest post was an uncaptioned photo of an aesthetically pleasing cup of coffee posted just the day before. There was no tagged location, but I knew that counter, and I knew that blurry kitchen cabinet. She was at her home in Portsgrove. A few times, I went to hit Reply but didn't, or my finger hovered over the trash can icon. In the end, I closed the email. I went to bed early, and, like many other nights, I dreamed about Portsgrove.

CHAPTER 3

I spotted Teddy and his friends as soon as I pulled into the Matthews Beach parking lot.

They were basically naked; the guys wore tiny Speedos, while the girls had donned puffer coats over their swimsuits. Teddy's Speedo was lime green. He turned and winked at me, rubbing his arms with his hands in a frantic motion. He whooped and exhaled hot, steamy breaths out into the air. Luke jumped next to him like he was performing an invisible double Dutch routine. There were at least ten of them, more than I expected, and girls and guys. I felt my annoyance flare up. As I approached them, Teddy waved.

"There she is!"

I smiled. "You all look ridiculous."

Luke eyed my outfit. "Where's your bikini?"

"I'm here for moral support."

The group looked disappointed. One girl turned her head to another and made a comment I didn't quite catch.

"You'll be missing out on the most invigorating experience of your life," said Luke. "The cold water revitalizes the systems."

Teddy gave me the familiar look where he both pleaded and judged me at the same time. "It's like a bonding thing, you know?"

"A bonding thing?" I eyed a girl adjusting her bikini strap.

Teddy flinched. Of course, I was aware of how bitchy I sounded. I didn't care. "Here, I can bond! Watch." I slipped off my boots and rolled off my socks. My toes gripped the sand. I took a sharp inhale. "Whew! There! Now I'm freezing, like you guys."

The crowd seemed to groan, and each member turned to one another to continue the more celebratory mood I had interrupted.

"Look, I'm sorry," I said, my voice low. I scrunched my toes.

Teddy nodded and looked out at the water. "I know you don't like these kinds of things. I shouldn't have pressured you to come out this morning."

"It's fine."

The foam-tipped waters rushed toward my feet, and I stepped back before the ripples licked them. It wasn't the temperature I was afraid of; my naked toes were already numb, dug into the wet, hard gray sand. I forgot for a moment why I was standing barefoot on the beach in January, but the raucous yells reminded me.

The shorebirds danced at the water's edge. Their skittish legs side-stepped the white foam of the waves.

I remembered us on the shore.

The three of us girls, our too-long legs pushing the pedals of our secondhand bikes rushing along these roads, the salt air brushing our wild hair into unruly waves. We zigzagged down to the end of the piers and back up again, waving at our uncles and dads who worked the boats. We knew all the side streets and the unpaved paths down to the water where we could find the best sand dollars. In the summers, we ate french fries from Matt's Burgers in the deep, lush evergreen forests beyond the beaches. In the winter, we yelped as we whipped each other with the bulbous kelp strings that washed upon the shores.

For all I knew then, the world was composed solely of fog and salt and the inlet tracks engraved on my heart.

"Let's go!" Luke called, and the group rallied. Teddy placed his hands on either side of my face and kissed me square on before running. The ones wearing anything more than a swimsuit stripped off the few clothes they had. A yelp and they were off. I watched them run into the waves like a battalion into the throng of battle. Teddy and Luke led the pack with a war cry. They were the ones who swam out farthest, quickest. I wrung my hands and no longer felt the cold on my soles.

I wouldn't reply to Cara. It was easy to remember the good times; they rose to the surface, light and airy. I had sat with Cara's email for a week now. The easy memories floated away, like dandelion seeds caught in the breeze. They were beautiful to watch, to relive, as I had done so many times before. What was left once they were gone? The heavy things that couldn't take flight; the dying stems plucked from their soil.

I had watched Zee slather on makeup and wear short skirts so she would be the pretty one, just once. She and I would never be—only Cara, with her golden hair and tide pool eyes, could ever hold the title. Was there anything more insidious than the spaces between teenage girls? Sure, Cara could make us swoon with compliments, but she also shot poison-tipped barbs. Yes, she held us under the covers and wiped away our tears when the big feelings of girlhood became too much. Even when she was the one who had made us cry in the first place.

"Delia? Did you see it?" Teddy was in front of me, his hair dripping in his eyes, goose pimples covering his white naked skin. "Shit, I'm freezing! The towel!"

I stared, confused. "The towel?"

A girl with bangs, now wet and swept to the side, walked past me and picked up a towel laid across the sand. She threw it at Teddy with a smirk. "Thanks, Nicky." Teddy draped it around his shoulders. "Did you see?" He asked again.

I nodded, trying my best to feign interest and support. "It was epic."

"Maybe next year?" Luke asked.

Before I could reply, my world turned upside down, as, in one swift movement, Teddy ran at me and lifted me up and onto his shoulders. I clawed at his arms, the chest bare from the fallen towel left on the sand behind us as he ran us to the water. "Teddy, no! Please!" The group hollered in sick triumph.

He reached the waves, and the icy spray splattered my face as I continued to scream and plead. "Don't put me in the water! Please!" He laughed. I tried one more time. "Please, I'll drown!" With that, I fell, suspended in the air for a split second, then plunged into the freezing water. I was so unprepared for him to drop me, I felt my body shock at the sudden coldness. I gasped—exactly the wrong thing to do. Frigid water filled my lungs, and they went numb inside of me. I tried to scream, but I opened my mouth to more water. I felt myself lifted from the darkness. My head broke the surface. I vomited up seawater and bile.

"Jesus Christ!" A woman held me. I looked at her through blurred vision. It was the one Teddy had called Nicky. "She's drowning, you asshole!"

"She's in three feet of water," Luke sneered.

With apologetic eyes, Teddy ran to my side and took me by the arms. I fell into him and sobbed. The salt in my tears fell from my cheeks to the sand, joining the tide pulled out to sea.

—⚬—

In my apartment, on my couch with my wet hair piled up in a towel on my head, Teddy handed me a cup of tea. I cradled it in my hands. "Thanks."

"I'm so sorry. It was supposed to be funny. I had no idea you were afraid of water. In all the time we've been together, why not tell me?"

I stared ahead, unable to meet his eyes. "Tell you I can't even go into a hot tub without having a panic attack? Or my childhood best friend likely drowned in front of my eyes when I was fifteen?"

"Both. Did you say 'likely'?" He grimaced.

I took a sip of the warm tea and swallowed. "The official story is Zee drowned. But there was no body. We were all there—Zee, myself, and Cara, the third in our trio. We were swimming to the shore, and Zee and Cara raced. Cara and I made it, and . . . Zee didn't."

"Holy shit."

"It's fine." I traced the rim of the teacup. "It's something that happens. Isn't that what people say?" I set the cup down on the coffee table. I drew my knees to my chest and wrapped my arms around them.

Teddy scooted against me and reached his arm across my shoulders. "So that's where you've been all this time?"

"Where?"

"There. On the lake. Waiting for her."

With a hand, I moved his arm off me. I crossed my arms, and I took a breath. "I've been meaning to tell you something, Teddy."

I blamed my trauma. It was an easy card to play. He promised to fix it, said it with so much earnestness, and for a second, I forgot how many times I'd heard that one before. Finally, all the pleading and the apologies and the tears ran out for the both of us. He walked out the door with one last look back, his face red and eyes puffy. I watched through the peephole as he strode down the apartment hall and waited until he got into the elevator before I locked the door and sighed with relief.

In bed, I turned over and dimmed the brightness on my phone until I had to squint to see it. I typed out a quick response:

> From: Delia Albio
> To: Cara Snyder
> Subject: RE: We need to talk
>
> Cara,
>
> It surprised me to hear from you, but thank you for reaching out. I'm going to be in Portsgrove next weekend to visit my parents. Let's meet up?
>
> Delia

I texted my mom: I think I'll be coming home, after all.

CHAPTER 4

I caught the early ferry home and crossed the fog-covered water of the sound. I sat near the tiny cafeteria and bought a muddy liquid that could be called coffee only in the most active and forgiving of imaginations. While my computer joined the spotty ferry Wi-Fi, I watched families and couples go outside on deck, where the wind blew their hair and scarves about their faces and they laughed and ran back inside, rubbing their hands. My inbox loaded.

No reply from Cara.

It had been a week since I sent my response. Fair enough, since I had waited awhile to reply to her too.

Against my better judgment, I once again checked her Instagram. Her user description of herself declared her as a "Free spirit, committed believer in my Radiant Self." There were a couple of rainbow hearts and a link to the Artemis Wellness website. Besides the most recent coffee post in Portsgrove, her last post was from November.

It was a selfie taken on a windy Pacific Northwest beach. Her blonde hair whipped across her face, and a blue knit beanie was pulled down over her eyebrows. Her eyes were closed and her mouth pursed in a closed grin, as if she was smiling to spite the gust. She wore no makeup, and it highlighted her brown freckles against her cheeks, pink from the cold. It was so achingly Cara.

The posts preceding it were more staged. I tapped on one of Cara in the woods, hiking boot clad and leaning against an enormous fallen tree trunk, cut in a cross section to show the vastness of its rings. Against it, Cara looked tiny. She held a white thermos to her mouth while she looked at the camera with big, inviting eyes. She strategically held the thermos to show off a bold pink logo, some kind of bow-and-arrow motif. The caption read, Mother Earth feeds my Radiant Self. Who knew a simple walk in the woods could renew your soul? Will you join me? (Another link and too many star emoji, followed by a deer emoji.) Use the CODE: CARALOVESARTEMIS for a discount!

There were a dozen more photos shilling whatever Artemis was selling. I scrolled past.

I stopped at a photo. They had taken this one from a distance, of Cara in a long formal dress holding a glass of wine. Her arm was around a man in a suit who had his own arms around her in a kind of awkward embrace. It took me a moment before I recognized the man was Tom. Cara looked much younger here than in her more recent photos. I read the caption, which tagged Tom's username. I tapped. He had posted nothing in a year. His last update was from some concert in Central Park, while his profile picture was him smiling in a worn leather motorcycle jacket; the Brooklyn Bridge loomed behind him, which made sense since his location said New York City.

I swore to myself. He was even more handsome than I remembered from my teenage puppy love–obscured memories.

The horn blew and announced the ferry had arrived on the other side of the sound. I went downstairs and got back into my car for disembarkation. My tires clunked off the metal gangway and clattered along the wooden ferry terminal dock: the sounds of coming home. I drove through the streets, past all the familiar landmarks of a life lived in a small town: the mill, my elementary school, the pharmacy I'd stolen candy from, the same pharmacy I stole condoms from later, the trees growing taller, the people who grew older. The docks were quieter now than they had been in my youth. Blame the environmentalists, or the Democrats, but the industry that had brought Portsgrove to life was now dragging it down into the depths of unemployment.

I blinked at the Weyerhaeuser sign that had replaced the more familiar Snyder Mills during my absence. The Snyder money ran deep in the Portsgrove soil, like the roots of the old growth they clear-cut. The third generation, which included Cara's father, had sold their legacy. Weyerhaeuser had allowed the Snyders to continue running the day-to-day operations and even gave them a reasonable salary.

Whatever constituted the social ladder of Portsgrove, Cara had enjoyed a spot at the very top rung. Yet I never thought of her as the "rich girl." To be honest, the rift between the haves and have-nots wasn't wide in a place like Portsgrove, anyway. A house with an attached garage made you bougie. So, she was simply Cara until high school cliques mandated she become *that* girl.

Cara, Zee, and I had created an equilibrium. We balanced each other, allowing us to live up to our assigned roles within the micro-cosm of our trio. So, after Zee was gone, I watched from the shadows as my former best friend found like creatures to hang out with. It was an easy reason for our estrangement: the growing apart. Maybe it had had nothing to do with Zee, after all. Now I thought back and realized my timeline was wrong. Cara had left for boarding school on the East Coast partway through our junior year, after the summer we lost Zee. *Did we lose touch before or after? Why can't I remember?*

Upon arrival, Mom allowed me enough time to drop my overnight bags in my old bedroom before whisking me off as a companion on her many errands.

First stop, the only Asian grocery store in town to pick up the pancit noodles and the real fish sauce and the like, which wasn't sold in the local Shore Foods. The thick scent of fresh ginger in the air was familiar and comforting, much like the faded posters of K-pop stars next to the same Chinese zodiac calendars that had been tacked onto the walls since I was little. The elderly woman behind the counter didn't speak any English but recognized Mom and me. She threw in a box of Botan Rice Candy for me with a wink. I sucked on the sweet edible wrapper as we loaded the bags into the car. "What's next?" I asked.

Soon, we were weaving through the aisles of the Shore Foods in downtown Portsgrove. Mom consulted her written list. "Carrots and cabbage." She tossed the veggies into our cart. Mom pointed out the advent calendars on clearance. "Do you want some? Actually, never mind. I remembered I have one at home I meant to give you when you came for Thanksgiving! Of course, that's when I assumed you were still coming home for the holidays. I guess from here on out I can't make assumptions. You know what they say?"

I raised my eyebrows. Mom's passive-aggressive guilt trips had been in full force for hours now. It had to end at some point, I thought. Or it might go on forever. "What?" I bit out.

"Assholes make assumptions."

"That's not the saying at all. But I'm picking up what you're putting down, Mom."

"Can you believe I still got a four-pound turkey for me? I'll never get used to not having your dad around or my baby home for Christmas."

"Mom, this was the first year I haven't come home for Christmas. Besides, you weren't alone. You told me you went to the neighbors' and you had a pleasant time."

She ignored me. "My kiddo, a grown-up out in the big world. I hope Teddy and you can come see me next holiday season."

"I don't think it'll be a debate." I steeled myself to tell her.

"What do you mean?"

I chickened out. "Nothing. I mean it's twelve months away. A lot can happen." I couldn't confess my newly single status in the middle of the grocery store. The last thing I needed was another lecture on how I needed to stop pushing men away.

Mom clucked. "Maybe what you need is more girlfriends to dish with, huh? Wouldn't that be fun?" She leaned toward me.

I thought of the gaggle of girls from the polar plunge. "I don't need vapid girlfriends to waste my Sundays with at pointless brunches. Besides, I have Ren."

"I like Ren! I bet there are lots more Rens out there for you, dear. For example, if you went back to grad school—"

"Stop," I whined. "How many times do I have to tell you, I'm happy with my life as it is?"

She pursed her lips and pretended to be absorbed in examining produce. "Well, so to what do we owe this visit, anyway?" Her voice was icy.

"Cara emailed me. I'm going to meet up with her while I'm here."

Mom threw me a glassy glare, eyes squinted. "The truth comes out. And here I thought you were interested in hanging out with me." She pierced her heart with an imaginary dagger.

"You're so dramatic." I shook my head, smiling.

"I'm joking. Glad you're seeing Cara."

I didn't respond, and Mom walked around the corner.

Then, over the elevator music, a male voice. "Delia?"

I froze. Damn it. It was the one rule of visiting home—avoid running into a past acquaintance. Maybe the rule didn't count if you came to see an old acquaintance. "Yeah?" I looked up. *Oh, please no. Don't let it be.* It was. Tom Snyder stood in front of me, holding a red shopping basket.

"It is you." He smiled, and all at once, it plunged me back to a time where my existence hinged on Tom Snyder smiling at me. And here I was—my skin electric and my mouth dry, awed in his presence. Nothing had changed.

"Wow," I said, trying to appear unimpressed. "What are you doing here?"

"Uh, precooked deli rotisserie chicken." He sorted through his basket, like he forgot what he threw in minutes before. "Red Bull, instant oatmeal, your normal bachelor fare."

"I meant, what are you doing in Portsgrove? I didn't know you moved back."

"I didn't know you did either."

"Visiting," I said defensively.

"Same." He grinned.

My forehead hurt, and I realized I was frowning. I took a breath. "Not that I'm not glad to see you." I tried to salvage it. "It's nice to see you, Tom."

"Yeah, you look"—a sweeping study, a curious gaze—"great."

I might have passed away right there and then, had Mom not come around the corner and exclaimed, "Tom Snyder!"

"Ms. Albio, been a long time." She and Tom hugged while I continued to glare. He opened his mouth, but Mom interrupted before he got a word out.

"It's Delia's birthday weekend," she said.

"Well, shit," said Tom. "Happy birthday."

I muttered an inaudible *thanks*, while Mom continued. "So, what brings you to town? Are your parents here?" My mom searched the immediate vicinity for the elder Snyders.

"No, they're wintering in Phoenix. I'm here because of Cara." His voice lowered, and a cloud front passed through his eyes, darkening his gaze.

"Delia is seeing her this weekend," Mom offered. "They've been emailing. A reunion of sorts, I think."

Tom snapped to look at me. "She emailed you? When?"

"Beginning of the New Year. She didn't respond to my reply yet, but I heard she was back here, and I was hoping to see her while I'm in town. Is she around?" I hoped I hadn't missed her.

Tom breathed a sigh, like something had just flown out of his reach. "Cara's missing." He looked upward, avoiding our eye contact. "I'm here to help find her."

—⚭—

Mom invited Tom to dinner, because of course she did.

"This is unbelievable," Mom said as we drove home, shell shocked by the news. "Poor boy. Her poor parents. Another girl—missing? It's too much to bear."

At home, Mom walked me through the prep work. She pulled out the pork belly marinating in the tangy adobo made from soy sauce and vinegar. I washed the noodles and chopped up veggies, trying to ignore the pit of worry settling in my stomach.

I set the table for three, setting Tom's plate in the place where, until a few years ago, Dad's went. Soon, the aroma of Mom's food filled the house with its rich scent of pepper and homecomings.

CHAPTER 5

Tom arrived early and brought flowers for both me and Mom, hydrangeas like blue fireworks in my hands. I wondered how he had found them so out of season.

"This smells amazing," he said, seeing the table with the serving platters piled high with golden noodles and the adobo with bright flashes of bay leaves scattered among the pork. "I remember when Cara would bring home leftovers from your house. They were always delicious. What's this?"

"Pork adobo and pancit." The words clumsily tumbled from my tongue, spoken like an American would say and without the ring they had when Mom said them. It was a strange feeling, being half of something; even certain words didn't really belong to me. I only borrowed them while I served Tom a spoonful of each dish. He took a bite and his eyes rolled back, no doubt to Mom's unending delight.

"This is incredible," he said. "Seriously, Ms. Albio. You don't know how long it's been since I've had a home-cooked meal, and this is out of this world." He looked at me. "Do you cook this too?"

Mom laughed out loud. "I keep trying to teach her, but she's not interested. I tell her, When I'm dead, who will cook for you, huh?"

I inwardly cringed but managed to smile. "I do want to learn. Soon, Mom."

She looked at me with skepticism. Thankfully, Tom spoke before she could throw another barb. "Cara always said you were the best cook, Ms. Albio. She loved coming here to eat, and now I get it."

For a moment, her name didn't hang in the air like an approaching storm. For a moment, it was normal and we had forgotten: Cara was missing.

Then, we all remembered. I poured everyone wine and finally said, "Tom, tell us about Cara."

"I came home as soon as I heard the news. My parents were here for a while, too, but they left. My mom wanted to stay, but I convinced her I could hold things down here in case she turned up. Besides, there's always a chance with Cara she could be doing this on purpose. Always was a bit dramatic, you remember. Almost three months back, Cara told us she was moving back home for a bit. We were all a bit surprised, figured she needed a change of pace from Oregon."

"I thought she lived in the Bay Area?" I asked.

"Recently, she moved up to the Oregon coast, to this beach town where a bunch of her Artemis buddies lived."

"What is Artemis exactly?" I remembered the social media postings.

"Artemis Wellness. Their website will tell you they're a women's wellness and empowerment organization. Girl power and all that, but crazy expensive and crazy exclusive. It's a kind of self-empowerment thing she got into in the Bay Area, while she was doing marketing for a start-up called BloomWallet. One of her friends invited her to one of these seminars. You know how they're into all the alternative woo-woo down there. She told us it was the most exciting weekend of her life, and we noticed the change. When she came home for the holidays, she was a different woman. My parents said it looked like this Artemis thing was working, so who were we to judge." Tom lifted his wineglass and swirled it in the light. The red legs dripped down the glass, unhurried. He took a sip, then licked his lips. A jolt of lightning went up my thighs.

"Soon she left her start-up to join Artemis to lead their marketing and business development. She sold her condo and moved to Oregon to be closer to the Artemis founders. That was a year ago. My parents planned a trip to visit me in New York over the summer, and Cara didn't even respond to their calls to ask if she wanted to join."

He rubbed his hands over his dark stubble, then passed his fingers through his always-messy curly hair. "Complete silence until she called my mom and asked if she could live in the Portsgrove house. She was here for four weeks, I think? Then, nothing. Gone."

I considered the date of the email. Right before my and Zee's birthday. Knowing more about her involvement with this Artemis, the timing couldn't have been a coincidence. Maybe while searching her soul, she had decided to tell me something she kept secret all this time. "She emailed me in January," I said.

"If it was her, you might be the last person she was in contact with before she went silent." He looked into my eyes with a flare of scrutiny. "Do you know where she is? Did she tell you?"

"No." My heartbeat quickened under his sudden intensity. "Are you sure she didn't return to Oregon?"

"She's not there. That's about the only thing they tell us." He leaned back and dropped his shoulders.

"They?" Mom asked.

"Her friends and coworkers from Artemis. They say they haven't seen her since she left there to move back here."

"You believe them?" I took a sip of my own wine, noticing his eyes never leaving me.

"I guess I don't have any reason not to believe them. The authorities were involved for a minute and questioned some people there, but they came back without any leads or any reason to suspect wrongdoing." Tom looked down at his plate and took another bite.

"So, there's no missing persons case open or anything?" I asked, surprised.

"No, they said she's a grown woman, and without evidence of wrongdoing, there's nothing to investigate."

Mom sighed. "This is horrible. I can't imagine what your parents are going through."

"It doesn't make any sense." I recalled Cara's email. It didn't sound like someone who was planning on vanishing. "Do you know why she came back here?"

"No, like I said, my parents didn't ask questions. I think they were afraid of spooking her. She was already pretty deep into Artemis."

"What can we do to help?" I asked.

Tom looked surprised. "Help? This dinner is the best thing I've eaten in a while, Ms. Albio. And you have no idea how good it feels to get this all off my chest."

Mom clucked. "Like I said, I didn't know. If I knew, maybe I could have helped keep an eye on her while she was here. Cara was like a second daughter to me, once upon a time."

His smile wavered, and there it was—a small crack in his confidence. "Honestly, she's probably throwing a tantrum somewhere for attention."

Mom stood to clear the plates. Tom stopped her. "No, you sit and have some more wine. I'll clean up all this."

While we sat, and Tom cleaned, he told us more stories. Not about Cara this time, but about his own life in Manhattan. He told us about his full-time job doing marketing for a health-care start-up and part-time job as a bartender and his studio apartment in Little Italy, right above a sushi restaurant with twenty-four-hour karaoke. He told us how when he first moved there, he didn't own a proper winter coat, and now the three he had took up half his small closet. We laughed about his stories of surviving the subways, oohed at his various celebrity sightings. It was a life so different from mine, and I found myself enamored by the possibilities of Tom Snyder once again.

I excused myself to the bathroom, and when I returned, the lights were dimmed. A small chocolate cake was on the table, illuminated by a single candle. They serenaded me to the words of Stevie Wonder's birthday salutation. Despite my best efforts, I was touched and couldn't help but smile at the strained high notes.

By the time Mom excused herself to go to bed, we were close to bursting with cake. She gave Tom a hug. "It was so nice to see you. Please keep us updated."

I walked Tom to the door. "Thanks for coming and telling us about Cara. If there's anything I can do."

"I'll let you know. It was nice seeing you."

He opened the door and stepped down to the driveway. "Wait," I said, looking out. "Where's your car?"

"I walked here."

I shook my head, seeing an opening I couldn't resist. "And you were planning on walking home in the dark?" I grabbed my coat and called down the hall that I was giving Tom a ride home.

CHAPTER 6

Though we were adults, walking into the Snyder home in the middle of the night took me back to when I would sneak in, following Tom through the halls down to his basement bedroom. It had felt naughty then, and the thrill, aided by wine and powerful nostalgia, remained.

"I have to piss." As Tom left for the bathroom, I moved through the hallways I had galloped through as a girl. How lonely they seemed now. Back then, I hadn't stopped to look at the photos on the walls or the designed interiors. I'd never noticed the tired woodwork or the faded paint. From the kitchen cabinets, I took down two wineglasses. There was already a bottle of pinot on the counter. Carrying my glass, I went to the living room and examined the framed pictures of the Snyders.

A toilet flushed, and the bathroom door swung open. I started.

"Don't worry." Tom laughed. "No grown-ups around to catch us tonight."

"I can't believe I'm back here." I shook my head in disbelief.

"Without her, you mean? Weren't you here plenty of times after she left?" He grinned his stupid, irresistible grin.

"Not on the main floor." I emphasized each word, feeling my cheeks turn warm. I scrunched my brows. "Tom, aren't you worried about her? I am." The large empty house suddenly felt very cold. "Are your parents all right? I can't imagine your mom not being here while her daughter is missing."

Tom sighed.

"What?" I pressed.

"I didn't want to say anything in front of your mom, but I told my parents I've actually been in touch with Cara."

I balked. "You have heard from her, then?"

"No, but I told them I had so they wouldn't be up here and worrying to death when there's nothing they can do. Especially when I'm ninety percent sure this is just Cara throwing some kind of tantrum."

"Tom, you can't do that. What if something really is wrong? And you told them she was okay? Why would you lie about that?"

He shrugged, his eyes cast downward. "Cara can take care of herself. Trust me, this is her needing space. She'll be back and acting like nothing happened."

"You realize the last time you tried to convince me my best friend would come waltzing home again, you were wrong." His sudden flippancy about his missing sister was strange, considering his inquisition at dinner.

"How could I forget? What would you rather I tell you? The truth?" His voice almost a growl.

"That's the last thing I want to hear right now," I confessed. Maybe he had a point; his parents wouldn't be able to do anything more than it sounded like he was doing now anyway. Tom knew them and their relationship with Cara better than I did. "I don't like it," I said. "But I hope your judgment is correct."

Tom poured his own glass of wine and sat down on the armchair across the room from where I curled up on the couch. We talked in the dark about our work and lives. He didn't ask about boyfriends. I afforded him the same courtesy. The words came and went easily with him. It wasn't like with Teddy, having to keep him at arm's length. No, Tom already knew my damaged past, so why not let him in with open arms?

"Do you still sleep in the basement?" I asked with a grin.

"What was wrong with the basement? It was the best room ever." He smiled. "A separate entrance, bathroom, and enough room for a foosball table? A teenage boy's dream."

I swirled my wine. "You know your parents were fully aware of how many girls you snuck down there?"

"They didn't know about you," he said, his voice lowered.

I whispered back, "Maybe not."

Tom traced his forefinger along the edge of his glass. He stared at me, his eyes bright in the shadows. "I still think about us down there." He drank and swallowed.

The wine turned me brave; I stood up and crossed the time lost between us, setting my glass down on the coffee table as I passed it. I lowered myself onto his lap, hitching up my skirt to straddle him. He groaned under me.

He spoke through gritted teeth. "Do you have any idea what I've wanted to do to you from the moment I saw you?"

"No," I answered. "Show me."

A swift movement, and his fingers found their way inside me. I folded over him, lips gasping like the drowned against the skin of his neck; his palm ground hard against me, a pestle against a mortar. His free hand, the one not thrusting into me, lifted my shirt and stroked my curves. He was so familiar, like a favorite song from my teenage years. I welcomed him with a hunger, and he fed me with an urgency, as if all these years apart had only been a great obstacle we needed to cross to prove ourselves worthy to meet again.

—⚬—

When I emerged from cleaning myself up in the bathroom, Tom was asleep in his parents' bed. I dressed to leave. Just like the old days. Turning my head to check that nobody was watching, no parents were waiting to jump at me and turn me in for missing curfew, I went into Cara's room and flipped on the light. It was sparsely furnished, just a bed, desk, and drawer; the walls were still covered in all the girlhood posters.

When I opened the top dresser drawer, an orange prescription bottle rolled and clattered among a scattering of receipts. I held the bottle and read the label. Xanax, prescribed to Cara by a Dr. Nicklin, back in August.

The next drawer was full of her underwear and bras. I laid my hand on the softness of them and felt something hard underneath. I pushed aside a frilly pink pair of panties and revealed a workbook of some kind. I traced the unusual logo on the cover, a bow strung with an arrow—a small crescent moon in place of the arrowhead, set against a geometric deer facing me head on. Below the logo, the engraved words *ARTEMIS WELLNESS*.

I opened it and read the title on the first page: "Workbook 1: the introduction to authenticity." Underneath, it read "this journey belongs to:" and in the blank space, her unforgettable handwriting: "Cara S."

I flipped a few more pages, skimming the sections with subtitles like "Our Social Masks" and "Unlocking Goddess Energy." Her annotations and notes filled the margins and between paragraphs.

One page was titled "Our Biggest Fears." It offered the question, "What is your biggest fear?" Cara had filled out several lines underneath with her answer:

> After being told my whole life I was smart, beautiful and full of promise, I'm afraid I haven't lived up to any of it. It's a hard realization at my age. How long do I have to wait to become someone as great as everyone thought I would be? This isn't even my biggest fear. My biggest fear is my guilt will destroy me—I wasted a life when others had theirs ripped away before they had the chance.

I squeezed my eyes shut to hold back the rising wave of grief. This would be harder than I thought. I pushed the feelings away.

With a shaky hand, I placed the workbook into my bag to read later. Before I left her room, I looked at the collage of photos on her wall. I remembered lying on the carpet, sorting through that envelope from the Walgreens Photo Center. Scissors in hand, we cut along the outlines of us, then arranged the photos onto the wall with double-sided tape. We filled in the in-between spaces with clippings from magazines, our idols like Britney, and our dream vacation spots like Paris. It was a living vision board changing with the seasons and each finished disposable camera.

It seemed silly now, this altar to friendship.

I realized I was making my usual mistake when it came to Cara and Zee: glorifying the past. What did it mean, anyway, to have friendships in those tenuous pubescent years, when we weren't fully formed people, anyway? If Zee hadn't disappeared, would we all still be in touch now? Doubtful. Were we ever as close as the pictures and my memories made it seem?

A photo I didn't remember seeing before caught my eye. It wasn't from the fateful summer days at Blythe Lake but from the only trip all three of our families had taken together, up to the Harrises' mountain cabin outside of Leavenworth. We were thirteen at the time. Tom would have been seventeen. I remembered how much Tom had bitched and moaned about being the sole boy and too old for a lame family vacation. The first night, he hid away in the assigned Snyder room and played games on his computer by himself. By the end of the long weekend, he joined in all the hikes and even the family game nights, where the dads had sneaked him sips of their whiskey when the moms weren't looking. The photo showed us four kids outside the cabin the morning we were leaving. Our arms around each other's shoulders in the following order: Tom, Cara, Zee, and me. While we girls faced forward with wide grins, Tom's head was turned, and he smiled at . . . I looked closer. Was he looking at me?

I wondered if the Harrises still owned the cabin. Maybe they had sold it off when they moved away, because what was the point? I tapped the photo with a fingernail. *What I would give to go back, huh?*

I turned off the light and let myself out of the Snyder house.

Back home in my childhood room, I slipped out of the clothes that still smelled of him. I put on clean underwear and an oversize T-shirt, then crawled into bed. On my phone, I typed *Artemis Wellness* into the search engine.

The organization website was the first result. I clicked on the link labeled "About Us" and found the group mission statement:

> Woman by woman, we are a movement committed to a future where every individual has the power for success and self-fulfillment. Powered by the radical idea that transformative thinking can lead to transformative living, Artemis Wellness is a revolution in the making. To give a woman a view of her own motives and subconscious needs is the first step in a long journey. The true mission of Artemis Wellness is to give each woman not only a target with which to strive for but to arm her with an arrow of intention with which to succeed.

I balked. What did it even mean? I clicked on the link titled "Our Creator." A photo of a handsome older man appeared on my screen. Thin faced, with high cheekbones and intense dark eyes, the man appeared young. His hair was snow white. "Everett Ware" read the caption. Odd, I thought, a man creating a women's wellness group.

Everett Ware's bio read that he had been inspired to help his sister, who, at a young age, struggled with self-confidence and extreme shyness.

I closed the window and opened my social media apps in my normal bedtime rotation, liking all the regular posts and bookmarking new workouts from my favorite fitness influencers and recipes from the foodies, even though I knew I'd never open them up again. I opened the Artemis website again and tapped on "Upcoming Seminar." After I input my zip code, a pop-up was happy to inform me that there was a session a couple of weeks away in Seattle. What were the odds? It was a two-day-long "intensive," as they called it. There was no available agenda online. No price, either, I noted, but a field labeled "buddy code" and a pink button below: *Register.* I took a screenshot.

Do you know this company? I texted Ren. I attached the screenshot.

No, she replied. I can do some digging? Is this for business or pleasure?

NOT pleasure, I wrote.

I'll see what I can find.

I navigated back to the seminar page, and my fingertip hovered over the button. Register.

If Tom was right, Artemis was Cara's whole life. Maybe learning more about Artemis meant learning more about Cara, which could lead to finding her. Maybe someone at these seminars would know her or where she had gone.

I was about to tap on Register, then remembered. Opening Instagram, I confirmed and went back to the Artemis Registration page. I filled in the buddy code: "CARALOVESARTEMIS."

The site informed me I had unlocked a 20 percent discount.

Hey, every little bit counted. I clicked Register.

CHAPTER 7

I extended my visit home, and over a couple of weeks in Portsgrove, Mom and I worked in an easy routine. I woke up every morning to Mom panfrying longanisa sausages and pulling a tray of fresh-baked Filipino pandesal out of the oven. We shared a pot of coffee and watched *Good Morning America*. I set up my workstation at the dining table, after we cleared it of fruit and plates. The beauty of my job was that I could work anywhere, even in a dining room next to the living room where Mom watched K-dramas. At least I had a view of trees. On breaks, I accompanied Mom into town on errands or took a walk in the wooded neighborhood.

Sometimes, my walks took me to the Snyder house. I didn't knock anymore but went in through the unlocked front door. Depending on what time it was, Tom might offer me lunch and a coffee; more often, though, we immediately took our clothes off, not uttering a sound except those of impatience and pleasure. Tom and I found each other now with a ferocity we had lacked in our teenage days. After all, I wasn't a beginner anymore. I corrected the past missed opportunity to enjoy his body as much as he enjoyed mine. The selfishness of my sex had bothered and frustrated Teddy, but Tom found it intoxicating.

Afterward, I inevitably found myself back in Cara's room, sorting through more workbooks. One well-worn book was titled *Mentor Training Manual*. I wondered what a mentor was.

One page had instructions to write about a pivotal moment from their childhood. She had to have written about Zee, about that day, I thought. But as I began to read, I found her two pages, cursive letters bubbly and even, were about her leaving her hometown to go to boarding school. There was no mention of me or Zee.

I read more of Cara's words but found they didn't tell me anything about who she was at all. As if the education in Artemis had sanded over the edges that made Cara, turning her into something muted and docile.

"I think this is a bad idea," Tom said, the night before I was leaving for the seminar. We lay naked underneath blankets on the living room couch, passing a half-drunk bottle of wine between us, the movie on the TV having been paused a long time ago.

"You think anything taking me away from your bed is a bad idea," I countered with a soft and playful push to his chest.

He frowned. "I'm telling you I don't think you should get involved."

"I thought you wanted to find your sister," I shot back, immediately feeling the tightness the words left in my throat. "Sorry," I muttered.

His neck stiffened. "I make calls all day, chasing down Cara's old friends or coworkers. So don't act like I don't care about my sister."

"I'm sorry," I said again, petting his hair and breathing in his smell, tobacco and soap. We curled up and hit play on the movie.

—⚉—

The Artemis Wellness Introduction to Self seminar began early on Saturday morning and ended late on Sunday. The seminar cost $455 for the two days, inclusive of breakfasts and lunches. I caught a later ferry than planned and had to jog the mile to the downtown Fairmont Olympic Hotel on University Street. I arrived sweaty but right on time.

"Where can I find the Artemis Wellness seminar?" I asked at the front desk.

"Name?" The woman tapped on a screen without looking up at me.
"Delia Albio."

"ID?"

I fished for it in my bag and showed her. She nodded and typed and tapped and presented me with a hotel key card. "Artemis is in the Olympic Suite on the very top floor."

The elevator doors opened up to a typical hotel hallway. I waved the card in front of the reader on the suite doors and couldn't help but be surprised when it beeped and the door unlocked. I pushed the doors open.

Sunlight streamed through arched windows showcasing city views against the faint outline of the Olympic Mountains beyond. I blinked and saw I was standing in an enormous room, bigger than my entire apartment. There was a dining area with a long polished table and multiple bouquets of flowers adorning it, their clean fragrance heavy in the air. A small group of six women had already sat and were chatting in the living room area, which was filled with overstuffed plush white sofas and purple velveteen armchairs. My ears filled with lush ringing sounds stretched over one another in a kind of meditative loop—I recognized it as the steady tones of Tibetan singing bowls.

The women smiled and waved while I tentatively sat on one of the armchairs and held the pillow in my lap. My plans to be the kid in the back of the class were thwarted, as the sofas and chairs were arranged in a circle. The other attendees were chatting softly.

I don't know what I was expecting—maybe a dash of Brené Brown's production value and rabid self-help junkies. Instead, it was as if I had wandered into a bachelorette party's spa day. Except for a woman who appeared of Indian descent, everyone was white and blonde. I looked down at my hands and picked at my chipped nude-colored nail polish.

At last, the Indian woman stood. She was tall, with bronzed sepia skin and lush raven hair. She wore a striking maroon silk jumpsuit, fitted with a gray blazer, that looked like a nightmare to iron. Distractingly straight teeth filled her mouth, and she used them to impressive effect.

She beamed her toothpaste-commercial mouth at us, then held her right hand to her heart, laying it on her chest. The room hushed under her gaze. She nodded and lifted her other hand to us. We got the hint, and one by one, stood and also placed our hands in front of our hearts. Once we were all performing the motion, she bowed and announced, "Good morning, goddesses." She motioned for us all to sit down again. She took a stack of workbooks from a desk and passed it along; we each took one and shared around the circle. We were seven, not including the jumpsuited woman, and I noted one empty chair next to me.

I held the spiral-bound white notebook with the laminated cover like a present. It was like the one I had found in Cara's room. My fingertips traced the familiar geometric design: the moon, the bow, the deer.

"My name is Stacey Roy," the woman in the silky jumpsuit introduced herself. "I'll be your guide through this weekend's journey of self-discovery. I am so looking forward to getting to know each one of you, but first I would love to introduce you all to Artemis." With a game show wave, she brought our attention to the large flat-screen TV behind her.

The room dimmed and the video began. Electronic, moody beats filled the room, and panning shots of generic mountains and forests flew by. An unnecessarily sultry female voice-over began:

"From the beginning of time, man has struggled with the most unknowable of questions. Who am I? What is my purpose?"

The door opened, and a slash of light illuminated the room. "Sorry!" A panicked whisper. I squinted against the brightness and looked toward the door. "I'm so sorry!" the shadowy figure said again as they slunk into the room and slid into the armchair next to me, thus completing our circle.

"Hi! Hey! Where'd you get the notebook?" She struggled out of her jean jacket, which I noted was too light for February. She was Asian, and her black hair was pulled back into a high ponytail.

I motioned to Stacey.

"Thanks! Did I miss much?"

"The meaning of life." I pointed at the TV.

"Wow, giving the people their money's worth, am I right? By the way, did you have a discount code? I didn't sign up through the site. I had to pay full price, but the girl who sold me her ticket said she used a code. She said to ask for a refund to cover the discount I'm owed because it was a legit code even though she sold her spot—"

A shush came from the dark. My new neighbor looked at me, her eyes flashing in dramatic guilt. I had to smile. This girl was more my speed, if not a touch chatty.

"I'm Delia," I said.

"Nice to meet you. I'm Jenny."

I turned my attention back to the TV screen and saw the man from the website, Everett Ware. The caption below his face read "Founder." "My greatest gift to this world is Artemis Wellness," he said. His voice wasn't what I had imagined in my head. It was soft and musical. I leaned forward in my chair to hear more of what he had to say.

"If I can create a scientific process for a woman to follow to help her understand not only who she is but how she can use the knowledge of self-awareness to create her best life, then I want to give this knowledge to every woman I can! Not all women want to hear it. It's the fear that keeps us from understanding our true soul, what I call our radiant self."

"Let's hear it for Everett!" Stacey clapped when the video ended. We all followed suit, and nobody thought it strange we were clapping for a man in a video who couldn't hear us. "Everett is a true visionary and the man behind Artemis. As he explained, he and his sister, Sage Ware, came up with this extraordinary and life-changing course. I am so excited to share it with all of you this weekend.

"Now, I'll ask everyone to turn to the first page of your workbooks and read a note from one of our very happy Artemis students."

It turned out to be a testimonial from Golden Globe–winning actress Regan Elliot. Jenny gasped next to me. "She's my favorite actress!"

"So, are we ready to get into it?" asked Stacey.

Yes, dear God, please. The quicker we start, the quicker we can get this over with.

Stacey returned to her seat on one of the sofas. "What does it mean to be a woman?"

I sighed quietly. This was my nightmare.

"A mom?" a voice offered. Stacey nodded. More suggestions from the audience: "Girlfriend." "Sister."

"So, these are people who are women. I'm asking, What does it mean to be a woman?"

Silence. "I know, I'm starting off with the heavy-hitting truths, and it's not even ten a.m.!" Seriously, it wasn't even ten yet? I glanced at the clock like I was in high school math class again. This was going to be a long weekend. "What does being a woman mean to society?"

"Pressure," someone offered.

Stacey clicked her teeth and smiled. "What do you mean? What kind of pressure?"

"If I don't cook dinner for my family every night, I'm afraid I'm a terrible mom." Nods and murmurs of agreement from the audience for the woman I dubbed Red.

"Are you a terrible mom?" Stacey asked her.

"No!" said the woman. "I drive my kids to school every morning and pick them up from soccer practice every afternoon. I pack them lunches, and I try to buy organic produce when it's on sale."

"Someone who does those things can be a terrible mom, can't they?" asked Stacey. She wasn't wrong, I had to admit.

"I guess," said Red. "My husband is in the military, so it's my kids and me. I'm so tired in the evening." She paused, as if she were about to admit something shameful. "So, I order takeout. A lot of times I order takeout or pick up a take-and-bake pizza on the way home. What else can I do?" she asked, whirling a golden band around her ring finger with a shaky hand.

Stacey stood in front of her and took both her hands. "You are a wonderful mom," she told Red. "You are nourishing your children, and that's what matters. Don't let anyone tell you different." Stacey continued, "The pressures we put on moms can be overwhelming. We are here for you now. We can be the support system if you need it."

Red broke down. Stacey hugged her and led her back to her chair, where those nearest leaned over to tell her she wasn't alone. It was an intimate moment, like I was watching a group of close friends in someone's living room. No, we were all strangers who had paid a fee to find some affirmation.

The next activity was working on our personal statements in our notebooks. I halfheartedly wrote down financial goals for my copywriting business. I was grateful when we broke for lunch, which was brought in by hotel staff and served in little brown boxes. I unpacked half a brioche sandwich filled with microgreens and a slice of portobello mushroom, a tiny bag of dried apple slices, and a carton of spring water that reminded me of kindergarten juice boxes.

Another journaling exercise followed this; my hand was starting to get sore. I sighed with relief when Stacey said to put away our notebooks. From a large Tupperware bin hiding under a table in the corner, she began pulling out little pink drawstring gym bags and distributing them on the empty chairs. She handed me mine. "What's this?"

"Your ticket to relaxation." She winked.

Jenny squealed. "Swag bag!" She pulled out a pair of black yoga leggings and a pink tank top with the arrow motif emblazoned on the chest. We took turns going to the other rooms within the suite to change, while Stacey moved the furniture around and laid down yoga mats. With the lighting of a few tea lights and the return of the singing-bowl soundtrack, the suite was turned into a yoga studio. The last part of the day was dedicated to a gentle hatha yoga flow. During Savasana, Stacey announced it was the end of the first day. I opened my eyes and stretched my toes out. I hated to admit it, but I felt kind of amazing.

"What do you think?" I asked Jenny as we gathered our things.

She beamed. "I think I learned a lot about myself today."

CHAPTER 8

The cocktail hour was in the hotel bar, so we walked across the lobby in a gaggle. Jenny told me she'd flown up from Los Angeles for the weekend. "Artemis seminars are totally booked up all the time in LA," she said. "A few girls in my acting class have done them before, and they raved about them. They said all the A-list women in Hollywood know Everett. If you're in Artemis, it's like a networking thing, you know? I've been trying to get in for months now. Lucky for me, I was on the #artemiswellness hashtag on Instagram and a girl in Seattle posted, wanting to sell her spot in the seminar because she couldn't go anymore. I jumped on it and then even found a deal on airfare! It was meant to be, you know? It's like Everett says."

"Does he say that?" I looked at the special organic cocktail menu the bartender handed us. "Do you think you'll try the Coriander Cocktail? I'll have the Lavender Gimlet, please. Do you think it's weird an old white guy founded this whole thing? What can he know about being a woman?"

"Well, his sister cofounded it with him." She said it with a matter-of-factness, like it made sense a man might know a woman and, therefore, know women.

"So, you're an actress?"

"Aspiring. This will be my foot in the door. The girls in my acting class weren't even getting callbacks before joining Artemis. And now, they're getting booked for the career-making roles: Pretty Girl #1, Diner #2, you know?"

"Mm-hmm, I know." Our drinks arrived, surprisingly frilly and fluorescent for something labeled as organic. With the sprig of lavender garnish, I stirred the drink and watched an iridescent sparkly swirl around the highball glass.

We cheered with a clink of our glasses. Jenny took a sip and continued. "I'm finally going to break out from getting cast as Karate Girl in the background and . . . ugh, Geisha #6. I mean, I'm Chinese, for Chrissake. Oooh, okay, this drink is delicious."

I tasted my gimlet and had to admit, "It's tasty, yeah. I don't know why I was expecting it to be disgusting."

"Was it the edible purple glitter, maybe?"

I laughed and pretended to gag. "That was making me nervous. I didn't know glitter could be organic. Do I have glitter in my teeth?" My lips curled back like I was at the dentist's office.

Jenny examined my mouth. "Nothing in your teeth, but you're going to have the prettiest poos tonight."

An unexpected cackle of laughter escaped before I could stop it. Jenny put her hand over her mouth and laughed, her face erupting in a rosy flush. When I finally calmed down, I wiped tears from the corners of my eyes. It had been a while since I had laughed that hard; my abs were physically sore. In Jenny's easy company, my limbs and tongue were light and loose. "You know, my mom is Filipino, and she was kind of weirded out about me going to this thing," I confessed.

"Really? I thought you were mixed something, but I couldn't place it."

"Story of my life." I shrugged. "If I were in Hollywood, I would be going out for the roles of Ambiguous Ethnic Girl."

"Don't sell yourself short. You could also try for Tan Girl," Jenny quipped. "Surprisingly, my parents were supportive. They own a rental management company and take care of properties for owners who live primarily overseas. I grew up scrubbing laundry room floors and helping my dad repair leaky faucets. So, they're excited for me to pursue my dreams, even if it means they have to pitch in to cover my rent sometimes."

"That's amazing they're supportive of you."

Jenny stood up a little straighter and smiled. "Yeah. They would do anything for me."

I watched as Stacey arrived at the bar and was swarmed by the seminar attendees offering to buy her drinks. "Can I ask you something?" I lowered my voice. Jenny waited as I gathered my thoughts.

"Is this like Scientology or something? Isn't that big with celebrities too?"

"Oh God, no." Jenny dismissed this with a laugh. "I was in Scientology for about three months. This is different. Look at me, boring you with industry talk. Why are you here?"

"A friend recommended it to me. Has anyone you know ever met Everett or Sage?"

"One girl did. She went to the Artemis Retreat at their Salthouse property, and Everett was there in person! He's usually traveling, so she lucked out. She even got a personal one-on-one consultation with him. I was so jealous."

"Let me guess, a personal session costs extra?"

"Of course. Gurus don't hand out their time for free."

"Is he a guru?"

Before she could answer, Stacey spotted us and came over. "I'm so glad you both stayed for cocktails," she said. "Thank you for your time and attention and vulnerability today."

Jenny took her hands. "I've come all the way from Hollywood for this!" She repeated her story to Stacey, who, to her credit, listened to every word with rapt attention. At some point, a woman standing nearby overheard Jenny talking about LA and mentioned her cousin was living in Silver Lake. She and Jenny broke away in conversation.

Stacey turned to me. "And you? Have you come far?"

"No, I live here. I was meaning to ask you if you knew my friend? She referred me."

"Ooh, did you put her name down on your registration form? We want to make sure she gets credit for changing lives!"

"I did. Her name is Cara Snyder. Do you know her?"

Without a pause, Stacey answered, "No, I don't think I do." Yet the corner of Stacey's pink lips twitched, ever so slightly, while her eyes bored into me, unblinking. "I would love to meet her."

I nodded. "Sure."

Stacey sipped on her glass of white wine. "Is your friend also local?" she asked. "I mean, is she around, by any chance? I would love to thank her personally for referring you to us."

"No, she's not."

"It is unfortunate. If you see her, let her know I say hi." She offered modified prayer hands, one palm flat against her wineglass, and moved on to another woman waiting to pick her brain.

Maybe it was the yoga workout for the first time in too long for me, or the cocktails, but I opted to walk rather than take the bus home to my apartment. My body felt lighter, despite Cara still weighing down my thoughts. The city was brilliant, bathed in a low winter sun, and as I crossed busy streets, I began humming to myself in long, steady tones.

—◊—

For the second day of my seminar, the suite was still arranged as a yoga studio. The women, including Jenny, were sitting at the dining table. She waved and pointed to a Venti cup of Starbucks in her hands. "I visited the original store this morning!" she said. "And look." She showed me a selfie on her phone, the background a brick facade with millions of tiny globs of color. "The gum wall, so gross." She swiped and showed me a photo of her next to fishmongers in orange plastic aprons and sporting impressive beards. "I even caught a fish," she bragged. "Pike Place Market is so fun."

"You hit all the spots," I commented, sipping my own cup of Caffe Vita from the impressive breakfast buffet spread.

We had been asked to arrive in our yoga gear, and right on time, Stacey entered and led us in a vinyasa flow. After the fifth or so upward dog, my stomach was gurgling and I regretted my coffee for breakfast. Thankfully, after our practice, Stacey handed out chlorophyll smoothies. "Will this make me photosynthesize?" Jenny asked.

I shook my head and tried not to laugh at the fact I couldn't tell whether she was joking or not.

While staff cleaned up the breakfast spread and helped move the furniture back into place, I wandered to one of the windows overlooking the water. Gray clouds met my eyes as I stared at my reflection in the glass. The heavy rain front that hid the usual snow-capped mountain view also accentuated the dark circles that had settled underneath my eyes in the last couple of years. Especially since after Dad's death and my short stint in law school. I pushed the thought away, thankful Ren was the only thing remaining from those torturous nine months.

In the reflection, I saw Stacey move behind me. I turned. She smiled, and the corners of her mouth raised her broad nostrils, so her entire face, even her wide copper eyes, lifted. "How are you today, Delia?" With a delicate flip, she tossed her mane over a shoulder. She was still in her own leggings and tank top but looked as graceful as she had in satin.

"You know, I remembered," she said.

"Remembered?"

"Cara Snyder." She nonchalantly sipped her smoothie. My skin tingled, and I forced even breaths.

"Oh yeah?" I swallowed.

"So funny, I must have misheard you." Stacey leaned into the mirror, fixing an errant hair. "Of course I know Cara. She lived at Salthouse, after all. I was sad to hear when she left."

"Do you live there too?" I asked.

"I'm based out of our New York City location, but I do these intro seminars and training at our various Artemis offices across the country."

"Training for who?"

"Women aspiring to become mentors."

"Is it hard to become a mentor?"

"It takes years of studying. Unless you're uniquely gifted. As a mentor, I guide and train members. Sometimes, an especially gifted woman can rocket through the ranks. Part of my role is to intuit those who have a strong connection with their radiant self. Those women make the best mentors, we've found."

"Was Cara a mentor?"

"She was. She is a gifted woman, no doubt." Her voice wavered. She looked away from her reflection to me. "Do you plan on following her?"

I jolted, my mouth tilting open with only empty space. Stacey laughed at my dumbfoundedness. "I meant, are you thinking of joining Artemis?"

I giggled to cover my gaffe and hoped she thought I was a flake. "Maybe."

She tapped her watch. "Well, shall we chase the enlightenment some more?" She walked past me, her hair so close to my face, I caught the lingering scent of baby powder–scented shampoo. Without thinking, I inhaled deep.

—⁓—

I couldn't focus for the rest of the day. I tried to distract myself by participating in the never-ending flowcharts and mental exercises Stacey scrolled through on the screen, but my pen kept slipping in my sweaty palms. Why would Stacey conceal she knew Cara, then admit it so openly? I wondered if I had made a mistake in telling her of my relationship to Cara.

After all, I knew one version of Cara. Who Cara was to Stacey or Artemis, I was still discovering. Why hadn't I thought of it before? Maybe Cara was gone for a reason. Had she stolen money? Stolen intellectual property? The theories went wild in my head.

Finally, Stacey clapped her hands, and I emerged from my cloud of theories to find the seminar was ending. "It was such an honor to meet you and guide you all." She bowed, and the room answered with applause.

She nodded and smiled and pressed her palms against her chest. "If anything from this weekend resonated with you—" She clicked her projector remote, and a slide appeared. It read "Artemis Retreat at Salthouse Place: the next step in your journey." Ah, here was the closing pitch. A photo of a sunny Pacific Northwest beach appeared on the projector screen. The silhouette of a woman was backlit as she stood in the waves with her arms wide to meet the sun. My stomach turned at the very sight.

"While it's possible to continue your Artemis teachings at home with our workbooks or through remote webinars, we encourage woman-to-woman guidance. It's the best and fastest way to unlock your radiant self. Our next session at Salthouse Place is starting in a few weeks. And good news." She paused for effect. "Everyone here will get twenty percent off your registration fees when you sign up today."

Jenny gasped next to me. "I have to do it," she whispered, I think to herself.

"Even more exciting—" Stacey raised her voice above the din, and a hush ensued as the women straightened their backs in their chairs. "Each seminar, we choose one woman who has shown a unique aptitude for Everett's teachings to receive a scholarship to Salthouse Place."

Several women let out an "Ooh!" Jenny practically vibrated next to me. I glanced up at the clock.

"This year's scholarship recipient is—" Stacey let her gaze sweep over the room. Then those golden eyes met my own. "Delia!"

What did she say? Jenny gave a genuine whoop of excitement and clapped her hands with glee. "Good job!" she cheered. The rest of the room turned to me, arms folded and eyebrows knitted with disbelief. The silent girl who wouldn't have even earned a participation award had just received a free ride to wellness land.

CHAPTER 9

"Let's have the tea." Ren expertly gripped a Chinese soup dumpling in her chopsticks. "Figuratively and literally!" A curl of steam escaped as she bit a tiny hole in the top for ventilation before gulping it, broth and all.

I looked sideways, trying to hide behind my cup of floral jasmine tea. The University Village dumpling spot was our favorite place to meet, and Ren had been more than happy to meet me for lunch on Monday afternoon before I caught the ferry back to Portsgrove. I gave her a recap of the seminar and watched her eyes grow as large as the white enamel plate on which we piled our sautéed bok choy and noodles. When I told her about the scholarship, she laughed. "No offense, but I don't think it's your promising connection to a radiant self she sees in you." She rubbed her thumb and forefingers together. "Cha-ching."

I took another long sip of tea as she waited for me to finish. "Well?" She asked.

"Well, what?" I avoided her eyes.

She set down her chopsticks. "You are not going."

"Maybe—"

"Maybe, nothing. It's a scam."

"I'm not paying anything. They're footing the bill," I explained.

"Not now, you're not, but that's how they lure you in. There will be add-ons and fees and all manner of Karens trying to shill crystals. I don't know why you even signed up for the class."

I had to tell her. "I was gathering information."

"What information were you looking for in a self-help workbook?"

"Remember my old friend Cara?"

"I know you've mentioned her a few times in relation to . . . your other friend."

"Zee." I nodded. "Well, now Cara is missing." I told her about Cara's email and Tom's story.

"This is wild," Ren said when I finished. The tea had gone cold in my hands. "You think she's hiding at this Salthouse Place?"

"I think it's more likely that somebody there knows something."

Ren nodded. "Well, you asked me to research Artemis, and I did."

"And?"

"They're popular. Goop links to their blog articles, and Oprah listed the Artemis Essential Oils line as one of her Favorite Things for Christmas last year. The founder, Everett, was it? He's done lots of interviews and written for some big outlets. Though, it's funny you bring up Salthouse. If you sort through the Google results long enough, you start to run into local news articles about some controversy about Salthouse Place."

"What do you mean?"

"From what I read, in the early 2000s, an investor bet big on a coastal Oregon town forty-five minutes from Portland. They bought up ten acres of land as close to the public-owned beaches as possible. The locals were like, no thank you."

"Not great," I said.

"Not at all. Construction began, and they divided the lots up with string and stakes and poured driveways. The idea was the buyer would be able to custom build the house from a menu of choices."

I chuckled. "McMansions by the sea."

"They built a few houses as model homes. Some buyers bought townhomes, which were erected. Salthouse Place was populated with several new shiny houses intermingled among the empty dirt lots. In 2008, the investors went broke. The few families that moved in decided they didn't want to live in a half-finished artificial neighborhood and moved away. Salthouse Place became an eyesore and a burden for the town."

"Let me guess, the Wares to the rescue?"

Ren nodded. "In 2009, Everett Ware walked in and bought up the whole thing. He paid the town back for the utilities and back taxes. In his press release, he declared a vision informed him Salthouse Place would be the new home of Artemis and a destination for all their followers. But," Ren explained, "it's more likely he got a tip on some cheap land. The land title has Everett as a co-owner with at least five other parties, including a big-time tech CEO named Madelyn Brewer. The other listed co-owners seem like they could be shell companies. This guy is shady, Delia."

"Aren't all CEOs? What about Artemis? Anything about the company strike you as weird?"

"They seem to be on the up-and-up as far as their finances. I can't find any red flags there."

"So, what's your conclusion?"

"I don't know. My research tells me Instagram influencers love them and Regan Elliot credited them on an NPR interview for helping her get over stage fright." She stabbed a dumpling with a chopstick; the juicy pork broth oozed out into a pool onto her plate. "Why are you getting involved in this?"

"I don't know." Her jaw tightened, and I knew she was resisting the urge to tell me off. She understood friendship, more than most people I knew in my life. When I was drifting and drowning in my grief following Dad's car accident, Ren brought me dinner for two weeks straight. When I stopped going to class and my grades plummeted, Ren tried to tutor me in everything I was missing during lectures. In the end, she was the one who allowed me to say the words out loud: "I don't want to do this anymore."

She walked with me when I went to the registrar's office and officially withdrew from law school, and she didn't even flinch at the pitying stares and whispers following us down the hall. Our friendship was one of imbalance, I thought, one I often questioned in the beginning. I had nothing to offer her, yet she was there when I needed her. Why did I need to chase Cara when someone like Ren was right here?

Because it wasn't about Cara. Not really. "I have to find out what she knows about Zee," I said.

"What makes you so sure it's about Zee anyway?"

"It's too much of a coincidence," I said. "This year will be the ten-year anniversary of her disappearance, and the email came on my birthday week, which just so happens to be Zee's birthday week too. Then I check Cara's socials, and she posts a picture from her parent's house in Portsgrove. I know in my gut this is important."

Ren shook her head. "What could go wrong?"

I bit into a dumpling, tearing into the dough as the salty hot broth pooled in my mouth.

CHAPTER 10

I pulled up to the Roman-inspired pillars and a large concrete sign with gold-lettered cursive: SALTHOUSE PLACE. According to Google Maps, the road was paved in winding loops leading into various cul-de-sacs beyond.

I parked in front of an impressive circular building with a sign that read VISITORS' CENTER. There were stone steps leading from the center down to the beach, which I wandered along until they disappeared into the sand. Seagrass and dunes rolled down to the waves. My feet shifted, and the familiar clutch of fear tightened around my heart at the sight of the ocean. Yet I couldn't look away. The expanse of the Pacific stretched out before me and up to meet a dark sky. Ominous storm clouds hovered out at sea, their darkness seeming to threaten the land not already swallowed up by the fog. Although I knew otherwise, it was as if Salthouse was an island unto itself.

I pulled out my phone. No service. Of course.

"Welcome!" I jumped at the voice behind me. I turned to a woman at the top of the steps. She wore skinny jeans with an oversize white sweater and held a clipboard. "Are you Delia Albio, by any chance?" Her voice was a bubbly prosecco mixed with a southern twang of sweet tea.

"I am."

"Well, howdy and welcome! I'm Petal, a mentor here and all things operations." I climbed the steps to meet her. She shook my hand. "How was your journey? Did you come from far away? Let's get you checked in."

The inside of the visitors' center was painted in chic coastal grays and blues, though the decorator had thankfully stayed away from anchors or whale motifs. Instead, I walked on clean hexagonal tile and sat on a sleek leather love seat. Petal sat opposite me on an overstuffed ivory armchair. Behind her was a gallery wall of photos and paintings, the biggest being an artist's recognizable rendition of Everett Ware in a flourish of colorful oil pastels. Next to that, the largest photo was him and a blonde woman standing in front of an impressive brick building, which looked almost collegiate. The rest of the photos seemed to be of Everett posing with various famous people: benefactors, no doubt. Petal noted my interest.

"Pretty cool, huh? Everett has many famous friends who have found true peace with the Artemis teachings." She pointed to one photo of a woman on the beach, arm around Everett as they both smiled for the camera. "Madelyn Brewer," she said. Why was the name so familiar? "She runs BloomWallet," Petal added.

Now that she mentioned it, I recognized BloomWallet too.

"It's a tech start-up," Petal explained. That was right, Tom had said Cara worked for a start-up in the Bay Area before leaving to Oregon. "Madelyn is basically a badass Silicon Valley boss babe. She's been to Salthouse countless times."

That was it. Madelyn Brewer was one of the co-owners Ren had found listed on Salthouse Place's title. Cara's former boss was a prominent member of Artemis who also happened to be a co-owner of Salthouse Place? Clearly, the "friend" who Tom had said introduced Cara to Artemis had to have been Madelyn herself. I wondered how else they could be connected.

Petal moved us along the wall of photos. I pointed to the one of the large brick buildings. "Is that here at Salthouse?"

"No, it was a private college-prep school Everett and Sage ran for a time, the Ware Academy School for Girls. It's closed now."

I leaned forward to look at the photo. "That's Sage?" The photo was blurry and taken from a distance.

"You betcha. She's excited to welcome you new arrivals tonight at dinner." Petal handed me a packet of papers.

"I didn't realize I had dinner plans for my first night here." I sifted through my papers to find some kind of welcome agenda.

"Oh, you have dinner plans every night!" Petal laughed. "We eat lunch and dinner communally, right through there." She waved toward a set of large wooden doors. "Our gathering space. We call it the Forum. It's where meals, community meetings, or larger workshops are held. It's such a cozy space, you'll love it."

—⁓—

Petal instructed me to sign a myriad of waivers and agreements. Remembering Ren's advice, I read every word. Even with my fluency in legalese, they were vague and complicated. In the end, I gave up and signed.

Petal took the papers and inputted some information on an iPad. "And I see you've been a recipient of an Artemis scholarship! Congratulations! Artemis Wellness has covered all your expenses! Lucky you!" She tapped and scrolled.

"Would you like to put down a card? Having your card on file will also be helpful should you decide to stay longer than a month."

"I won't be staying any longer. Don't worry." I handed over my credit card, and she swiped it through the attached reader.

She handed it back in a flourish. "Well, now all the boring stuff's taken care of. Ready to go see your new digs?"

Though the sun was still out, it was raining in earnest by the time we left the visitors' center. The raindrops sprinkled against our skin, lit up like fireflies against the sun shining down between the droplets. "You know what my grandpa called this?" asked Petal, holding up her hands to catch the drops. I shook my head. "The devil is beating his wife today." She giggled.

As we walked down the road, my suitcase rolling behind me, she continued with her welcome script. "Every quarter or so, we offer this intensive Artemis retreat. It's a very special time, and you're very lucky to have snagged a spot! The first week will be, true to its name, intense. We like to call it a boot camp for the soul. Clean eating, exercise, and reflection. You and your cohort will work through some very tough feelings, and not everyone will make it past the first week. After the initial cleansing, those who have survived will be ready to live among the community and enjoy the benefits of life at Salthouse."

I could only nod and hope my face wasn't showing my obvious despair in the group project. "When do I achieve nirvana?" I asked.

She grinned. "Ah, a skeptic. Don't worry. You'll be in good company. Since you are here, I reckon you're not as closed minded as you think."

With a sharp realization, I noted there were no utility poles or power lines anywhere. "There are no streetlights," I said, mostly to myself.

"Oh no," said Petal. "Certainly not. We believe such things are visual pollution. The electrical lines run underground, and all trash needs to be taken to the Forum on a weekly basis for garbage pickup."

She was right: I didn't see any garbage bins against the outside walls of houses, only neatly trimmed green lawns. There were no cars in any of the empty driveways. I remembered my cell without any service.

"So no phone service?"

"No service or Wi-Fi in the larger community. We find our members are more successful when they don't have the distractions that constant contact allows. Not to mention the fact that outside influences can sometimes, er, pull focus away from our own journeys. You can use the phones and the computers in the Forum at scheduled times, though we would encourage you to take advantage of a digital detox."

Of course.

We reached a fork in the road. To the right, there was a house bigger than all the others. Petal noticed me staring. "The Ware residence. Isn't it grand?"

"It's something."

"Well, you are neighbors!" We took the left fork and paused at the first townhome. "Here's your new beachfront home."

"Well, we can't see the beach anymore . . ." I craned my neck to look behind us. Petal either didn't hear me or wasn't listening. I followed her inside.

The town house was nice, I had to admit. The interior was as chic as the Forum, with slate-gray walls and silver accent lighting; the living room was immaculate; and the navy-blue sofa looked inviting. Though somebody, perhaps a former #goddessintraining, couldn't help herself and had nailed onto the wall above the TV a painted driftwood sign that read BEACH DON'T KILL MY VIBE.

I nodded my approval, and Petal led me upstairs. We passed two rooms with open doors. Peeking in, I spied suitcases and various personal items in each. I was the last housemate to arrive, it seemed. Petal opened the last door on the right, and I followed her into a good-size bedroom with a door leading to an en suite bathroom. I set my suitcase next to the full-size bed, made with stark white bedsheets. I ran my hand over the gossamer fabric and imagined the thread count was something very high. A small desk and chair were in the corner with a pocket-size white notebook placed on top. The logo was a bow and arrow, similar to the workbook from the seminar. It was also like Cara's. I picked up the notebook and traced the logo, wondering if she had done the same.

"A small welcome gift." Petal nodded to the notebook. "There are complementary essential oils in the bathroom for your enjoyment, as well." Petal pointed out the window, which looked like it might provide a view of the water if you pressed your face on the glass hard enough. "Imagine you'll be waking up to this every morning now." She smiled serenely. "Do you love it?"

I didn't know how to answer her or where to begin. Should I tell her I was happier not looking at the ocean on a daily basis? The front door opened again, and voices entered. "I bet those are your roommates!"

To my surprise, I recognized one woman as soon as we got back downstairs. "Jenny?"

"Delia!" She jumped and hugged me. "I heard a rumor I was going to be rooming with you! And by 'heard a rumor,' I mean I requested you as my roomie. I'm so excited! This is Gillian," Jenny said, introducing the woman beside her.

"Nice to meet you. Jenny has told me all about you!" Gillian gave me an earnest hug. She didn't look like the other Artemis members I had met so far. Bright-red tassel earrings hung from her ears, and her lipstick matched. Something about her was genuine, and somehow, I was grounded in her touch.

"It's so nice to meet you too," I told her. My roommates weren't so bad after all, I thought. A piece, albeit small, of anxiety floated away.

"Here is your key. I'll leave you gals to it, and we'll see you at dinner tonight!" Petal bid us farewell.

Gillian and I sat in the living room while Jenny dug around in the fridge. "I'm starving," she said. "I thought we had more string cheese in here, Gil!"

Gillian shook her head. "No, we need to pick more up. We ate it all last night."

A bubbly laugh emerged from my mouth. "You have no idea how much I'm identifying with you both right now. And thank God, because Petal was beginning to weird me out."

—⁂—

Jenny and Gillian had both arrived a couple of days ago, in order to settle in before the first day. Upstairs, I hung up my clothes, lined up my toiletries on the bathroom vanity, and plugged in my phone charger, only to remember that was useless. Last, I took Cara's old workbook and carefully slid it underneath my mattress. After a change of clothes and a deep breath in and out, I met my roommates downstairs.

On our way to dinner, Gillian walked through the schedule. "We eat breakfast at the house. They serve lunch at noon and dinner at six p.m. sharp every day. All the food comes from the kitchen, made by the on-staff chefs. They follow a custom-made menu created daily by Dr. Nicklin."

"Who's Dr. Nicklin?"

"He's the community physician. He's our primary care provider and dietitian, and he leads a yoga class every Wednesday," Jenny chimed in.

"How do you both know so much already?" I asked.

"We took turns reading the welcome booklet and new member manual last night."

"Sounds like a wild night. So where did those string cheeses come from?" I asked, half joking.

The girls exchanged guilty smiles. "Technically, the kitchen here provides everything we need, even pantry staples and snacks. We might have snuck out to the local grocery store," Gillian said.

"Might have?" I loved that their rebellious streak included contraband dairy products.

"It was so weird." Jenny whistled. "Everyone was staring at us at the store in town."

"Why?"

Gillian paused. "Let's say it would seem the relationship between Artemis's Salthouse property and the town isn't the greatest. I don't think they support Everett's vision here."

I wanted to ask what exactly the vision was, but we arrived at the Forum. The sudden appearance of the entire Salthouse population in one place took me by surprise. There were more women than I expected, at least a hundred, of all ages and color. We joined the line and filed in.

Jenny had made several friends already and was soon engaged in a conversation at another table. Gillian and I went to fill our plates without her. I piled on some brown rice and picked out seasoned chicken breasts and bright-green steamed broccoli with a heaping spoonful of Greek salad. Gillian's plate contained a mountain of spring salad, shining with balsamic.

"So, I know Jenny's story," I told Gillian when we were seated at our designated house table. "How did you find Artemis?"

"A diagnosis of depression led to my divorce a couple years ago; my ex-husband couldn't deal. So, I was doom scrolling one night and saw a picture of this woman on a beach. It was a sponsored ad, of course, but something about her. She was gorgeous, of course, but it was her look of peace with herself. The caption was something about empowerment and it mentioned the Wares and that book he wrote, *The Artemis Method*. I did more research, and I wanted in. Did some seminars in my hometown, San Diego. For the first time in years, I was motivated. Even my kids noticed. I stopped taking my depression meds. Artemis Wellness has helped me more than any doctors I've seen. So, I applied for the retreat. I didn't expect to get in. It's competitive." She took a bite of her greens. "What about you?"

"I went through a breakup." It was the first thing that came to mind, and, after all, it was true.

"Oh, you poor thing." She placed her hand over mine. "Hear from me, it gets better. He was trash anyway."

I smiled, my lips a thin line. "Where's Sage?" I asked. "Petal said she would be around tonight."

"I don't think the leadership have come in yet. You would know if they did. Sage is a wellness celebrity. I'll be the first to admit fangirling over her."

As if on cue, the doors opened, and the room hushed into reverent silence. They entered in a line. I recognized the woman in the middle; it was Stacey, the teacher from the seminar in Seattle. Behind her was a man, the only man at Salthouse I'd encountered so far. He wasn't Everett, that much I knew. It clicked that he must be Dr. Nicklin. Behind him were a few other women I didn't recognize, including a petite white woman with gossamer wavy brown hair flowing down to her shoulders, framing her face like a lion's mane.

Everyone's eyes were on the woman leading them, the woman who I recognized from the website and the woman who I knew could tell me about Cara. It was Sage Ware.

She was tall and lithe, and I guessed she was in her mid- to late thirties. Her blonde hair was cut in a severe bob, with edges threatening to slice the equally sharp jawline it glanced against. She wore no makeup, yet she glowed. The group stood at their table, and the room held its breath. Sage bowed slightly, and the room bowed back. Gillian and I exchanged glances and bowed too.

Holding her pressed palms in front of her heart, Sage spoke. "I want to say to all our new sisters, we are so happy you've taken the first step to wellness, to your radiant self, and to truth. Welcome to Artemis."

Applause broke out, and everyone sat down.

While women moved around from table to table socializing, Sage stayed in her seat in the center of the Forum. The room seemed to both orbit around her and be repelled by her at the same time. Jenny returned, and she, Gillian, and I continued to chat. After our plates were cleared and I noticed women drifting out, Gillian suggested we also head home. "You must be exhausted," she said. She was right: I felt everything catching up to me.

At the Forum door, I turned. "I'll catch up. I forgot something."

I walked up to Sage, still at her table, and we locked eyes. "You're new. We're so happy to have you here." Her voice was quiet and soft, her blue eyes piercing. The air around her felt both welcoming and electrifying, like running into a long-lost friend. Was this an aura? If I wasn't a believer in Artemis at that moment, I became a believer in Sage.

"Thank you." I held out my hand. "I'm Delia Albio."

She ignored my hand and sipped her wine. "Wonderful to meet you."

"A friend referred me to Artemis. Maybe you knew her? I think she did a lot of your marketing . . ."

"Who?"

"Cara Snyder."

Sage smiled. She stood and brushed past me; did I feel a spark on my skin as the fabric of our clothing touched? "Good night, Delia." She walked out into the night.

CHAPTER 11

The next morning, the intensive week began, much like the seminar, with a yoga session.

It was led by the lion's-mane brunette woman from the leadership lineup, who introduced herself as Robyn. I was excited to continue this new practice I had discovered during the Seattle weekend session. In the days after, I'd found myself searching for YouTube yoga classes and attempting to stretch myself into awkward asanas in my living room.

As we lay down for Savasana, Robyn put on ambient forest sounds and said she would come around to each of us with a small blessing. I let my bones settle into my sweat-soaked mat and found my usual racing thoughts were absent and my muscles were a happy kind of exhausted. *Yoga,* I thought. *Who knew?*

Soft pads of feet approached, and Robyn's voice softly spoke into my ears. "Artemis welcomes you to this journey to your self. Walk in peace and intention." I felt a wet, cool dot on my forehead, and then she ran a finger across to each temple. Then, a strong scent of floral potpourri hit my nostrils. I held back a tickle in my throat. "Hrrmm, what's that?" I whispered.

"Our proprietary Artemis blend of bergamot and lavender essential oils."

"It's so . . ." I couldn't hold back anymore and jolted up, coughing and gagging. Robyn jumped back, and the roomful of yogis sat up to stare at me while I wiped the vile scent off my face.

"Well, it's not for everyone," Robyn admitted. She cleared her throat and moved on to anoint the next woman.

We broke for lunch, wild greens salad and roasted herb chicken, with a journaling session following. Without forewarning, the next activity was an aggressive Tony Robbins–style confessional. I cringed at hearing various traumas teased out of reluctant attendees. I didn't understand the purpose of making women regurgitate these regrets, these ugly scars.

I became more agitated at Robyn's open-ended questions: "And how did you feel?" or "And did you think that was fair? What did it mean to you?" Like an uncredentialed therapist. Then, a small realization, tears, and applause, like a breakthrough had happened before our eyes, when it was really someone having room enough to speak that was the medicine here.

Robyn found me in the audience and locked onto me. Shit.

"You there." She pointed. "Would you stand?" I did. "Tell us about yourself, what you do for work, where you're from." Her smile gave me an instant cavity.

"Uh, I'm in the legal field. Seattle."

"Cool, a lawyer," said Robyn.

"I'm not a lawyer." I corrected her with my familiar refrain. "I write for lawyers. Websites, blogs and things."

"You have some legal training, no?"

"I did . . . attend law school for a short time. I dropped out, though."

"Why?" The inevitable question.

"My dad passed away. I went home to be with my mom and stayed."

"Wow. That must have been hard. How do you feel about your decision now?"

How did I feel? Years on, and I still hated myself for the choice. It hadn't been a choice at all. I couldn't be away from home, not with Mom alone and Dad gone. Because what I never said out loud was, *If*

I hadn't left for law school to begin with, Dad would still be alive. "Fine," I answered.

"Did you do okay in law school before your dad's passing?" she asked.

"Sure," I lied. No, I didn't do okay. I developed anxiety and depression over the sudden intensity of the curriculum. Used to easily skating by academically, I found myself shrunken into a tiny fish in a very big pond. Mom had said more than once I was using Dad's death as an excuse to run from law school, but what did she know?

"Were you concerned your decision disappointed your family?"

I softened my tone and tried again. "I knew my mom was disappointed, but it was done, and I couldn't take back the choice."

"And your friends? Especially the one you lost?"

I blinked. "What did you say?"

"Did you think about the friend you lost and whether your choice would disappoint her?"

My breath caught in my throat. How did she know? "How do you mean?" I stammered, feeling the sweat beads forming on my forehead.

"I mean," she said, "did you feel guilty at all she wasn't around anymore to accomplish these kinds of things, while you, alive and well, were affirmatively choosing not to do what she would never have the opportunity to?"

I stared in jaw-dropping silence. I swallowed. It wasn't possible.

"It's okay." She nodded. "It's a lot of feelings, I get it." I wanted to punch her. Instead, I steeled my barrier for another assault. To my surprise, she turned away, back to the crowd, and chose another victim. I couldn't hear another word, only Mom's voice when she called me that night. *Delia, there was an accident. Your dad.* It replayed infinite times in my head, alternating with memories of Zee on the lake. It drowned out the rest of the day. When we arrived back at our house, I fell onto the couch and covered my face with a cushion.

"What about the homework?" asked Jenny.

"We have homework?" I moaned through the cushion.

"Didn't you hear Robyn?" said Gillian. "The workbook."

I sighed. "Okay, let's get it over with. How long can it take?" We didn't finish until midnight. Even after I laid my head on my pillow, I heard the whispering in my mind. *They know.*

They had researched me, found my business website, read my bio, like I had done to them. They had looked up my hometown and, no doubt, found the articles from Zee's disappearance. Where had they found my law school records? I thought about my social media—maybe they'd read that I had attended law school for an inordinately short time. The only explanation would be something happening, like me leaving. It made sense. Though, did I have the law school and my dates of attendance on any of my profiles? In my haze of aching bones and aching heart, I couldn't, for the life of me, remember.

The week went by in a fever dream. Late-night bedtimes and 5:00 a.m. wake-up calls took a toll physically, while the mandated emotional exploration compounded my weak state. I almost didn't believe Jenny when she said, quiet and flat, on our walk to the Forum in the dark morning air, "Last day."

That morning, Robyn asked us all to gather on the beach rather than in the Forum. I chewed on my lip as we approached the steady hum of the wild Pacific. We took off our shoes to walk through the sand. A wave crashed like a cymbal, and I flinched but kept walking.

We stood on the sand, where Robyn led us in a triumphant parade from the Forum. She lined us up in three rows facing the water. Without her microphone, Robyn yelled against the wind while walking back and forth in front of our rows, an army commander addressing troops about to go into battle. As we got closer to the waves and it became more and more apparent what the exercise entailed, I shrank to the back.

"To mark the completion of the first-week intensive, we will perform a group walk into the water." She flourished her arm toward the dark sea. "Like a cleansing, we, the apprentices of Artemis, will be anointed in the seas of Mother Goddess Earth!" she screamed fanatically.

"I can't do this," I hissed at Jenny frantically. "I can't do this."

"Do what? We're going to walk into the water. I'm not a good swimmer either—"

"It's not about swimming!" I said. My heart threatened to beat out of my chest. Why didn't they get it? My mind raced back to Teddy, dropping me into the lake while I pleaded and screamed. "No," I said again, breathing harder.

My heart beat louder than the breaking waves. When Gillian and Jenny moved forward, I grasped their arms, and my heavy bones remained stuck into the sand.

Jenny signaled to Robyn. "She can't swim." She pointed at me, frozen in place.

Robyn turned her fearsome attention to me. "I'm not asking you to swim. I'm asking you to walk, one step at a time. Trust your feet and your mind to keep you steady against waves you won't be able to control. Don't listen to the fear! Your body is a liar. Your mind has to be stronger than what your body tells you."

"No, no, no, no," I repeated, to nobody but myself. I lowered myself onto the sand, spreading my fingers through the rough grains to anchor myself somehow to the earth. *She's out there, I know it.*

"Who's out there?" Robyn asked.

Had I said it out loud? *I'm too tired,* I thought, *getting mixed up.* I shook my head again. "I can't do it."

"What if your new sisters help you?" Robyn suggested.

Gillian and Jenny cushioned me by my armpits, and, limp as a rag doll, I allowed myself to be lifted. "I don't know," I mumbled to Gillian. She stroked my hair and eased it from where it had stuck onto my lips, slick with lip balm.

"You can do this," she said. "You've done an entire week of hard work. Dipping our toes in the water? Now, this is nothing."

I looked up. Women were returning from the water. Some of their clothing was wet from the knees down, others from the waist, a visual mark of their limits of bravery. They laughed and caught each other, their feet slipping against the shifting sand beneath them. They looked happy.

And what was I? I was tired.

I wanted to be as happy as the women returning from the ocean. I nodded my head ever so slightly, and Robyn caught it. "I know you can do this," she said with the conviction needed for the both of us. I rose to my feet and, in a delirium, willed them forward.

Clutching one another, we moved to the water. Gillian and Jenny were repeating encouragement to me as we approached; all I heard was the roar of the surf. My toes sunk into wet sand; the water pooled around my foot as it compressed the sand down. I wondered if the polar plunge hadn't gotten something right: my clothing weighed me down. I pulled at my shirt, like I needed to shed my skin.

Then there she was. In the waves slapping against my legs, in the wind that left my throat dry and as hoarse as the day I had yelled for her for what seemed like hours. Lost in the cascading roar of the memory, my legs gave out, and I hit the sand.

I slipped away to another time as I was pulled out of the depths.

CHAPTER 12

Then

After the police put a closed stamp on the case, nobody knew how to move on. The lack of a body might have been a problem for most. For the family, it was a small lifeline allowing them to stay afloat on a slowly capsizing hope: Zelda could walk through the door at any moment. They were adamant no funeral take place, but the church convinced them to have a memorial. They even called local news crews. I thought it was smart. "If she's somewhere, watching," I told my mom on the day of the memorial, "she'll see how much we want her to come home." My mom was silent as she pulled into the church parking lot. I watched a look pass between her and Dad. The fleeting glance between parents they never think their kids see, but we always do.

As a family, we retrieved our candles from the cardboard box set up on the welcome table in front of the church steps. Mom and Dad greeted and hugged Zee's parents, Ella and Walt Harris. They looked like zombies, I thought. I didn't know then the unnaturalness of it all—a parent losing a child.

A child myself, I was more concerned about how I would go on in Zee's absence, at least until her return, which I was still adamant would happen soon. Any moment. I gave my sorrys and hugs to Ella and Walt, who were like a second set of parents to me. My mom rubbed Ella's shoulder and told her, "You're so strong."

Ella evaded her comfort. "They're not even looking anymore." Her voice lowered in a growl. "You know they would still be diving for the body if Zee looked like *her*."

Her husband shushed her. "Not now, Ella."

"No, I won't shush," Ella said. "It's no secret if Zee was white, like Cara, they would have brought her home by now."

From the corner of my eye, Walt jerkily gestured to me to remind the adults that I was still here and very much listening. Ella fell silent.

I looked at my mom, her eyes shifting from candle to candle. She spoke, her voice barely above a whisper. "What about the lawsuit?"

"We don't know," replied Walt. "We got a second opinion, and the lawyer told us providing alcohol to a minor was a tough sell to a jury for wrongful death. Especially when the girls took it without anyone knowing. Besides, the Snyders have money to draw out any legal stuff. We can't afford it."

I left before I could hear anything more. I couldn't handle the infighting. The parents had been as close as we girls were. Now, here they were, going at each other worse than any of us. I walked along the periphery of the crowd; the entire town had turned out. Everyone was nervous, on edge. If Zee had been taken, then, at best, someone here knew something more than they were saying. At worst, there was a murderer among us.

Suddenly, there it was. In between the flickering flames and the shadows of the growing dusk, there she was. I looked around me to see if anyone else had noticed her. All faces were turned downward in respectful prayer. I moved toward the outer edge of the candles, toward the shadowy figure. I bit my tongue to keep from screaming out and inciting a panic.

How did everyone miss her? I had left the immediate churchyard now and was almost back in the parking lot. She was gone. *I'm going insane,* I thought. *I'm seeing things.*

I spotted her again, at the edge of the crowd. Her long black curls, and, I swore, a glance toward me with those unmistakable eyes.

I dropped my candle. The flame extinguished on the wet pavement between my feet. I ran to her, only to have her dissipate once again into the shadows between the lights.

I gulped at the air and rubbed my chest, where my heart was aflame. With blurred vision, I looked around for my parents but saw only her. I turned to go back to our car. I would sit and wait there. As I approached it, I heard it behind me, the steps following my own. *Here she is,* I thought. With a sudden dread, I realized it wasn't her this time. The footsteps heavy, the gait all wrong, I knew. The dread entered me, and my thoughts accelerated along their twisted tracks. It was him. Whoever had taken Zee was now stalking me because I knew the truth—she was still alive.

I had to get back to the memorial and tell someone. I spied a route between cars back to the main lit road. There, I could double back to the church and tell someone. So, with a bolt of adrenaline, I ran. When I hit the sidewalk of the main road, my feet flew from circle to circle of streetlamp light. I reached the other side of the church and glanced back in the direction I came from. There was nothing there. Nothing in the parking lot except dark car shapes.

I turned back. Then I ran into him.

I screamed. My body pressed against a strong square chest.

"Delia? It's me! It's okay."

I found myself in Tom Snyder's arms.

"What are you doing?" He looked behind me and around us. "Why are you running?"

"I thought I saw . . ." I gasped to catch my breath to explain everything. As I breathed easier, I knew it was no use. The stalker was gone. So was Zee. "Never mind."

"Hey, you all right?" With a finger, he wiped away a tear from my cheek. I looked up and couldn't speak. Nobody had asked me. I wasn't all right. I wasn't sure if I would ever be all right again. Tom tilted my chin up and whispered, "Shh." He pulled me into an embrace, my hot face buried in his jacket, which smelled like cheap cologne and canvas. "Do you want to get away from this place?"

I had never wanted to be somewhere else so bad in my young life.

In his basement, beneath the floorboards where his parents flipped through prime-time television and his sister cried over Zee, he asked me, "Are you sure?"

"I'm sure." So, I lost myself then and there in his bed. I struggled to move against his weight on top of me, like a current holding me down. Every push inside of me was a reminder to breathe, and I gasped for air.

"Are you okay?" he asked me when it was over.

"It's like drowning in someone," I said into his skin. I was hurting and dizzy, but I knew at that moment we had emerged from a dark undertow. My head lay on his arm. He nodded and kissed my forehead.

CHAPTER 13

The kiss felt soft against me. When I opened my eyes, it wasn't Tom at all who was facing me.

"There you are, Delia," Sage cooed, her voice a purr as gravelly as the sand I was crumpled upon. She licked her lips, the salt from my own wet skin having transferred to her. I blinked, disoriented.

"Thank God." Jenny sighed next to me.

"Thank Goddess," Robyn corrected with a head tilt.

Gillian held my limp wrist between her fingers. "Your heart rate is back to normal. You fainted. Probably dehydration."

"Facing our radiant self can be overwhelming," Sage said.

How long had I been out?

"I'm sorry," I said. "I just—"

"Don't apologize," said Sage, stern as a parent. "Your strength is found in not having to explain yourself. The water will be there when you're ready." She stood and held out her hand. I took it. She lifted me up.

Light headed, I grasped onto her and floundered for a moment on my unsteady legs. My heart was still pounding, and a heat was flaring in my chest. She and Robyn would have pushed me into the water and let me drown, I thought. All in the name of a bonding exercise. In a swift movement, I pushed her arm away from me. "I got it," I snapped. Looking down, I slapped my thighs with my palms to shake off the sand.

Robyn held something toward me, and before I could focus on what it was, I felt her slide it over my head and around my neck. "What is this?" I looked down and saw a soft leather necklace holding a teardrop-shaped opalescent pendant. I picked it up and noticed how the sunlight and even the blue from the water seemed to flow right into the middle of the translucent stone. Then I saw Jenny and Gillian had the same necklaces hanging from their necks as well.

"You earned it today," explained Sage. "It's a moonstone, helpful for clarity of thought and an ancient symbol of new beginnings and the feminine divine. All apprentices receive this amulet after successfully completing the first-week intensive."

I dragged my hands over my face, nodding through shaky breaths. My thoughts and memories were entangled in my brain. I touched a fingertip to my forehead, still tingling from Sage's lips.

Jenny shifted and held her hands gently on my shoulders. "Let's get you home," she said.

CHAPTER 14

I was warm in my bed, staring at the white ceiling above me, naked except for the moonstone settled in between my breasts. I could hear Gillian's shower running through the wall her bathroom shared with my own, washing the Pacific salt off her skin. I thought about showering, too, though I had already tracked clumps of gritty sand in and dirtied the pristine white sheets. I wiped as much as I could off the bed, while my mind kept wandering back to the Snyders. I had always thought Tom saved me that night. Saved me from a phantom, saved me from my grief. While he pulled me out of the depths of my mourning, who was watching out for Cara?

Cara.

She had been where I was now. I knew she'd gone through the Artemis training, faced her demons, walked into the ocean. Did it have to do with what she knew about Zee's disappearance? *Why, Cara?* What did she need from Artemis? Or, I thought with a twist of fear, what did Artemis need from her?

—※—

I hadn't set an alarm, but I needn't have bothered, anyway. I woke up to Gillian and Jenny invading my room and throwing open the curtains to the sunrise. I groaned and tried to hide under my pillow.

"Up, up." Gillian poked me. "The girls will be here in thirty minutes for the very first Coffee."

"What time is it?"

"Six thirty a.m."

They had divided the houses up for morning group sessions, euphemistically called Coffees. The houses took turns hosting, and today we were up.

"You mean I have to talk about more trauma?" I whined.

"Only if you want to, I think," said Jenny.

I shivered, remembering Robyn's brutal interrogations during the intensive week. I wanted to ask when we got to work through and process *that* trauma.

Gillian snapped her fingers. "Come on, get dressed. You can help me bake some muffins."

I sat up. "Okay, you should have led with muffins."

I wondered if we were pretending it was another normal morning. Was it better that way? I didn't know.

Despite every muscle in my body crying for more rest, I got up and dressed. I washed my face with the fair-trade linen washcloth in my bathroom and made sure to accidentally knock the essential oil bottle over into the trash can. The kitchen was soon bustling with activity, akin to hosting a dinner party but at an unnecessarily early morning hour. While Jenny said she needed to go for a quick walk, Gillian employed my help in whipping up a batch of blueberry muffins in record time. I was comforted by her giving instructions like Mom did. We rearranged our living room seating into a circle.

Jenny returned with a handful of wildflowers.

"Where did you get those?" I asked, surprised.

"Along the dunes, close to the forest. Isn't it amazing how flowers can grow in impossible places?" Jenny arranged them in a mason jar on the coffee table. "Camas and ocean spray blossoms. This is our first Coffee, and I want to impress Robyn."

The group members soon arrived, bringing more unsolicited breakfast pastries. I had met most of the women already, but there were a few I didn't know. They waved and greeted me warmly, shouting out their names in turn; I immediately forgot them all. They unwrapped themselves from multiple layers of jackets and rain shells. There were ten of us. Gillian had created a buffet-like space on the counter, and the women marched in line and filled up their plates.

Robyn arrived later than the main group, and Jenny met her with a cup of coffee at the door.

I took a seat on the couch with my muffin and coffee. Robyn joined me. "How are you doing, Delia?"

Oh, you know, I thought. *Just busy being a failure, and thank you for bringing that to my attention.* "Fine. Everyone is very nice here. My roomies and I get along."

"We try to be welcoming. After all, if you don't feel safe at a women's retreat, we've failed miserably." She smiled. I didn't find the sentiment as comforting as she obviously did.

Jenny called us to sit in the living room. Balancing gluten-free muffins and coffees, everyone took their seat in the circle of armchairs and a sofa and a giant beanbag.

Robyn called the meeting to order. "Good morning, sister goddesses."

"Good morning, sister goddesses!" the group, myself included, replied in unison. I widened my eyes and looked at Gillian over the rim of my coffee cup, but she was focused on Robyn.

"Let's begin with the daily schedule," Robyn explained. "Aside from Coffee and the self-led meditation and reflection times, how you spend your time here will be up to you. We refer to this second week as a self-led path of discovery. You'll find open activities and groups you can sign up to work with this week. The rest of your day we hope you intentionally fill with positive activities promoting spiritual growth. I know there's a forest bathing session in the late morning, and I would highly recommend joining."

I made what-the-hell eyes at Jenny, and she stifled a smile.

"For now," Robyn continued, "I want to continue building on our past days' conversations about image and expectation. Specifically, I want to know what it means when we're exposed to so many toxic images of women in media and online."

Jenny slowly raised her hand. "I can speak about this topic. I live in LA, and I'm an actress. Or aspiring to be a successful one, anyway. Everywhere I go, I see images of what I'm supposed to look like. I'm not Nicole Kidman, and I'm not Kim Kardashian. Of course, people say, 'But you chose this industry.' True. I wish sometimes the industry would change for women of color like me, instead of me changing for the impossible standards of the industry."

"What standards do you mean?" asked Robyn.

"Tall, blonde, and white," said Jenny. "When I walk into auditions, the casting director doesn't see me. They see a stereotype or, sometimes, a fetish."

"What would happen if you didn't let them see?"

Jenny was quiet, glancing down at the mugs on the table.

Robyn went on. "Don't let yourself give in to the lie you have to look a certain way to be successful or taken seriously. Don't allow their preconceived notion to be part of your vision."

"A little hard when those images are everywhere," chimed Gillian, clearly self-conscious as she held a cushion against her stomach. "I mean, Kim Kardashian doesn't even look like Kim Kardashian. It's all Photoshop!"

"Exactly," said Robyn. "Let's not focus on what we can't change. Instead, let's choose not to see. Simple."

Jenny furrowed her brow. "I don't mean this to sound rude," she said. Robyn nodded. "It's hard not to see. Gillian's right. It's everywhere and, well, I have eyes."

"Let's turn our gaze toward ourselves. Jenny, name a couple things you love about how you look."

Jenny sat silent and stoic.

"Nothing at all?" Robyn prodded. "I could tell you fifty things I find beautiful about you, Jenny!"

Jenny looked at Robyn, her eyes like glass. "I'm not beautiful." A chill went through us all. I glanced at Gillian, who frowned back at me with worry.

Robyn sighed. "Of course, we can all find beauty in images and in the mirror, but more often, beauty is found in the places we can't easily see into. So, cover your eyes with your hands. Let's all practice not seeing with our eyes but seeing with our hearts." I rolled my eyes behind my eyelids. "Say it with me now: no more eyes. No more eyes."

The group began chanting together in rhythm. "No more eyes. No more eyes. No more eyes."

"Enough," said Robyn. "Our new eyes don't see the harmful or the toxic. Only the good and worthy. Open your new eyes."

I blinked, and light shone into my world again. There was a sniffle next to me, and I turned to find Jenny fighting back tears. "Are you okay?"

She burst and let out a wail. Surprised, I froze. Gillian swept in between us and took hold of Jenny. "Shh, shh, you're beautiful, love. You're so beautiful."

—⁐—

Gillian and I washed dishes while Jenny rested upstairs before we were due for the forest walk. "Isn't that a problem, though?" I asked Gillian. "When an attractive white woman tells you to 'not see color' or 'not see sexism'? That's privilege." I tempered my argument. "I don't mean to attack white women. It's more the attitude."

"You mean, since I'm also a privileged white woman?" Gillian smirked.

I relaxed. "I understand, but she's trying. She's trying to open our eyes—"

"Close our eyes."

"Whatever. It's funny how white women co-opt practices like yoga and preach about it, but when there's a water crisis in India or Indian women are being assaulted on a mass scale, it's crickets on their Instas."

"Well, I'm not like that," Gillian said.

"I didn't mean—"

"A couple years ago, I gave to a GoFundMe for an Indian village to get a working water pump." Gillian handed me a wet mug to dry.

My lips formed a soft "Oh!" And I looked down at my hands and traced the rim of the mug with my fingers. I allowed a small whisper of a thought to form. "Do you think they research us?" I asked.

Gillian's head snapped up. "What?"

"They knew I lost a friend," I explained. "And they wanted to talk about toxic media in a group where there happens to be an aspiring actress? Is it coincidental?"

Gillian shook her head. "I think we see connections we want to see."

CHAPTER 15

Petal was leading the forest bathing excursion. We all met at the farthest end of the Salthouse Place beach before the cliffs, where the sandy dunes were infiltrated by meandering Sitka spruce roots. The trail dropped dramatically into a coastal forest; you might miss it entirely from the beach. Once you got to the trailhead, you were able to see the path leading into a dense underbrush of outstretched ferns, wild rhododendron, and salal. At this point, Petal stopped the group and explained, "Now, despite what you might be thinking, the act of forest bathing does not entail lying down, covering yourself with moss, and taking a nap."

The group of women giggled.

"Actually, it has to do with intention and connection. We will step into the forest, and instead of being focused on a destination, we will mindfully observe and become a part of the forest. We will let the forest invite us in, and nature will show us how to put aside our worries and fears." Petal's melodic voice intermingled with the birds and wind around us.

"Shall we begin? Follow me."

Petal began narrating from the front.

"Make sure to feel the stones and roots beneath your feet as you step. Are they sharp? Do they put you off balance? Instead of pushing branches and leaves out of your way, gently move into them, feel the leaves against your skin, the resistance of the branch against you. How can we move with our surroundings, instead of in opposition?"

After a few turns along the winding path, even the sound of the ocean disappeared against the thick wall of fir and spruces. I gazed up to where the tops of the trees ended. The sky fractured into blue stars against the branches.

Soon, I fell into the very rear of our pack. I liked the peace away from the main group, and, following marching orders, I took my time in investigating a beehive constructed inside a fallen tree trunk. I wandered off the trail, pushing ferns aside. The group's chatter faded. Only birdcalls filled my ears.

A patch of unnatural color against moss caught my eye in the distance. A flash of blue. What was it? I walked toward it. A single sneaker. Dirty and weatherworn, it had been out here for some time. Who loses a single shoe in the forest? I ran my finger across the faded blue suede, still bright enough to stand out in the muted forest colors. As I looked around at the area, something felt wrong. The vegetation around me was disturbed, flattened, I realized. Even though I was sweating from the hike, my skin flashed cold. A chill blew across the back of my neck. Where had this come from? I turned it over in my hand.

"You're not supposed to go off the trail."

I looked up to see Petal. "Sorry," I said.

"Don't be sorry. Wandering and observing is the assignment. I just can't lose any of you." She saw the shoe in my hand. "What's that?"

"Not sure," I said.

"Probably an animal dug something up, or it fell out of someone's backpack while hiking. In fact, I would drop that and make sure you wash your hands later."

I let go. It landed with a thump and disappeared under a clump of ferns. What kind of animals were in this place? I wondered.

"Have you done a lot of hiking before?" asked Petal, leading me back to the trail.

"Not really." I thought of the photo in Cara's room. "Although a friend of mine had a cabin in the mountains. We and our families would go stay in it sometimes. It was beautiful up there. Though I'm spoiled, I guess. My hometown, Portsgrove, is pretty picturesque too." I hoped she would recognize the reference.

"Portsgrove?" Petal glanced upward. "Why does the name sound familiar?"

"I know a member who was also from Portsgrove. Do you know Cara Snyder?"

Petal smirked and leaped lightly over a root in the path. "Ah. I was wondering when you would ask me."

My heartbeat skipped. Petal was the very first to admit Cara existed at all. "So you knew her?"

"Of course, we all knew her."

"Why did Robyn and Sage pretend to not know who I was talking about?"

"I can't speak for them, though you should know asking about Cara won't make you very popular."

"Why?"

Petal stopped, her voice tense. "I know she's missing. Trust me when I tell you it has nothing to do with Artemis. She may have left Salthouse under tough circumstances, but she was very much alive and well when she left."

My stomach dropped. "Why did she leave? I thought Artemis was her life."

"I think it would be more accurate to say Sage was her life." As soon as she spoke, Petal sucked in air through her teeth. "Shit, forget I said that. Look, I like you. I think you'll enjoy being here, and I think we can help you. Don't let Cara's messes get in the way of your journey here, okay?"

"What messes?" I asked in exasperation.

"Hey," called a voice from farther up the trail. Gillian appeared and waved. "Hurry up, slowpokes."

"Coming." Petal began walking again and called back to me, "Come on. Rotten egg and all that."

I hurried up the trail. The group was stopped ahead, grouped around something. I came closer, and their bodies moved to reveal the objects of their wonder. A deer and her fawn. The animals stood silently off the path. The mother watched her baby gently prod a backpack with its big round nose. They weren't afraid.

"We spoil all of them around here," said Petal softly. "These deer know people mean snacks." To prove her point, she reached out and gently stroked the doe's ear. The doe stretched her neck and then shook her head, so her ears flapped. We let out a collective and involuntary "Aww."

After a time, the deer got bored with us and tiptoed into the undergrowth and continued on their way. We continued with ours. The path cut and wound upward suddenly in a sharp rise. After a turn in the path, I gasped.

"Isn't it magnificent?" Petal stretched out her arms. "A giant western red cedar!"

It was the tree from Cara's post. I walked toward it and placed my palm on the ancient wood. *She was here,* I thought. In this spot— though I couldn't feel her. Only the wood worn smooth from passing hands like mine; only the cool of the forest air hitting the sweat on my face.

"Delia?" Robyn was staring at me. "Are you okay?"

"Yeah." I backed away and took out my phone to snap a picture. Just like her photo, but without her. The shape of her absence jarred me. I traced the outline of where she had stood against the scene.

We reached a clearing in the path. "It's the lookout," said Petal. The lush green trees parted, revealing a rock plateau overlooking the beach below. My mouth opened in amazement. The panorama before me was like a painting come to life; rocks below met the shore, which met the water in large brushstrokes along the landscape. Clouds piled upon one another in the endless sky. I felt the radiance of the earth and my place in it, which was so unbearably small.

"We call this place Flat Rock," said Petal.

We all sat on the smooth rock, taking in the view. "What is it used for?" I asked.

Petal's lips tightened. "Um, we don't use it for anything."

Jenny drew a half circle with her arm, outlining the plateau in the air. "It looks like a stage," she noted.

Cara must have been here. She must have felt the pull, like I did; heard the wind in her ears and the ancient trees at her back, whispering "one step closer." Maybe she had stepped off and flown away. I scooted and leaned closer to the rock edge. Wind bit my skin and threatened to carry me over.

"Delia?"

The spell was broken, and I leaped back.

"Jesus, you're scaring me." Jenny laughed. "Don't do that again, daredevil."

Petal passed around a large thermos and metal cups she pulled out of a backpack. I sipped the hot tea she poured. We all sat in silence and drank our tea, then walked single file out of the forest.

When we made it back to the beach, I looked up and scanned the cliffside. From my angle, I couldn't see the rock plateau at all.

—⚉—

In the evening, I sat in one of the Forum phone booths at my prescheduled time slot. My heart wanted to call Mom or even Ren, but my brain protested; I was too tired and overwhelmed to try and defend my choice to come here. In the end, I called Tom.

"Hello?"

"Greetings from the mother ship."

"Hardy har har. How are you? Do they have you confessing your deepest, darkest secrets yet?"

"I'm fine. It was pretty rough, but I'm fine now."

"Yeah? You sound exhausted. What did you do today?"

"Ate muffins, had group therapy, and then we all went for a bath in the woods."

"Typical spa-retreat shit is what you're saying. Anything about Cara?"

"That's the part I wanted to talk to you about. Did Cara ever mention anything about Sage Ware?"

"No, I don't think so."

"She's the cofounder and leader of Artemis. I asked her about Cara, and she ignored me. So, I asked another woman about Cara today, and she told me Cara left under tough circumstances. Something isn't right here."

"Baked goods and hikes? Doesn't sound so insidious to me. Anyway, happy to hear you made some friends on your first week at school."

"It's a bit like being the new girl, you're right. I suppose there are worse places I could be infiltrating." We said goodbye, and I went back outside, pulling my coat closed against the cold air and the incoming mist.

I thought about the house where Jenny and Gillian were chatting on the sofa, holding their cups of tea, my own waiting for me on the coffee table. There was something here, in this place. Maybe not magic, but something that pulled and endeared itself to me, even this early. It was familiar. I had been the new girl before, the child gazing with sadness out the car window while the city faded and the forests drew near. I remembered how much I had hated leaving Seattle when my parents told me we were moving, plucking me from the fifth grade and everything I had ever known. In the end, it had taken the painful move for me to be where I knew I was meant to be. It brought me to Zee and Cara.

CHAPTER 16

Then

Even as a fifth grader, I understood that this part of the state was a place I didn't want to be. It was in the middle of nowhere, deep in a forest it took us hours to drive to in our U-Haul truck. I missed the city already. How many times had I insisted I wasn't moving? Yet there I was, one backpack strap hung on my shoulder, shuffling my squeaking tennis shoe soles on the alternating red and white square tiles of my new school. When Mom finished the paperwork, she got down on one knee, eyes level with my own, and gave me a hug. "You're going to have such a great first day."

"I hate it here," I sniffed.

Mom forced a flimsy smile and stood, grasping her coat around her.

Soon, I was being whisked through the halls by a bald, sour-faced principal, off to meet my new teacher, Mrs. Alesley. I walked into the classroom, and a sea of uninterested faces turned to meet my own. "Well, here she is now, class. Delia, I was just telling the class we are having a new friend join us today. Would you like to tell us where you've moved from?"

I looked down at the toes of my shoes, wet with pine needles from the walk from the parking lot. "From Seattle," I muttered. I glanced up, and while Mrs. Alesley was smiling, nobody else was. A few kids leaned across the aisles of desks and held hands over their mouths to whisper to one another. Stares slipped over me, assessing, judging.

"All the way from Seattle," said Mrs. Alesley. "We are so happy to have you in Portsgrove."

In the back of the class, a Black girl and a white blonde girl slouched together across the aisle, so close their shoulders were touching. When one turned to whisper into the other's ear, her blonde hair fell across her face so she didn't even need to hide behind her hand. Whatever she said made the Black girl smile, but not in a mean way.

"Here's your seat, Delia." Mrs. Alesley directed me to a desk one row in front of the girls. As I dropped my backpack and slid into the hard metal chair, Mrs. Alesley told me I could borrow a math book from Zelda until she assigned me my own. "Zelda, I'm guessing that's okay, and you'll share with Cara?"

"Yeah, Mrs. A."

I turned, and the girl with the tight shiny black curls was holding the book toward me. I took it, and we locked eyes for a split second; it was all it took for us to see the loneliness in one another. I turned, face cast down at my shoes again, and tried to focus on fractions.

My brown paper bag lunch and I did exactly one lap around the cafeteria before I spotted the girls, Zelda and Cara, sitting in a larger group at a full table. I passed by slowly and pretended to look straight ahead, to not notice them; I pretended I wasn't waiting for them to ask me to sit. I passed by, and they hadn't noticed me. Or if they had, they weren't interested in inviting me to eat with them. I found a lone table and sat down by myself. Had I misread Zelda in class? I picked at my peanut butter and jelly, which I had insisted my mom pack instead of mechado leftovers. The last thing I needed as the new kid in school was to explain to everyone that I was eating larded beef in tomato sauce.

Two older boys approached my table and sat on either side of me. I put down the sandwich and looked back and forth between them, my heart beating and my muscles twitching.

"You're Delia, right?"

I nodded. "Yeah."

"Hey, welcome to Portsgrove," said one.

"Thanks."

"I'm talking to you," the same boy said.

I scrunched my brows. "I heard you."

"Well, here it's polite to look at people when they talk to you." He almost kept a straight face before letting out a chuckle, which he stifled quickly.

"I don't . . ." I turned to look at the other boy, hoping he would explain.

"Open your eyes," said the other boy, sternly. The other one burst out with laughter. I shrank and pulled my arms into my rib cage, as far as they could go without breaking through. A flush went through me, all the blood rushing right beneath my skin.

The boys continued. "Oh shit, your eyes are open? How do you see?" Then, like I knew they would, they both pulled on the outsides of their eyes, stretching them to slits. They danced around laughing, and soon, kids turned and began to laugh too. I froze, feeling the water rising to my eyeballs.

"Hey, dickheads, quit it," a girl's voice yelled. It was her.

The boys stopped, even though they were twice her size. "Hey, Zee, we were playing around. We weren't serious."

Zelda and Cara stood side by side, confronting the boys. "Go play with yourselves somewhere else," Zee ordered. The room had fallen quiet; everyone turned to watch what would happen next. What happened next was that the boys relented.

"Whatever," they mumbled, walking away. "The new girl is so lame anyway."

I pushed back the tears that had come so close to escaping. Zelda and Cara sat down next to me. "You okay?" asked Zelda. "Those guys are the worst."

"It's fine," I said. "Thanks for saying something, but you didn't have to."

Cara flipped a lock of golden hair. "They really were playing around. They can be jerks sometimes, but it's like they said, just jokes."

Zelda frowned at Cara for a second, so quickly I wasn't even sure I saw it. "Come sit with us," Zelda said. "I've been to Seattle before. Did you live by the university?"

When the last bell rang, I followed Zelda and Cara out to the parking lot and waited until Cara got picked up in a big black SUV by her mom. "What now?" I asked Zelda when they had driven out of the school gate.

"Where's your house?" she asked.

I pulled the little sticky note Mom had put inside my back jeans pocket. "Eighteenth Avenue North."

"That's out my way," Zelda said. She grabbed my hand. "We can walk together."

We journeyed down the street, wet with afternoon rain and copper leaves falling around us. The way home took us down Main Street and past the water. Zelda talked and pointed out the important landmarks. "There's the saltwater taffy store where the owner throws in a couple extra pieces for free. There's the movie rental store where the guy who works the Tuesday shift will let you rent the rated-R movies if you're a girl. Once we pass this boat launch, there's a trail to a secret beach where we camp on warm nights. I'll show you in the summer."

The road soon led to a residential area, small ramblers scattered among the trees, often with more than one car parked in the yard. There were no sidewalks, so we walked down the middle of the street. Zelda pointed out who lived where, though I didn't know any of the names. "Keene Stevenson lives there." She motioned to a blue house with several bikes piled on the porch. "Keene was one of the jerks who was talking to you today. I'm sorry about that."

"You don't have to be," I said, my shoulders tensing and raising up to my ears. The weight of my backpack, now filled with books, was heavy against my back. "They were joking, like Cara said."

"Cara doesn't know what's joking and what's not," she said quietly, looking ahead. "She doesn't know those kinds of jokes hurt." She didn't point out any more houses. Instead, she turned and took a big step, almost leaping. "Tell me about Seattle! Do you think you'll go back and visit?"

"I hope so," I said. I actually hadn't even thought of that. Would Mom and Dad let me go back to see the friends I'd left? Suddenly, I missed having other kids who were brown and Black and white and all of the in-between. Here, my otherness was exposed in a way it hadn't been before. "Is everyone here like Keene?" I asked Zelda.

She didn't even seem surprised by my question. "No, but some are; most aren't. I know you're thinking *This is a pretty dumb little town my parents dragged me to*, huh?"

"That's exactly what I'm thinking." I laughed.

"It's not so bad. I'll show you the good parts. Like Blythe Lake! It's one of the deepest lakes in the state. Full of microorganisms." She blushed. "That was pretty nerdy, sorry."

"What's wrong with nerdy? How'd you know that, anyway?"

"My mom is a biologist for the forest service. Did you know when we get to high school, they have a science fair, and if you win it, you get to go compete in a bigger science fair at the University of Washington? I would love to do that." She smiled. We stopped in front of a two-story Craftsman. It was well taken care of, and a thorny rose bush grew by the porch steps. "This is me," said Zelda. "Want to come in and watch TV or something and stay for dinner?"

I hesitated. "Um, no I should probably get home. My mom is kind of strict about everyone eating dinner together and everything."

"No problem. Eighteenth Avenue is two streets up from here. Want to walk together tomorrow too?"

"Yeah. Cool." I hitched my bag by my straps and waved. "Bye, Zelda."

She wrinkled her nose. "Zelda? Call me Zee."

CHAPTER 17

I smelled like dirt. On my knees, I dug my fingers deep, the tiny bits of soil packing underneath my fingernails. A pink, squirming tendril of flesh peeked out from underneath a dead leaf. I swept a handful of dirt over it and reburied the little earthworm.

The community garden was in what used to be one of the vacant lots in between houses. When asked to choose our own paths for the second week, we had mulled over the list of options. Jenny had finally landed on a somatic therapy workshop.

"What does that mean?" I asked.

"The description says it's about using awareness of our body's movements and therapeutic touch to transform," Jenny read. "'Somatic therapy awakens the body to help tell the story of your self.' This actually sounds perfect for honing acting skills. So much of conveying feeling is in those tiny movements. Dr. Nicklin is teaching it. You guys down?"

I frowned. "I was hoping to find something less introspective, if that's a thing at a wellness retreat." I kept scanning the list.

"Question for you," Gillian said, pointing to an activity. "What color is your thumb?"

It was objectively not green, but I knew after a claustrophobic week inside the Forum walls, I was more than happy to hang out with Gillian outdoors.

So, Gillian and I, along with several other women, knelt in the dirt and turned over the beds to ready for planting in the coming warm spring weather.

"Sure you don't want gloves?" the head gardener asked for the second time.

"No, thanks, Lainey. I like the feeling of the earth between my fingers." I paused as she broke into a wide smile. "Is that weird?"

"Not at all. You may have missed your calling, girlie." Lainey had lived in Salthouse the longest, aside from the Wares and Robyn. I guessed she was in her midfifties, though I bet she would easily beat any of us younger women in any contest of physical strength. Her face, maybe once white and soft, was as browned and weathered as driftwood. Her silver hair was in a long braid thrown over her shoulder.

"Okay, gather round, newbies," she called. Gillian and I lined up with several other new gardeners around Lainey.

She delegated tasks and assigned me the task of spreading manure across the garden beds. She held up a laminated sign with a red tomato. "Tomatoes are here." She placed the sign next to the bed I was working at.

Gillian groaned. "As a note," she said, "I'm mildly allergic to tomatoes."

"Stock up on your antihistamines," barked Lainey. "The tomatoes grow like nobody's business here, so hope everyone likes caprese salads come August."

"Why do you grow so much?" I asked.

"We used to sell our excess crops in town at the farmers' market," explained Lainey. "Last year we tried to renew our permit for our stall, when the town council told us they were already full. We went and counted the stalls, and there were the same amount as the previous year, minus us."

"What does that mean?" I asked, trying to work out what they were suggesting.

"It means the town didn't want the likes of us in their market. I heard they thought we were poisoning our veggies with a mind-control drug! Like we would be interested in their small minds . . ." Lainey's voice continued into unintelligible murmuring before she shook her head and clucked at us. "What are you staring at? Less gossip and more manure."

"But you were the one telling us—" She was already over to the next group, instructing on the building of a compost heap.

The women chatted while we tilled and dug, the sounds of our chattering punctuated with the gritty sound of our trowels slicing through the dirt. It seemed like we were on a different planet altogether now from a few days before. How could this be the same place? The same people? These women around me were fun and helpful and sweet. I wondered if the intensive had helped to weed out those who weren't serious about the program.

The stench of manure filled my nose, though it wasn't revolting to me. Mixed with the sweet scent of dirt and the ocean air, it was invigorating.

I was ordered to move some bricks for bed building. I piled the bricks into a wheelbarrow from a spot near a large garden bed in the corner, covered with a plastic tarp. I picked up a brick and jumped when a worm wriggled from underneath. Actually, no. Not a worm. I gripped it with two fingers. A broken shoelace. Old, covered with dirt.

I looked to the bed next to the pile. The tarp was tied down. I slid my fingers under to lift it up a bit to peek inside. I bent down and held it up—

"Delia!" Lainey barked.

I jumped and turned on my heels. "Jesus, you scared me. What?"

"I need the wheelbarrow over here."

I stood and emptied the rest of the bricks before wheeling it over. Lainey rolled up her sleeves and put her forearm to her head, blocking the sun and surveying our work. I noticed a small tattoo on the inside of her wrist. She caught me staring. She smiled and held out her arm.

"Is that the Artemis logo?" I asked, surprised. She nodded. "What, an act of devotion or something?" I asked, half joking.

"I wanted to do it as a reminder of what I'm working toward," she said. "I haven't had the easiest ride, trust me. Everett found me at rock bottom. A small reminder to keep the faith, I guess you could say." I was trying to decide whether to ask if she knew Cara. Petal's warning on the hike had given me pause.

"Are you going to tonight's fireside?" Lainey asked.

I nodded. Petal had impressed upon us the necessity of attending the "fireside." She billed it as a casual hangout at Sage's house. Everett had done them weekly until he went away.

"It was a significant chance to get some face time with him," Petal explained. "Everett would give a teaching, and then it was social time, like a little party!"

I thought about how a couple of weeks ago, the very word *party* might have sent me into a mild panic. The thought of having to meet and make conversation with people I didn't know in an unfamiliar setting would cause my anxiety to go rampant. Every scenario, however unlikely, would play out in my head until I decided not to attend at all. Now, I was surprised I was looking forward to it. Who was I? Artemis was breaking down my barriers, despite my best efforts.

The other day, I had been walking out of the house to go to dinner, and I'd peeked into the bathroom to check myself in the mirror, lest I forgot to apply mascara to one eye or some other disaster. Both sets of eyelashes were appropriately mascaraed; I did a double take for another reason. I caught myself smiling. For no reason at all, I was smiling. Was I happy now? I wondered at this woman I was becoming. An Artemis woman, Petal would say. In moments like these, I found myself excited to meet her.

—∞—

In the afternoon, I had another appointment in the phone booth for some long-overdue phone calls. The Forum was empty in this midafternoon hour, a lull between lunch and dinner. The only women around were Artemis staff.

I signed in on the clipboard hanging on the handle and walked into the small room, closing the door behind me. It really was a booth, barely bigger than the old-school phone booths I used to see on the streets. I wondered to myself when they had disappeared.

I dialed the number from memory.

"Hello?"

"Hi, Mom."

"My God, are you okay? I was worried, honey. I hate that I can't contact you when I want to."

"I know. It sucks for me too. It's so we don't get distracted by the outside world—"

"So, I'm a distraction?"

I sucked in my breath. *Maybe this is why I don't call,* I wanted to say. Maybe a couple of weeks ago, I wouldn't have hesitated. Instead, I softened my voice. "Sorry. You're not a distraction. I miss you. That's why I'm calling. How are things?"

"Fine. The same." A pause. "I don't understand what you're still doing there. You didn't find Cara, did you?"

"Not yet, no."

"Then come home."

"I can't. The program is a month. I can't leave right in the middle. Besides, you knew how long I was going to be gone, so I'm not sure why you're freaking out now. It's actually beautiful here on the coast. I'm meditating and learning how to garden. I'm eating healthy, way more healthy than I have in a while. We take hikes all the time. I think I've lost a lot of weight."

"That doesn't sound healthy! You were a perfect weight. Did they tell you to lose weight?"

"No," I said in exasperation. Why was I bothering? She couldn't understand what this place was or what Artemis was about. My mom was too old and too set in what she believed it meant to be a woman.

Honestly, I wasn't sure why she wasn't remarried already. That would make her happy, I thought. Someone to take care of and boss around who wasn't me. "I'll—I'll be home soon, Mom." Then, in an effort to salvage the conversation, "How far are you on *The Great British Bake Off*? Can you fill me in on what I've missed? I hate not having Netflix here."

We spent the rest of the call on our differing opinions on trifles and matcha cake, and we even exchanged *I love you*s. I felt guilty to be relieved as I hung up.

I dialed Tom. Voice mail. Annoyed and slightly jealous, I dialed again. Still no answer. I sighed, chasing my knee-jerk worries away.

Finally, I made one last call.

"This is Ren."

"Heya. Guess who?"

"Delia? What the hell is going on? Where the hell have you been? Jesus Christ, I thought they murdered you and dumped your body into the ocean!"

"I miss you too."

"Are you okay? Seriously, where have you been?"

"I'm sorry, I'm so sorry. I didn't realize I get zero service out here, and there's no internet for me to even email from my computer—"

"That's weird. You don't think that's weird?"

"It's a kind of digital detox."

"Sure, okay, so you're out, right? If you're calling me . . . by the way, what's this number you're calling from? Did you get a new phone?"

"I'm not out. I'm calling from the Forum—"

"Forum?"

"It's our community center. I'm sorry I haven't called. It's been so busy here."

"Busy?" She sounded hurt. "I was worried about you, and you were just busy?"

"Not what I meant. We have a schedule of activities all day, so it doesn't leave a ton of time for me to do my own thing."

"Did you forget, you asked me to research this group? They are shady. Something is wrong with them, and it's alarming you don't see it. Your mom called me. She hasn't heard from you, either, and she's worried too."

"I spoke to Mom and explained it all to her too. Don't go scaring Mom; you're both overreacting. I'm fine!"

"You're not acting fine."

I sighed. "I'm sorry I've been ignoring you. I've been focusing on working on my issues here. It sounds crazy, but it is a retreat, right? So, maybe not so weird that I'm trying to get away from the real world and figure some shit out."

"Maybe you're right," Ren said, reluctance in her voice. "As long as you promise you're all right?"

"Promise."

She took a deep breath in and released it into the phone in a hiss. "You can't ghost me again."

"I won't."

"Well, look, please promise you'll meet with me for lunch or dinner or pizza delivery when you're back? I want to hear everything."

"Deal."

"Okay, good. Week after next, right?"

I grimaced. I thought about returning to my work and spending day after day alone and in front of my computer.

"I'm thinking . . . ," I said. No, it was a crazy idea.

"What?" Ren asked.

"Nothing," I said, unable to say it out loud. "And yes, see you soon in Seattle."

"Keep in touch," Ren ordered. "If you need anything, if you get into any trouble, please call me."

"I will," I said. I would have said anything to get off the phone.

CHAPTER 18

The fireside chat was the event of the season, it seemed. Dinner was buzzing about whether the turnout would be like when Everett had moderated them. Some women said they admired Sage for reviving the fireside chat to keep Everett's tradition alive. Though I wondered if it was more an assertion of her leadership in his absence.

Our trio arrived at the Ware residence later than we'd planned, on account of Jenny returning late from her somatic therapy workshop, held at Nicklin's clinic. Her face had flushed red when she saw Gillian and me sitting in the living room, ready to go. "What are you doing?" she asked, out of breath, as if she had run the entire way home.

"The fireside-chat thing."

"Shit." She smoothed her ponytail back. "I didn't realize we ran long. Let me shower quick, and I'll be ready."

"You don't have to shower," Gillian called up, but Jenny was already in the bathroom.

"I'm sorry," Jenny said as we hurried to leave the house. She wrapped up her still-wet hair into a messy bun.

"I don't think it's a formal event. Don't worry about it," Gillian had assured her.

We heard the buzz of activity and conversation even before we reached the front door, which we had to push hard to open against the pile of shoes that lay on the entryway floor. "This is like going to an Asian party," laughed Jenny.

"It's true." I snorted, happy she had come out of her odd mood.

We removed our own shoes, and I stretched my bare toes on the cold tile. The layout of Sage's house was like ours on a larger scale. We walked into the living room, with tall picture windows draped with pulled-back sheer curtains. In the daytime, they must have revealed impressive beach views, though right now, they were imposing black shapes looming over the gathering. I wandered behind Gillian and Jenny. Several women sat on the white cotton sectional and some on the oversize oak coffee table. Orange flames danced in the stone fireplace, keeping the coastal damp at bay.

Moving into the kitchen, we helped ourselves to wineglasses and filled up from a bottle that we realized too late was only sparkling cider, the only choice besides water. I spotted Lainey at the dining table socializing. She spotted me and waved. I waved back.

"Who knew Sage threw the hottest party in town?" said Jenny.

"It's the only party in town," I said to clarify.

"Hello, ladies." I turned to the voice and found Robyn behind us.

"Robyn!" said Jenny. "All of this is exciting, isn't it?"

"I forgot." Robyn smiled, all saccharine. "This would be your first fireside chat, right? Well, it's all of our first without Everett at the helm. I hope he can feel our energy tonight. We're all thinking of him in his extended meditation trip in Bali."

A bell rang, and the room hushed. "Gather round, please." I recognized Petal's voice. We moved along with everyone else, who squeezed even farther into the living room. This time, Sage was sitting in a plush armchair next to the fire. The flames illuminated one side of her face while throwing the other side into shadow. She looked like some kind of enchantress, with all of us under her spell.

Our trio found room on a windowsill to sit. Petal kept waving people in, alternating with prayer hands for good measure. When everyone seemed to be settled as much as possible, there were a good twenty of us squeezed into the living room. "This turnout is amazing," commented Petal. "We are so happy to be hosting the return of our fireside chats."

A small round of applause broke out. "I know, right? Although we are very sad Everett is away and unable to host them as usual, we should all be grateful to be getting the next-best thing, Sage!"

I winced, though nobody else seemed to think twice about Petal's awkward word choice. Everyone clapped as Sage rose from her seat. "Thank you, all. I want to open with some housekeeping before we get right into it and allow open dialogue to occur. First, as Petal noted, Everett is still gone on his pilgrimage. This doesn't mean we sit idle in his absence." Nods and murmurs. "We grow as individuals when we grow as a group! I needn't remind everyone that as an Artemis member and as a woman, it's your duty to hold the door open for other women on your way to the top. Or in this case, on your way to enlightenment." The group giggled.

"I look around, and I know who's here for the right reasons. I could point them out to you right now. I can also tell you who's not supposed to be here."

The hairs on the back of my neck stood. Sage lifted a slender, manicured hand. She straightened her finger and pointed straight to a woman sitting in front of her. "You're here for the truth, aren't you?"

"Yes," the woman breathed without hesitation.

"The truth is," said Sage, "if you're in this room, you're here for the truth." She clapped her hands and sat back down in her chair, the fire's shadows licking her face. "My topic tonight is loyalty."

Another chill swept through me, and I shuddered.

"Loyalty. If there's one thing Artemis can teach us, it's that we, above all else, must be loyal to ourselves! And who are we if not the embodiment of the teachings of Artemis? By honoring yourself, you honor me. If you dishonor yourself, you dishonor your inner radiant self and all of us." Her voice, light and conversational before, had turned stern. She was a preacher upon her pulpit, and the brimstone burned behind her, bright.

"How can we honor ourselves? I'll tell you what is not honoring yourself. Lying. When we lie, we don't just harm ourselves. We harm each other. And we all know the problem with liars is they can't stop lying. So much so that after a while, they believe all the lies they've told themselves are the truth. It's so tragic, the distorted world liars weave for themselves." I caught my breath as her eyes swept across the room and fell, for one second too long, on me.

"Secrets." She hissed the word like poison. "Keeping secrets is another thing that dishonors us all. There are no secrets in a family, and you are all my family. So, now we know what loyalty isn't. So what it *is* is a beautiful acceptance, an adherence and vow we make to one another." The darkness in her voice faded, and her face relaxed again. The room breathed a heavy sigh, as if the storm had passed like I had imagined it. "By practicing loyalty to who we are as women and each other, we can build upon our strengths and grow the word of Artemis. So every woman learns how she can change the world."

Applause rang out, and she placed her hands over her heart in prayer. "Thank you for listening to my truth." Her voice back to a lilting song, she clapped her hands with a smile. "Now, let's open up for Q and A."

Lainey brought up the farmers' market in town. A long discussion ensued about town relations, one I couldn't quite follow and had nothing to contribute to. While a couple of women I didn't know argued about whether we should boycott the local grocery store or try to set up a farm-to-table garden pipeline with them instead, I sneaked away to refill my beverage.

As I poured more sparkling cider, I could hear two women speaking in hushed tones in the kitchen doorway. Over the Q and A in the other room, I heard the distinct words "Cara" and "Everett." I drew a sharp breath and, still holding the glass, sidestepped slowly toward the women.

"—so obvious. They ran away together to get away from his sister."

"You think so? I heard he's still living at Salthouse but moves around in the empty houses. He's watching us all the time."

My hand jerked suddenly, and the bottle hit my glass. A shrill ring sounded. The women spun around and gaped at me holding the bottle, cider spilled across the counter. "Whoops." I went to grab a kitchen towel hanging from the fridge door. When I turned back, they were gone, thankfully. I sighed and mopped up the spill. Then I took a long drink from my glass. I tried to steady my breathing.

I returned to the living room. After more discussion, Petal concluded the chat, though encouraged us to stay and have some more cider and engage in more discussion among ourselves. I sighed with relief. Maybe too loudly; Jenny elbowed me gently in the ribs.

I checked my phone. "I can't believe it's midnight. Before we leave, I have to pee."

I knocked on the main bathroom door only to be met with an "Occupied!" I knew there was another one upstairs, if the layout of the house was like ours. I paused at the bottom of the steps, looking up into the darkened hallway. At the top of the stairs, I faced a hallway with doors all shut. The soft hum of conversation from downstairs floated to my ears. I turned my head and followed a separate line of voices coming from one room. I softly stepped down the hall and was passing the first door when I heard two voices coming from inside. Pressing my ear to the door, I held my breath.

"—not buying it anymore. Why hasn't anyone except you had contact with him?" It was Robyn. She was speaking in a hushed, urgent tone. It was also clear who she was referring to. I held my chest to stifle the thundering sound of my heart beating fast.

"He's my brother." Sage.

"He's my mentor, and he wouldn't abandon me like this—"

"Nobody has abandoned you. It's going to benefit the group as a whole. He told me he's writing again."

A pause. "Writing? Another book?"

"Possibly. It depends on how long he can be away and let the words come to him, as they do when he's able to access his deepest inner voice. He needs isolation to do so." Their voices were turning softer, and I pressed my ear harder against the door, my brain refusing to think about what would happen if I was caught.

"This just isn't like him at all. I'm worried."

"It's a safety concern that his location remains private, so no need to worry. All you need to know is that he's not going anywhere and he's still very close to us all, in spirit. And trust me, I inform him of all the recent developments when we communicate. Myself, Everett, and his protégé are all in close communication."

My mouth opened in surprise; she was talking to him. Was she talking to Cara too? And who is his protégé?

"So, he knows about the bills," Robyn pressed.

"We will pay everyone." A hint of annoyance. "It's not your concern."

"Everett made it my job to do the books, so it is my concern. What's your plan to deal with the bank notices that come across my desk every day? We are bleeding money, and there is no plan. We need to talk to Madelyn. It took Everett a decade to build Artemis, and with him gone, you'll let it burn down in a matter of months." I drew in a silent, staggered breath.

"It's mine to burn down if I want to," Sage stated, like it was a well-known fact. I felt a chill go down my legs.

"Not for long, if you keep at it like this."

I jumped as the handle turned. I pressed myself into the wall just as Robyn stepped out. In the dim hallway, backlit against the light coming from the room, she wiped her eyes and slipped away, as an embarrassed child would do. I watched her go until she disappeared down the stairs.

I swallowed hard. The door was still wide open, and Sage was steps away from catching me eavesdropping. My heart raced, and I crossed sweaty hand over sweaty hand along the wall and gently stepped backward to the stairs, not daring to breathe until my feet were on the ground floor. So, there were financial problems within the company, which Sage clearly wanted to be kept under the radar. I wondered if Cara had discovered the money situation.

"What were you doing?" Robyn asked. She was standing just around the staircase, hidden by the banister. I started and spun to face her. "What were you doing upstairs?" she repeated.

"I was using the bathroom. The one down here is—"

Robyn stepped toward me, and my back hit the wall. Robyn didn't stop advancing. Soon, her face was within inches of my own. "It was a timely talk tonight, don't you think? I wonder sometimes who is telling lies, spreading mistruths. I wonder who is keeping secrets." She stepped back. "Don't you?"

"Actually"—I regained my composure and lifted my head—"all the time."

Gillian and Jenny appeared from around the corner. "Oh, there you are!" said Gillian. "Did you pee? Oh, hi, Robyn. Have a great night."

Robyn smiled. "Have a lovely night, ladies."

On the quiet streets home, Jenny asked, "What were you and Robyn talking about? Looked kinda intense there."

I held my arms tight around me to stop my body and voice from trembling. "Loyalty," I said.

CHAPTER 19

The next day, I ventured out of the community for the first time since my arrival. As soon as we turned out of the Salthouse Place entrance and onto the highway, my phone found service and dinged with texts and messages waiting for me. After the lashing from Mom and Ren the other day, I dutifully sent out proof of life to both of them.

Gillian eyed me in the rearview as I put the phone down. "You okay?"

"I'm fine," I said, biting on a fingernail. "Though I would be better if people stopped asking me if I was all right." My teeth ground against themselves at the thought of Mom or Ren not believing I was okay here. I was a big girl. They should trust I would know when I was in danger. There was nothing dangerous about Artemis so far. Sure, there were rules, and leadership was intense. The initial reluctance of people to talk about Cara didn't seem so strange anymore. Like Petal had told me on the hike, it sounded as though Cara had stirred up drama between members. It was no wonder they didn't want to revisit bad memories.

I thought about the exchange overheard at Sage's house during the fireside. While Robyn had seemed a tad aggressive over cash flow problems, there didn't seem to be anything more to it. Maybe I would be upset at me, too, for nosing into other people's business.

Besides, I would be lying if I said I didn't connect with the women here. It was a camaraderie and a sisterhood I hadn't experienced in years. Not since . . .

I rolled down the window and leaned my head against the door. My hair whipped out with the spring winds. We drove along the coast, and the salt air seeped into my skin. Everything here clung to me. From the grains of soil underneath my fingernails and the leaves I pulled from my wild hair after a hike along the forest trails to the strings of affection for the women here I could feel wrapping around my heart at night while I slept. Despite my fears and suspicions, I sensed that this place was much more than just inspirational quotes that looked pretty online. I longed to walk toward the way those words made me feel. Artemis was changing me in ways I both resisted and desperately wanted.

Maybe I should stay. I needed to know more about everything. I had some savings and credit cards, if it came to it. Suddenly, my chest felt lighter, and my thoughts cleared. I wasn't ready to leave yet. *There is something here, Cara,* I thought. My sudden remembrance of my friend caused a ripple of guilt. I pushed it down—I wasn't getting distracted. Just the opposite. There was more to find out, and staying meant I would have time to get more information. That was it. I was staying for Cara.

As we parked in the lot of Top Foods, I remarked on the weird normalcy of the town. I realized it was my first time outside, off the property, since my arrival two weeks before.

The stares bored holes into our backs. When I looked up, the faces turned away. When we left an aisle, the whispers followed us. Jenny read off our list. "What kind of apple is your favorite?"

"Gala," Gillian said. She bagged several and set them in our cart.

I gathered vegetables, calling them out to Jenny to cross off. "Don't forget the kale," she said.

Looking through the rainbow of produce displayed, I couldn't find the kale. I approached a woman wearing a green vest and a name tag. "Where can I find the kale?"

She didn't make eye contact, only looking at the moonstone pendant around my neck, and nodded to a corner I had missed. I swallowed. "Thanks," I mumbled.

A small hand pulled on my hip. "I don't think we need kale after all." Jenny pulled me away.

"Let's get our shit and go," Gillian whispered.

I realized the stares were glares. We shopped and paid in silence, practically threw our bags of groceries into the trunk, and locked the doors with a satisfying click.

"What the fuck," Jenny breathed. "It wasn't that intense when Gillian and I went last time."

I offered to drive. With shaking hands, my natural anxieties aflame, I started the car and turned out of the parking lot. The tires squealed as I pulled out and navigated back onto the main road, turning back to the highway.

"You turned the wrong way," Gillian said.

"Shit." I hit the steering wheel. I turned into a strip mall parking lot and did a loop to double back. A tired storefront with the neon word **BAR** in the darkened window caught my eye. "Does anyone else need a drink?" I offered.

—᠁—

Tucking our pendants underneath our shirts before we entered, we walked into what turned out to be a sports lounge with an identity crisis. Slim red sofas lined a dirty dance floor; talk radio blared from speakers, and TVs above the bar were playing a UFC fight. At least it was close to empty, though the few pairs of eyes peering out from the shadows watched us as we entered. The girls slid into a booth in the back, and I took a seat at the bar to order.

"Three shots of Jack and three cans of Rainier." I flashed my ID. The tall bartender in a white T-shirt with rolled-up sleeves glanced at the ID and took his time to study my face. I stared back at his blue eyes, his blond buzz cut, and the pine tree tattoos on his biceps.

"You girls from our favorite local wellness community?" He grinned.

I tucked my hair behind my ear. "We're from Salthouse Place, if that's what you're asking."

"Didn't know they allowed you to drink."

"Why wouldn't we?"

"Ah, rebels." He chuckled to himself. "I'm joshin' you. Here you go." He gave me the beers. I hated that I noticed his dimples.

I placed cash on the bar and carried the drinks to our table. "Let's drink fast," I suggested. "Cheers."

"Cheers to what?" Jenny asked.

Gillian raised her glass. "Cheers to friends."

I followed her lead, and the three of us clinked our shot glasses and tipped our heads back. The liquid fire burned as it went down my throat. I shook my head, which was immediately clearer.

"To friends." We cracked open the cans and sipped the crisp and comforting drink. "I would not have survived these past weeks without you two. I never would have imagined when I came here, I would find two amazing women." It was so corny, even if I meant it. Every word. "It's been a long time since I've had good girlfriends," I breathed. Why was I on the verge of tears?

Jenny reached her arm around me and squeezed. "You read my mind and my heart! I knew when we first met in Seattle we were going to be best friends."

"I didn't expect to make two new best friends as a forty-something divorcée!" Gillian clapped her hands over her heart. "You girls are going to make me cry!" She waved her hands. "I'm an emotional wreck, I'm sorry."

"Are you kidding?" I took another drink. "We've been facing inner demons nonstop. I would be worried if we weren't emotional wrecks." *Never mind the shots and beers on empty stomachs,* I thought.

The door opened, spilling light into the dim space. I looked up as a group entered: two guys and a girl. They looked to be my and Jenny's age. Locals, no doubt. I lowered myself in my seat. Gillian looked over and shook her head. "Sit tall," she told me. "Let them know we're here."

Gillian was right. I straightened and caught the eye of the bartender again. He smiled at me, and I looked down at my beer.

"Are you going to stay, Delia?" Gillian asked.

"I'm so jealous! I wish I could afford it," Jenny said.

"I don't know if I can," I confessed. "I want to stay longer." I looked at Gillian. "How do you do it? Or, sorry, that was rude."

"No, no." Gillian shook her head. "It's fair. Is it bad if I admit it's all on credit cards? Turns out divorce is expensive. I know I should get a proper job and save; it's hard when this is the first thing that's made me feel normal in a long time."

Jenny exhaled. "Right? I'm so happy you said it. In fact, I'm getting nervous thinking about going back to LA. There's a lot of pressure waiting for me." She covered her eyes with her palms and whispered, "No more eyes. No more eyes." She took a deep breath and removed her hands, her makeup smudged.

"Does that work?" I asked.

"It did for a little. I'll admit, the no-internet thing helps. I binged all the social media on the car ride here as soon as I could connect to service. My roommates in LA got cast for a modeling gig, and they had to lose a few pounds for it, and now they look so good." She drew out the words and stared at her beer. "And here I am, drinking my calories."

"Stop," said Gillian. She looked as if she was about to go mother hen on Jenny, when we looked up to see one of the dark-haired men staring at our table. He was looking at Jenny. She cleared her throat, and they glanced away.

"I think I need another," said Jenny, pushing away her empty can.

"I'm on it," I volunteered. At the bar the newcomers moved to the middle, and I ordered another round of beers.

The bartender tilted his head. "What's your story, anyway?"

"My story is I'm here having a drink with my girlfriends."

"You know what I mean." He winked. Heat rose to my cheeks. "Why are you at that Artemis place?"

"It's a wellness retreat and self-help group. I'm there because . . ." I didn't know what to say. *Because I'm looking for my friend and dealing with repressed childhood trauma?* ". . . because I needed to get away."

He nodded. "You needed to be verbally abused and harassed for donations?"

"You read some blog?"

"No, one of your members told me. She was trying to leave. She seemed scared, freaked out."

"Trying to leave? If someone wants to leave, they can leave. And there's no reason to fear anything going on at Artemis, trust me. Unless meditation and forest bathing scares you."

He shrugged. "I don't know. She didn't seem too sure. She came in here a lot, is all. Didn't seem so happy with the self-discovery happening over there. You and your friends seem . . . too normal."

"Normal as opposed to what?" I tapped my fingernails on the bar. My skin was feeling too tight. It was too hot in here, I thought. I pulled my hair back and flipped it over one shoulder.

"She seemed like she needed someone to talk to," the bartender went on, not answering my question. "She would spend hours here alone, drinking and sitting in the back there."

"Right," I said. Where the hell was he going with this?

"I haven't seen her for months."

"Wait." My hairs pricked up, and my mouth went dry. "What did this girl look like?"

"Blonde hair. Pretty. Your age, I think."

Before I could ask what the girl's name was, a scream. Shattering glass.

I whipped around to look at our booth. Jenny and Gillian pushed through the two recently arrived locals, while the third was cursing and wet with beer. Pieces of a pint glass were strewed across the floor. He yelled back at Jenny, "What the hell?"

"For God's sake," muttered the bartender.

"You're an asshole!" Jenny pointed at him and stomped through the glass toward me as Gillian followed. "We're leaving now!" Jenny snapped at me.

"Are you okay?" I asked.

She nodded and kept walking. Gillian held her hands up at me and ran after her. "Shit," I said. "What's your name?" I asked the bartender.

"Brayden," he said. "Now, if you'll excuse me, I have to go get my mop."

I turned to follow my friends out, when I stopped. Instead, I walked over to the man wiping beer off his shirt with a handful of napkins. "What did you say to her?" I asked.

"Nothing," he sneered.

The glass crunched beneath the soles of my feet as I walked closer. I stared at him and softly repeated myself. "What did you say?"

He said, backing away with a smirk, "I asked her if your guru dude took turns with all the women, or if you all did it at the same time."

A deep breath. I stepped back with one foot as my arm reached back with my closed fist taut and ready to swing. He didn't even try to move. I couldn't do it. My arm fell to my side. He sneered and snorted.

We drove home in silence. As we turned past the Artemis sign, I realized Tom had never called me back. The three of us put away the groceries without a word. Afterward, Jenny ran upstairs. The shower started.

"How can they judge us?" I asked, sitting cross-legged on the couch. "They know nothing about who we are. They just make fucked-up assumptions. Maybe it's because they hate to think we're a group of women bonding and finding strength in ourselves. And in each other! I knew the world was ugly. Why would anyone think what's going on here is bad? Everett's not even here, after all. And even if he was? He was the one who started all of this! He's helping women!"

"Exactly." Gillian joined me. "Some people hate to see other people happy and fulfilled. My ex only liked me when I was docile and dumb.

This female-empowerment stuff drives him up the wall. Men hate it when women realize their power."

I half heard her. I couldn't shake the bartender's words; he had to have been talking about Cara. Who else could it be? *Cara was there. He knew her.* I cursed the ignorant asshole at the bar for ruining my conversation with Brayden.

The more I learned, the more questions I had. And the more I thought about it, the more I knew—it was her. I had to go back to town.

CHAPTER 20

Robyn tapped her pen on the notebook open on her thighs. I sat across from her, in her own living room, for our one-on-one mentoring session. Since our encounter after the fireside, Robyn and I had avoided one another or circled each other like felines when forced into the same room in the Salthouse confines. Today's one-on-one mentoring session was unavoidable, however. She cleared her throat. "What would you like to talk about today?"

I slumped in my chair, a sleek suede love seat the color of the sand outside. I dragged my nail across the surface and left behind a scratch as light as an old scar. "Nothing is top of mind."

She flipped through her notebook, biting her lip. "Actually, I was wondering something." I stiffened and rose a bit in my seat. "Looking through my notes," she mumbled. "Ah, yes. Here it is. I wrote something you said way back during the first week here. Do you remember? I was asking you about loss."

How could I forget? "Yeah," I answered, lifting my chin.

"I was wondering—"

"How did you know?" I interrupted. "How did you know about Zee?"

Robyn stretched out her legs before her. "Zee?"

"You asked about the friend I lost. You knew. How? Did Cara tell you, and you knew you could use it to catch me off guard?"

"I think you are under the impression we pay way more attention to you than we actually do," she said, her tone flat. "That being said, of course we heard about Zee from Cara."

I knew it on some level, though hearing it said out loud made me shiver, my muscles gone cold. *They knew about Cara and Zee, and, of course, they knew about me.*

"We do our homework on the women we invite here," said Robyn. "To help them. Not to use your trauma against you." She sighed, and her gaze softened. "Believe me."

I didn't.

"So, tell me about Tom."

My mouth gaped. "How—" Robyn smiled, her lips thin. Cara had told them about my crush on Tom, too, then. A bloom of heat crossed my neck and up to my cheeks.

"How old were you when Zee disappeared, again? How old was Tom?"

"Fifteen and eighteen."

"Was he your boyfriend?" she asked.

I almost laughed. I shook my head.

"You became close with Tom after Zee died?"

"After Zee disappeared." It was an important distinction.

"So, how did it make you feel when this man used your grief to take advantage of you?"

"What? No, that's not what happened." I shook my head. "He comforted me."

"You were a secret," she stated matter of factly.

My hair fell across my face, and I pushed it behind my ear with a shaky hand. "You're twisting it so it sounds like something wrong," I mumbled.

"I'm sorry," said Robyn. "As a third party hearing this for the first time, it sounds like you were a child who was enamored with someone and the someone took advantage of a confusing time."

"That's not what happened," I snapped.

"It's hard to realize you were a victim, I know. It wasn't ever your fault. He was a predator, and you were underage. Men go to jail for doing what he did to you. Maybe he should have—"

"Screw this. You don't know me enough to judge me or my life." Shaking, I leaped from my chair and walked out the door.

—⚐—

On the beach, I sat on the bluff, looking out to the ocean and wishing I'd had the wherewithal to remember my coat. The sharp wind cut through me, and the dampness of the air seeped into my skin. A summer storm was approaching. A lone figure walked along the water, sidestepping waves and hugging a long sweater tight around her. Sage. As I stood to sneak away, I looked back at her and saw her spot me. I wiped my eyes with my sleeve, leaving black mascara smudges.

"Ahoy," Sage called out, her voice barely making it to me against the wind. She scrambled up the rocky slope to where I stood and turned to face the ocean, matching my gaze to nowhere.

"Tough day of introspection?" she asked.

"How'd you guess?"

"It's been known to happen around here."

I was tired of her bullshit. "Where's Cara?" I asked. "Why does everyone pretend to not know who Cara Snyder is?"

"We all have bad days. We all eventually find ourselves trapped and forced to face the demons we are usually so good at running from. Sometimes we've become so good at hiding from those demons that we convince ourselves it's other people who are to blame. It's called projection. It's Psychology 101."

My blood was boiling all over again, and Sage could only give me her stupid, mysterious smile I knew she practiced in the mirror every morning. "I want to talk to Everett. If you won't tell me about Cara, maybe I'll ask him instead."

"As we all know, he's in an unreachable location in Bali. When he returns, I'll let him know you would like to speak with him."

A realization stopped me cold. "Is he with Cara? Is she his protégé?"

The crack appeared in her rehearsed grace. Her smile became strained, her voice lowered. "Listen, I'm not sure why you've come here. It sounds like you were someone who was close to Cara, so I'm sorry to hear she's no longer keeping in touch with you. Please listen to me when I tell you chasing after them will only bring you more pain."

"What does that mean?"

She walked away in the direction she came from. "Wait," I called, scrambling down the rocky slope after her. My foot caught a loose rock. I fell. My side hit hard, and I slid down, catching myself with both hands grasping the hillside for a hold. I slid down farther and finally righted myself on the sand. I ran to catch up to Sage.

"Where are Cara and Everett?" I demanded. "Tell me or . . ."

She turned. "Or what? You'll bludgeon me?" Her gaze glanced down to my side.

"What?" I looked down and gasped to find a large, jagged stone in my hand. *No, I picked it up as I fell. I wasn't intending . . .* My arm and hand wouldn't let it go. It was as if my body parts were no longer under my control.

Sage came close, close enough for me to breathe in the scented shampoo in her hair, for me to see the lines in the corners of her eyes. "I loved Cara. Do you understand? We all did. That's why her leaving came as a betrayal. She hurt many of us. So, is it surprising to you her name is bringing up some bad blood? We've all tried to put it behind us."

"This isn't some distant past; this is now. I don't know if you know—"

"I know who you are. I know you've spent your life keeping people away and keeping yourself angry because of what happened to Zelda."

My fingers squeezed the rock tight against my palm, the ragged edges cutting into my skin.

"Maybe for your time here, you could try accepting the fact that you are loved."

My fingers released the rock, and it fell from my hand onto the ground with a crack. "What did she tell you about Zelda?" I choked, my vision filling with tears.

"Cara had a lot to heal from too. There's no shame in asking for help, for forgiveness. Give what we do here a chance, and try to take advantage of what we can offer you."

"Which is what exactly?"

"A place to belong, of course." She stepped toward me, holding out her hands. I rooted my feet to where I stood. She wrapped her arms around me, gently pushing my head against her own. She smelled like salt and forest. We stood like that for a long time, and her long graceful fingers found their way against my scalp, tangling themselves in my hair. When I pulled back, she kept one arm around me while raising her other hand to wipe dry the tears running down my wind-chapped skin. At last, she released me. I immediately craved her again.

"You should get home," she advised. "The storm is almost here."

Taken aback and disoriented, I nodded. I turned to walk back up the slope toward home. I reached the top and quickly turned to look at Sage one more time, but my foot caught a loose foothold, and my weight shifted beneath me. This time, I couldn't catch myself and landed hard, my right foot jutting out and twisted beneath me. I cried out into the empty air. Holding back tears, I forced myself to my feet. I could barely put weight on my ankle. *Shit.*

True to Sage's warning, the storm caught me as I limped home. The rain was a steady mist that coated me in sparkling droplets, somehow bypassing my skin and seeping directly into my bones. I looked out across the neighborhood before slipping inside; the houses were dark geometrical silhouettes against the shifting cloudburst.

I staggered into the doorway and slid down the wall. It was dark and quiet inside. A note was on the kitchen counter from Gillian that read they had gone to dinner without me and would bring me back a doggie bag. I lifted my foot tenderly while lowering myself to the ground, then stretched out on the cold linoleum. Turning my ear to the floor, I breathed through the pain until the throbbing of my ankle and my heartbeat synchronized with the electric drone of the refrigerator.

CHAPTER 21

The waiting room of the infirmary was actually a living room in yet another townhome repurposed as both a community health center and Dr. Nicklin's residence. I signed in on a clipboard attached to the wall in the entryway and followed the signs instructing me to take a seat on the sofa until called. I made myself a cup of watery coffee from the Keurig in the corner and sat on the love seat, which faced the windows. The infirmary was in the outer ring of houses and so had a view directly to the beach. A gaggle of women were on the beach doing Pilates or something. They lay on towels and lifted and lowered various limbs while the instructor looked on and occasionally waved her arms in some kind of encouragement.

"Delia?"

I turned. Nicklin was standing in the doorway with a manila folder. He wore a pair of blue jeans and a tucked-in white polo shirt, looking like an irritating school guidance counselor.

"Nice to meet you. Come on in." I followed him to an adjacent room, which had been retrofitted into a convincing examination room. He motioned for me to sit on a small plastic chair while he turned and washed his hands at the sink in the countertop, which ran along one side of the room. On top of the counter sat all sorts of medical accoutrements: glass jars filled with cotton balls and swabs and tongue depressors, and stacks of boxes with blue gloves pictured on the outside. A kind of exam table stood in the middle of the room; it looked like a portable massage table. I shifted in my seat, and a sudden cold moved over my skin. Even the homey touches like the canvas paintings of flowers on the walls couldn't quite make me relax.

"Now," said Nicklin, drying his hands and turning to me. "What can we do for you?"

"I tripped on the beach." Raised my injured foot. I didn't want to spend any more time in the room with Nicklin than necessary. "I iced it, but the swelling hasn't gone down. My roommates convinced me I had to get it checked out."

"Jenny is your roommate, isn't she?" His lips parted slightly. "She's a great girl. Now, let's take a look." He sat in his rolling chair and motioned for me to put my foot on his lap. I did, and he unlaced my sneakers, then slowly rolled off my sock. I took a sharp breath through my teeth as his fingers gently prodded my ankle. It burned like fire. "How did you even walk over here?" he asked. "Your ankle is sprained. I can wrap it up properly and give you some painkillers."

Shit, I thought, the last thing I needed. I thought of my shitty freelancer health insurance. "How much are the painkillers?" I asked.

He looked up, surprised. "How much? Did they not tell you medical care is included in your Artemis membership while at Salthouse?"

"Are you serious?" My freelancer heart did a flip in my chest.

"The Wares believe in universal health care. As long as we're able to provide you with the proper medical care you need here in the community, you won't pay a penny."

"Amazing." I sighed with relief. Before he released my foot, his fingers traveled upward along my calf. He squeezed it briefly. "Everything else looks wonderful."

I swallowed and pulled my leg away, careful to hide my grimace at the sudden movement.

He turned away to open a cabinet, though I caught the smirk he was trying to conceal. After returning with a bandage, he wrapped up my ankle and foot. When he finished, the support of the bandages had relieved a bit of the pain.

I placed my foot on the ground and applied a gentle pressure. Despite my skepticism about Nicklin's credentials, it wasn't nearly as painful anymore. "It feels better already. Thank you."

"Of course." He opened another cabinet. I tried not to gasp upon seeing the contents: rows and rows of little orange bottles. He picked out two and promptly locked the door before handing them to me. I looked at one of the bottles' labels and raised my gaze. "Oxycodone?" I noticed the label was in French. "For a sprained ankle?"

"They're five-milligram tablets. I trust you're responsible enough to take the amount prescribed. Or do you have a history of addiction I should know about?"

"No." I looked at the other bottle. "What is carisoprodol?"

"A muscle relaxer. Very routine for this kind of injury. I think you'll be back on your feet in a week or so."

"Thanks," I said quietly, wondering if Nicklin often handed out these kinds of medications to members. I turned the bottles over in my hand as he went to the counter to write notes in my file.

"The Wares believe we all have enough to deal with as it is. No need to worry about our health. In fact, many of our members take advantage by engaging in the various healthy-living options I provide through the clinic." He paused, obviously waiting for me to respond.

"Uh, like what kinds of options?"

"Glad you asked. Somatic massage therapy is the most common request. I teach the workshop, you know. I also do acupuncture and nutritionist services. For example, you look like you could use some help in portion control and healthy eating choices."

"Excuse me?" I was taken aback.

"I don't mean to be rude. You'll find I'm a straightforward person. Tell you what, I'll build you out a personalized guide with daily exercise routines and some diet help, such as macro counts. I think you'll find a healthy body and physical wellness can be a benefit in the journey to our spiritual wellness. Now, what do you say about the somatic massage therapy? I can actually begin now, if you'd like. You're my last appointment for the day." He leaned toward me, too eagerly.

I eyed the door. "What kind of massage, exactly?"

"I'm glad you asked. Often, women find their spiritual and physical states are out of alignment. I"—he rested his fingers on my arm—"help to align the chakras through erotic touch. The release of erotic energy can be extremely freeing and, often, essential to full spiritual awareness."

I jerked back and shook my head. "No, thanks. Is that an official Artemis therapy?" I thought back to Everett's book and the seminar; nobody had mentioned anything like this.

His lips pressed into a thin line. "It's true that some people do not believe in its full potential as a therapy." His voice turned low. "But without concerning myself with naysayers, I am perfecting the practice."

I clutched my pills. "I think I have to head out now. Uh, thanks for looking at my ankle."

"No problem at all!" His normal grin reappeared. "Check your email tonight for your diet regime. Otherwise, let me know if your ankle gives you any more grief after a few days." He wheeled his chair over to a file cabinet, unlocked it with his same set of keys from his pocket, and slipped my file into the middle of a hundred other identical files.

He walked me out, extending his hand at the door. I shook it. He held on a little too long, and I pulled away and hurried down the drive. I looked behind me. Nicklin was still standing at the open door, his eyes fixed on me. He held up his hand and waved. I turned back and continued walking, the metallic chill of the exam room still in my bones.

—⁂—

"One of Dr. Nicklin's nutrition plans?" Jenny gestured to the pdf I had opened on my laptop screen. She walked past me to the kitchen countertop and set the kettle on the stove.

"Yeah, how did you know?"

"He did one for me. I also signed up for the massage therapy package. We had our first one last week. It was amazing."

"Really? When did this happen? Where was I?"

"Not sure." She tilted her head, thinking. "If today is Monday, then it was a week ago exactly. In the afternoon."

I thought back on the week. "Oh, I think Gillian and I were doing a foraging course."

"We were," confirmed Gillian. "Remember, the kitchen made a mushroom quinoa from the wild mushrooms we all gathered. It felt so affirming to eat food from the earth!"

The kettle whistled, and Jenny poured the hot water into a mug, tea labels hanging from the rim. Gillian took a bag of Flamin' Hot Cheetos from our pantry and crunched happily, peered over my shoulder.

"Apparently, I need to eat more earth-based foods." I clicked through Dr. Nicklin's personalized menus. Gillian slowly lowered the Cheetos.

She balked. "Twelve hundred calories per day? Seems low."

I nodded in agreement.

Jenny voiced her support. "Dr. Nicklin is fantastic at his job. Delia, I think you should try it. Your body is capable of amazing things."

I shut the laptop. "I don't know if his massage . . . thing is really healthy. Did you know what it was before he did it?"

"Not exactly," Jenny admitted. "It was a little surprising, for sure."

I ground my teeth. "Jenny, I think you should be careful around him."

"Don't be silly." She laughed. "Isn't this experience about trying new things? Now, I have to journal." She curled up with a notebook on the couch, marking the conversation as over. I looked at Gillian. She seemed tense.

Feeling guilty, I joined Jenny on the couch while Gillian took the other side, all three of us with our legs touching.

"I'm sorry," I said. "I didn't mean to sound judgy there."

Jenny threw her arms around us both. "You girls are like my family now," she said.

"I always wanted sisters," Gillian said.

I leaned against Jenny's shoulder and looked across to Gillian, who gazed back at me. For a moment, I was safe with them. Like we had been meant to find each other.

CHAPTER 22

Classes and activities filled my days. I had notebooks filled with thoughts from my full-day chakra exploration course and recipes saved from the daily healthy-cooking classes. Still, I never attended the oceanside meditation classes; I preferred the meditation time inside the Forum's yoga studios. During free time and as my healing ankle allowed, I walked along the many forest trails, often finding myself completely alone in the lush greenness.

Some mornings, I woke up without even thinking of lost childhood friends, only to remember with a deep pang of guilt just hours later in a quiet moment. Those days I would lock my bedroom door, pull out Cara's notebooks, and scour their pages for a clue, a code, anything. But I hadn't come across anything yet.

I stared at my reflection in the mirror, my skin blemish-free and my hair windblown from the ocean air. "Get it together," I hissed at the girl staring back.

The next fireside was even more popular than the first one. Upon arrival, I fell in with some women from my Coffee group, and we chatted about nothing in particular. Gillian found me shortly after.

"I've extended my stay here," said one woman. We all pounced with our questions.

"Wow, congratulations! Did you quit your day job?"

"What does your husband think?"

"Do we get a discount as existing members?"

She explained she could move to part-time remote work, her husband was super supportive of her journey, and she could get us 10 percent off with her buddy code.

I made a mental note to check my credit card balance.

Gillian and I moved away from the group. "I think I'm going to sign up to extend my stay," I told Gillian. For Cara, I told myself again. I dreaded telling Mom and Ren. *Shit, Tom,* I thought. He was the one person who could talk me out of it. I missed him. His laugh, his attention, his touch.

"Let's align our dates," suggested Gillian. "The band stays together."

I laughed with relief. "I'm so happy you're going to be here with me. You and Jenny. Where is she, by the way?"

We walked through the crowd and didn't see her anywhere, though Gillian pointed out she was petite and hard to spot sometimes. I noticed the sliding glass door to Sage's backyard deck was open.

Two figures leaned against the deck railing. The smaller of the two held on to a drink in one hand and gripped the railing. The taller one was talking animatedly. They laid a hand on the arm of the other, a quick touch, but enough that the other person ever so slightly, almost imperceptibly, flinched. If they hadn't been backlit by a moonlit night, if there had been any more to them besides a black outline to emphasize their movements, I would have missed it. I didn't. I glanced over to Gillian and saw from the flash of anger in her eyes that she hadn't either.

"Jenny?"

They turned into the light. Jenny's face was red, caught by surprise.

"Hi there." Nicklin put both hands in his pockets. "Didn't notice you come outside. Lovely night, isn't it?"

Gillian took Jenny by the arm and pulled her away. "Will you come and look at something with me?" Jenny nodded as if in a trance. Not knowing what else to do, I followed my friends. We retreated to a corner.

"Are you okay?" asked Gillian.

Jenny looked at us with mixed amusement and shock.

"Delia?"

We all turned to find Sage standing nearby. "Sorry, am I interrupting?" she asked.

"No," said Jenny. She and Gillian disappeared.

"Can I chat with you for a moment?" Sage asked.

"Of course." I followed her out and upstairs. My heart jumped when I realized we were going to her office. *She knows I was listening to her and Robyn,* I thought. *She's going to call me out.* Sage offered me a seat on a cream armchair facing a small coffee table, while she took a seat in the one mirroring it. On the other side of the room was her desk, sleek and glass. A transparent chair with a white furry throw over it was at the desk and angled toward a laptop sitting closed. Several houseplants surrounded us, and a framed photo of her and Everett sat atop the coffee table. I leaned forward and picked it up, studying the face of the man who seemed to be everywhere and nowhere.

"I'm a little confused," began Sage.

"About?"

"You."

I set down the picture and leaned back in my chair. "What do you mean?" *I should confess now,* I thought. *She's playing a game to see how long I hold out.*

"I didn't mean to eavesdrop," I blurted out. She didn't blink. "You and Robyn, the first fireside," I continued. "I was just looking for a bathroom, I promise."

"There's one downstairs."

"It had a line. I didn't even hear that much, but when I went back down, Robyn caught me."

"So you think she spoke to me about it?"

I paused. "She didn't?"

"Didn't she?" Her eyes, cerulean like the sea outside our door, held steady. I didn't let myself look away. I was afraid to even try. Our staring contest ended after what seemed like ages when Sage spoke. "What is it you're here for?"

My lips parted to answer. I found myself tripped up on my own tangled stories.

"I ask because," said Sage, saving me from the damning silence, "you seem so interested in what Cara was doing here. I sometimes wonder if you came here for her and not for yourself."

Caught. My mind whipped around itself as I tried to think of a response to absolve myself. "I wanted to experience what she did," I said. It was part of the truth, after all.

Sage nodded. "It's understandable you would come here looking for answers about where she went. This was the last place she was, after all. We told her parents they were welcome to come and bring the authorities with them."

"Her parents were here?" This was news to me.

Sage shook her head. "No, they never took us up on our invitation, unfortunately. I think Cara's brother correctly spoke some reason and convinced them they would be wasting their time. Too bad, though. I would have liked to meet them. Cara was . . . special."

Her brother? Tom convinced them not to look further into Artemis? But then I caught her mistake.

"*Is* special."

"Huh?"

"Cara is special. Not was . . ." The implications hung in the air between us.

"That's what I meant," Sage corrected herself. "So, I was thinking. Since Cara is so special, I think her friends are special as well. She surrounded herself with extraordinary women. I wanted to tell you, even if you came here for her, I've seen big changes in you, Delia." She pointed toward me to punctuate the statement.

"I have found a lot of value in Artemis," I admitted. "I love the women here. It's been a long time since I had friends like this."

"Cara led you here for a reason," Sage said. "Maybe you will realize it was your own self you came here to find. What I'm saying is, we've noticed you, Delia."

"We?"

"Leadership."

"Really?" So, this wasn't a visit to the principal's office at all, I realized.

"We have an assignment for you."

"What kind of assignment?"

Sage relaxed into her chair, her demeanor changing from a close girlfriend having a chat to that of someone about to provide a business proposition. "How do you like San Francisco? Stacey has a seminar there this weekend, and we want you to accompany her."

"Stacey Roy?" I asked. "She led my first Artemis session in Seattle." I remembered her fondly and realized she hadn't been in Salthouse at all since my arrival.

"We know," said Sage. "We thought it made sense. Stacey often travels and conducts our seminars and workshops all over the world. She's been asking us for a long time for help. We think you could be an asset to our outreach program, much like Stacey. Assisting her with this event would be a good way to get your toe in the water, so to speak."

"Why me? I'm so new here." Not to mention, still not a genuine believer, so to speak. "There's nobody else?" I realized my glass was empty. I set it down on the table.

Sage shook her head. "Why are you so quick to dismiss this opportunity as something you haven't earned? You're smart, and your dedication to Cara has been very clear, which says to me you're loyal." Loyalty. There it was again. "I'd like to earn your loyalty. Tell me you'll go to San Francisco."

"I'll go."

She clapped her hands. "Perfect. We already booked your flight, so I'll ask Petal to forward you the details. Thank you, Delia. Artemis appreciates your commitment."

I placed my hands on the arms of my chair, about to stand to leave. The meeting had clearly concluded.

"One more thing." Sage raised her hand. "While you're in San Francisco, I would love for you to visit someone. A former Artemis member. I have something for her. Do you think you can find time to deliver it?"

"Sure. What is it?"

"It's a letter, if you want to know. I think she would be touched if it were hand delivered on my behalf. Now that I think about it"—Sage's head cocked to the side, and she grinned—"you and Madelyn might have a lot to talk about."

"Madelyn?"

"Yes, Madelyn Brewer." The BloomWallet CEO. Cara's former boss before she left for Artemis. "Don't look so suspicious," snarked Sage, my surprise written on my face. "It's a letter of gratitude. Madelyn has been a wonderful benefactor of Artemis. Even after she left, she's been one of our greatest supporters. Please say you'll pay her a visit?"

Sage was right. Madelyn might have more information on Cara. "I'll do it."

"There's my girl," said Sage ever so sweetly. "Let's get downstairs, now, shall we?"

—◊—

After the fireside concluded, Gillian and I went to the Forum for late phone booth appointments. Neither of us had said anything when we saw that Jenny remained in Sage's living room, riveted by a story Nicklin was telling.

In the booth, I rang Ren to tell her about my trip.

"You don't think it's weird, they're sending you on a vague mission? You need to look at that letter." I could hear her chewing something over the phone, probably a late delivery dinner at the office per usual.

"I'm not looking at anything," I said. "Sage trusts me."

"Exactly why you should look. She won't suspect you if she trusts you, unless it's some kind of trap."

"Why would it be a trap?" I rubbed my temple. "Sage isn't what I thought she was." Her embrace lingered on my skin still. "The truth is, I've connected with the women here. I don't know, maybe I had it all wrong. I'm starting to think nothing happened here with Cara. Maybe she couldn't deal with the truth she was learning."

Ren's voice was flat. "Case closed. So, when are you coming home?"

"I'm going to sign up for more time." I spoke quickly, so she couldn't interrupt. "To see it through is all. After this next session ends, I'll go back home. Back to real life." Back to my one-bedroom apartment; back to one friend, a lonely job, and the occasional random date. Why was I going back, again?

"Why not come home now?" Ren asked. "I'm worried, Delia. The longer you stay there . . ."

"What?" My voice was sharp, a dare.

"The more brainwashed you'll become."

My breath came out part scoff, part laugh. "They tell us about people in our lives who want to block us from becoming better people. I never thought you'd be one of them."

"Stop—"

"No, you stop trying to keep me small and afraid, so I have no one except you. You crave me depending on you as my only friend."

"No, it's not like that," she pleaded.

"Goodbye, Ren." The clang of the receiver as I slammed it down reverberated against the booth walls. I swung open the door and stomped outside. "Gillian, you won't believe the bullshit I just heard." I stopped short. Gillian was leaning against the wall of a booth, her face in her hands, weeping.

"Hey." I held her hands in mine. "What happened?"

She spoke through sobs, her shoulders hunched and shaking. "My husband, er, ex-husband—I called to speak to the boys, and he wouldn't let me. He found my bank statements and learned how much I was spending on Artemis classes and now this retreat. He was livid."

"Oh, Gil, I'm sorry." I shook my head.

"He's right. My cards are maxed out. He threatened to use this to take custody—" She couldn't finish the words; her cries echoed through the Forum, empty save for us at the late hour.

I hushed her and walked us to a couch, where we sat together. "I know it must be scary to think about," I reassured her. "It's going to be okay." I repeated it so many times, I began to believe it myself.

CHAPTER 23

It was noon on a Wednesday, and walking into the dingy bar from the bright sunshine of the day was like walking into a cave. Brayden waved at me.

"Hey, you're my first patron of the day. Here to drink or just break more of my barware?" he asked.

I slipped onto a barstool. "None of the above. Though I do have a very important question for you."

He looked at me quizzically.

"Are you interested in the word of our Lord Jesus Christ?"

He chuckled. "Nah, I'm good. Although I would reconsider if you asked me if I were interested in discovering the secrets of my radiant self instead."

I pretended to laugh, though his words stuck in me. He knew our terminology. He really wasn't lying about knowing a member.

"I have a present for you." I reached into my pocket.

"Please let it be a buddy code to your next webinar."

I placed the ancient piece of technology on the bar. His eyes went wide with amusement. "Is that . . . a pager?" He held it up like an artifact, which it was. "I think my dad had this same one when I was in middle school." He furrowed his brows at me. "Thanks?"

"If your dad pawned his at the local Gold Star Pawnshop, it might be one and the same. And you're welcome."

"Do you want a drink?" He softened, looked at me with something like guilt. "It's on the house, of course, to apologize for the assholes who gave you and your friends shit the other night. You know, nobody around here, including me, is a fan of Artemis or the Wares, but nobody deserves to be disrespected for their beliefs. No matter how weird. They aren't hurting anyone."

I couldn't believe he was apologizing on behalf of those guys. Despite his prickly sarcasm, maybe Brayden could be an ally after all. I needed as many as I could find. "I'll take a pale ale," I said in a tone that told him all was forgiven.

Since we were alone in the bar and Brayden assured me we would most likely be the only ones for a couple of hours, we took our beers to one of the red pleather couches along the wall across from the bar.

"When's the last time she was in here?" I asked. "The one you said was trying to get away from Salthouse."

"It's been months." He scratched his temple.

"So, she got out?"

"Or she didn't." His voice was dark.

"For Chrissake—"

"I mean, one day she appeared out of nowhere. She kept coming in to drown her sorrows; then she didn't anymore." He tapped the pager. "So, what's the deal with this?"

"If you know anything about Salthouse, I'm sure you know there's no cell service out there. No Wi-Fi either. If she comes back, I need you to let me know." I pointed to the pager. "I'll give you the number for it. I need you to page me if you ever see her again."

"You mean I don't get to keep the pager?" He feigned betrayal. "You told me you got gift for me!"

I laughed, and I meant it. He was funny. "I guess I didn't think about that, sorry. I guess I led you on there, didn't I?"

"If only." He winked. He took out his phone. "Okay, I promise. Give me the pager number." I watched him enter the digits and then pause as he was about to save them into his contacts. He raised his eyebrows at me. "Should I put in Mysterious Girl as your contact name?"

"Delia."

He typed in the letters, each syllable rounding on his lips. *Dee-lee-uh.* "Huh, I liked mine better. So, real talk," he said. "Why are you at that Salthouse place? You seem pretty normal, no offense."

"None taken." I clicked my thumbnail against my forefinger's nail. "You don't have to go bartender mode on me." I smiled. "Besides, I think you already asked me what my story was, and I told you the truth—rest and self-reflection."

He chuckled. "Trust me, I'm not expecting a tip for listening to your woes. I'm interested in what draws people to Artemis. It's a big topic of . . . speculation in town."

"I've noticed."

"So . . . self-reflection." I opened my mouth. He laughed and held up his hands. "Hey, it's your story, and you're sticking to it. I get it, I just work at a bar. What do I know about the finer things in life, like spa retreats and enlightenment?" He spoke with a smile, though I could hear the disdain behind it. He thought I was some rich lady paying for the privilege of forgetting my worries.

"My dad worked as a sawyer at our local mill," I said. "Even though he had a college degree in business. He and my mom met in Seattle, and they moved into a crappy studio apartment downtown next to a freeway overpass. When I was born, my mom convinced my dad to move to this tiny town on the Olympic Peninsula. She wanted to raise her child among the endless evergreens. There was nothing like that in the Philippines, where she was from. Of course, the only job in town was in the industry cutting down all those trees she loved so much. So, he took a job leagues beneath him, and he never missed a day and never complained, all because he loved her. He grew old cutting trees into planks. Sometimes he would bring home freshly cut tree rounds from a trunk, and we would count the rings. Sometimes there were hundreds, and I couldn't comprehend the ancientness, no matter how hard I tried." Even though my throat had gone dry, the words flowed so easily out of me.

"Of course, it was only a matter of time before there was an accident. A forklift malfunctioned carrying a pallet of lumber, and when the wood hit Dad, it dislocated his shoulder and broke a couple of ribs." I winced at my own description, speaking quickly now to get it said and done.

"He was in the hospital for as long as the workers' comp would pay for it, which wasn't long enough. Disability wasn't enough, either, and he went back to work too soon. One day, while working a double shift, he took a larger dose of painkillers than normal, even though they made him drowsy. He finished the shift and then fell asleep at the wheel on the drive home. They said he didn't feel a thing when he rammed the electrical pole at sixty miles per hour."

"Jesus," Brayden breathed. "Where were you?"

"Too far away." I clenched my fists and dug them into my thighs as I remembered my mom's call in the middle of the night, when I was still awake over a contract law textbook. "If I had been home, I could have convinced him to stop working. Or at least given him rides to work, or helped him regulate his meds." *Where were you?* I had hissed at Mom. *Why weren't you looking out for him?*

Brayden let out a low whistle. "Is this what you talk about at Artemis?"

I remembered Robyn's grilling the first week. "A little. I don't talk about the details to anyone. Not like this." I felt tears threatening to fill my eyes, and I blinked them back, but he saw.

Brayden laid his hand on my arm. It was rough against my skin, and the tiny hairs on my forearm tingled. With one tug, he pulled me close. I laughed as my clothes stuck and squeaked against the plastic pleather. He smelled like cheap deodorant and cheaper cologne. I relaxed into him, into the feeling of strong arms at my side. "I'm sorry I'm dumping this on you."

He furrowed his brow, and his lips thinned. "I don't know if that's why you're in that place, but you should know. You're not broken. You don't need anyone to fix you."

"I know," I said, trying to hide my surprise at his genuine concern. He nodded and caressed my skin, his fingers following the underside of my forearm all the way past my shoulder, where his fingertip touched my bare neck. I flinched and moved back. *Of course,* I thought. *I should have known.* His eyes widened as I stood.

"Anyway," I said, sniffing and rubbing condensation from my cheeks. "Keep me informed, please." Before he could say anything more, I walked out the door.

CHAPTER 24

I boarded the plane to San Francisco, settled into my seat, and popped in my earbuds, ready to indulge in free Wi-Fi. Artemis Wellness had been invited by a big consulting company to do a workshop during their annual conference, and they had sprung for business class. I stretched my legs out and enjoyed my extra two inches of space. On my phone, I entered into the search bar *Bloom Wallet and Madelyn Brewer*. BloomWallet was a chic start-up whose website's mission statement included hip tech speak like "disrupt the financial industry." The company had been born from Madelyn Brewer's own experience of finding herself fresh out of grad school with a bona fide knowledge of engineering but clueless about the reality of being an adult in a capitalist world. I watched her latest TED Talk in my seat on the plane, thankful I was in a different row from Stacey, though I was still careful to angle my screen toward the window.

Madelyn Brewer was a tech darling and one of the youngest Silicon Valley CEOs to make her start-up a unicorn, a company with a million-dollar valuation. This was even before she married a local councilman rumored to be the next state senator for his district. In fact, this was an election year. When I googled, a campaign photo popped up with Madelyn, husband, their two adorable children, and even a family golden retriever. Madelyn Brewer, bankroller of Salthouse Place and Artemis member. Besides her photo, framed and hanging in the Salthouse Place Forum, there was nothing to connect her to Artemis or the Wares. Maybe it made sense. Actresses like Regan Elliot were happy to lend their faces to Artemis. That was their currency, after all. Madelyn provided a different support—cold, hard cash.

―∞―

Our hotel was in Union Square, a popular San Francisco city landmark. I sat on the balcony, watching the families below eating the Halal Guys takeout in the park, while irreverent teens skated at dangerous speeds through the throngs of tourists taking pictures. It was 5:00 p.m. on a Friday, close to dinnertime for tired travelers who had been sightseeing all day. Below me, they fell into all the usual spots. Places that someone wouldn't normally choose to eat at in their own city but provided a familiar oasis while traveling. Across the way, at my room's exact level, the Cheesecake Factory outdoor dining was overflowing with midwestern parents. I clocked them by their colored visors and stuffed-full backpacks, how they were trying to herd rambunctious children back to the table and back to the massive plates of pasta. Interspersed were businesspeople drinking chain-restaurant cocktails to shake off the week and getting deals done, all while dodging the tourists and children.

A knock at the door.

"Hey." I let Stacey in. She wore the same flowing red silk pantsuit I remembered from Seattle. Her hair was curled and her makeup done tastefully.

"Wow, I think you have a cooler view than me," she said, stepping out and gazing down. "Are you going to be okay on your own tonight? Sorry I couldn't get you a spot at the dinner with such late notice. Security is strict."

"I don't know what I'll find to do in this one-horse town. Of course I'll manage." Truth was, it relieved me to not have to attend a corporate conference dinner party. Stacey had a purpose in going. She was a keynote speaker for them, and she could schmooze and put on the recruiting charm.

"You would be bored out of your mind anyway," she said. "Tomorrow will be much more fun. You'll be manning a table in the main conference area, so you'll be meeting lots of people and handing out Artemis swag. Way better than trying to remember which fork to use for your salad versus your dessert. Meet me downstairs tomorrow at seven a.m. sharp so we'll have time to set up." She took one glance at herself in the mirror and left.

—◆—

Before I dressed, I tried Tom one more time. I had called him twice while waiting at the airport, and each time the call went straight to voice mail. No answer. Muttering curses, I put on my coat.

It was a beautiful night, so I told myself I would walk as far as I could through the city and north to the BloomWallet coworking building on the Embarcadero. The noises of traffic and busy sidewalks were jarring to me. I felt like I had lived in isolation for years in the orderly houses in Salthouse. This, I remembered with a jolt, was the real world.

I signed in with security on the ground floor of the coworking space, and they gave me a visitor's badge; they directed me to the sixth floor. The doors opened to a shiny lobby. The company logo and lettering were emblazoned in rose gold along the hallway as I exited the elevator. A front desk stood in front of a glass wall, revealing an open space filled with women and men gathered around tables and sitting on pink couches with their laptops. I squinted and imagined Cara crossing the open floor, her laptop balanced on one arm. She would dress in chic high-waisted pants and a silky blouse. She would wear thick black-rimmed glasses, not because she ever needed glasses but because they looked elegant against her blonde hair and complexion.

"Can I help you?" The front desk clerk appeared. "We're closing for today. You can come back Monday at nine a.m."

"I'm here to see Madelyn," I said.

She hesitated. "Ms. Brewer isn't available right now. Would you like to make an appointment?"

"No," I insisted, thinking quick. "I'm only in town for the night. Please tell her Sage Ware is here to see her." I paused as the clerk jotted the name down on a Post-it. "I think she'll want to make time for me."

I watched the girl walk back into the open area, to a corner office with glass walls. The woman inside, half-hidden by an oversize monitor, turned to the messenger. She almost leaped up and followed the clerk back to the lobby. To me. To her credit, Madelyn's poise didn't falter when she saw I wasn't Sage. She held out her hand. "So nice to see you. Follow me."

We passed a group of workers heading home for the day. Madelyn waved and told them all good night. I scanned for Cara, imagining her behind a table and closing her laptop for the night, grabbing her bag to follow her coworkers out for happy hour and waving goodbye with her bright smile. Normal stuff. It wasn't until we were in Madelyn's office and she'd shut the door that she turned on me. "How dare you," she hissed. "You people will stop at nothing. Coming into my place of business? Who are you? Because you sure as hell aren't Sage."

Her rage caught me off guard. "My name is Delia Albio." I glanced at the shelves behind her, photos of her and her staff in front of the logo I had walked by on my way in. "I'm in Artemis."

"No shit. Why are you here, and what do you want? Sage knows I'm paid up for this quarter. I can't give you assholes one more penny."

I stammered, and I looked from her to my shoes and back again. At my obvious confusion, Madelyn took a deep breath. She sat back down behind her desk.

I was the one to break the silence. "You're paying Artemis? For what?"

She balked. "If you don't know, then why are you here?"

"Sage sent me." I didn't know what else to do besides give her the envelope. She held it tenderly, fingertips only, teeth clenched. While she slowly opened it, I glanced at the framed photos behind her desk of her husband and kids.

She removed a single piece of paper and scanned it. Then her hands reached in again. She widened the envelope to see inside. A shudder. She slammed the envelope onto her desk. She breathed hard and shut her eyes tight again. Her voice trembled. "Tell Sage I will be in touch."

I sat frozen. What had Sage sent? Whatever it was, I couldn't waste this opportunity to talk to Madelyn. "There's something else," I said. "I'm a friend of Cara Snyder's."

Regaining her composure, Madelyn settled and clasped her hands in front of her on the desk. Her face softened and turned pretty again. Her breathing steadied. She was back in her CEO mode. I had caught her off guard for a moment; it was clear she wouldn't allow it again.

"Is she back at Salthouse?"

"No. Nobody knows where she is."

She nodded, her lips pursed, like she was offering condolences. "Her brother reached out to me about her. I said I knew nothing about where she might be, and I told him I thought she'd be home soon enough. I'm sorry I was wrong. Well, it looks like Sage found a quick replacement, someone else to do her bidding."

"I'm not doing her bidding," I said. "She asked me to deliver something, and I did."

"So, then you'll be leaving—"

"I also had some questions," I blurted.

"So, Delia Albio, ask." Her fingernails tapped impatiently.

I could tell I didn't have time to mess around with Madelyn. She wasn't like Sage; her patience for talking in circles was limited. "Why are you funding Artemis? You're a co-owner on the Salthouse Place title."

She laughed. "Oof, you don't start with the softballs. Are you a journalist? No? Maybe you missed your calling. I'm not funding Artemis. I support the mission, and I give donations reflecting the same. As for Salthouse, I didn't buy it for Artemis. I bought into the property as an investment, and Artemis functions on the property. It's a business relationship."

"Why would you, a savvy business person whose entire persona is built on making smart financial decisions, buy a half-built abandoned subdivision in Oregon? Doesn't sound like any kind of smart investment I would want to be a part of, if I'm being honest."

"Well, maybe you need some financial advice. Have you checked out the BloomWallet app? It could help you research the recent boom of wellness communities and the fact that they are a hundred-billion-dollar industry—a pretty smart investment, actually."

"So they pay you rent?"

Her nostrils flared, and her neck muscles tensed. "I don't have to tell you any of this. It's confidential information. Now, can I do anything else for you or—"

"Cara is missing. Everett is missing—"

"So, they're together."

"No. They're not."

"If you believe that, then you don't know Cara as well as you think. I'm sorry Cara is missing. Frankly, I'm sorry she got wrapped up in Artemis." She paused and looked down at her desk. "Have you met Everett?"

I shook my head.

"It's better that way. He was something . . . He really saw you, you know?"

"Why would someone as successful as you need a self-development guru to see you?"

"Because he didn't act like everything I said was brilliant, like the yes-men, and he didn't treat me like I was a wild uncaged animal to be tamed, like the sexist pigs inhabiting the venture capital world. He spoke to me like . . ." She scoffed. "It sounds so silly. He spoke to me like a whole person."

I thought of Sage and her warmth, her way of looking at me and seeing only me. "I know what you mean."

"They got me. I was all in. And I wanted every other woman to feel the same warmth. The world was a better place when I was close to Everett. Cara saw it, too, felt it too. We talked about it. We would visit them in Salthouse and then come back here to the cold city. I should have seen it coming. It felt like a betrayal when she quit to move there. I don't know if I was more jealous that I was losing her to him, or that she would get to be with him all the time."

"Wait," I asked. "Was Cara . . . in a relationship with Everett?"

"Don't you know?" Madelyn looked at me with confusion about how I could be so unaware. "They're all with him."

My stomach wrenched, and a furious rush of blood coursed to my brain. *No, it's not true. She wouldn't . . .* I shook my head. "That can't be true."

"It's why, when Sage asked me to join Sorority, I accepted right away."

"What sorority?" It was moving too fast.

Her face fell. She searched my face for some recognition. I could give her none. *Please don't stop talking,* I prayed. I was close to something here. She looked around her with a sudden panic, like she had wandered in front of me in a dream and I had rudely awakened her.

"Who are you?"

"I'm just trying to find my friend."

"Forget it, she's left you behind," Madelyn said, hard as stone. "You need to leave now." She signaled to someone beyond her glass windows, and I glanced to see a man in a security uniform coming toward us.

I held up my hands. "It's fine. I'm leaving." I gripped my bag and bolted out. At the street level, I pushed through the doors. The cool air hit me. My hands on my knees, I breathed in the fresh air in gasps.

CHAPTER 25

I tossed and turned all night. By the time I had to meet Stacey in the lobby, I had slept two hours.

Cara had had some kind of an open relationship with Everett. And she was best friends with, or extremely close to, Sage. Had Sage facilitated the pairing, or was it done without her knowledge? Maybe Sage had found out and told Cara to leave. Everyone was with Everett. That's what Madelyn had said. What the hell had been in the envelope? Whatever it was, she was wrong. I wasn't Sage's mere messenger to do her bidding. Madelyn had admitted she'd fought for the Wares' attention. She was jealous, even now.

Fighting every fiber of my body that wanted to remain in the bed, I showered and dressed. I put on a high-waisted pair of black trousers and a silky white blouse with a pussy bow that puffed up elegantly right under my neck. I noted how the pants were a little loose. I guessed Dr. Nicklin's program was working. I hadn't worn this outfit since long before Artemis. It was a good thing I had even packed it in the suitcase I'd taken with me; otherwise I would have been at a loss when Stacey had instructed me to pack a business-chic wardrobe.

As I rode the elevator down to the lobby, I kept thinking about Madelyn and Cara. Was the secret sorority why Cara had left? I didn't even know if I was asking the right questions. Maybe the sorority was a deeper level, another exclusive Artemis program. Maybe it's where Cara was.

When I met Stacey downstairs as arranged, she put me to work organizing worksheets and reviewing the workshop agenda.

"Did you have any vodka in your minibar?" asked Stacey, rubbing her temples. "I brought my own tomato juice mix and would have killed for a Bloody Mary this morning." I shook my head, though I hadn't even opened my minibar. Stacey's workshop was taking place in a larger version of the hotel conference room where I'd first met her a few months before. I wondered at how long ago it felt, like a different person's memory altogether.

The company's diversity and inclusion committee had reached out to Artemis to specifically book a session on how their female professionals could lean in, as it were. So here we were. The group was a good seventy women, mostly middle aged to youngish, with cardigans and wraps layered on top of their business wear to combat the overzealous hotel air-conditioning.

It surprised me to realize the men of the company wouldn't be attending. Even if the workshop itself was about navigating working while female, it seemed to me the boys could listen in and learn a thing or two about how they might change or act more inclusive of their coworkers (read: not be sexist assholes). Silly me to think they would ever ask the men to put in the work. It was the women who needed to do the changing.

"Remember," Stacey said, as she adjusted her mic clip on her blazer. "Be on the lookout for the big fish. The girls who would be assets to Artemis. This is a recruitment trip as much as a speaking engagement."

Despite my other worries, I was drawn into Stacey's talk. I remembered being Stacey's student back in Seattle. Her warm glow and how it made me feel so special. It was disappointing Stacey wasn't returning to Salthouse when I was. She was a steady anchor and a foil to Sage's recent unpredictability.

There was a brief break before Stacey's "Negotiating like a Bad Bitch" session. I washed my hands in the bathroom and retied my wilting bow in the mirror.

"Are you really a member of Artemis Wellness?" asked a girl who was washing her own hands next to me. She was young, maybe fresh out of school herself.

I nodded. "I'm just a newbie, though. I'm no Stacey."

"Oh, she's incredible. You both are," she gushed. "I'm Constance. When I heard Artemis was doing a workshop, I couldn't believe my luck."

"Ah, don't give luck credit, remember?" I smiled and wagged my finger.

She laughed, caught. "Oh my God, you're right! I'm the one who deserves the credit." She gave a tiny fist pump.

"Exactly. You worked hard in school, and you hustled to get this job at this company, and nobody except you got yourself a seat out there today." It was fun playing teacher.

Her voice dropped to a whisper. "Actually, my dad owns the company. And I don't know why I'm whispering because everyone knows it's how I got this job."

I fought to keep my smile up, teeth showing, and nodded.

"Anyway," she said, her voice returning to normal levels. "See you out there."

"See you out there." I wondered if Stacey knew. Eagerness, excitement, connections, money. Constance was exactly who we wanted more of in Artemis. I instantly felt guilty for the thought. Could I see her living, thriving, in Salthouse?

I fiddled with my bow some more until I had tangled it hopelessly. In annoyance, I gave a tug to one end, and it unraveled completely. I didn't bother trying to fix it and left the bathroom with the two ends hanging down the blouse.

They would chew Constance up and spit her out. I walked back into the conference room.

"Quick, quick, hand out the slide printouts," requested Stacey. I grabbed the stack with the appropriate sticky note and began my round.

After the workshop, we set our booth up in the middle of the main thoroughfare conference goers had to travel through to get from room to room for the various sessions. However, the more I thought about Madelyn, the more handing out our little flyers made me sick. If the workshop was interesting and absorbing enough to keep me from my own thoughts, the table duty was excruciating.

"What's wrong with you today?" Stacey asked.

I said the first thing that came into my mind. "Uh, I'm on my period."

"Did you just blame your shitty performance and attitude on your menstrual cycle?"

I shrugged. "Not feeling empowered when my uterus is trying to kill me."

"I don't know what part of the Middle Ages you beamed in from, but modern women succeed despite biology, Delia. No, no, they succeed because of it. Our periods are pain, yes, but we learn, from a very young age, to put the pain aside and work through it. Women win gold medals during their period. They argue court cases on their period. So, I think you can hand out pamphlets and look fucking happy to be alive on your period."

"Yeah, you're right," I agreed, genuinely frightened.

"Menstrual power!" said Stacey with a fist pump. Several men glanced over at us, foreheads wrinkling. "You know, I think I might develop a module on this. See, periods are inspiration."

"Whatever you say."

Stacey knelt down and began rearranging our boxes of swag underneath the table, muttering something about someone needing a Midol. I spotted a familiar face walking toward us across the patterned industrial carpet. "Hi again!" Constance waved.

"Hi there," I greeted her, less than enthusiastically.

"I wanted to tell you again how awesome you ladies are."

Stacey perked up. "So sweet of you," she said. "I'm not sure I got your name. Forgive me."

Constance was about to respond when a hotel worker in a uniform walked by. "Oh, Stacey," I exclaimed, pointing at the employee. "Weren't you wanting to talk to someone about your minibar?"

"Oh, it's not—"

The worker stopped. "Did you need something?"

Stacey waved her hands. "No, it's nothing."

I looked at her. "Why are you minimizing your problems? Don't be afraid to assert your needs." I thought for a second she would only laugh at her own words being said back to her. Thankfully, she took my genuine tone to heart.

"I didn't have any vodka in my minibar," she explained to the hotel employee.

With Stacey distracted, I turned to Constance. I grabbed an Artemis-branded Hydro Flask in one hand, gave it to her, and took her wrist with my other hand. I whispered into her ear. "Don't you ever speak to us again."

She froze in horror, gripping her new pink water bottle. Slowly, she stepped back, then turned and walked away.

"Who was that again?" asked Stacey, her conversation regarding hotel amenities concluded.

"She wanted the Hydro Flask," I said matter of factly.

Ten minutes later, the hotel staff returned and gave us each a complimentary mini bottle of Tito's.

I thanked the volunteers when it was time to pack up and catch our flight home. Stacey had another workshop in LA the next day, so while we waited in the airport lounge together, I would go back to Salthouse alone.

Over our twelve-dollar beers, I asked her, "Do you think we caught any big fish today?"

"Maybe, maybe not. I have some emails I'll follow up on and refer to our marketing team. Sometimes earning trust takes a long time. They might not be interested now, so it's smart to network and make connections. You never know when someone will show up and say, 'I went to an Artemis meeting five years ago, and it took me this long to get the courage to do this for myself.'"

She misread my face. "Does the terminology bother you? Forget fish. I know Artemis is big on feel-good euphemisms. I remember no matter how many inner goddesses we unlock, this is still a business. Like any business, we live and die by sales."

I was taken aback by the frank admission. "You can't mean that," I said. "Sure, it's a business, but Sage and Everett have something here, right?" I scoffed. "Was I a big fish when I walked into your conference room in Seattle?"

She looked at me with surprise that I could miscategorize myself so badly. "No, you were just lost."

It was me, then, who balked in surprise. "Wow, thanks."

"I'm not being facetious," said Stacey. "I know I gave you a whole biz dev talk, but I still believe in what we teach. And you, when you walked into my conference room, were so indescribably sad. I wasn't lying when I told you I saw potential for change in you. And look how you've proved me right. I hear you're a rising star at Artemis."

"What? Who says?"

"Little birds. It's a new dawn in Artemis. Whatever you've done to endear yourself to Sage, keep it up. Before she left, Cara was so close to Sage. We wondered if one day, Cara might even take her place. It made sense, since Everett had his own protégé . . ." She stared past me. "But now, who knows how long Everett will be gone."

His own protégé? Nicklin, of course. Did Sage and Everett really plan to turn the reins of Artemis over to Cara and Nicklin? "Has he done this before?" I asked. "Left for this long without telling anyone?"

She shook her head.

"Was he ever married?" I asked, taking a drink from my beer. I peered over the rim, but Stacey had no reaction at all.

"No, I don't think so. I don't know if he would have the time. He seemed to never sleep. He was so busy with Artemis. When he wasn't writing books, he was traveling for speaking events, and when he wasn't doing that, he was giving therapy sessions to his chosen ones."

"Chosen ones?"

Stacey's cheeks reddened. She was drinking too much, saying too much. I prayed she wouldn't put down her beer.

"Everett himself picked and groomed the mentors. He's very particular about who conveys his message."

I winced at the word *groomed*.

"Were they the women in the sorority?"

She licked her lips. "Now what would you know about Sorority?"

"I've heard about it, is all . . . ," I said.

"I don't think so," Stacey said with a frown. Then she lit up with a realization. "Cara told you about it." I held her gaze, allowing her to believe it. She extended her pointer finger and wagged it from side to side. "That was a no-no."

"How do I join Sorority? I have to be picked by Everett?"

"No, Sorority operated separately from Everett. They didn't involve him at all. Once you became a mentor, Sorority noticed you. You have to be invited by someone who's already in it," she said. "You're not supposed to know about it. It's a secret society kind of deal."

"You're in it, aren't you?" I surmised.

"They initiated me, yeah. I don't think it's active anymore. After . . . some women left, it kind of fell apart."

"Madelyn," I said. Then, I took a gamble. "And Cara."

Her eyes confirmed it.

A bell rang, and an automated announcement sounded through the lounge speakers; Stacey's flight to LAX was boarding. "I don't know what else Cara told you," said Stacey, standing. "I hope she was a good enough friend to tell you to leave it alone. Take care of yourself." She gathered her bags and left toward the A gates.

I downed the rest of my beer in frustration. Aside from confirmation this secret sorority existed, I had failed to learn anything more, and now my trust with Stacey was most likely broken. I regretted bringing it up with her. I regretted not making more of an effort with Cara after Zee was gone. It had always been Zee and me against Cara, maybe too much. That's why it had all fallen apart. Now it might be too late.

The sorority had to be part of the reason why Cara left. I knew it. She was either running away from something, or she had been chased out and was in hiding. Either way, I feared she was in danger. And finding her was how I fixed things.

CHAPTER 26

Then

The mirror surface of the lake was crystal clear, and for one split second, Keene's body was perfectly reflected in the water before it crashed into itself. The waves rocked the little pontoon boat we were piled onto, the canopy from which Keene propelled himself. Cara was next off the canopy, her scream echoing from the cliffs on the far side of the lake as she jumped with arms out wide.

Cool splashes licked my face, and I cheered as Cara emerged from the water. She climbed the ladder back onto the boat, where I handed her a new beer. The radio played bouncy pop beats barely audible over Keene's and Jason's yowling as they wrestled, trying to toss each other overboard.

Cara and I clinked our bottles and cheered to the summer before our sophomore year. We drank and leaned over the edge, looking to see where Zee was floating nearby on an inflatable raft tied to one side of the pontoon. She lay on her tummy, feet hanging off, her hands making gentle strokes in the water. She was looking down, focused on something Cara and I couldn't see.

"What are you looking at?"

Zee looked up. "Give me a cup."

"Beer or this gross Smirnoff thing?"

"No, an empty cup."

I tossed one overboard, and it fluttered down, dipping into the water. Zee paddled the raft and retrieved it. She scooped a cupful of lake water.

"Ew, what are you doing?" Cara scowled.

"I think the algae here is different."

"What are you talking about?"

Zee sat up on the raft and, hand over hand on the rope, pulled herself back against the boat. The red cup appeared over the side, and I took it so Zee could climb inside. Removed from the sun and separated, the lake water was a dull opaque brown with green furry specks floating.

She took the cup from me, then placed it in the cooler between beer bottles and packed it into place with more ice. "Keene, you have to drive slowly on the way back, okay? I don't want this to spill. Do you think we can swing by the north shore too?"

"Whatever," Keene grunted, avoiding a karate chop to the crotch from Jason. "Really, dude?"

Jason glanced over. "North shore? There's nothing over there."

"Exactly," said Zee. "I was thinking, the north shore has those big cliffs but no beaches, unless you count the rocks as a beach. No beaches people hang out on, which means no trash or booze or God knows what else goes in the water. I want to get some algae from over there too."

I knew where she was going. "The science showcase. Are you thinking of a project?"

Cara groaned. "Ugh, you guys are literally the nerdiest ever. Why can't you enjoy the summer without thinking about school?"

"We're going to be sophomores, which means I can finally enter the competition. The showcase is the last Thursday of September, so I don't even have that much time once classes start."

"It's the day before homecoming. You're going to spend homecoming week working on this science thing instead of going to parties with me and Delia? We made a promise to go to the game and then to the homecoming dance together as a threesome." She side-eyed me for support. I only shrugged.

Jason and Keene giggled. "Threesome," they said in unison.

Zee rolled her eyes. "We can still go! Because when I win—"

"Yeah, yeah, you get to compete at the state showcase. If you want to visit the UW campus so badly, I'll get my brother to drive us there. I know you'd love to have him as a captive audience for an afternoon." She stuck out her tongue.

"Not the same," Zee muttered. Before she closed the cooler lid, she took a beer bottle and popped the bottle cap off with an opener.

"Sure, whatever," Keene said again. "We'll drive by the cliffs."

"Maybe I don't want to," whined Cara. "And it's my boat, so my vote should count for more."

Jason scoffed, "You mean it's your dad's boat."

"Shut up," Cara shot. She sat on the seat opposite us and crossed her legs.

"It's not a big deal," I said. "It will take five minutes, Cara." I leaned against the boat's edge, next to Zee. "I think it's a cool idea. Besides, you've been talking about the showcase forever."

"Huh?" Cara called. "I can't hear you over the music. Why are you guys whispering?" She stared over the top of her oversize sunglasses, one of those Cara stares that could have been inspiration for the legend of Medusa. "You always take her side, Delia."

"Chill, Cara," whistled Jason. "You know Deels is the innocent, smart one."

"What?" I scrunched my nose.

"In your threesome." Jason laughed again.

"I'm the what?"

Keene nodded in agreement. "Everyone knows it." I wanted to ask, *Is it because I'm Asian?* I held my tongue and took a sip of cheap beer instead; it was heavy in my mouth.

"Zee is the cool Black girl," Keene continued. "And obviously, Cara is the spoiled rich girl."

"Get fucked," Cara spat. Keene sat next to her and held an icy beer bottle against her bare side, and she arched forward with a yelp. The tension broken, we all laughed.

We did drive by the north shore of Blythe Lake as the sun began setting and we were all too drunk to remember to argue. Keene parked the boat back in the slip with ease, even after a day of summer drinking, since most boys from Portsgrove had spent their lives on the water, in one form or another.

"Sure you don't want a ride back?" he asked Zee and me as I dragged the empty cooler from the boat to his truck. Zee was holding her precious samples, which had miraculously survived.

"We're cool to walk," I said. "Besides, it'll help us sober up before we get to Zee's place."

Cara gave us a hug, one arm slung around each of our necks. She kissed us each on the cheek. "I'm riding with the boys."

"We know," Zee said with a smirk.

Cara pouted. "Wow, jealous much?" Cara gave Zee a spank on her ass. "Will I see you sneaking into my basement later?"

I glared at Cara. We all knew Tom's room was the whole basement of the Snyder house. Cara regularly made fun of the steady rotation of girls he sneaked in and out of there. I felt my cheeks redden. I was aware Cara and Zee knew about my little crush on Tom, but Cara's jab felt like it was a low blow and a sting to both of us.

Zee's nostrils flared. "That's not funny."

Cara waved her hands and snorted. "Seriously, both of you need to relax and have a bit of fun sometimes. Don't you know every girl in this town would die to spend a day on the lake with two senior guys? They don't get to; we do. Maybe start appreciating it."

Jason put an eager hand on Cara's hip. "Let's go." She hopped into the truck and flipped us off from the window until we couldn't see them anymore.

In Zee's room, we lay side by side, sun-toasted skin against skin, flipping through magazines. I stopped at a glossy ad of a supermodel, pale and blonde. Zee leaned over. "Looks like Cara," she said.

"Do you think she's right?" I asked.

"About?"

"Not being so nerdy." I laughed halfheartedly. "Do you think we're missing out on, like, our teen years or something? Or, like, boys?" *Innocent one,* I thought.

"Delia is thinking about boys?" Zee teased. Unlike both Zee and Cara, I hadn't even had my first kiss yet. Her voice softened with something almost sad. "Don't be in a hurry, Deels. Sometimes, boys aren't that great at all. Like, sometimes they are, and sometimes you have to go with it, even if you might not really want to, you know?" I nodded, but I didn't know at all. She breathed in, and I saw the words on the edge of her teeth. "Like one time . . ." Her voice drifted.

"Zee?" I asked softly. Cara's joke was stuck in my mind, and I couldn't help it. "Have you actually been in Cara's basement before?"

"No," she said quickly and firmly. I turned and studied her tightly knit brows and twisted frown. I instantly felt horrible for even asking. "You know Cara is just a bitch."

To try and lighten the mood, I offered, "I think your lake-water idea sounds really cool. I'm excited for you to enter the showcase."

She brightened. "You know why I want to do it, right? You know why I have to win?"

"Well, of course, to win. And to go to Seattle."

"I have to get first at our local showcase to compete at state, then top three at state to win the scholarship money and to put it on my college application. With a state science showcase place, I would have such a good chance at being accepted to the university. Cara can drink and go with boys and not worry because she'll get to go anywhere she wants. We can't, Delia. We don't get to go anywhere we want, and I want to get out of this town so bad." Her face contorted into a sob, and she sank back. Instinctively, I reached forward and caught her.

She breathed heavy into my shoulder. "It's okay," I told her.

As quickly as she had crumbled, she recovered. She sat up straight. "Sorry, I think I might still be a little drunk." I nodded, though I knew she had drunk the least of all of us. "Don't tell her," she said. "I love Cara. I just think you get me a little more."

"I won't," I promised. "And I do." We turned off the light and didn't talk about it anymore. Zee turned to face away from me, and I settled into her, resting my cheek on her back, still warm from the summer.

CHAPTER 27

My plane landed at PDX late at night. I disembarked, found my car after forgetting which parking garage floor I was on, drove to Salthouse, climbed into my bed in the dark, and lay in the familiar quiet.

Overflowing with questions, my brain refused to turn off and let me rest. I turned on the bedside lamp and reached underneath my mattress to read more of Cara's words.

I flipped to a section of the workbook about happiness. It prompted, "Write about a time you were happy at home." I almost glossed over it, assuming she had written about her family. Then I caught my own name. The first time in all her pages I'd read it in her handwriting. Then I almost stopped breathing when I saw *her* name next to mine.

Cara had written:

> Not a happy moment at home, but in my home-town: I was happy the time Delia, Zee and I went to a football game and then got drunk at a bonfire on the beach. I was happy the time we went to Zee's family cabin in the forest and whispered to each other from our sleeping bags. I was happy once upon a time. I was happy before.

Holding her words against my chest, I found myself smiling. Happy about at last finding proof that Cara might have longed for that time as I did, even just a little.

—⁂—

It wasn't until morning that I walked down the hall and glanced into Gillian's room to see her bed stripped and bare; her desk cleared; in the closet, her luggage gone. Jenny walked out of her room, fresh out of the shower, one towel wrapped around her as she used another to dry her wet hair.

"How was your trip?" she asked.

"Where is Gillian?" I snapped back.

Jenny yawned. "She left."

"Left?" I repeated, thinking I had misheard. Jenny nodded. "She moved into another house?" I added, my brain trying to make sense.

"No, she had to leave Salthouse. Something about canceled credit cards."

I stared at Jenny. "So . . . ?" I held out my hands.

"She couldn't pay anymore. They asked her to leave." She shrugged.

The floor felt like it had disappeared right from under me. My heart dropped, and I felt my stomach churn. "There must be a mistake. She has to stay." I shook my head.

"She's already gone." She squeezed her hair in her towel and walked back into the bathroom. I remained in the hall, hands clenched into fists at my side.

"You should get dressed," Jenny called out. "Coffee is at Petal's house this morning, and I know everyone is dying to know about your trip." Any excitement I had over telling Jenny and Gillian about Sorority faded into a pit in my stomach. I bristled at Jenny's flippancy. How could she be so calm when one of us was gone? I realized I didn't even have Gillian's cell phone number to call her. No email, no address. I might never see her again.

—⟋⟍—

I mustered as much enthusiasm as possible, telling the women about San Francisco and the conference. Nobody mentioned Gillian's absence. For the rest of the session, Petal reviewed breathing exercises to help us through stressful moments. Then Coffee was over. Petal pulled me aside. "Delia, when you have a moment, Sage would like you to pop over to her place."

She wanted a report on Madelyn, no doubt. "I have an appointment at the phone booths and computer lab, so I'll go afterward."

"Great. By the way, I'm not supposed to tell you this, but Stacey gave you a glowing report." She gave a thumbs-up.

"She did?" I tried to hide my surprise. After I had shown my cards about Sorority, I was certain Stacey would tell everything to Sage.

Jenny walked to the door and waved bye to the few of us left lingering. "I've got to head to my shift at the Forum now. See you all later."

"Hang on," I said. "I'm going there, too, if you want to walk—"

Jenny shut the door before I could finish my sentence. I turned to Petal, whose eyes widened. She carried an armful of dirty plates and mugs to the sink. "Don't take it personally." She placed each dish into the soapy water in the sink. "Can you help me clean up, Delia?" I nodded, and the last of the women waved at us and said their goodbyes.

"Did it hurt you?" Petal asked. "Jenny being short with you?"

"Gillian is suddenly gone, and she doesn't even care." I wiped a lip print from the rim of a mug with a sponge. "I thought we were all friends."

"Think about it. Everything here runs on strict hierarchies and rules. And then you, a brand-new member, get tapped for a task that seems like it should be given to someone more senior. This isn't anything against you, Delia. I think Jenny is getting exhausted at watching women other than her get opportunities."

"I didn't ask for any opportunities here."

"I know." Petal paused. "Everyone knows you were friends with Cara Snyder."

"You mean to say people think I'm getting special treatment because I knew someone here? Everybody knows someone here. Besides, if people are paying attention, they would see me knowing Cara isn't exactly a golden ticket. Not everybody liked her."

"If the Wares liked her, that's what matters, right?"

Was it? I marveled at this place that operated at the whim of two people. Well, one person.

Still, there was something in Artemis that pulled at me. I didn't have the freedom of my little apartment in Seattle anymore. Far from it. I had a daily schedule and an assigned job, gardening and growing food for the community, and it turned out I wasn't bad at it. I woke up knowing exactly what the day would bring and, most days, went to bed with sore muscles and an exposed heart. Salthouse Place and Artemis worked because they were built on structure and rules that everyone knew and accepted.

Months ago, I had balked at the idea of daily group therapy and self-important navel-gazing. Maybe it was exactly what I needed. If only I hadn't come here with a different mission. I wished Cara would appear somewhere, anywhere, alive and well and with lots of apologies. *Funny story,* she would say, *my phone died, would you believe it? Just now got service.*

Did I want her to appear so I could end my search and go home? Or did I want her to surface so I could find my place at Salthouse on my own terms, without her shadow stalking me at every perfectly designed cul-de-sac?

I walked to the Forum without my coat, my bare feet slipped into a pair of Birkenstock sandals. It was warm, even at midmorning. There was no wind at all to cool the small beads of sweat forming at my hairline.

It seemed the glowing ember of spring was at last about to ignite into summer.

My sandals crunched along the sand-dusted sidewalks. I waved to the women I passed, all whose names I knew by heart. In late May's bright light, it was inconceivable that the rolling streets and pastel-painted townhomes could conceal anything insidious.

In the phone booth, I prayed for the voice on the other end to answer.

"Hello?"

I breathed a sigh of relief. "Tom, it's me."

"It is you." I felt his own relief across the phone. "What's been going on?"

"A lot." I told him everything. He didn't interrupt once. I finished with my conversation with Stacey.

"I don't like this," he finally said when I finished. "Whatever is going on with Artemis and Sorority, I don't think you need to be a part of it anymore."

"What do you mean?" I asked, my words short. I picked at the seam of my pants. "I thought you would be excited I'm getting so close. Madelyn was scared. You should have seen her eyes. Something happened, Tom. And it's all connected to Cara, I know it."

"And you'll place yourself in danger to find out more? It's stupid." He paused. "If you think Everett saw Cara as a future leader, then who's to say Sage isn't behind both of their disappearances? Maybe Sage was tired of waiting for her turn to be in charge."

I scoffed. "They didn't make Cara disappear. It's widely known that Everett is off somewhere writing. I certainly don't think they're going to do anything to me."

"They've let you get this close already. What's the endgame?"

"What do you mean?"

"Think about it. They knew you knew Cara. They correctly assumed you were coming to Artemis to look for Cara. And if so, why did they let you in? They knew you were a risk, that they were exposing themselves. And then—Sage sends you straight to Madelyn? And she basically tells you to ask Madelyn about Cara? She must have known there was a chance she would tell you about Sorority. No, Sage was counting on it. It's so obvious. We have to assume Sage is also counting on you wanting to join Sorority to continue to search for information about Cara. This is all a trap, and you are walking straight into it. I'm coming to get you today."

"No," I snapped. "You're not coming down here. Maybe it is a trap, but I have to walk into it to find out where Cara went. Don't you get it?"

Tom breathed into the phone. I imagined his face flushed, his intense blue eyes flashing with anger. "This isn't up to you. I'm so sorry I even told you about this. It's gotten way out of hand. Cara is not your responsibility."

My face flashed hot, and I pressed my eyelids to stop the tears from flowing. "I have to go," I choked. "I'll call you later."

"Wait, don't—"

I slammed the receiver down. *How dare he send me here, tell me the answers were here, and now, now that I was so close, he tells me to abandon it all?* I caught my breath before emerging from the booth.

The computer lab was right next door, so I signed in on the clipboard, and the attendant pointed to an empty computer. I signed into my bank account. I did the math on my savings and my credit cards. It would be a stretch, I knew. I copied and pasted a response to all my client emails sitting in limbo that, because of unforeseen circumstances, my absence would continue for at least three more weeks. Thanks and screw you very much.

Ren's voice was in my head, warning me I was committing career suicide. I wrote her and Mom a quick email to check in and let them know everything was going fine.

On my way out of the Forum, I spotted Jenny in one of the plush chairs I'd sat in when I first arrived. She sat cross-legged, her eyes glued to her laptop.

"Hey," I said softly, like she was a creature who might be spooked if I moved too quickly.

"Hey." Jenny shifted in her seat. "What's up?"

"Just saying hi," I said, feeling her coolness. "I'm supposed to be in the garden in a few, but do you want to go for a quick walk or something? It's beautiful today." I wanted to ask her more about Gillian and hoped for an opportunity to ask her what was going on between us.

She chewed on her lip in irritation. "I'm kind of busy."

"Of course. Maybe at lunch? I can come back when you're free." I smiled.

"I'm kind of busy . . . all day." She looked at me blankly and gazed back at her screen. The conversation was over.

I stiffly pressed my elbows to my sides and swallowed. It was her coldness that hurt the most. I nodded. "Sure. See you at home."

—◊—

The door to Sage's house was cracked open when I arrived. I peeked in and knocked.

"Come on in!" her voice called, singsong and light.

I slipped off my sandals in the entryway. I realized it was the first time I'd been in Sage's home by myself, not for a fireside. Sage was in the kitchen with a large chef's knife in one hand, an apple in the other. She wore black leggings and a slouchy gray T-shirt, looking like a girlfriend I was meeting for brunch after yoga.

She placed the apple on the cutting board in front of her and swiftly chopped it in half with a thunk. "Have a seat, Delia."

I slid onto a barstool. *Thunk, thunk.* She picked up a slice and bit it in half with her perfect white teeth; juice dripped down her chin. "Apple?"

"No, thanks."

"Come, come." She put the other slices into a bowl and beckoned me to the living room. We sat down on her overstuffed couch. In the daytime, the large picture windows let in the sun, which cascaded across the room, illuminating the mistress of the house in a buttery haze. "So," she said. "Tell me about San Francisco."

She nodded thoughtfully as I went over the workshop and conference. I told her about Madelyn. She didn't move a muscle. I kept details sparse, relaying the broad takeaways to save myself embarrassment.

"You did fantastic work," she said, nodding. "Madelyn will come around."

"Come around to what?"

"She pledged us her support," said Sage. "We're merely asking she keep her promise. You'll find there are lots of people who want the rewards without the work. That was the problem with Madelyn. Her presence got to be toxic for everyone. It's why Everett asked her to leave."

This was new information to me. "She didn't leave on her own?"

"Ha!" Sage threw her head back in laughter. "No! Oh my God, she would have never left if it were up to her. She was obsessed with getting close to Everett. Even if it meant stepping over and onto her Artemis sisters."

"So, why do you want her support?"

"She promised a partnership with BloomWallet. An Artemis and BloomWallet collaboration could be a boon for us and for Madelyn. I don't believe our personal differences should impede a mutually beneficial opportunity."

"What was in the envelope you asked me to give her?"

"A business proposal." Sage didn't miss a beat. "Like I said, I think she'll come around once she's thought about it some more. Thank you, Delia."

"For what?"

"Being willing and able." Sage smiled. "You remind me of her, you know."

"Who?"

"Cara, of course. I can tell why you were friends."

"I wanted to ask you about something," I said. Sage nodded for me to go ahead. "I know Cara was in Sorority." I paused. Sage didn't react. I wondered if it was because she was expecting me to ask, like Tom said. "I want to be in Sorority too."

"Not possible," Sage said without even having to think about it. "It doesn't exist anymore," she explained. "You might have heard about an exclusive group called Sorority. It was a short-lived exploration of a potential Artemis modality that didn't involve Everett. That's all. Cara and Madelyn were involved in it, yes. They were also much more senior in Artemis than you are now."

"So, what if I paid for the advanced workbooks and worked my way up after the fact?"

"Sorority is defunct," Sage said again, her voice a little louder, more final. She'd finished with her apple slices, and I was sensing she'd also finished with our brief visit.

"What did Sorority do?" I asked before she could ask me to leave.

"It was a group of high-ranking women who were ready to go beyond Artemis's current teachings. We were ready to think of and develop new philosophies for a modern woman. Everyone knew Everett's way was becoming irrelevant in a Me Too world." Sage's eyes glassed over, as if she were imagining what could have been. "Word got out, and . . . feelings got hurt. We decided it was best to shut down."

My head was spinning. *Beyond Artemis's current teachings, new philosophies, modern woman.* It had been an inner group without Everett, outside of his influence. When it somehow got back to him, he'd made Sage stop.

A sharp ringing pierced through the room. I almost leaped out of my seat. Sage laughed. "Someone's jumpy. Only my phone alarm for my next appointment." She waved her phone. "If you'll excuse me, I have a meeting I have to call into now. Let's keep talking, Delia. I enjoy our chats."

My head was spinning as I walked to the garden. I rotated the pieces around in my mind and watched them fit together. Was Madelyn the one who had told Everett about Sorority? Had Sage made her leave in retaliation? Or had Everett asked her to leave? I could see it play out. Madelyn had thought Everett would reward her for spilling the secret about the offshoot group that existed right under his nose and out of his control. Sage (or Everett) had ousted Madelyn. If Everett had promised her protection from his sister, he either wouldn't or couldn't keep his word.

—⁓—

Once in the garden, I scooped out a little hole in the earth and plopped in a small cherry tomato start, covering all the roots in a tiny mound of mulch. My hand rounded into a fist, and I stamped it into the dirt to pack it tight.

"Those are going to be some angry tomatoes." I looked up to see Lainey over me. "Everything okay?"

Nothing was okay. "I hate when things change," I muttered.

Lainey squatted down next to me. She popped another tomato start out of its compostable cardboard seed tray. "That's kind of the whole point of this place. Change is hard, but it's the way of nature."

I rolled my eyes at the platitude. "Doesn't mean I have to like it."

"I know I'm not your mentor, but you can talk to me. Trust me, I've been through it all and come out the other side with only a few broken bones." I couldn't tell if she was kidding. "Does this have to do with your trip to San Francisco with Stacey? Heard it was a good mission."

I paused. Mission? What would Lainey know about my mission? I shrugged it off as small talk. "It was fine. When I got back, Gillian was gone. I'm kind of in shock."

"Sorry to hear that," said Lainey. "She was a good one. These things happen. People come and go in this place. It's not for everyone. Especially not everyone's wallets. I'm pretty blessed to have a good stipend from Artemis."

"You live here full time, right?"

Lainey nodded. "I owe everything to Everett and Artemis. Salthouse is the only steady roof I've ever slept under. Lots of women have come and gone in that time. Maybe you'll meet Gillian again."

"The only steady roof?" I repeated.

She nodded again. "I experienced homelessness for a lot of my life. Ran away from an unpleasant home situation and learned to become hard on the streets. When Everett found me, I was like a wild animal. He tamed me, and I learned how to become soft. He gave me a role here, and here I've stayed. I've had to change to allow myself grace. Sometimes grace means letting go of people you thought you needed but who were holding you back in your bad habits."

"I'm sorry about how you grew up." We were silent for a moment. I straightened the stalk of a tomato plant leaning askew, adding a stake to hold it upright.

Something compelled me to continue. "It's Jenny." How could I explain her distance? "She's not the same as she was a few weeks ago."

"Change," Lainey said again. "Maybe she's processing something heavy she's never had to deal with until now."

I shook my head. "I wouldn't know. Maybe she misses her family. It sounds like her parents are invested in her, emotionally and financially. She has told me there's a lot of pressure on her, as a first generation, to be successful."

Maybe it was Nicklin. Had Cara consented to his therapies too? Maybe he was doing to Jenny what he had done to Cara. What exactly that was . . . I couldn't be sure. But it wasn't anything good. I considered Tom's theories. Maybe Nicklin was growing frustrated with Everett's way of doing things. Had he suggested his own ideas that Everett disapproved of? Like the somatic therapy? If Everett had promised Nicklin his own ascent in Artemis, maybe Nicklin had simply grown tired of waiting for Everett to hand over the reins.

And where did that leave Cara?

I had to get into Sorority, somehow. *I know it is still going.* I thought about what Sage said about Madelyn. *She was obsessed with getting close to Everett. Even if it meant stepping over and onto her Artemis sisters.*

"I have to go," I said. I stood and swiped the dirt from my pant legs.

"Where are you going?"

"I have to visit someone." *Someone else I know who I suspect would be willing to step on some necks to get to Everett.* I walked past Lainey without stopping. I pretended I didn't hear her calling after me.

I'd never been to Robyn's office at the Forum before. She tilted her head when I came around the corner. "Delia?" she asked. "Are you looking for someone?"

"You." I sat in the chair opposite her.

Her chin jutted forward. "Okay, one moment." She double-clicked her laptop keypad a couple of times. Robyn's office was spartan. Scattered copies of *The Artemis Method* lined the white pine bookshelves behind her. "So, what can I do for you?" she asked, focusing her attention on me.

"I want to join Sorority," I said.

Like all her well-trained colleagues, she didn't flinch. "Sorority is defunct. If it weren't, I'm afraid membership wouldn't be available to a member of your status."

"Yeah, that's what Sage said." I could see the very name rubbed her the wrong way. Good, I could work with this.

"So, what does this have to do with me?" Robyn threaded her fingers together. She released them and laced them again, her knuckles a tiny mountain range.

"Tell me how to get an invitation. Is it a matter of contributions?" I asked.

"Hardly."

"There has to be something."

"Again, if it existed, why do you want to join so badly? You don't even know what it is."

It occurred to me that honesty might be the best policy here. "Cara was in it." Then, I had an idea. "Madelyn told me."

Robyn's facade cracked as easily as her voice. "You saw Madelyn?" I nodded. "Shit," she said. "Of course. That's why you were in San Francisco." She gripped the armrests of her chair and asked me, though she already knew the answer, "Sage sent you?"

It was a dangerous game. I had no plan left. "She did," I admitted. "She said I was the only one she could trust."

My barb landed, and Robyn snapped her eyes to me again. "She said that?" The betrayal was clear.

"She did." When Robyn didn't respond, I continued, "I gave her an envelope. I don't know what was in it—"

"I do." Robyn knew? She went on. "Listen, Delia." She picked at her fingernails while she spoke. I'd gotten to her. I knew it now. She was nervous. "I know Sage has . . . taken a liking to you. She's not who you think she is. Everything has changed since Everett left. I've been trying to keep Sage on track; she won't listen to anyone. Cara was maybe the last person who could hold her accountable."

I said nothing. Even when I wanted to break down and demand that someone tell me what had happened to Cara.

"The more I think about it," said Robyn, "the more I'm convinced that if we find Cara, we'll find Everett too. Right now, there's nothing I can do for you."

I was crestfallen. I suppose I had known better than to expect anything. "Fine." I stood up and left without another word.

—∞—

Since I was in the Forum, I logged on to email and relished the indulgence of connecting to the internet twice in one day. There were only a few new items since the morning. Mom replied to my earlier note already, so I sent her another follow-up. As I was about to log off, I got a new-email notification from an anonymized address; the subject read because of SF. I almost moved it immediately to spam. As my cursor hovered over it, I gave it a second thought and opened it.

It was three lines long.

> you are hereby invited to join the illustrious Sorority of Artemis.
>
> be at the Flat Rock trailhead on Monday.
>
> twilight.

Because of SF. My heart leaped. *Thank you, Stacey.* Tomorrow was initiation day.

CHAPTER 28

The trailhead glowed. In the fading daylight, it looked magical from my distance on the beach, like a portal to another world. As I approached, I saw the trees around it hung with glittering fairy-light strings. Lanterns marked either side of the entrance, and a path of more lantern lights unfurled along the trail.

Last night and the entire day, I had focused on this moment. I had put in a few hours at the garden to make it up to Lainey for being so flaky yesterday. I helped clean at home and didn't even make a weird face when Jenny said she was heading to the clinic for her physical therapy session with Nicklin.

And now I was here.

I'd been on this trail dozens of times, but it was different in the impending twilight. The lights, which I assumed had been laid down by Petal, did more than make it pretty—they illuminated the possibility I was going somewhere secret and special. When I stepped off the beach, I would be a different person than before I made the journey.

So, I crossed that threshold.

My feet were sure on the dirt path, and it wasn't long before the sound of the surf was far behind me. It was eerily quiet in the darkening forest. I followed the lights to the familiar markers I knew from our hikes, the bend here and the big fern there. I stepped over a supine log and knew I was close to the fallen petrified tree.

I paused at the tree to catch my breath; I hadn't realized how fast I was moving. From between the trees a figure in a white flowing dress appeared. She held a lantern in one hand and a bundle of white fabric in the other. She emerged from the shadows so abruptly, for a moment, I was convinced she was a ghost. Or a veritable goddess. Only after I stared for a good ten seconds did I realize it was Petal.

"Jesus, you scared me," I said.

She threw her bundle at me. "Put this on."

It was a gorgeous white dress, like the one Petal wore. It fell around me and drifted like sea-foam. I gave myself one indulgent twirl, like a little girl on Easter, and forgot about the goose pimples up and down my bare arms.

—⁂—

At the top of the trail was the ghostly pantheon, Petal, Robyn, and Lainey, standing in front of the sheer rock platform. Lainey was shockingly regal in her gown, especially since I had only ever seen her in overalls and covered in fertilizer. On the rock platform itself, surrounded by more lanterns, was Sage. Even with her hair, illuminated and glowing as brightly as her dress, and her eyes piercing through the night right at me, she wasn't what I couldn't keep staring at—it was the young deer next to her, a loop of thin rope around its neck. Sage held up her hands, the end of the halter clenched in her fist.

The deer shuffled, one hoof over the other, white steam puffing from its flared nostrils. It was small, with two budding horns on its head. A male.

I stepped forward.

"Welcome, initiate," said Sage. Her voice was powerful and reverberated through the air. I thought that everyone asleep at Salthouse must have been awake now. "The Sorority of Artemis invites you to join our society. It is customary that goddesses unite with common bonds. To display these bonds, symbols of Artemis are used to represent our shared beliefs and recognize one another. However, to members of Sorority, the symbols have more significant meaning."

Lainey stepped forward and held a bowl with a white substance. She licked her two forefingers and dug them into the bowl, then raised her fingers to my lips. I opened my mouth, presented my tongue, and licked her skin. Salt. My lips puckered around her fingertips.

"The namesake of our community," said Sage. "Salt signifies the harshness of the world and the suffering we all endure."

Lainey stepped back in line, and Robyn approached, carrying a glass glinting in the light. I took it, and my nose was treated to a warm aroma of cinnamon and orange with some kind of herbal mixture.

"The drink of goddesses," said Sage. "An elixir to help us unlock our inner radiance. Drink the tea," Sage ordered. I paused, opening my mouth to ask what was in a goddesses' elixir, but before I could speak, Robyn poured the drink between my lips. The warm liquid was bitter as it went down my throat. "All of it." Sage gestured to my glass, still half full. I swallowed the rest.

"Finally," Sage continued, "the deer, signifying the innocence and strength of the huntress." She gestured, and I followed her hand motions. I gave the deer a pat on the head. His hair was bristly and sharp. He snorted and sniffed my sleeve. I moved back to my place.

"Now," said Sage. "For the sacrifice." She moved from the rock. The deer followed her. She gently fastened the deer's halter to a low tree branch.

My heart jumped as she pulled a knife from the folds of her gown. The blade glistened in the moonlight. She pointed the knife tip at me. Deftly, she turned it around and offered me the handle. "One quick cut," she said. "Then, you are one of us."

All eyes were on me. I didn't know what else I could do, so I took the knife. It was a proper hunting knife, made for the tearing of sinew. As my fingers wrapped around it, heavy and cold, someone—Petal, I think—began to cry. I held back my own tears and held the knife tighter so it didn't slip through my sweaty hands. The deer sensed the danger now; he pulled against the leash, and his panicked eyes flitted back and forth between us all and back to the thick forest again. Then he screamed. I hadn't even known deer could scream. It was a high-pitched, agonizing trilling. I winced, moving forward. I looked back, and Sage stood tall and watched, urging me on.

I turned and held out the knife in a limp hand.

"I can't," I whispered, clutching the neckline of my dress.

"You must do it," said Sage, like a threat. "It's a sacrifice, Delia. It's necessary—"

"For God's sake." Robyn walked toward me in long, sure steps and plucked the knife from my open hand. In one swift movement, she sliced upward. The blade sang.

The deer shuddered once before the light left its eyes. I clasped my hands together, suddenly feeling sick. Robyn motioned to Petal, who hurriedly brought the bowl of salt over to her. She placed it underneath the deer, collecting the blood pouring from its neck as its legs buckled and it sagged to the ground. Robyn threw the knife to the ground with a clatter that echoed over the cliffside.

Sage picked up the knife and, without hesitation, drew it along her own palm. It left a deep red cut in her hand. She turned to Lainey and did the same. Then Petal, then Robyn, and finally she turned to me. Against my own will but unable to stop myself, I held out my open hand.

I flinched against the sharp sting of the blade. I was feeling more and more sick, like my own legs would fail at any moment. Petal was coming around now with the mixture of blood and salt. She stopped in front of Sage and dipped her fingers into the bowl, which had now become a paint-like substance. Sage lowered her head, and Petal moved her fingers on Sage's face. When she was done, Sage had a red crescent moon of blood drawn on her forehead.

Petal repeated this on the other women, then me. The blood was warm still on my skin.

"Now our pledge," said Sage. She held strips of gauzy fabric. I tried to steady my breathing. *How many parts does this wild ritual have, anyway?* I just wanted to be back home and out of these woods.

Next to me, Petal and Lainey clasped their cut hands together, while Sage bound the hands with the fabric strips. She spoke as she wove them together, hand in hand. "We bind ourselves to Sorority. We give ourselves to each other, to our radiant selves, and to him, our leader."

I shot a glance to Robyn, whose face hadn't wavered. But Petal and Lainey were shaking their heads. "That's not part of the pledge," said Petal, almost in a whisper.

"It is now," responded Sage.

Who was *he*? Who was the leader? Nicklin? Was I wrong in thinking Sage was trying to take Artemis for herself? It had to be Everett still, wherever he was, and she was still loyal to him after all. And now soon, I would be, too, bound by blood oath.

After a sharp look from Sage, Petal and Lainey repeated the pledge. Satisfied, she turned to me.

Robyn approached me and held out her hand. It dripped with blood. I swallowed but didn't lift my own hand to meet hers. She reached forward and grabbed my hand, squeezing it tight so my wound stung.

Sage wrapped our hands, and the blood seeped out from between us, darkening the fabric in a crimson stain. "We bind ourselves to Sorority. We give ourselves to each other, to our radiant selves, and to him, our leader." Sage nodded to us. Our turn.

Robyn and I said it together. "We bind ourselves to Sorority. We give ourselves to each other, to our radiant selves, and to him, our leader."

My heart was jumping, and I felt light headed. What had I done? What did I just commit myself to? Sage clapped once, a sharp crack in the silence. "Now we are sisters for life, empowered by Artemis, the blood of the sacrifice and the salt of the ocean. As long as we never break this bond with one another, we are unstoppable. As long as we never refuse an order from our leader, who knows all, we will reap our deserving rewards."

What is she even saying? Petal pulled at her bindings. Robyn followed suit, and our strips fell away to the ground.

Sensing the women were at their limit, Sage lowered her head. "That's right. Go in peace now."

Robyn sighed. "Come on," she said to everyone. "This is over."

We all followed her. All of us except Sage.

Our strange silent party marched back down the trail, the spell broken. This was not an enchanted forest. It was a hiking path decorated in cheap fairy lights.

"Should we blow out the candles in the lanterns?" I asked. I regretted asking, not wanting to leave Sage without a lit path to follow home.

Lainey rolled her eyes. "They're battery operated, girlie."

When we passed the large tree, I grabbed my crumpled clothes. I looked behind only once, to see if Sage was following. She wasn't. I wondered if she was going to dispose of the deer. By the time we got to the beach, the moon was high and the surface of the water was silver, like a pool of mercury spreading onto the sand. The puddle grew and grew, and as I strained my eyes to focus, my brain turned fuzzy.

The others stopped and were staring at me. When I tried to reach out to Lainey, my arm only floated to my side. I tried to take a step and faltered; the world dipped around me. The tea.

What did you do to me? I said, though it came out as only a half-formed mewl. I bent over and retched into the sand. Everyone was staring as I slow-motion crumbled to my hands and knees. My fingers held on to the slipping grains of the sands of my consciousness, while the sky slipped underneath me and the ocean flowed above me. *This can't be happening.*

"Shit," someone said from beyond. "What are we supposed to do now?"

The cold closed in, and I couldn't keep my eyes open anymore. I fell into the darkness, into the waves, and I felt better. They were old friends, after all.

—⁓—

The pounding of the surf echoed through my skull. The sunlight through my eyelids was too strong. I pulled my arm over my face to block the light, as well as to hold my mouth closed against a pushing sickness.

When the nausea passed, I pushed myself to sit.

I was on the beach. A woolly blanket was pulled over me, though I was still in the dress from last night. Last night. At least I thought it was last night. How long had I been out?

"Good morning." Petal was sitting a little way from me. No longer an ethereal figure, she'd changed into sweatpants and a thermal shirt and was drinking from a thermos. "How are you feeling?"

I struggled to stand. My limbs were concrete. Catching my breath, I sat back down. "What the hell did you do to me?"

"Sorry about that," she said, like she had rung me up twice for bananas at the grocery checkout and wasn't sure what the fuss was.

"You're sorry? You drugged me!"

"It's a part of the new ritual. We didn't think it through." She held out her thermos. "Coffee?"

I waved her away. The thought of putting anything into my stomach made me feel even more sick. "I want to go to bed."

Petal helped me up, and we trudged along the sand. Last night came back to me in pieces, then in a tidal wave. Sage, the tea, the deer. "Where did Sage go last night?" I asked.

Petal shook her head. "Robyn is calling an emergency town hall this morning." Her breath was visible in the cold air. "She's suspected for a long time, and now leadership agrees, that Sage is no longer fit to lead Artemis. We'll have a public vote of no confidence at breakfast. You have a couple more hours to rest and change, if you can."

My sore muscles felt a little lighter when my house came into view. I didn't know if I could fall asleep again with everything going through my head. "What did you mean, you didn't think it through?" I asked Petal.

"I don't know," Petal evaded. "Normally, we would have a little after-party at the Wares' to celebrate a new sister. We didn't think it through because . . . we haven't initiated anyone since Everett left. Things have changed."

She looked down at her feet.

"Why would you drug someone and take them to the Wares'?" I asked.

"That's where the men would be waiting."

"What would they be waiting for?" I asked, though I already knew the answer in the pit of my stomach. It was a dark, swirling mass lodged in my gut. "But Sage," I protested. "He was her brother. Even her?" I don't know why I asked her. Maybe I needed her to say it out loud.

But she wouldn't, or maybe she couldn't say it, even if she tried. Instead, Petal looked at me. "Stop pretending to be stupid." She walked away.

CHAPTER 29

Everything about Artemis was connected to the Wares. I woke again, in my bed this time, and sensed it in my bedroom walls; the very air buzzed with a change in pressure, sensing the quiet insurrection about to take place. It turned out my exhausted body had no problem going back to sleep once I'd stumbled into my room. Now showered and changed into normal clothing, I felt like the whole initiation had been a dream.

We walked to the Forum with the usual morning crowd, and though Robyn had instructed us not to say anything, I felt as if everyone already knew. Instead of the usual morning chatter, lips were still. *They're all looking at me differently, aren't they? They all know what happened at Flat Rock, and they all know what Robyn's about to do.*

I pushed my spinach and egg substitute around my plate; the thought of eating made me ill. Petal and Robyn sat stone faced and silent at the center table. I spotted Nicklin at the buffet, heaping tempeh and fruit onto his plate. He wasn't speaking to anyone, but he wasn't looking distressed either. If he knew what was going on, he wasn't acting like it.

Sage was nowhere to be seen.

Robyn stood and tapped her spoon against her glass like a bell; the room fell silent. "Good morning to all," she began. "I know this is unorthodox; however, there is something that needs to be addressed here today. It's now been six months since our leader, Everett Ware, left

Salthouse Place to follow a path set forth by his radiant self. He's in a deep meditative state in a protected location.

"In his absence, his sister has stepped in as our leader. Sage isn't only a cofounder of Artemis; she was the actual inspiration for Everett's mission to help women around the world. She has always been, and always will be, a pivotal member of Artemis." *Always will be.* The room erupted with a soft buzzing as the whispers began.

"This is outrageous," interjected Nicklin. His face was red, and a vein in his neck bulged as he leaned over the table toward Robyn. Her surprise attack had worked. "It's highly inappropriate in this setting—"

Robyn continued, cutting off Nicklin and speaking louder. "Since Sage has stepped up as leader in Everett's absence, membership rates have plummeted. This is because of a series of questionable decisions on Sage's part. For example, Everett spent years working with those in town and forming a relationship with them. Sage has ended all efforts to work with those in town, and it's brought even more scrutiny and judgment on our community. Her newly instated curfew is unfair and pointless, to be frank. Under her watch, two well-regarded members in leadership parted ways with Artemis."

She meant Cara and Madelyn, I knew. I bristled at the thought of Robyn twisting their stories to serve her agenda.

"And so, it's with a heavy heart that I have to bring to leadership, in this public forum, a vote to declare our loss of confidence in Sage Ware."

We gasped—even those of us who had known it was coming.

"She doesn't have the best interest of our group at heart. She has, I'm sad to say, lost her way and is not fit to lead us anymore. So, I pose a vote for those in leadership. All those in favor of removing Sage from her leadership role, say aye." Robyn paused, then raised her hand. "Aye."

Nicklin sputtered and again leaned toward Robyn, an irate finger pointing at her. "You have no right," he spat.

Petal raised her hand. "Aye." The crowd turned to ask each other, Is this happening? Jenny met my eyes as if to say, *You were right.* The noise settled, and we all looked back to see who was next.

I knew Lainey would vote nay. Robyn looked like she might be the next de facto leader. If just Nicklin and Lainey voted no, the vote would pass; Sage was out.

Lainey stood and yelled, "Nay."

Nicklin had stopped protesting. "Nay," he said. "And Sage is a nay too."

"Sage isn't here," said Petal.

"We should postpone until she's here to defend herself against this would-be mutiny," Nicklin declared. "What would Everett say if he knew you were turning against his sister?"

"He would thank us for being loyal to Artemis," Robyn said. "Sage could have been here. She chose not to be."

"Even so," said Nicklin. "It's two against two. Stalemate. The vote doesn't pass."

Robyn folded her arms, smugly pursed her lips. Her jaw muscles tightened, and she turned to Nicklin. "You're right."

Nicklin nodded, sweating like he'd dodged a bullet.

"Except there's one more member here with voting rights," Robyn stated.

"Since when?" demanded Nicklin.

"Since last night."

Her eyes fell on me.

The room followed her, all turning to me. It wasn't Stacey. It was Robyn who had invited me for this small leadership group vote. She had been planning this for who knows how long, and she knew the math. She needed more votes. So, when I'd asked her for an invitation, she'd finally known where her tie-breaking vote would come from. *You could have warned me before using me as your pawn.*

"So, Delia? How do you vote?" Robyn asked.

My mind raced. She was right, I knew. I had fought against the instinct that Sage was dangerous. Madelyn had told me as much and, somehow, I knew Cara had known it too. I also knew I had gotten very little traction in my search for Cara with Sage blocking me at every turn. If she wouldn't help me, maybe Robyn would. Especially if I did her this favor.

I opened my mouth to vote, despite feeling out of place.

The doors of the Forum slammed open. We all turned, then stared transfixed at the sight in the doorway.

It was Sage. She looked like the final girl straight from a horror movie; she was still wearing her dress from the previous night. The fabric was stained rusty dull brown from dirt and sweat, a shade that extended to her face and bare arms and hands. Women turned to each other and whispered.

She emanated a sweet wild aroma of moss and earth. Her feet were bare and left footprints, dirt mixed with blood. She must have wandered through the forest and beach all night, I thought. Where had she gone? Or what had she been looking for?

My eyes followed Sage in terror; when she passed our table, she met my stare. Surprisingly, she looked more confident than ever.

Sage stopped in front of the table. Robyn hadn't moved, and a tiny smile ached to unfurl at the corners of her lips. This was good for her, she was thinking. If this crazed appearance didn't prove she was exactly right, then nothing would. Sage continued around the table. Nicklin hurriedly cleared a space for her and offered his chair, which she ignored. Standing with head held high, despite her face dirty with soil and her hair hanging down like wet yarn, she raised one hand. The murmuring silenced. Her back was pole straight, and her words were sure when she finally spoke: "I've had a vision.

"I saw Everett in the forest last night. He told me that he was moving on from Artemis and giving it to me to lead into the future."

The entire room erupted into disorder. Robyn began yelling at Sage, and Nicklin began yelling at Robyn. I couldn't discern any words over the cheers and applause. I looked at the rest of the women, surprised at the reaction. For the most part, they were looking at Sage without revulsion, only hopeful smiles. A handful of women were visibly distressed at the news; a couple walked out. At last, having delivered her message,

Sage turned and left, as nonchalant as she had arrived. Robyn turned, agitated, to me. She shouted above the din. "Well? Delia? The final vote," she said, hands gesturing, fingers grasping at an invisible ballot.

Sage's show of strength had worked. I couldn't vote against her, not anymore. She was still powerful here.

Loud and clear, my voice rang out. "Nay."

I stood and turned my back to the uproar. I ran after Sage. When I caught up to her, she looked at me and knew I'd made my choice. Of course, she had known all along what it would be.

We walked to her house in silence. In her bathroom, I helped her strip down. The dress was heavy; the hem was caked with mud and earth. We still didn't speak. *She's in shock*, I thought. I looked at her to see any evidence of a transformation. Of course, there was nothing to show it, only her lean ivory torso and the sinewy angles of her muscled limbs.

She didn't pull the shower curtain closed when she started the water, so it sprayed beyond the bathtub and pooled on the tile at my feet. In the tub, the deep-brown dirt and red residue swirled around the drain. I faced away and wiped down the counter, stealing a glance up in the mirror, and found her eyes waiting for me in the fogging reflection.

"Are you good?" I asked, wanting to leave.

She leaned out of the shower stream, wiped her eyes and face, then slicked her hair back with both hands. Her day-old eye makeup ran, streaking her face in black charcoal. "What?"

"Are you good? I mean, being left alone in here?" I asked again.

"Yes, why wouldn't I be?" She opened her mouth wide, and the water fell on her tongue. Dropping her head, she mumbled, "It was a sacrifice. It was necessary."

I slipped out the door. Outside the en suite bathroom, I wandered around. The decor was as generic as that of any of the town-homes around; the photos on the wall were all landscapes. Books on the shelves were self-help treatises with the occasional visitor's guide to the Pacific Northwest. Out of sheer frustration at wanting to find something unique, I gently pulled open the top drawer of her oversize dresser. Socks, all paired, and a stack of nude-colored bras. I lifted two unbranded bras, thinking there might be a white underneath. Nothing. There was no personality here. No Sage at all.

After a thorough tour of her room, the shower was still running, so I found sweatpants and a T-shirt in her dresser and peeked into the bathroom. Sage was out and sitting naked on the toilet, dripping, her arms pulled around her chest. "Hey." I pulled a towel around her. "You're okay. It's okay, let's get you dried." I rubbed her hair with another towel until her blonde strands stuck up like straw. "I'm surprised you didn't get hypothermia being in the woods all night. What were you thinking?"

She pointed to the medicine cabinet above the sink. I opened it, and sure enough, a prescription bottle of pills sat next to a tube of face cream. I read the label: alprazolam—generic Xanax. Prescribed by Nicklin, 0.5 milligram pills to take as needed. I opened the bottle and handed a single pill to her. Her hand stretched out from beneath her towel and took the entire bottle. She dumped out several pills and jammed them into her mouth.

"Jesus, slow down." I reached for the bottle. Sage thrust out her hand and grabbed my forearm. The strength of her grip caught me off guard.

She pulled me close until I could smell mint on her freshly brushed teeth. "You. You're the only one I trust now." I breathed, sucking the air inward. Her words echoed my own to Robyn. "They're trying to take it all away from me," she said, staring straight ahead, her eyes glassy and blank. Her fingers loosened and fell away from my arm. I rubbed the indentations on my skin as they faded before my eyes. I helped her pull her clothes over her bruised and scratched skin. I imagined her fighting through brush and over roots, with only the moonlight to lead her through the old growth.

"Where did you go last night?"

I led her to the bed, and she crawled in, pulling the covers up to her chin. "Were you worried?" She closed her eyes, drifting away on a drug-induced wave.

I was about to leave when she stirred again. "Everett and I built it all. I will never let them have it. For him."

I knelt against the bed and held her face. It was delicate in my hands, all her hard angles smoothed against my palm. "Did you see him?" I asked.

"He's so close," she said. "Closer than anyone thinks." Her words rocked me, and my skin was buzzing. *Everett is close.*

"Is he coming back soon?" I got only a snore in return. *Shit.*

Sage sleeping soundly, I drifted through the Ware home, free to leave, unable to make myself step out the door. I explored the rest of the upstairs, the guest bathroom, and two locked doors. Everett's, I assumed, all secrets safe and sound behind those doors.

I went into Sage's office, hoping to find a key. I looked through her desk. The top drawers were locked, and the bottom drawers only hid a stash of pretzels and various office supplies. I sat on her office chair and twirled around. Her shelves here, unlike her room, were filled with framed personal photos, plaques and awards, and other knickknacks. I walked over and scanned them. There were a lot of her and Everett, even as children. Then, a photo of a group of young girls, teenagers, with Sage and Everett on either side. It was like a class photo in front of a redbrick building. I remembered Petal had spoken about the short-lived Ware Academy School for Girls. This had to be their inaugural, perhaps the sole, class. Sage was very young there, just out of college herself. I touched the faces under glass, all blonde, one by one. My finger landed on her.

Standing right next to Sage in a white uniform. I would know her anywhere. It looked just like Cara.

A sudden weight dropped onto my chest, and I struggled for air. I picked up the picture and examined it closer. Maybe I was imagining things, going as crazy as Sage. But there was no mistaking her. There she was; Cara had known the Wares from before.

The boarding school she'd attended was the Ware Academy.

—⁂—

I was floating, unmoored. I took the picture and sat on the office couch, my feet tucked up against my bottom, and held the picture close like a child. I cried. Everything was resurfacing, and before I could catch myself, I was the scared and lonely girl with a dead friend and a missing friend—all over again.

You should have stayed, Cara. We were a trio, and when we weren't anymore, it should have been the two of us helping each other heal. You should have stayed with me.

CHAPTER 30

Then

Cara left me for boarding school to wander the high school hallways alone, whispers at my back while I stored my textbooks in my locker and tried not to look at the photos of Zee taped up on the inside. I stayed home on the night of the homecoming dance, even though Keene Stevenson asked me, out of pity, no doubt. We had promised each other we would go as a triple date like we did every year. It seemed wrong to go solo. My junior year, I had lost Zee, Cara, and myself in that order.

In November, after homecoming, as finals were wrapping up for Christmas break, I came home and found the envelope on my kitchen counter; I picked it up and held a piece of my heart in my hands. I took off my chunky knit hat and slipped out of my rain shell, letting it fall to the floor. With a fingertip, nail painted kitten pink, I followed my name and address, written in her unmistakable flowery writing. The return address some town in Massachusetts. She wrote about the fall colors in the Northeast and asked who I'd gone with to homecoming. She didn't say if she was coming home for the holidays. It was a page long.

I wrote her back that Keene and I had an amazing homecoming night and he even rented a hotel room for the after-party. I wrote that I missed her.

The next morning, I dropped the letter in the mailbox and raised the tiny red flag. Later that afternoon, in the Snyders' basement, I hung my bare legs over Tom's chest, and we shared a joint. I told him about the letter.

"Huh, Cara's never written me."

"Why would she write to you?" I asked him, prodding him with my toe. "She barely spoke to you when you lived in the same house."

"Damn," he winced. "Here I thought I found myself a nice girl." He passed the joint.

"I didn't get mean until I started hanging out with you, Tom Snyder." I took a long drag and winced when the sharp, smoky sting hit the bottom of my throat. Tom laughed when I coughed. When I caught my breath, I asked him, "Why did she leave?" It was the first time I'd asked him, the first time I'd asked anybody.

He shrugged. "How should I know? Ask her yourself."

"I mean," I backtracked. "I know why she left. I guess I don't know if it was because of all the town talk or if she needed a change of scenery." I waved away the smoke Tom blew over in my direction.

"What do you mean town talk?" he asked.

"How people said they didn't try hard enough to find Zee. If it were Cara, they would drain the damn lake dry." Tom's face told me I was going too far. The joint had made me brave, or stupid. "Admit it, Cara disappearing would have been a big deal—the Snyders' daughter, beautiful, rich . . ."

"White?"

"Well, yeah."

"Enough, Delia." Tom snubbed the joint into an ashtray on the bedside table and got out of bed. Naked, he walked over to the minifridge next to his entertainment center and pulled out a beer.

"What's wrong?" I asked.

"I don't know why you get like this sometimes." He shook his head, his brown curls brushing along his forehead without a care.

"Like what?"

"It's not healthy to keep talking about this. You're obsessed."

"With what exactly?" I sat up in bed.

Tom cracked the beer can open and took a drink. "About her. Isn't it time to move on?"

"Her name is Zee, and I can't move on. It just happened. How can you be so cold?"

"I don't understand why you're remembering her like she was an angel and Cara was so awful."

"Cara wasn't awful." I stuck my chin out. "Just, out of the trio, Zee and I were closer."

"That's rich." He only laughed and took another drink. "They made fun of you all the time, Delia. To your face, sure, but behind your back too. They thought you were a goody-two-shoes prude. If only they could see you now." His eyes scanned my naked body in a way that made me feel dirty.

"That's not true." I gathered the surrounding sheets, feeling suddenly exposed.

"I heard them talk shit all the time. Hey, sure, go on and think Zee was such a good girl and it was the two of you against pretty white Cara."

I hugged my knees close to my chest, and I cried.

"Shit." With a heavy sigh, Tom crawled back into bed and laid his head on my shoulder. "I'm sorry," he said. I buried my face in the crook of my elbow. "I didn't mean it, okay? You're right. She hasn't been dead all that long, anyway."

Not dead, I thought. *Gone for now.* I wiped my eyes and took a deep breath.

"Forgive me?" He kissed my neck, nuzzling underneath my armpit so he could see my face I'd hidden. His hands came searching along my side, then found their way in between my thighs. Of course, I forgave him.

I would even forgive him when he left for the East Coast, after the New Year. His parents were fed up with him hanging around the house and taking one community college class a semester. He was going to a new school, he explained. One that would have him even though his test scores were shit. His dad had made some calls, and besides, he would be closer to Cara. His parents wanted him to keep an eye on her, he said.

I got over it. Teenage girls are resilient, if nothing else. By senior year, I had made new friends. Yet I still longed for the closeness shared between myself and Zee and Cara.

So, if I kept grieving for Zee that year and all the years following, I grieved for the living, too, when Cara's letters became fewer and further apart, before they stopped altogether.

I tried writing Cara one more time before graduation. I wanted to tell her congratulations on her own graduation and ask where she had decided on going to school, to say that if she was going home to go to the University of Washington, we could finally be in the same city again. Weeks later, my letter reappeared in the mailbox with a big red stamp over Cara's name: RETURN TO SENDER.

CHAPTER 31

When I ran out of tears, or maybe energy, I could only stare and trace the edge of the picture frame.

How could Tom not have told me about Cara's prior relationship with the Wares? They knew everything, he'd said. Did they know because he told them? If Cara knew the Wares, Tom must have too. It was a trap, he'd said. Maybe it was worse. Maybe it was a trap of which Tom himself had been involved in the makings.

Sage had said she could trust only me. I felt I no longer had anyone, only the memory of Zee and the idea of a grown-up Cara I didn't really know.

I had to call Tom again.

The Forum was still buzzing, and there was a line for the phone booths. Were women calling for rides home or telling their friends to come join them?

I walked back to the town house. While the Forum was chaotic, the neighborhoods were uncharacteristically quiet. I passed the empty garden. When I reached home, Jenny was waiting. "What the hell is going on?"

"I took Sage home and helped her clean up. She isn't going anywhere."

"The understatement of the year. What's going to happen now?"

Startled by a loud vibration against my side, I reached into my purse and found the pager I'd forgotten I had. I read the screen: *911*. I looked at the number and knew it must be Brayden.

"I have to go," I said with no explanation.

Jenny balked. "Where?"

"We'll talk when I get back, okay?" I didn't wait for her response.

By the time I reached the bar, it was almost nine o'clock, and it was busier than I'd ever seen it. Generic country-pop music blared over the speakers, and there were even a few folks using the tragic dance floor.

I walked through the throng of townies, who stared as I passed through them. A tangy, sticky odor of microwaved BBQ sauce hung in the air next to the aroma of cheap beer.

Thankfully, Brayden spotted me. He waved and gestured for me to come over, and this simple acknowledgment from him put people at ease: I was here by invitation of one of their own. They returned to their conversations, even if they kept one eye on my back.

"You got here just in time. She's nervous. I thought she was about to run," he said, his voice low. "I promised her you'd come."

"Yeah, I'm here, along with what seems like the entire town." I looked around, searching. I didn't see Cara anywhere.

"Sorry," said Brayden. "It's ten-cent wing night."

"Of course it is. Where is she?"

Brayden tilted his chin to a booth in the very back, out of my line of sight from the bar. I stepped a couple of feet back, and I saw it—the back of a blonde head, sitting alone.

"Are you sure it's the same girl from before?" A glance told me he was right; it had to be her. "Thank you," I told him.

I walked to the booth, not even a length of eight feet. As I closed the distance, my heart threatened to explode. I'd found her. She was here.

I rounded the booth and exhaled.

"Madelyn? What are you doing here?"

CHAPTER 32

Madelyn Brewer sat in front of me, holding an untouched beer. "Delia, thank God." She lifted her face back and breathed a sigh of relief.

"You have come here before? You told Brayden you were scared and were trying to leave Salthouse?" She didn't answer. "If you were so frightened, why are you here again?"

"Brayden told me he knew how to get in touch with you. I had to see you."

I sat down in the booth, which provided a small barrier from prying eyes. Madelyn noticed me scanning the room. "Sorry, I didn't know this place would be so busy. I forgot there aren't many other options for a drink in this town."

"It's ten-cent wing night," I said.

Her head tilted in recognition. "Of course, every Tuesday," she said, as if she were an idiot for forgetting.

I waved away her attempts at stalling through small talk. "Why are you here?" I asked again.

Madelyn shivered, though it wasn't cold at all. I wiped small beads of sweat away from my hairline, then gathered my hair together and swept it over my shoulder.

"I have to tell you the truth. You asked if Cara was in a relationship with Everett."

I nodded, remembering her answer with disgust. *They all are.*

"She was—all the women in leadership are too," Madelyn repeated.

All of them? I wondered.

"The initiation," I said. "The last part of the initiation ceremony into Sorority is . . ." The words stuck in my throat like a bone.

"Surrendering to Everett." Madelyn finished the sentence for me. "I did it. And it wasn't the last time we would have sex together." Her eyes flashed in defensiveness. "I see you pitying me," she said, her nostrils flaring. "Like I was so taken advantage of, poor lonely woman who couldn't see the con. I did it of my free will. I thought being with him physically would . . . unlock something in me. Potential, promise, I don't know what."

"They told you that?"

Madelyn nodded. "Everything flowed from Everett. To be glanced at by Everett meant the sun was shining on you and you alone. So, the thought of being touched by him . . . God, it was life changing." A distant alarm sounded inside of me. *Life changing.* "Leadership became a snake's nest of jealousy and allegiances. His bond with Cara . . . was different. It was deep. Like an instant connection, lightning striking, in front of all of us, over and over again. It made all of us feel so small next to her light." I knew what Madelyn meant. Cara was like that, too, so bright she cast shadows over us all.

"All with Sage looking on, both behind the scenes and on the sidelines," said Madelyn.

"Meaning," I said, "she controlled the women but couldn't control Everett."

"Sort of. It was more that she couldn't control Cara." Madelyn shook her head. "Cara was getting too close, too brave with flaunting her closer relationship in front of the other members. Then, he told us one night, Cara and he were going to be joined."

"Joined?"

"Married. He said this wouldn't change his relationships with the rest of us; it would mean that Cara would step up as his counterpart. Which meant Sage would be, well, stepping down. Cara would be the fresh face of Artemis, he said. She would be the rebirth, the new generation."

"No, no, that can't be."

"I left that night. I told Sage I was leaving. I couldn't take it anymore. The place I came for self-care and healing became too toxic for me. My jealousy was taking over. I was neglecting my business. I knew I had to go. Sage lost it when I told her I was leaving."

"Because if you left, your money would go with you."

Madelyn reached into her purse next to her and placed two things on the table. One was the envelope I had given her back in San Francisco. The other was a silver flash drive.

"Sage told me I wasn't going anywhere. Sure, I could leave Salthouse if I wanted. Nobody was a prisoner there. If I left, I would still have to pay dues. That's the word she used, *dues*. Then she told me."

"Told you about what?"

"All the hidden cameras in Everett's bedroom." Madelyn slid the envelope to me across the sticky beer-stained tabletop.

My hands shook as I opened it and pulled out a single glossy photo, blown up to letter size. It was grainy and slightly blurred, but there was no mistaking it. It was Madelyn, her naked breasts exposed and her legs straddling a man who was clearly recognizable as Everett, his face in the throes of ecstasy. I shoved the photo back into the envelope and pressed my knuckles against my eyelids to stop the tears.

How would Silicon Valley investors react to seeing her like this? It could certainly cost her her reputation and maybe even her company. I thought of Madelyn's politician husband; photos like this could ruin his career. Sage had used me. "I'm sorry I gave you—"

"Don't be silly. I knew you didn't know what you had, even if you have a mean poker face." She gave a smirk. "I was still going to leave, even at the threat of blackmail. I wanted to know what I was dealing with. Sage forgot I'm an engineer by trade and know the brightest minds in Silicon Valley. It only took my people a day to hack into the

Artemis archives and download all of Sage's revenge porn. They're all there, everyone." She laid a finger on the flash drive.

Everyone? "Even," I ventured, "Sage herself?"

Madelyn nodded, her eyes cast down. My stomach turned. "And it wasn't just Everett. Both of them . . ." She shuddered. "And other men who thought they owned us."

I nodded. My suspicion that Nicklin was involved was confirmed.

Everyone. Even Cara. Cara with her carefully laid plans and hidden traps. How many had been Everett's or Sage's, and how many had been her own?

I pulled out my phone and showed her the photo. "You said you were the one who took Cara to her first Artemis seminar. It's not true. She knew the Wares from before. That's why their bond seemed so deep. Because it was. It went back a decade."

Madelyn shook her head. "I can't believe it. Why keep it secret?"

I didn't have an answer, aside from a small guess. "Maybe Cara was recruiting women in powerful roles: CEOs, recognizable names, women like you."

"That's absurd," said Madelyn. "She applied, and we interviewed her along with a handful of others. There was no guarantee she would get the job. And even if there was, how could she be sure she could lure in the boss?" Her voice shrank as she spoke.

"Where did she work before?" I asked.

"Another marketing start-up, I think. And I don't recall another big-fish CEO in Artemis."

"Maybe this is the first time it worked," I said. "It looks like it was worth the time and effort." I turned over the silver flash drive in my hand. "Why should I believe any of this?"

"Because I've been silent for too long. I've been so afraid to say anything because of what they have against me that I've become complicit in all of their dirty deeds. It was selfish of me. If I came forward right away, when I left Salthouse, maybe it would be different. Maybe Cara would still be here. I won't do it any longer. I don't care if it ruins my career and my company. Artemis won't hold me prisoner any longer."

Madelyn snapped her head suddenly toward the door, like she had heard something, though it was impossible over the incessant country and western tunes. "I have to go. I've been here too long. Someone has been following me. Ever since I touched down at the Portland arrivals gate. They know I'm here, Delia. And if they know I'm here, then they know I'm talking to you. Be careful." She took the flash drive and placed it in my hand. "In case anything happens to me, this is yours. Use it to find out what they did with Cara, then use it to make Everett and Sage pay."

In a sudden rush, she snatched her purse sitting next to her and slid out of the booth. Before she was out of reach, maybe for good, I clasped her arm. She paused and leaned into me, so close I smelled the beer on her breath and the fear from her pores.

"How can I trust you?" I asked.

She took my hand from her arm and squeezed. "You can't. You should know by now you can't trust any of us."

CHAPTER 33

A group of revelers surrounded us, and our hold was severed. I was pushed back into the booth by the insistent group, which was too drunk to notice the table was occupied. "Wait," I called over the table to Madelyn, who'd almost been swallowed by the crowd, bodies pressed against her. Had someone turned up the music? She spun.

"Do you think she's alive?" I asked.

"I do."

"Be careful. There's a lot at stake for the Wares. I'm not sure what they would do to hold on to Artemis."

She stepped back into the sea of flannel and denim, and she was gone. The top of the door opened and closed again. When I made my way back to the bar, Brayden slid me a pint of a dark ale. "Did you get what you needed?" he asked.

"I think so. Maybe more." My fingers wrapped around the flash drive in my pocket. If Madelyn was telling the truth, this tiny storage unit had the capacity of a ten-ton bomb. Now, I had to decide where to aim it.

I was about to thank Brayden again when a scream shattered the country chorus. A squeal of tires. The crunch of an impact. A group of patrons near the front of the bar, next to the windows, yelled. "Call an ambulance!" someone screamed. "Someone hit a woman."

I fought my way through the charged throngs. When I reached the open door, I didn't have to step outside to see it.

She was staring right at me. Madelyn's body lay crumpled on the sidewalk, limbs arranged in unnatural angles. There were black skid marks on the pavement next to her, and the smell of burnt rubber stung the hairs in my nostrils. A single stream of red flowed toward me from her ear; it ran so bright and smooth. I could kneel right here and touch it, and I knew it would be hot.

A powerful hand landed on my shoulder. I spun around to find Brayden. He mouthed a single word: *Run.*

He was right. In just a moment, the locals would remember the girl who nobody knew, the stranger from the retreat up the road. They would happily tell the cops how I was talking to the woman moments before a car smashed her to pulp and left her dead. I felt for the flash drive in my pocket. Only when I confirmed it was still on me did I slink back through the people on their phones, taking pictures of the dead body, and duck into the bar, now empty. I headed toward the back, past the bathrooms, and out the back door. In the fading light of the evening, I jogged around the back of the block to the car.

What now, Delia? I was too numb to cry, let alone think. *Drive to Portland and get a hotel room. Hell, I can drive all the way to Portsgrove. I'll give the flash drive to Tom and tell him Madelyn's story. He'll know what to do. Except he won't. Remember? He didn't tell you Cara knew the Wares. He might be in on the whole thing; I have to work out how.* The more I thought of a way out, the more it became sickeningly clear.

I could not see a way out.

If Artemis could follow Madelyn all the way from San Francisco and find her here, they knew she was meeting with someone. *Maybe they knew it was me, maybe they didn't. If I don't go back to Salthouse tonight, they'll know for sure it's me.*

Even the confidence I'd had in the flash drive wavered. It was evidence. Evidence of what? Consenting adults who liked to make sex tapes?

I held my breath as headlights appeared in my rearview mirror, flashing for a bright, blinding second before passing. I started the car and shifted into drive.

When I reached Salthouse, I parked in the nearly empty Forum parking lot, a sharp contrast to the busy exodus I'd left. I'd come back to a ghost town. I turned the car off. I couldn't make myself move. I sat staring out the window. The beach was visible under the very last reaches of the lampposts around the Forum. Where the light ended, the beach dissolved into shadow, then blackness.

I fished around in the center console and came up with an empty sandwich baggie, previously home to potato chips or maybe cookies. I pulled out the flash drive from my pockets. The pager and my phone were missing—they must have fallen out during my dash from the bar. I dropped the flash drive inside the baggie and sealed it—I knew the perfect place.

I avoided the streetlamps and walked in the shadows.

In the neighborhood, a scattering of lit windows glowed like tiny lighthouses in the night. I wondered if Sage was asleep. I knew her better than that. She was awake; I felt it. There were too many moves to make now.

In the garden, I buried the flash drive in between tomato plants in the middle of the bed.

I turned onto my street and wondered why I hadn't met one other person. I was sure someone had missed me at dinner earlier.

—◯◯—

Footsteps. I stopped and crouched at the edge of the sidewalk until the sharp branches of a bush scratched against my neck and back. A figure came into view under a streetlamp. Nicklin. What was he doing walking around at this hour? And coming from the direction of my house? Even after his shadow was long gone down the next street, I huddled in the bushes, breathing into my sleeves.

At home, I peeked in Jenny's room to find her asleep and nothing disturbed. Exhausted, I shrugged my dirty clothes onto my bathroom floor. I turned on the shower and let the hot water run over me until my skin glowed pink, though I still didn't feel clean. My muscles were restless with agitation; my mind raced. I went downstairs and proceeded to clean the kitchen counters. I sprayed cleaner and wiped them down over and over again until my head was dizzy from the chemical smell. I knelt down to scrub a dried spill of something on the floor.

My foot hit something, and a metallic object clattered across tile and underneath the counter. I bent down and looked, fishing with my fingers. When I pulled them out, a shiny set of keys hung from my finger. *Whose are these?* It contained a Toyota key fob and three other small silver keys. Upstairs, I set the keys on my desk.

I tried to sleep, but every time I closed my eyes, I saw Madelyn's battered and broken body, her blood flowing toward me.

CHAPTER 34

Breakfast. Twenty-four hours ago, we had lived in a different Artemis.

The Forum was quiet. I picked at my plate and pushed the tempeh hash around with my fork while my other hand slipped down to my thigh, where I traced the vague outline of the key ring I had stuffed into my pocket.

However, Jenny was interested in making conversation, much more so than the past several days. "Where were you yesterday, anyway?"

"Needed a change of scenery. Sorry, I should have told you. I think I panicked."

Jenny shrugged. "Where did you go?"

"Nearby beach."

"Well, I have news. I got a scholarship for Artemis! I can stay for another few months." She smiled.

I didn't know what to say. I lowered my voice. "Do you think staying is a good idea?"

Jenny's face fell. Her smile turned into a scowl. "I knew it. I knew you couldn't be happy for me. He was right."

"He?" I knew. Who else? "Nicklin?"

Jenny nodded, and a flush spread across her face, like I'd said the name of her secret crush.

"What about LA? Your agent?"

"I've parted ways with him. I emailed him yesterday. He wasn't the one for me—Nicklin helped me see that. As far as LA goes, I've told my roommates to look for someone to sublet my room."

"You did all this because Nicklin told you to?"

"He sees something in me. And he also sees you only want to keep me small."

Madelyn's words echo through my brain. To be noticed by Everett was to have the sun shining on you; to be touched by him would unlock her promise and potential. It seems Nicklin had learned more than philosophy from Everett. I wanted to yell at Jenny that she was being used. As I opened my mouth to say the things I'd regret, the Forum doors opened, and Sage walked in.

She was no longer the wet and exhausted body I'd put to bed yesterday. She was a thing reborn. With Nicklin in tow, she strutted to the head table, and it was all I could do to keep myself from leaping at him and clawing at his eyes. Jenny watched him like a puppy dog. I wondered suddenly, Did he have cameras set up too? Was there a trove of videos from all his therapy sessions?

Behind Nicklin, the rest of leadership followed, including Robyn, to my surprise.

"Good morning," Sage said. "I had prepared to say something about a new day and a new vision for Artemis. I was going to thank all of you for your steadfast loyalty. However, our celebration will have to be for another day. I've received word of a terrible tragedy.

"I learned this morning one of our past members and generous benefactors was killed last night." A wave of gasps went through the room. Sage placed her hands over her heart and sniffled, then looked to the sky before she continued in a shaky voice. "So many of us knew and loved Madelyn." Voices talked over one another. Sage put out her hand, and the room silenced. "Madelyn was a sister goddess and a friend. It's with great sadness I have to tell you she was the victim of a vicious attack last night. I can assume the attacker was one of the many critics Artemis has attracted. It's people like her attacker, her murderer, who wish to do us harm. Please be vigilant. I'm asking all of you to observe what's happening around you at all times and to report any suspicious behavior you witness. I wish I didn't have to say this. We should not rule out the possibility that enemies are in our midst."

This was too much. The women in the room glanced around, considering each other, knowing that maybe these women, friends—no, *sisters*, moments before—weren't safe anymore. Sage kept talking, but I didn't hear her anymore. My ears filled with an echo, like I was underwater.

"Delia?"

I snapped into focus. "Sorry, I need some air."

Outside, it was calm and warm, one of those early-summer days that made me want to curl up and sleep on a grassy sunlit patch somewhere. Bees bumbled along a growth of wildflowers blooming along the Forum walls, blissfully unaware of the ungodly activities of their human neighbors. The sky was large above me, and I took a deep breath.

I remembered the keys in my pocket. I wandered through the parking lot. In the middle, I pressed the unlock button on the key fob. *Click.* I scanned the cars. Nothing. I pushed the lock button. *Click.* Still nothing. I walked along a little more, changing my angle. *Click.*

There it was—the glimmer of lights; headlights flashing. I found myself in front of an older tan Toyota Camry. The passenger's side headlight was cracked. I knelt down and looked closer. It looked like someone had done a poor job of wiping it down, almost as if they had been doing it in the dark. I could see the tiny trace of dried brown blood on the inside of the crack in the plastic. Madelyn's blood.

Suddenly, even the outdoors with the wide-open sky was collapsing in on me.

I went to the phone booths. I dialed and hit my fist against the wall over and over. "Pick up, pick up, pick up," I mumbled.

"Hello?" answered Tom.

"Tom." I breathed out. If he was in on it, I didn't care anymore. I needed something to ground me, someone to catch me. Besides, everything was different now. Someone was dead.

"Delia, what is going on?" Tom asked. "I've been using the pager number; why aren't you calling me back?"

Before I could explain to him what had happened or confess that I'd lost the stupid pager, there was a hammering at the door. I jumped, gasping into the phone. "What's going on?" demanded Tom.

I opened the door. "Robyn? What are you—"

She squeezed past me and slammed her hand down on the hook. My call ended with a devastating dial tone as hopeless as a flatline.

"Are you crazy?" I snapped.

She closed the door and pointed to the phone. "We're listening."

I shook my head. "It's not true. They can't do that."

"It is true. We can and we do. We listen to and record all calls. I've listened to your calls, Delia. Every one since I've been here."

I was at my breaking point. I couldn't hold it in any longer, and the tears fell down my cheeks. "What do you want?"

Robyn wiped one away. "To be in control." She laid her fingers against my cheeks; they were soft as her voice. "You need to leave. Sage will find out you were with Madelyn last night."

"How do you know where I was last night?"

She smirked, and her hand fell back down to her side. "You weren't at dinner. I knew you went to see Madelyn in San Francisco. So, who else would she come back here to see except for you or Sage? And the latter was in a drug-fueled deep sleep. I put it together pretty easily. Sage will too."

"You knew?" I asked her.

"No, her office informed us this morning. They knew she was traveling here, and it surprised them to hear she never made it to Salthouse."

"Why? Why kill her?"

"I can only imagine whatever it was she had to say was very dangerous information to have. For both her and whoever she told it to."

"Why are you telling me this? Why are you helping me now?"

"Because this has gotten out of control." She took a deep breath. "I don't want to see anyone else get hurt."

Could I trust Robyn now? I didn't know if I had a choice; my allies were dwindling.

"It was Everett, wasn't it? He's still pulling strings from wherever he's hiding." I lifted the keys from my pocket. "Whose are these? They go to a tan Camry."

Now it was her turn to be surprised. She eyed the silver Toyota logo on the fob. "If you mean an ugly Camry from the nineties, they're Nicklin's. Why do you have them?"

I sniffed. "That son of a bitch must be trying to frame Jenny. Last night, he was slinking away from our house in the dark; then I found these on our kitchen floor. Robyn, we have to go to the police, we have to get help—"

"No!" she snapped. "Absolutely not. The local police are in Artemis's pocket. They let the Wares do whatever they want here as long as they get paid. If you go to the police, they either won't care or they'll personally deliver you to Sage herself."

I was at a loss. "What now then?"

"Leave."

Of course. *Will they let me?*

"Tell Jenny to get out too," Robyn said matter of factly. "I'll try to talk to you later. I have to get back." She left as abruptly as she came in.

I thought of all the conversations Robyn had overheard. So, maybe Tom wasn't involved; it wasn't the Snyders; it was the Wares . . . plus Cara. I was confused. I caught my breath and left the Forum.

It had been a mistake to return. I should have left. I should have left a long time ago. I was going to take Robyn's advice.

I walked home and opened the door. "Jenny?" I called.

"Here," Jenny answered from the living room.

"Jenny," I sighed with relief. "Hurry, we have to—" I halted dead in my tracks. She was sitting on the couch, and Nicklin was beside her. I tried to cover. "Oh, hi, sorry—didn't mean to interrupt. Jenny, can I talk to you?"

"Whatever you have to say, you can say it here," she said. "In fact, we were just talking about you."

"About me?" I rubbed my hands; they were cold and clammy.

Nicklin stood. "Jenny told me you were out pretty late last night. You didn't go to town, did you?"

I shook my head, chasing away the images of Madelyn in the street. "Nope. How sad about Madelyn. I hope they catch whoever did it." I stared defiantly at Nicklin.

He was the first to break eye contact. "Nevertheless"—he took a step toward me—"Sage wants to check in on a few things." He crossed the room and took hold of my arm.

"Don't touch me." I pulled my arm back.

He smiled and held up his hands. "No need to fight."

I was still closest to the door. I couldn't bring myself to leave Jenny. Not with what I knew now. "Fine."

Jenny didn't move as Nicklin walked me outside. He followed me all the way to Sage's house, like the executioner following the prisoner to the hangman's rope.

—⁂—

Sage wasn't in her bedroom. I stepped into her office, and it was empty as well. A single item caught my attention on her otherwise clean desktop—a single antler branch, splitting into two tines. I glanced my finger across one point and drew it back with a sharp gasp; on the tip of my finger was a drop of red, the scarlet blood bubbling up through the wound as small as a pinprick. I put my finger to my mouth and tasted it, a tiny metallic tang, like licking a penny.

Back in the hall, I noticed the door to Everett's office was open. I glanced behind to see Nicklin still following, but he stayed in the hall when I entered the office, conveniently blocking my exit.

My heartbeats thundered in my head.

Sage was at his desk, flipping through a stack of papers. Archive boxes lay open throughout the room. Were these all of Everett's records? What was she looking for? She glanced up, then back to her papers, as if she couldn't be bothered. "Do you have information on Madelyn's attack?" she asked.

I had to say something to shake her or, at the very least, distract her. Maybe there was still a way to get back to the Sage I first met, to get her to help me. "I want to talk to you about Jenny."

"What about?"

"I think Nicklin has been manipulating her. I think the therapy he provides is bullshit."

Sage broke her attention away from the mess of files. "I thought Jenny suffered from hysteria. Nicklin has told me she's been responding well under his care."

"Hysteria?" I scoffed. "You're diagnosing women with hysteria in this century? Do you understand the misogynistic connotation of that? Not to mention, it's flat-out wrong."

"Whatever name you want to attack with, these women find great relief in working with Dr. Nicklin. He uses a variety of physical therapy methods."

The massage sessions, Jenny's sudden attachment—my stomach recoiled in disgust. He was abusing her. "Nicklin needs to be in jail," I said. "I know he's Everett's protégé and you're protecting him like you protected your brother."

"What do you know about my brother?"

"I know he's a predator too."

"My brother was a genius. But he could only do so much. I'm going to bring Artemis into a new era, like he never could. It's time a woman was leading Artemis. Funny . . ." Her voice drifted.

"What?"

"Everett wanted it to be Cara." Her lips lifted a bit at the corners, a hint of a smile. It made me furious.

"Where is she? I know you know," I demanded.

"I don't know why you refuse to believe me; I've told you multiple times I don't know where she is. Delia, maybe it's time we accept that wherever she is, it might be better if she stays there. She doesn't want to be found."

I sensed movement behind me and spun around to see Nicklin in the doorway. He smiled a toothy grin.

My frustration and despair churned and erupted inside me. Still, I trusted her. I had to try. "It's him," I said. "Nicklin is the one who killed Madelyn, and I think Everett told him to do it and frame Jenny. Sage, I know Everett made you Artemis leader, but he's still going to keep controlling people from wherever he is. You have to convince him to stop before more people get hurt."

Sage stared at me in silence, then let out a thick, velvet laugh. The heat in my cheeks grew even hotter with embarrassment. Was I so wrong? I remembered that Sage was the one who had revealed Everett's cameras to Madelyn, and Sage was the one who had sent me to blackmail Madelyn one more time. The conclusion was unbearable: Sage was working with Everett. She knew everything.

I played the last, the only, card I had. "I have the videos."

Her laughter stopped. "What videos?"

"The ones where your brother conducts his sessions with Artemis members. The ones you used to blackmail former members. I know everything, Sage. So, you better tell me where Cara is, or I'll make sure everyone knows about you and Everett and that Artemis Wellness is nothing more than a hunting ground for sick men to victimize vulnerable women." My words hung above us like knives about to drop.

"Now you've gone too far," Sage muttered, almost too quiet to hear. "Now I'm bored with you."

Nicklin moved on me fast; he grasped my neck in his hand and squeezed hard. I screamed and tried to turn. I was reaching to pry his grip from my throat when I felt a sharp prick below my ear. Nicklin released me, and I tried to move forward. A wave of nausea hit me, and I held out my hands to steady myself. I put my hand to my neck, and when I pulled it away, a tiny bead of red was on my fingers. I looked back to Nicklin, who was holding an empty syringe.

"What did you do to me?" I asked. Or I think I did. My tongue seemed to fill my entire mouth. I tried to look back at Sage, and my vision blurred. The room spun upside down, and my body hit the floor, helpless. From above, Sage's sapphire eyes came into focus, peering down at me. I reached my hand toward them to claw them out. It was too late, and everything went black.

CHAPTER 35

I dreamed of Zee.

This dream was different. I was treading water in Blythe Lake. It was winter and snowing all around, yet I was in my swimsuit. Then I saw her. She was splashing and kicking, and her head kept breaking the surface only to disappear again. I turned to find Cara next to me. She laughed and swam after Zee. I followed her. *She's right there.*

We reached her and each grabbed one arm. Clutching one another, we turned and swam toward the beach. In our arms, Zee had regained her footing, her stroke. We were a multilimbed organism, swimming together in perfect coordination. We had three brains and three hearts between us, six lungs heaving in the frigid waters until, at last, our feet found the shore. The wet sand sucked in my legs, like being caught in concrete as the sand tightened and compressed against my calves. I stumbled and got pulled down by the waves again. Zee and Cara pulled me forward. The swirling waters cleared for a moment, and I gasped the precious air and spat as a wave departed from my face. "Stand," I said. Collectively, we surfaced, emerging from the lake. When we caught our breath and looked around, we found the water was barely above our waists. We were floundering in the shallows.

—ᴍ—

I woke up in bed, and even in the darkness, I was relieved I could tell it was my own. First, I put my hand to my neck. *What did that bastard inject me with?* My fingers flew to the side of my bed and underneath the mattress.

Cara's journal was gone. I tried my pockets. Keys, gone.

The door opened. It was Nicklin. "How is the patient feeling?" He flipped on the overhead lights, and I winced at the sudden flood of illumination.

"What did you inject me with?" I demanded. I swung my legs over the side of the bed to sit up; the simple action left me woozy and out of breath. With one hand, I steadied myself.

"Ooh, I would take it easy if I were you." Nicklin strode to the window and looked out. "You got a good dose of xylazine, which is a muscle relaxer and sedative. It will drop your heart rate and blood pressure, just like that." He snapped his fingers. "If you happen to be an *Equus caballus.*"

"You gave me horse tranquilizer? You could have killed me." A realization dawned on me, and it was all at once hilarious and terrifying. "Wait a minute, are you a fucking vet? Oh my God, you're not even a proper doctor." I giggled like a madwoman at the absurdity of it all.

Nicklin's face turned boiling red. "You won't be laughing for long, bitch."

"Now, now." Jenny came in the door. "You know her; she can't help herself sometimes."

"Jenny?" I blinked to check if this was still a dream. "What are you doing?"

"Carrying out my duties as a member of Sorority," she snapped. "What am I doing? What are you doing? You're not a believer. In fact, you're a bad influence. I thought we were friends, but you're not a friend at all." Nicklin moved to Jenny's side and slid an arm around her. She shrank against him.

"Don't touch her." I tried to stand. Cymbals crashed inside my brain, and stars exploded into my sight. I gripped the bed frame and lowered myself back down. "Jenny, you can't trust him," I mumbled through the pain. "He's trying to frame you for murder. I found his keys in our kitchen. The keys to the car that killed Madelyn."

"He doesn't have to frame me," Jenny said, her head tilted in confusion.

I shook my head. Maybe my hearing was affected; I didn't understand.

"Because I did it." ·

No. "Jenny, no." My heart thumped against my chest.

"Sage asked me to eliminate the threat against Artemis and Sorority. It was a great service."

I breathed in sharply. "Jenny, how could you? She was a person. Don't you understand you killed a person?" My voice rose, shaking.

"I understand she was an enemy of Artemis." Her gaze was cold and distant.

I couldn't understand the words she was saying. My grasp on consciousness slipped again. The darkness was so warm, so inviting, and I was so tired. *Delia? Delia, can you hear us?* Their words floated away from me, and I, once again, fell into the depths.

—⁓—

Delia? Delia, wake up!

The darkness swirled around me. Hands reached for me, grabbing me. I opened my mouth to scream. A warm palm clasped itself onto my face, stifling my call.

"Shh! It's me, Robyn. You have to wake up now!" Her voice cut through the shadows, and I opened my eyes. It was still black. As I blinked and looked around, my eyes adjusted. It was nighttime.

"How long have I been out?" I asked, my voice hoarse and my words slurred.

"For a full day," Robyn said. "I thought you were going to die from how much Nicklin gave you."

"Where is Jenny?"

"They moved her to another house. She's safe for now. After all, Jenny's not the one holding Sage's interest." Robyn was sitting on the bed and holding a folded pair of clothes. "I raided your closet."

I took the clothes and began stripping. "How do I leave?"

"Walk out the open door."

I glanced behind Robyn. She was right—I could see the small crack of light coming through the door left ajar. "They left me to guard you," she explained. "They think I hate you for voting for Sage and allowing her to stay in power." She paused to reflect. "Though, now I say it out loud, yeah, I'm still kind of salty."

"I'm sorry," I said because I didn't know what else to say, and because I meant it.

"You don't have to be sorry. You don't think your vote would have changed anything, do you?" No, I didn't. It was clear to me now that Sage would have held on to Artemis no matter what it took. Robyn went to the window and looked down. "Hurry up."

With my T-shirt and sweatshirt on, I stood to pull on my jeans. Too fast; all the blood rushed to my head. My legs swayed like jellyfish tendrils. Robyn steadied me.

"How am I supposed to escape like this? Besides, they have my keys."

"Getting out of Artemis will be the hardest part. Sage has panicked everyone with Madelyn's murder. There are women all around the neighborhood as lookouts for suspicious activity. Nobody is getting in or out via the main roads. If you go through the backyards and skirt the parking lot by going around through the undeveloped areas, you should be okay. Once you hit the main highway, start running. Get as far away as you can and find a ride to town."

The thought of relying on an odd passing car on the seldom-used road going to Artemis seemed like a long shot. I prepared myself to have to run all the way to town in the dark.

We went downstairs, and I chugged a glass of water. By the time I finished the glass, I could feel my muscles rehydrating, and if I were a video game character, my little life icon would have filled up—a pale green instead of the flashing red from moments ago. I slipped on my sneakers. I placed my hand on the back door handle, then paused. "Come with me," I told Robyn. "You can't let them know you let me escape."

"I'll manage," she said.

I didn't know what else to do, so I hugged her. She froze, then relaxed into me and squeezed me hard. "Please be careful." I pulled away and nodded. With one more look over my shoulder at the place I called home, I walked out the door.

The fresh air hit my lungs, and the drug-induced cobwebs cleared from my brain. And for the first time in a long time, I knew what to do. I was getting the hell out. Our fenceless yard led straight to another one, so I stalked along the backs, taking care to take my time along those with fences where I could afford to linger. The first yard I came to, I watched the windows for a long time before I thought it was safe to sprint across. I crouched on the other side behind a tree for a good minute before I forced myself to keep moving.

When had my limbs become so heavy? It was a cloudy night but a quiet one, so each snap of a twig under me seemed to echo through the houses. Luckily, the ever-present surf provided cover to my missteps. I came to where the yards now curved along the cul-de-sac, and paused; I was closest to the beach. I needed to cross a couple more streets to get to the highway side.

The first street was empty and silent. I darted across and flattened myself along the bushes to make my way through an undeveloped green belt between cul-de-sacs. I picked up the sounds of voices talking. Crouching down, I eased some foliage out of my line of sight. There was a group of three women walking down the middle of the street, each holding a flashlight. Robyn wasn't joking. Sage had installed guards to ensure I didn't make it out.

They passed, more interested in talking than doing a proper sweep. I couldn't hear a thing they were saying, though I had a feeling my name was on their minds and tongues. I was frozen to my spot even once they were out of sight; my feet were getting pins and needles from squatting so long, yet I couldn't compel myself to move. Across the street and a few hundred feet of dirt and shrub was the highway. *This is crazy. I'm going to run out into the night not knowing what lies ahead? Would Sage harm me? Truly harm?* I stared into the open night. I couldn't hear the ocean anymore. It was silent.

The devil you know . . .

A car horn blared. I jumped as it continued in a long uninterrupted siren, then broke into short, quick blasts. It was an alarm. I'd been missed. Without wasting another second, I broke for it. I crossed the street and ran into the undeveloped stretch of land, deep blackness ahead of me. I couldn't tell how far I'd gone or how much farther I had left to go. I dared not look behind me. If before I couldn't force my feet to move, now I could not stop them.

I didn't quit until my feet hit firm blacktop. The white lines reflected in the moonlight, like a runway in front of me; there was a bright flash of headlights in the distance. I ran toward them and waved my arms frantically. They closed the distance between us fast. Faster than I realized. I wouldn't stand aside. This might be my only hope. The lights blinded me, and the engine roared in my ears. I held out my hands and prayed.

The brakes squealed. The car stopped with a creak of metal under strain, mere feet from me. The heat from the engine was warm on my outstretched palms. *Thank Goddess.*

A head in silhouette craned out from the driver's side window.

I gasped between heaving breaths that turned to clouds in front of me in the cool night air. "Tom? Is that you?"

The door opened, and the driver stepped out.

"Are you kidding? It's me. Now, get in the car!" Gillian pulled me around to the passenger side and pushed me inside. She ran back to the driver's side and pulled a U-turn, the dirt from the side of the road grinding beneath the tires. I placed my hands on the window and watched as the lights from Artemis pivoted behind me. Then we were gone.

CHAPTER 36

Once we left the local highway and joined I-5, Gillian asked me where we were going. I told her north, and I would let her know when we'd gone far enough. She didn't ask me anything else, so I leaned against the window, too exhausted to sleep, and watched the night part before our never-ending headlights.

After a couple of hours in silence, I told her to follow the signs for Portsgrove. We drove up the west side of the peninsula so there would be no need for a ferry. Our car pulled into town as the early-summer dawn was sprawling through the misty evergreens. When she cut the engine in my home's driveway, the front door opened as I stepped out onto solid ground.

Mom was in her pajamas; she took one look at me, dirty and disheveled, and cried. That's when I cried too. I was too embarrassed to walk inside, so she walked to where I was on the driveway and held me. When she finally led me to my bedroom, I barely noticed myself falling into bed before I fell into a dreamless slumber.

My nose regained consciousness first. The peppery warmth of fried rice: I knew it anywhere. On cue, I heard an egg crack against a pan edge and the sizzle of the yolk hitting the grease. I couldn't remember the last time food had gone into my stomach. I was starving.

When I opened my eyes to stare up at my ceiling, I realized somebody had dressed me in clean gray sweatpants and a tank top. My photo-collage walls and trinket-adorned bookshelves caught my attention, and I wrapped myself in the comfort of all of it. I'd never been so happy to be home.

There was a gentle knock on my door, and it cracked open with a squeak. "You up?" Gillian peeked through.

"Yeah, come in." As soon as she entered, I threw my arms around her. "Thank you. You came back. You saved me."

Gillian embraced me back. "Silly thing. Of course I came back."

"How did you know?"

"I kept calling that pager of yours, but you never called back. Someone named Brayden texted my number and asked who I was. I told him I was your friend, and I was trying to reach you. He told me something crazy happened, and a woman was killed after she met with you." She shivered. "I was so scared for you, Delia. I had to go back to make sure you were okay."

"Thank Goddess you did," I said with a smirk.

She grimaced. "Too soon." She sighed and rolled her eyes at me. "What was with that 'Tom, is that you?' Come on!"

Even I had to laugh with her. "Was it so pathetic?" Her wide eyes told me it was even worse than I remembered. "To be fair, I was terrified and in desperate need of saving," I admitted. "I should have known you're the only knight in shining armor I'll ever need, Gil."

"Don't you forget it. Come on, your mom is making us breakfast."

"I smelled it. Please tell me she has bacon and Spam and every kind of processed breakfast meat out there." I paused. "Gil?"

"Yeah?"

"Did you tell her?"

She shook her head. "I figured you should be the one."

In the kitchen, Mom put down her spatula and wiped her hands on a dishrag before wrapping her arms around me. I wondered what kind of horrible daughter I was to have ever been annoyed at her hugging before. She held my face with both hands; they smelled like dish soap and spices. "Are you okay?" she asked.

"Yes, I am." I looked at the table. "I'll be even better after I eat all of this."

Gillian handed me a cup of coffee, and I held it like a treasure. After we inhaled all the fat, grease, meat, and dairy, Gillian and I sat back in our chairs, so full we could only sigh about how full we were.

"Thank you, Ms. Albio," said Gillian. "Your cooking is amazing."

"Of course," said Mom. She reached over and held Gillian's hand in hers. "Thank you for bringing me my daughter." She bit her lip and released Gillian, patting her hand. "I'll bet they didn't feed you like this in the cult!"

"No way," Gillian said. "I've been out of there for a few days now, and I still haven't eaten like this in a long time."

"You're a superb cook, Gil," I said. "Mom, her pastries are to die for."

"I haven't been baking much," said Gillian, her eyes looking down at the table. "Not as much fun to bake for one." She stood and began collecting our plates and silverware. "As thanks, I'm on dish duty."

I rose to help. She pointed a spoon at me. "You, sit. Maybe you can tell your mom a story."

So, I did. I told her everything. I told her about Sage and her missing brother, Sorority and Madelyn. I told her about Cara's history with the Wares and how I couldn't exactly figure out why Tom didn't disclose that. I told her how I had escaped in the night. She listened silently. By the time I got to the end, the dishes had long been dried and our coffee was cold. And, in the end, there was nothing to say, nothing for anyone to say except "I'm sorry." So, Mom and I kept repeating it to each other: "I'm so, so sorry." To which we then each responded, "It's okay. How could I have known? The important thing is you're okay. It's okay." And, in that moment, it was.

—◊—

It took me three days to work up the courage to leave the house. Portsgrove Main Street was the same as it had ever been. Gillian and I walked down the covered boardwalk, passing Puget Sound on one side and the kitschy tourist-souvenir and antique shops one expects in a small coastal town on the other.

I bought myself a pay-as-you-go phone from a drugstore so I could at least have some contact with the outside world again. I gave Gillian my new number and set up access to my email.

Children basked in the June summer heat, clutching bright Popsicles and ice cream cones that dripped onto their fingers and down their forearms. Their parents pushed them forward along the sidewalks to the next shop or into line for the whale-watching schooners departing every hour from the Portsgrove piers. While couples from the city embraced on the boardwalk benches or canoodled in the beer gardens, Gillian and I slurped milkshakes and passed a takeaway bag of Matt's Burger sand french fries between ourselves.

"Okay, you weren't lying." Gillian licked her fingers. "Those fries are to die for."

"Matt's is a local secret around here." I smacked my lips. "They've been around since I was a kid, and no Portsgrove summer is complete if you don't gain at least five pounds from eating at Matt's."

"I don't know why I never pictured Portsgrove like this."

"Like what?"

Gillian raised her milkshake and gestured generally. "This. We're walking along the ocean, surrounded by lush green mountains. Kids are getting their faces painted at a booth over there, and there's a golden retriever licking up someone's dropped ice cream cone over there. It's a slice of Americana, for God's sake. I didn't picture it so perfect."

"It's not perfect," I scoffed.

"It is."

"Salthouse had the ocean and the mountains. We lived steps from the beach. You're saying it wasn't perfect?"

"Artemis was trying to create a community out of obedience and control. That's not what community is." She paused, taking a deep breath. "I've been seeing a therapist. They're helping me work through all of this. My time away helped me clear my head of all the garbage they fed us. I didn't want it at the time, but them kicking me out was the best thing that could have happened. It helped me see that as much as we wanted to believe, Salthouse wasn't our home."

"I know that. Now."

A boat scooted out of the docks; whale watchers in khaki shorts and tank tops pressed against the railings and held out their phones to capture the land drifting away from them. "Ever done those whale tours?" asked Gillian.

I nodded. "A few times. Sometimes you see lots of whales; sometimes you'll go for hours with nothing. The trick is to keep your eyes on the water. Sometimes, there's a whale right below the surface. You'll never see it if they don't want to be seen."

"Well, that's terrifying."

We walked out to the pier and sat down, right on the ground between pilings, and let our legs hang down over the water. After a long while, Gillian asked, "What are we going to do?"

"We shouldn't do anything, right? We got out, and we should be thankful we didn't lose more than some money and some dignity, right? Some weren't so lucky."

My chest tightened as I thought of Madelyn. Her death had been reported widely, but attempts to get the local police to act were met with silence. As far as they were concerned, it was an unfortunate hit and run. Robyn had been right.

I sucked my straw for more milkshake. It gurgled and delivered air. Maybe Gillian was right. Only days had passed since I watched the houses of Salthouse disappear behind me; only now, in the bright light of the summer sun, did it feel far away. It was a slow and tenuous fading, like the sharp edges of a picture being blurred by a spray of seawater.

Why is it I can't stop picking at the threads? "You ever think—"

"Delia, don't."

"Gillian, Jenny is still there. God knows what's going to happen to her. And Robyn told me to find Cara . . ."

"Are you forgetting someone died?" Gillian's voice was like a belt against my skin. "Cara is the reason you almost died too. Don't be stupid."

We were silent for a long time.

"What did your ex say when you told him about the money?" I don't know why I asked it. "That's why you had to leave, right? Your money is gone?" Maybe the sting of her earlier reprimand made me want to throw my barb. As soon as I said the words, I regretted it. She squinted her eyes and looked out toward the water, away from me. I could still see her tears.

"He was happy I was okay. After weeks of not hearing from me, I think it relieved him I was alive. Once I told him about the money, he was mad. He said all the things, told me I was brainwashed and I was an idiot, and they're all true, so I didn't argue with him. He got me a small apartment outside of Portland, so at least I can have the boys sometimes."

"It's all that matters, right?" I reached over and laid my hand on hers. She gave it a squeeze.

"I'm afraid they'll never forgive me," she said, wiping her tears.

"They will," I assured her. "Your family has no idea what you went through, but they have to know you're stronger for it."

My new phone buzzed with a text message. "That's weird," I said. "Who has this number? I just got it." As I reached for it, my heart froze for a moment—was it someone from Artemis? Had they found me that easily?

The text read, hi from Oregon. I still have your phone and this vintage pager. Any chance I can get it back to you?

My mind raced. Huh? Then another text came in.

Oh yeah, it's Brayden.

I turned to Gillian. "You didn't," I said.

"He has a point, you need your phone back! Besides, he kept texting me and making sure you were okay. He seems genuine, for what it's worth."

"I don't know if I'm ready." I chewed on a fingernail. "Though he is tall and rugged and hot, and *oh damn it.*" Gillian gave me a shove on the shoulder.

When we reached home, Mom must have thought we were bringing twenty hungry guests with us, because she cooked a meal for as many. We were up for the challenge. I piled pancit and adobo on my plate, nearly on the verge of tears again when I remembered it was what she had cooked when I first came home all those months ago. When we had Tom over for dinner and this whole thing had begun. I squeezed my eyes shut and felt the warmth and flavor of the food against my tongue. After all the "clean eating" at Artemis, eating like this again felt like a great indulgence. It tasted like home.

We ate and drank while Mom told embarrassing stories from my childhood, though I insisted none were true. When the last of the wine was poured, I gathered up the plates for my night of dish duty. I was elbow deep in bubbles when there was a knock at the door.

"I'll get it," I yelled.

I opened the door, and, though I shouldn't have been, I was surprised when Tom's blue eyes were the ones I was staring into.

CHAPTER 37

"Thank God," Tom breathed. He stepped through the doorway and wrapped his arms around me. I was frozen, still holding a wet dishrag in one hand. His velvet voice caressed my neck and hair. "I was so worried." He was a spell, because I couldn't break out of my trance; he was a poison, because I didn't want to.

"Tom?" Leave it to Mom to break up a reunion. We both flinched, and I turned to see her and Gillian, arms folded, in the hallway. "What are you doing here?" Mom asked, stern and suddenly sober. I remembered relaying my suspicions of Cara and Tom being more involved in Artemis and the Wares than he'd let on.

Tom shifted, well aware his welcome in this house had worn since his last visit. "I wanted to be sure Delia was okay."

"How did you know she was here?" Gillian asked.

"I went to Salthouse to check on Delia, and they said she left days ago. I was worried, so I emailed her to find out what was going on."

"It's okay," I stepped in. "I emailed him back a couple days ago and told him." Both Gillian and Mom exchanged judging glances.

"Can we have a minute?" I asked. Like a guilty teenager, I took Tom's hand and led us outside.

"What happened?" asked Tom once we'd made it down the drive and outside of eavesdropping range.

"What happened was you lied to me."

His face was blank. "What are you talking about?"

"Your family knew the Wares," I said. I reached for my phone, only to remember I didn't have my old one with my photos on it anymore. "Cara went to the Wares' boarding school. I had a picture of her with Sage and Everett. You knew she was more intimately connected to Artemis, and you didn't tell me."

"I didn't know they were the same people," he stammered. "If I knew, I swear I would have told you."

"Where have you been?" My question reeked of a jealous girlfriend. I didn't know how to make it sound any different. "I kept calling you. I needed help, don't you understand?" Robyn's words echoed in my mind. "They were listening to us. They knew I knew you, and they knew the whole time I was looking for Cara. Why did you send me there?"

"Wait a minute. I didn't send you there. Don't you dare put that on me. I told you to leave weeks ago."

"So you could console me when I returned, heartbroken when I couldn't find Cara? So you could do now what you did then?" It was all coming up, like a geyser roaring through my innards and out of my mouth. "You took advantage of me." I couldn't stop myself.

"I don't know—"

"After Zee died, you manipulated me, and you're doing it again."

"You're embarrassing yourself," he snapped. He sucked in air through his teeth, then closed his eyes, raising his palms to his forehead. "Let's reset. I understand you've been through something. I'm sorry you think I led you on. I didn't manipulate you into anything. You made your own choices." Slowly, as if stalking a woodland creature, he moved toward me, his hands outstretched. "You're a strong woman. I couldn't make you do anything you didn't want to."

He smelled like smoke and old furniture and the Portsgrove air itself. In his arms now, I thought I could be strong. I was wrong. "Did you drive here?" I asked.

"Yeah. Why?"

—⁂—

The Snyder house was messy, on its way to being a true bachelor setup. The roll of condoms so easily accessible from the nightstand drawer told me Tom wasn't short on the company of summer girls coming through Portsgrove. Damn if those eyes under the harsh overhead light didn't drink me up and make me feel like the only thing he needed in the world.

We consumed each other, and the world exploded and righted itself again. We both fell back onto the sweat-covered sheets, gasping for air. He kissed me some more before he turned off the light.

When his breathing evened out and his muscles twitched against my back, I lifted his arm and crawled out from underneath. I picked up a blanket and wrapped it around me as I walked to Cara's room; nothing had changed since I left it last. I sat on the floor and let my arms and neck flop onto the carpet.

Just let go. Just let them both go.

The pastel dawn found me curled on the floor, not having slept even to see my vanished friends in my dreams.

After I dressed and before I left, I went back to her room and touched a finger to the photo that hung on her vanity mirror of all of us at the Harrises' cabin. A time Cara was happy. With a slight tug at the corner, the double-sided Scotch tape gave, and the photo pulled away in my hand. I slipped it into my jacket pocket.

—⁓—

The door to home creaked open, and I stepped in gingerly, as if I were a teenager sneaking in after a night out. I spotted a blanketed bundle lying on the couch in the living room. I laid my hand on Mom's shoulder, and she stirred underneath the multicolored crocheted throw.

"Delia? I had a dream you didn't come home."

"No, no. I'll always come home, Mom."

She sat up, blinking at the morning light streaming through the mini blinds. "I'm sorry I drove you away after your dad died." Her eyes looked down at her wrinkled hands.

The suddenness caught me off guard. "You didn't," I lied.

She knew better. "I was so angry. Angry at your dad's manager for scheduling him a double shift, angry at your dad for taking it, angry at you for being angry at me. I let my grief become a tower, trapping me inside and keeping me so far removed from everyone else. I was so hurt when you didn't come back here to save me; how could I have ever expected you to climb those walls?"

"I was angry too," I confessed. "I blamed you for moving to Portsgrove. Can you believe it? I blamed Dad's death on a decision the both of you made before I was born. Because if you stayed in Seattle, he would work in an office instead of a mill."

"Accidents happen everywhere."

"Of course they do. Maybe it was silly of me to imagine a different life."

"I'm sorry you weren't happy here." She took my hand. "My one job as your mother, and I failed."

"No, you didn't," I said. "I was happy here. I'm so sorry I didn't tell you more. I love you, Mom. Maybe I was trapped in my tower." *Maybe I still am.*

I looked out the window and thought about my mom leaving her tiny island home and coming to a strange place for a new life. I thought about how, here in the forest, she became another kind of island. "Weren't you lonely here?" I asked. "Even before Dad . . . Did you ever regret it?"

"I will never regret the choices that led me to you," she said. "Of course I was very lonely sometimes. Parents have to make sacrifices for the future."

We embraced. She pulled away to smooth my hair back. "Grief can look like a safe space for a long time," she said. "It's easier to watch the world go by from a faraway vantage point than to face what's happened. Sometimes our grief turns to fear without us even realizing. Make sure you're not so busy living in the past that you don't even notice the open door in front of you. All you have to do is make the choice to walk through it."

Was it so easy? I wondered at the choices we made, even as teenagers, that made us who we were now. A tragedy that had shaped my life and the choices Cara and I had made afterward had led to this point. For almost a lifetime I had held my grief preciously, like a thing to be nurtured, never knowing it had long rotted into fear. And if Artemis taught me nothing else, it was to not give in to fear. So, maybe it was time to join the world again. Who would I choose to be now?

But an image from the past lingered in my mind—a group of four teenagers in front of a cabin in the woods. "Do you remember that cabin that Zee's family owned? We all drove up and stayed there one summer?"

"Sure," said Mom. "That was fun. A little crowded with three families."

"Think it's still out there? Did Zee's parents sell it after they moved away?"

Mom shrugged. "I have no idea. So sad how they left—"

I laid my fingers on my jacket pocket. "Do you remember where it was? I know it was around Leavenworth, but would you have an address?"

"Why the interest in the cabin all of a sudden?"

I pulled the photo from my pocket and slid it over to Mom. "After Zee, I was so bitter toward Cara for moving on like she did. But maybe she didn't. Maybe she was just really good at pretending she was okay. And after all this time, maybe I'm not the only one who wished I could go back to when we were all together."

With a heavy sigh, she placed her fingers over our smiling faces, as though to reach back to comfort us for what we now knew was to come.

CHAPTER 38

Then

Second place.

After the applause and the congrats and after the lights went out in that auditorium, Zee threw her second-place ribbon into the garbage can outside the high school doors. Cara and I hung back with her dad while she and her mom argued in the parking lot.

"She really wanted it," he said. "I don't know how to tell her second place is just as good."

I knew. I knew it wasn't close to just as good. All these years of dreaming, all the late nights when I helped her paint green algae bloom circles on the poster board or proofread her abstract. "Eye opening," said the school board judges after Zee presented her findings that the popular beaches had more aggressive types of algae blooms that were potentially harmful to the fish and other lake fauna. They thanked her for her entry into the science showcase and said they looked forward to more research into ways to curb pollution on the lake.

"I have it," she had told Cara and me during the deliberations. "I've fucking got this." Despite all her bitching, Cara had come to support Zee. Of course she had. She jumped and clapped her hands when Zee was called to the stage as a finalist. We clasped each other's hands tight as they read the results.

Second.

"Maybe you girls should head on home," Mr. Harris said. We watched Zee bury her head in her hands against her mom's chest, and we agreed.

"I feel awful," Cara said, putting on her seat belt. She put the car in drive, and we pulled out of the parking lot slowly, with small waves to the Harrises. Zee didn't look up.

"I thought she had it," I confessed. Zee didn't return my calls that night.

The next day, Cara arrived at my house with face paint and ribbons. "Do you think she's still coming over to get ready for the game?" she asked. I separated a lock of Cara's hair and threaded a red ribbon through into another loop.

"No idea."

We arrived at the pep rally at the stadium fully decked in high school spirit, red and white glitter stripes under our eyes and ribbons braided into our long pigtails. Even though we weren't cheerleaders, we wore knockoff cheerleading uniforms, and my bare legs had goose pimples all the way up and down from the nighttime fall cold. "Do we look super slutty?" I asked her, pulling my skirt down so it would at least cover my back thighs.

She nodded. "Yes, and I love it."

We hadn't heard from Zee. We filed into our seats in the bleachers with the rest of our friends. "Do you see them?" Cara asked, craning her neck to see where Jason and Keene were warming up on the field. I rubbed my hands and regretted not bringing a hand warmer. Was that Zee's responsibility? I wondered. It seemed like something we would have thought about.

Cara wrapped her arm around me. "Cold?" I nodded. She rapidly rubbed her hands up and down my arm. "So, maybe the sleeveless shirts weren't the best idea."

I laughed and stuck my cold nose against her neck. She screeched.

"What up, bitches?"

I turned. "Zee?" She was wearing an outfit that matched ours and had a face full of dark eyeliner and bright-red lipstick. "You look different," I gasped.

Cara shrieked, "You're here!" We gave Zee a group hug, our foreheads all touching. "We're so sorry," Cara said. "You should have won."

"Thanks, guys. You're the best. I'm over it."

I looked at Cara, who gave me a wary glance back. "Your project was brilliant," I said.

Zee broke our hug. "I'm freezing my balls off. Who has the booze, anyway?" A flask appeared from somewhere; Cara whooped. Any apprehension dissipated for her as she suddenly saw a good time to be had. Maybe she thought this was exactly what Zee needed. Maybe it was, but Zee's sudden act of not caring was throwing me, and I didn't know how to react. I wasn't buying it. So, I simply watched while she and Cara took sips from the flask and sat on boys' laps, Zee laughing at jokes she wouldn't have before.

At halftime, we were winning, two to nothing. I walked with Zee to the bathrooms and pulled her aside once we were away from the crowd's noise. "Hey, are you okay? What's up with you tonight, anyway?"

"Get over it," she snapped. "That whole thing was so stupid, and I can't believe I even had a chance. I'm stuck in this town, Delia. So, I might as well enjoy it and have some fun, like Cara says."

I put my hand on her shoulder. "This isn't you. We have fun with Cara and love her, but you're not her. Is this because of the showcase?"

She swiped my hand away.

I persisted. "I know you want to go to college and do something bigger. The showcase was only one path out of here. You can still do whatever you want to do. You think I plan on hanging around Portsgrove with Keene for life?"

"I'm not you, Delia. Remember?" She stuck her finger into my chest, her cheeks flushed and words hot. "Innocent, smart one. That's you. I'm the cool Black girl. Not the smart one, even though I'm the one who was obsessed with water conditions in a lake. Nope. Not me.

So, I'll go be the cool one, and I'm gonna go back and hang out with the spoiled girl. Let's all accept who we are for once." On unsteady feet, she stomped back to the bleachers. I watched, suddenly hot, even in my dumb skimpy outfit, as she found Cara and they put their heads together to talk.

A weight shifted in my chest, and an unseen balance moved in our trio.

When I finally returned to my seat, it was clear the game was going to be a blowout. The fourth quarter was going to end quickly, and Zee was already down at the end zone to meet the victorious players. Cara had stuck around for me. "Come on," she said. "We're all going to a bonfire at the beach to celebrate."

I didn't say anything when we packed into a boy's truck and drove to the beach. In the sand, with the flames burning and the beer pushing down my unease, I began to forgive.

We were best friends, after all.

Cara and Zee took my hands, and we danced around the fire, spinning until we fell into a pile. We stayed there, tangled on top of each other. I began to laugh so hard my entire body ached, which got Cara and Zee going too.

"I love you girls so much," Zee said once we had sorted ourselves out; we sat side by side against a piece of driftwood, passing a bottle between us, underneath a blanket that wasn't ours.

"I love you too," echoed Cara, between Zee and me; she put her arms around us both. "Let's be friends forever."

"We will," I said, so sure of myself. "We will always love each other like we do in this moment." When the bottle was empty and most everyone else asleep on a dune or long gone, we were still there, laughing and holding one another under the stars.

God, I believed myself when I said it would always be that way. I think we all did.

CHAPTER 39

Gillian and I walked down Main Street together for the last time, passing a farewell bag of Matt's french fries between us. The crowds from earlier had dissipated, and the boardwalk's throngs consisted of locals and couples without kids who weren't beholden to school schedules.

"You don't have to do it," said Gillian. "You can stop."

"Don't you see?" I answered. "I can't."

"And your mom? You're leaving her again?"

"I'm coming back."

I understood Gillian's defensiveness about Mom. In the days she had stayed with us, they became fast friends, bonding over their general concern for my well-being as well as a love for feeding me.

Of course, my announcement at last night's dinner that I was going to the Harris cabin to look for Cara hadn't gone over well. Both Mom and Gillian were stone faced at first, escalating to outright forbidding me.

"You almost died," Gillian said as we argued over the chicken, which was growing cold and untouched on the table.

"When will it end, Delia?" Mom asked, tears in her eyes.

"After this," I promised. "If she's not there, it's over. I promise."

"Will you keep sleeping with Tom? He kept secrets from you—"

"I'm keeping him close," I had lied. "Just to find out what he knows. When I say it'll be over soon, I mean all of it. Even Tom." How could I begin to explain to her that Tom was even more addictive than Sage and her sermons? That my body was never more radiant than when it crashed against his? Maybe he was right about it all being a trap, and he was the bait.

Now, the ocean waves lapped and churned beneath us, black and mysterious as ever. I hated that I knew I would fall for him every time.

A shiver ran up the base of my skull. I turned to Gillian. "How do you feel about going home?"

Gillian was leaving the next day too. "I'm excited to see my boys and begin to repair what broke down while I've been gone. I'll miss you. I'll worry about you."

"Don't," I said. "It's all going to be okay."

She nodded, looking down into the greasy french fry bag, where a couple of stray fries remained.

—⁓—

I had one stop before heading to the ferry. I parked in the Snyder drive-way and called Tom. When he didn't answer, I knocked on the front door and the back door too. I peeked through windows; the house looked empty. *Fine, be an asshole.* As I opened the car door, I heard the front door open and his steps on the porch.

"Tom," I called, turning. "I'm going. Last chance to come with."

"I'm not going with you," Tom said. He walked down the steps, his curly hair tousled and his clothes wrinkled, as if he had just woken up. "I'm done supporting this delusion of yours, Delia."

I sighed. "It's not delusional if she's there. Have you looked there yet?"

He shook his head. "No, nobody even thought of that place, if it's even still standing. You're the only one who remembered a random family vacation in the forest a decade ago."

"I know she's there. It's the only place left."

"You *knew* she was at Salthouse," he mocked.

I tapped a finger on the car door. "No, I knew they would have information—"

"How did that work out for you?"

My voice rose. "Pretty shit, actually. No thanks to you." Why was he discouraging me now?

"This is you repeating history."

"She's your sister. You are the one who started this whole thing. How can you not want to see it through?" I was practically yelling.

Calmly, in the most maddening way, he stood steady and spoke through his teeth. "I didn't start anything, so don't put it on me. You decided you were going to find her. I never understood your obsession, not with the whole Zee thing and not with Cara now."

"The *whole Zee thing*?"

He paused. "I'm going back to New York soon."

I stopped short. "When?" I asked, scared of the answer.

"Not sure. Soon. One day, you may drive up here and I'll be gone." He looked past me, out to the view of Blythe Lake. "Sick of this shithole."

"Well, cheers to history repeating." I got in the car and slammed the door shut.

———

The shapes of the mountains were overlapping blues against the endless black ribbon of highway. I had been driving for hours when the GPS told me I was getting close to the cabin.

Miraculously, after a search, a decade-old address book shoved into the back of the kitchen junk drawer had contained the location. Mom's face had fallen as she flipped to the *H* tab and there it was, scribbled into a margin next to Zee's old home address and marked "cabin."

I took an exit off the freeway to a local road and then to an unmarked county back road before my GPS lost service. I switched to my handwritten directions copied from Google Maps. The sun would set soon. The bright summer greens of the trees towered around me and melted to languid jeweled tones against the approaching dusk.

How had I forgotten those long barefoot days in moss-covered woods, chasing each other and braiding wildflower wreaths? At night, we'd eaten s'mores until we almost threw up. I remembered the long hikes with the families. Even the hike Zee'd had to skip because she was so ill one morning. The parents had thought it was from too many s'mores the night before and not the sips of whiskey Tom kept sneaking us from the flask his parents didn't know he had. When we got back, the parents had taken naps, and we stole beers from the fridge and drank them down on the shore of a nearby creek.

I drove at a snail's pace now and squinted to make sure I didn't miss the address marker. I nearly passed it but glimpsed the weathered signpost at the last second. The turn veered onto the gravel driveway. There it was.

The cabin was in a state of disrepair. It was impossible that someone lived there, I thought. I parked in the empty drive. Unruly flowers lined the path leading to the front door, gone feral with neglect. Shingles had fallen from the roof; I kicked one from the porch step into knee-high grass. There was moss in between the windowpanes, while two broken Adirondack chairs sat on the wraparound porch that reeked of damp. I sighed out loud. This was a waste of time and hope.

I had turned to return to my car when a glint of reflected light caught my eye. The silver of the door handle. I looked closer. It was clean. Not a speck of dust or dirt on it. I curled my fingers around it and turned and pulled. The door opened.

I stepped inside.

CHAPTER 40

"Hello?" I called.

It was dark inside; I couldn't remember if there had ever been electricity in the cabin. I remembered we used lanterns, but maybe that was for the ambiance. I traced my hand against the wall and found it. *Click.*

The inside was homey and clean, or at least the layer of wet was almost undetectable underneath a fake lemony scent of cleaner and something akin to microwaved meals.

It was exactly like I remembered.

The main room of the cabin contained a small kitchen and a living room with a wood-burning stove. A pair of jeans draped over the sofa, while a pair of women's boots lay on the floor right inside the door. I walked into the kitchen and opened the fridge. Sure enough, there were some vegetables and a gallon of hemp milk inside. I opened the freezer, which housed a good stock of Amy's-brand frozen dinners. On the counter, a cup half-filled with cool tea. From this angle, I spotted an errant pink sock underneath an armchair in the corner.

She was everywhere.

I noticed there were no photos anywhere. I wondered if it was the Harrises or Cara that had taken them all down. *How long will I have to wait?* I wondered. A horrific thought crept in—what if she had been here and left? What if I'd missed her and I was back to square one? Or maybe when the door opened, it would be Madelyn again—not dead at all, here to find me and bring me back to Sage. Maybe this was another trap, the photo of all of us at the cabin planted by Tom to lead me here, right where they wanted me.

It turned out I didn't have long to wait at all.

The footsteps were light and slow on the creaky porch steps. She would have seen my car; she could turn and run. I held my breath, staring at the door, willing the knob to turn. And when it did and the door opened, letting the light through in a cascade of sun, she stepped through it.

I wanted to yell her name and run to her to embrace her; my legs crumpled underneath me. "Is it—" I croaked.

She crossed the room like a bolt to catch me. "Shh," she said, stroking my hair away from my face. "Yes, it's me, Delia. It's me."

I'd found Cara.

—⁂—

I stared into the milky gray of the tea. She sat next to me on the sofa.

Cara Snyder is sitting right next to me.

"How did you find me?" she asked. "Where's Tom?"

"He's in Portsgrove. I remembered this place from the photo in your room," I said. "Funny, I didn't remember ever seeing it before. I thought, when I saw it, if I were trying to get away, that's where I would go."

"Why were you in my room?" Maybe it was a fair question, and I hated that she was asking it, such a silly question, when it was me that deserved answers to much more important questions. Her blue eyes looked so much like Tom's. They were sunken and ringed by a tiredness. Her shoulders poked through her white linen button-up shirt. She turned to move a throw from behind her, and I could count the vertebrae of her neck underneath her golden hair heaped up in a messy bun. I wondered if she was ill.

"I went home to see you," I said, not answering her question. "Because of your email."

She closed her eyes, searching for a long-forgotten thought. "My email?"

"The one you sent about life-changing news." I leaned toward her. "I went home to find you in January, but I was too late. Have you been here the whole time?"

"That's why you've been searching for me?" She sucked in her cheeks. "That's why you went to Salthouse?"

I'm not surprised she knew. "Sage told you?"

"We spoke not long after you arrived. Every now and then I make a trip to town to get groceries. I use the pay phones to check in with Sage. Or I used to. I haven't talked to anyone in a long time. Until now."

"Sage knows you're here?"

"No. She asked, constantly. Demanded, even. I didn't tell her. She wants to save me, but she can't. Nobody can."

"What did you do?" I reached out to her, and she shrank from my hand. "I'm not them," I assured her. "I'm not Artemis. I left like you did." I laughed, thinking about everything that had led me to Cara. "You know," I said, "you owe me an explanation, Cara. What are you running from?"

She took a sharp breath and looked me in my eyes. "I killed Everett."

The space between us took shape and crashed over me. *It's not true. It can't be.* Her gaunt face and stormy eyes said different.

I realized she wasn't sick at all, just guilty.

With the truth at last before us, Cara took a deep breath, as if she hadn't had air in some time.

"I met Sage and Everett at the boarding school I attended."

"I know," I said.

"Of course you do. You also know how they get inside your head. I was so fucked up after Zee, you know?"

I remembered Cara's would-be confession after the disappearance. *It was because of me. I think I kicked her.*

"Sage helped me get through the rest of high school. There were some dark times when I couldn't imagine going on—how could I?"

I knew the thoughts well; I'd thought I was the only one.

Cara continued. "Sage showed me I could graduate; then she inspired me to go to college and pursue a career. Unapologetically too. When my parents couldn't be bothered to deal with me and sent me away so they didn't have to look at my mopey face all the time, Sage took me under her wing and became a second mother to me."

"I thought you and Sage . . ."

She chuckled. "Were girlfriends? Yeah, many people did, because of how close we were. You can find intimacy without romance. Sometimes, it's even better and more fulfilling that way." She sipped her tea. "So, I grew up. I kept in touch with Sage now and again. I got the job at BloomWallet, and afterward I got an invitation to join Artemis. Go on a retreat at Salthouse. I went, skeptical it would do anything. After all, I had the job, the city apartment. What more did I want? It turned out to be amazing. It was so beautiful, and I met so many fascinating women. And Sage and I reconnected as if we hadn't ever been apart. Eventually, they asked me to bring my boss in, and Madelyn loved it too. When I joined Artemis as an employee, I thought it would be the best job on earth. And it was for a while. Hell, I lived on the beach and created content and shared late nights with Sage."

She paused; dark clouds formed across her face. "She told me the truth one night, after too much wine."

"The truth of what?" I asked.

"She took out these journals from a locked drawer in her desk. Old, from when she was in college, she said. They were essays really. Pages and pages examining the patriarchy and what it meant to be a woman in our society. She was taking what she was learning in her classes and applying it to her everyday life, examining how other women could do the same. It was brilliant. As I read it, I realized I had read the words before. Then I realized—it was the text of *The Artemis Method*. Not word for word, but it was all there." She hunched over, placing her tea on the floor by her bare feet. Her arms crossed over her knees, and she rested her head on top.

I gasped. "Everett stole her work." I remembered looking through Sage's things the day I'd helped her clean up from her night in the forest; I remembered trying to open those desk drawers, and I wondered whether those old journals were still there.

Her head shook on her arms as she spoke in a flat voice. "He passed it off as his own. She denied it. She snatched the journals away and made me swear to tell no one. How could I forget? It was all a lie. How could he do that to his own sister? Soon I would find out that Everett couldn't bear to let his sister have anything for her own, even me."

She stopped and sat up to take a deep breath, as if coming up for air. Her eyes were the same blue pools, magnified by the glistening teardrops they were filled with. I flexed my hands, realizing I was gripping my mug so tightly the muscles in my palm were aching.

"When he proposed to me, he didn't get down on one knee or anything. He told me he wouldn't demean me like that. He presented it as a business venture, a partnership. Artemis membership was dwindling, and he thought it needed a fresh young face. He said times were changing and a women's movement needed a woman's face. I told him I didn't want to marry him for business or any other reason. I didn't want to be the face of Artemis. It turned out it wasn't a choice. He threatened to show these . . . pictures." Her voice broke, and my heart with it.

"I was so stupid. He told me he would send them to my dad and all his business colleagues and friends. I had no choice. When I told Sage, she was furious. She couldn't stand up to him either. She never could." She looked at me, her face a mottled red. "Sage and I decided for Artemis and for us, we had to go along with it."

"So, how did it happen?" I asked.

"Everett, Sage, and I were on a hike up to Flat Rock." I recalled the photo of Cara in front of the fallen tree, the roots extending from behind her. I imagined them now as tentacles, moments from enveloping her in their darkness.

"I don't even know how it came up," she said. "Sage had wandered away from us. We were alone in the forest. He asked me for money. I told him I was all paid up on my dues, and he said he needed an investment, since we were to be partners, after all. I remember I laughed and said I didn't have any money. He should know. I was on his payroll, after all. He told me I should ask my parents for access to my trust fund. It shocked me he even knew I had one."

Her voice was now even and controlled, though she spoke through bared teeth.

"That's when it clicked, when the fog lifted. Such a simple thing to bring me out of years of brainwashing, but once I saw it, God, it was so obvious. I told him I wasn't giving him another cent. In fact, I was going to reveal to everyone he was a fraud. I told him I knew he didn't come up with any of the Artemis philosophy and his bestselling book was a lie. He could blackmail me all he wanted; I didn't care anymore. In fact, I dared him to show the entire world those photos, because then they would know he was a predator who manipulated women with sex and power. He made some joke, tried to brush it off; then he saw how serious I was. He grabbed me, began yelling, and the look in his eyes terrified me. I've never seen it before . . . the hate."

Chills ran through me as I waited for what she would say next; my thoughts were scattering in all directions.

"We fought, and at one point, I gathered all the strength inside of me to push him away. He tripped over something, a root or a rock, and fell. Except he didn't get up. So, I tried to help him up, and that's when I swear a piece of his scalp fell away, and the blood beneath . . ." Cara paused, a pained grimace across her face.

"Jesus, Cara." I stumbled, not knowing what to say.

She continued, her eyes still closed. "I screamed, and Sage found us. I told her we had to call the police, but she told me I would go to jail if we did. She told me to run, and I did. I hiked down and left Salthouse and didn't look back. I called her once I got to Portsgrove, and she told me not to worry, she was taking care of it; I had to keep hidden and not contact anyone from Artemis until she said it was safe. I kept waiting for a news article about his death. There was nothing."

Cara collapsed back onto the couch. Setting down my tea, I moved close and touched my fingers to hers. Her eyes opened, staring at our hands.

"She was keeping it a secret until she figured out a way to secure her place as his successor," I said slowly. Despite the confession, I didn't know where Cara's loyalties landed.

Cara shook her head. "That's not it at all. She was keeping it a secret to protect me. She knew I would be a prime suspect. Don't you get it? I've killed before. Sage knew about Zee. I got away with it once, but a second time . . . ?"

"You don't know what's happened at Salthouse," I said. "They killed Madelyn on Sage's orders."

"No, you're wrong. Why would they?" She withdrew her hand.

"Because Madelyn was done staying silent." My muscles tensed, and I crossed my arms, my fingernails digging into my biceps. "She gave me a flash drive of Everett's photos of women. She was going to expose them all."

"You have them?" asked Cara, eyebrows arching.

I sank back, deflated. "No, they're at Salthouse."

Cara let out a groan. "I brought Madelyn to Artemis. Her blood is on my hands, too, Delia."

"Stop it," I insisted. "They manipulated you. Don't blame yourself for Madelyn. I know how easy it is to fall for Sage. Trust me. For a moment, I was almost lost at Salthouse too."

Cara nodded as if she half believed me. "Delia?"

"What?" I asked.

"I miss home."

I moved close again and draped my arm around her, my childhood friend. She leaned her head onto my shoulder. I had more questions now than ever, but for this moment, we were still.

CHAPTER 41

The morning light filtered through the leaves, a golden, hazy hue. For a moment, I forgot where I was. It didn't take me long to remember.

I didn't know how long we sat there, entwined and huddled together on the couch; and when we moved again, it was twilight. Cara lit lanterns for the ambiance and made two microwave dinners. We ate in silence. I kept wanting to ask her about the email, about her news. Now, when faced with the chance to hear it, I realized I didn't want to know anymore. I was too scared. I knew too many dark secrets already. I needed a little more time to make space for this one.

I brought in my overnight bag from the car, while Cara made me a bed in one of the spare rooms. It was a big room with two twin beds in it, where we had stayed when we came up here with Zee's family. Of course, we had zipped all our sleeping bags together and slept on camping pads on the floor.

In a moment of weakness, once Cara had shut the door, I lay down on the floor, staring up into the wood-beam ceiling and trying to imagine our laughter. I listened to Cara brushing her teeth in the bathroom next door.

I slept hard without dreams.

A kettle whistled, and it was a few moments before the sweet scent of coffee permeated into the room. Even inside, the morning mountain air was crisp, so I put on a sweatshirt and black leggings. I padded outside to discover the main room was empty, with a carafe of fresh pour-over coffee and a clean mug on the counter. I made myself a cup with a splash of milk.

I found her sitting on a blanket in the yard, among the tall grass and dandelions.

"Good morning," she said, patting a spot next to her.

"Good morning. It's beautiful here." I sat, stretching my legs out in front of me.

"It is. Though I think it's time I moved on."

"I think so, too, Cara." There was a mournful birdsong somewhere above us; it filled the treetops. I picked a blade of grass and twisted it between my fingers, feeling the dulled edge. "Where will you go?"

She didn't miss a beat. "Salthouse."

"You can't be serious?" I balked. "Because she was asking you to? No, you can't. It's not the same as you remember it. If Sage wants you back there, it's for a terrible reason."

"Maybe she realized it was an accident and there's nothing for me to be afraid of."

"That's bullshit, and the fact that you're still here proves you don't buy it either." I crushed the blade of grass; it left a stain of green on the skin of my forefinger and thumb. "No, she needs you. Maybe you knew a different Sage. Trust me, you don't know her now. She wants Artemis, no matter the state she gets it in, no matter who she has to hurt."

Cara turned. "You're wrong about her. She's a good person who helped a lot of women. It was Everett who was bad. And now he's gone. She's in mourning. He was her brother, after all." She drew a circle in the dirt with a stick. "No police came around while you were there or anything? No reporters or . . ."

"Nobody like that."

"And people don't know what happened to Everett?"

"No. Sage spun some story about him going on a meditation retreat."

She stabbed the stick into the earth. "I have to go to her. I thought she was asking me to go back because the police got to her or someone found out about Everett. If you say none of that happened, then she needs me."

"First, Sage is not genuine about anything. Second, we are not going back. It's a trap. You don't know what's happened—"

"So tell me."

I didn't want to, but she needed to know. I told her everything. She listened in horror and interrupted to insist that couldn't have happened, not in Artemis. I finished and took a deep breath. With every retelling, I noticed, it was already getting further away. Like it was somebody else's story and not mine at all.

"I have to see for myself," Cara said.

"No," I said. "That's the opposite of what we should do."

"She needs my help," she repeated. "I can talk to her. I can make it right."

"Cara, it's madness to go back there. We can't go—"

"I didn't invite you." She stood and walked toward the cabin. Before the door, she turned. "In fact, I never invited you here, period. What exactly were you hoping to find, again?"

"You!" I followed her and offered my arms again. "Your family is looking for you. You're my friend—"

"We haven't been friends in a long time." She said it like a hard truth. She was right. Enough of the pleasantries. I lowered my hands and held my elbows instead.

"I already told you. It was your email. So go ahead, I'm ready. Tell me about the life-changing news."

Cara shook her head. "I don't know what email you're talking about."

"God dammit, Cara. If I had my phone, I would show you the email you sent me." I recited it from memory.

"I know it's been a long time! Like everyone, life got in the way, and you should know that despite busy days, I've been thinking of you! I know we haven't talked, but I wanted to connect. I've appreciated your support through the years and wanted to get your thoughts on something . . . Maybe you'll think me dramatic, but I have to say . . . It's something life changing."

"That email?" said Cara.

I nodded.

Her pink lips parted, and laughter cascaded from her mouth. She walked inside and knelt in front of the coffee table. From the stack of books piled underneath, she pulled out what she was searching for. She returned to the door and put it in my hands.

It was a familiar large white binder with the pink logo on the front. Text under the logo read "Artemis Marketing Manual."

"Maybe you'll find your answers in there." She patted the top of the binder in my hands.

I sat in the old chair on the porch; it creaked and shuddered as my body rested upon it. It took me ten minutes, maybe less, of flipping through the large binder. I found it under the section titled "outreach templates." It was the exact email, with a blank space for the name of "your contact" and space at the bottom to "personalize your email with anything else that might resonate with the potential member."

It had all been a scam.

It was a marketing email. I had imploded my life for spam. Didn't our friendship mean more than a cheap mass email for her marketing job? As I wiped away the hot tears running down my red face, I knew she wasn't to blame.

It was me who had created the fantasy of Cara harboring a secret that would bring me closer to Zee.

There was nothing to tell. We would never know the truth about Zee. Zee, who was dead. Zee, who was gone.

Cara was no better: a ghost walking here on the land instead of on the bottom of Blythe Lake. The morning air was no longer refreshing. It was a dampness that chilled my bones, creeping in through the pines and wrapping its tendrils around me. I couldn't be here any longer, knowing what I knew, that there was no solving Zee's death. It was like everyone said it was: simply a thing that had happened.

I ran inside to get my things. I was leaving.

"What's wrong?" Cara called as I passed through. "Not what you were hoping to find?"

I couldn't help myself. "I turned my life upside down for you. I know you didn't ask for it. You didn't have to. I thought you were contacting me to tell me something, and yes, I assumed it was about Zee. I guess that's on me for thinking you would reach out to me for something besides a selling opportunity. When I heard you were missing, I went to find you. When everyone stopped looking for you or thought you were doing your own thing, I knew something was wrong. I joined Artemis to find you, Cara. I did all the fucked-up shit they asked of me so I could get closer to you. I escaped God knows what and made it home, and I was safe. I had to come here to look for you; one more chance to find you. And then I get here, and you don't listen to a word I say and want to go right back to the place I barely fought my way out of? No, you ungrateful bitch, this is not what I hoped I would find."

Her head didn't drop, not for a second, and her clenched jaw only tightened, the muscles of her neck quivering. "Stop pretending you did all that for me. You did it because your life was boring and meaningless and you wanted the attention. You were always like that, whining and craving attention, yet you were incapable of doing anything interesting enough to earn it. Zee said so herself. You were the boring one. The miserable wet blanket. We were friends with you because we felt sorry for you."

Her words cut me to the bone, even if I knew she was lying. *It's not true. Zee and I were closer than the two of them ever were.* The hurt held me tight, and I wanted to hurt her back, to make her feel as bad as I felt. "Tom thought I was interesting enough, especially when he was in between my legs."

Her chest rose with a deep breath, and I knew I had cut her too. "Wow, you're right. I would have never guessed." I marched past her and into the guest room, where I threw my things into my bag and headed to the door.

Cara continued. "I would never guess about you, that is. Tom, well, I think you must have been the very last one of my friends to make it into his bed."

I stopped.

The very last one of her friends.

The photo of all of us in front of the cabin. Tom peering over Cara and smiling at me . . . Wasn't he? Of course, it was obvious. He was smiling at Zee. They were both sick the day we all went on the big hike. They'd had all day together. A roaring noise grew in my ears, as if I was back at the beach with the crashing surf. I held my hands over my ears and shook my head. Cara met my gaze. I expected her to be smiling, some triumphant grin, but she wasn't. She was as disturbed as me.

"We were only thirteen when we came here," I said.

"I know." Cara's lips quivered. "They didn't know I knew. I saw her leave one night from my bedroom window. It went on for years. Well, until . . ."

A weight dropped onto my lungs. "That day on the lake. We went on the boat with the guys, and you accused her of sneaking into your basement." I spoke haltingly. Slow panic rose in me. "She denied it."

Cara breathed out. "Of course she did."

Zee had lied. Cara had known the whole time. I wanted to throw up. And Tom.

Why didn't he tell me? A numbing emptiness filled my bones. Robyn had been right: Tom had taken advantage of not only me but Zee as well. If he had done it so easily then, did it mean he was doing it still? Did he know all along I wouldn't resist him, that I would always be pulled to him by our history like light to a black hole? How easily he let me drive away; how often he told me he was leaving. All of it meant nothing. I had never known he could be so cruel. It turned out I had never known him at all.

With a crushing weight on my chest, I realized Tom was the same as Everett and Nicklin, blackmailing Madelyn and gaslighting Jenny and God knew how many others. Who were they to do with us as they pleased and then throw us away?

I hated them.

I hated their lack of consequences.

Everett was dead, and nobody knew it. He would never be held accountable. Nobody knew who he was behind the image. *But I do.*

More importantly, I had proof. Madelyn had given her life to give me the evidence. I owed it to her. The image of Madelyn rushing out of the bar, scared and vulnerable, turned the glowing ember of grief in my ribs into a low flame. A righteous fire. If nobody else was willing to hold him, to hold *someone*, accountable, then it would have to be me.

"You're right." I clenched my teeth.

"About what?"

"We have to go back to Salthouse. Maybe you're right that we can help Sage. If we tell her we can help her get out of the mess her brother made and make Artemis a good place to be again. She doesn't have to continue his legacy. Would you help me do that?"

Cara thought, then nodded slowly, her face lifting to the sun. "Let's do it."

CHAPTER 42

We left that afternoon. We didn't stop to call anybody or even to inform her family that Cara was alive and well—her choice. I was too afraid that if I let us take a moment to breathe, we would collapse under the reality of what we were doing and turn around.

The mountains slumped toward the sound, and we reached Seattle. I didn't mention to Cara that I still paid rent on my little one bedroom in Queen Anne, though I hadn't been there in months and I'm sure my plants were rotting in their pots. I didn't even look at the highway exit as we passed. Neither of us mentioned it when we passed the sign for the Portsgrove ferry turnoff.

The asphalt of the never-ending highway was comforting, even if we moved toward uncertainty. At least, I knew, the road also led back. I'd followed it away before.

Somewhere between the Columbia River and the turnoff to Artemis from Interstate 5, Cara asked, "Do you remember our promise the night Zee disappeared?"

I did. "We promised we'll get through this together. No matter what, I'll stay by you."

"I'll stay by you." She nodded her head.

—〜—

Artemis was empty. The silence of nothing hung between Cara and me. Even the usual distant buzz of the waves seemed quieter, as if they were holding back to see what happened next. Cara wandered toward the Forum. A peek inside the front doors revealed it to be as abandoned as the parking lot. No smell of a meal cooking in the kitchen, no hum of women working in offices or chatting in the computer lab. I worried we were too late and Robyn was gone, maybe Sage herself.

"Where is everyone?" I asked, afraid something else had happened in my absence.

Cara looked at her watch. "The season is over," she said, confirming a date. "There's a weeklong break to prepare for the next arrivals." We walked along the Forum toward the houses. The sky was gray over Salthouse, the ocean a deeper shade of the same. A figure was standing silent and leaning against the Forum back wall.

"Lainey?"

If it surprised her to be confronted with two would-be ghosts, she didn't show it. She took one more drag from her hand-rolled cigarette and dropped it to the ground. Her sneaker snubbed it out, dragging it against the concrete; it left a gray streak of ash.

—⚊—

Lainey sneered. "Cara. You've returned. Sage said you would." Her face softened. "She will be so happy to see you. Come on."

So Sage was still here. "Where's Robyn?" I asked.

"Gone. Like everyone else."

We walked through the empty houses, tall and somber, some with front doors left open as if the residents had evacuated in the middle of a disaster.

"Where did Robyn go?"

Lainey shrugged. "I didn't do an exit interview with everyone, you know?" She gazed at me. "You didn't bother to say goodbye either."

Cara searched my face as I stared ahead.

—◦◦◦—

Sage was in her kitchen when we arrived. She was listening to pop music and dancing barefoot, holding a glass of wine, dressed in a red satin jumpsuit I remembered her wearing from my very first night in Salthouse. She twirled, and it gathered around her curves, flowed over her skin—a queen holding court for nobody in a ruined kingdom. Cara grabbed my hand and squeezed, along with a glance. Her eyes were wide. I nodded, like, *Yeah, this isn't the half of it.*

"I brought some friends," Lainey called over the sweet synth beats.

Sage snapped her head toward us. "Ah! My friends are here," she sang to the tune of the music. The wineglass sang as she placed it a little too hard on the stone countertop. Lainey, with a frown, located the speaker and turned the music off. Sage gathered us in an embrace. "More than friends," she said, slurred. "My prodigal sisters return."

I peeled myself from her arms. Cara remained. She rested her head on Sage's shoulder. "I missed you and this place." They unfolded. Cara brushed a piece of hair from Sage's face. "Hey," she said. "What happened?"

Sage's eyes narrowed. "What happened was a mutiny attempt. An insurrection. I'm so glad you weren't here to see it, Cara. Don't worry, I took care of it all."

With a flip of her wrist, she tossed the glass over her shoulder. It shattered across the floor; the wine spilled like blood. Cara flinched against me, her fingers trembling as they searched for mine.

"Ooh, I have something to show you. Come, come." In a manic burst, Sage jogged past us and up the stairs.

"I think we've seen enough." I directed Cara toward the door. Lainey blocked us.

"Probably best to go upstairs," she muttered.

"So, you were next in line for lapdog when Nicklin left?" I asked Lainey. Her expression remained the same. Cara and I reluctantly walked up the stairs.

CHAPTER 43

Sage's office was covered with papers. If one were to squint, it might look like a snowfall had occurred in the room. Loose documents were tossed across every open space. Sage sat at her desk and invited us to sit across from her. I spotted the deer antler on top of a pile of papers, a deadly paperweight.

She presented us with a folder. "Here." She opened it and flipped through papers that looked to be legal documents. "It took me forever to find them. He didn't want me to know," Sage said, almost chuckling. "You'll never believe it. Everett took the steps of drawing up papers as if you were already partners. So, in the event of his death, you are his beneficiary."

"Me?" asked Cara. "I don't understand."

"He left his share of everything to you. You're a fifty percent owner of Artemis."

Cara shook her head. "I don't want it."

"That's what I knew you would say." Sage nodded. "So, you have to do the right thing here, Cara." She handed her a pen and riffled through her stack until she found the right page. "Here. Sign there, and all of this is over."

Cara took the paper and stared blankly before looking to me. "I don't . . ."

"Let me see." I read it quickly. "This says you relinquish your ownership to your share in Artemis." I shook my head. "Cara, this is why she needed to find you. She needed you to sign this document."

"That's all you wanted?"

"Don't be silly," Sage cooed. "Cara, I missed you so much. I called you home as soon as I thought it was safe. Think about it. But then again, Everett is still missing—"

"Cut the bullshit. I know everything," I said. The flash of panic in Sage's eyes was beyond satisfying.

"Then you know how much danger Cara is in," she said. "Who do you think the authorities will look at first when they see Everett changed his last will and testament to leave Cara everything days before he was murdered?"

Cara inhaled. "It was an accident," she whispered.

"Was it?" Sage asked. "I can't protect you forever, Cara. The smartest thing to do is to sign it over and cut all ties with Artemis. It's not too late to start over."

"Wait a minute," I interjected, remembering my purpose of retribution. "Maybe Cara is owed for the emotional and physical trauma she endured here. And I don't think she's the only one. Cara, you can take your share of the profits and repair the lives destroyed by Everett."

"Ridiculous," laughed Sage. "We hardly destroyed her life. In fact, we were there when she needed us most. Where were you, Delia? Where were you when she needed you?"

"Enough," snapped Cara. She turned to me. "Delia, she's right. Artemis and Everett helped me get through a dark time. They're a part of who I am, and I owe them this much. Especially after I"—her eyes filled with tears—"what I did. Don't you see? I took her brother from her. I can't take his legacy from her as well."

I couldn't argue anymore. We had spent too much time here already. "So sign," I said. "And let's get the hell out of here."

Cara took the pen and signed. Sage grinned and cradled the paper in both hands. "I knew you'd understand, Cara. There's no need for you to go. I want you to stay here. You can help me rebuild, stronger than ever. I need you."

I stood and held Cara's arm. "Come on," I urged. "We need to go home."

She peeled my fingers from her skin. "Don't you see how badly she needs my help?"

"What do you mean?"

"I mean, I am home."

Enough, I thought. *I can't save her if she doesn't want to be saved.* "Fine," I said, my skin hot. "Goodbye, Cara." *I have to get to the garden.* I held back the coming tears as I turned to leave.

The door opened, and in walked Jenny, holding a tray with two steaming mugs.

"Ah!" Sage clapped her hands. "Who's thirsty?"

"Jenny?" I gasped. "You're here?"

"Why wouldn't I be?" She set the tea tray down on the desk and gave a cup to Sage. The scent was familiar, orange, cinnamon and herbs, though I couldn't quite place it. I watched Sage take a sip of the drink. Jenny gave the next cup to Cara, who drank with glassy eyes. When Jenny offered me the third cup, I placed a hand on her arm.

"Are you okay?" I asked.

"Why wouldn't she be?" a male voice said from the door. A voice I knew too well. "Cara?" he said. "Is that you?"

"I'm asking Jenny," I told Nicklin.

"It's okay," Jenny said. "Nicklin and Sage love me. They won't hurt me." She held my gaze steady. "Or leave me."

Unseen fingers of guilt gripped around my neck, squeezing hard. "I had to leave, Jenny. I was afraid of what they were going to do—" She shoved the teacup into my hand; a hot splash spilled over my hand, and I sucked air through my teeth. I muttered to Cara, "We have to go."

"First, a toast," said Sage, standing and holding out her drink.

Cara stood and raised her hand as well. I joined, keeping one eye on Jenny and Nicklin standing in the doorway. I would not be surprised with a needle again. Our cups clinked, and I put the rim to my mouth, pretending to allow the spicy warmth to flow into my mouth and throat. I put the cup back on the tray. "Now, let's go."

Cara hesitated. "Delia . . . she needs me."

"You don't owe anything to her. Leave with me now."

"I can help her." Cara looked to Sage.

Sage smiled. "It's true, Delia. Soon, I'll be alone. Everyone is leaving. It's a new dawn at Artemis. Lainey is moving to our East Coast offices to lead the new reforms I'm implementing. When I reach Stacey, I'm ordering her to be in California permanently to head a new push for recruiting." She glanced down. "If you haven't noticed, our numbers are down. Not for long! And of course, I'll be lost without Dr. Nicklin, who's leaving tomorrow for Laos."

Jenny's eyes widened and her mouth hung open. "You're leaving? What's in Laos?" she asked, stunned.

"Besides a lack of extradition laws?" I added.

Nicklin ran a hand through greasy hair and looked down. "Ah, well, I was going to tell you, Jen. It was a surprise—"

"For both of us?" Jenny asked, her eyebrows raising.

"Of course not," I scoffed. I looked at Nicklin. "Tell her."

Nicklin stammered, "I thought I'd check it out first for us and let you know when you could join me."

Jenny shook her head. "No, no, you promised you wouldn't leave me." She let out a tortured cry. "Where will I go now?"

Sage jumped in. "I'm sure Nicklin can get you a ticket back home to LA." It was brutal; even Sage didn't want her anymore. Nicklin's damaged goods.

"LA?" Jenny paused. "I have nothing in LA anymore. Because of you. You told me to break my lease and fire my agent . . ."

"And think of the growth it allowed you," Nicklin said. He was creeping around the room, putting distance between himself and Jenny.

"This is what he does," I said, sensing Jenny was so close to seeing it all. "He uses women to get what he wants. It's what Everett did, too, Jenny. Artemis is nothing but a way to make those men feel like gods and assert their will over others. We were all tricked, Jenny. Even me."

"You!" screamed Nicklin. "You were jealous of Jenny. You wanted to ruin everything for everyone else because you got hurt once." Jenny walked by Cara and me, toward Nicklin, who was now braced against the windows that framed sea and sky. She was whimpering and nodding.

"I understand," she said.

"You do?" Nicklin's face lifted. She was directly in front of him now. "I knew you would. It's why I like you the best, Jenny."

Her movement was so swift, I almost didn't see the antler in her hand, the knife-edge point raised. I hadn't even seen her pick it up from the desk as she passed. Her body stayed still while her arm arced and pierced the spike through Nicklin's chest. Nicklin's muscles racked against the sudden penetration. He fell against the glass. He opened his mouth, but only thick blood poured out.

Cara screamed.

Nicklin looked down at his chest and watched as Jenny pulled the antler out; bones crunched, and he let out a sharp scream. She raised her arm to inflict another blow. As she brought her hand down again, Nicklin held his arm out. The antler glanced off his forearm, bone ricocheting off bone, and her blow fell hard against the glass above his shoulder. The window shattered. As Nicklin's body fell through the cascade of crystal shards, he grasped toward Jenny. His fingers hooked through the loop of her moonstone necklace, pulling her with him.

A terrible explosion of metal and glass as the whole of the window fell, with the two of them at the center; then they were gone.

Cara, Sage, and I ran to the edge, as close as we dared, and looked down. On Sage's overgrown lawn, Jenny and Nicklin lay next to one another, a dark pool forming around each of their heads. *No!*

Cara lurched forward onto the carpet; she held her head. "I don't feel so good . . ."

The tea. Cinnamon and orange and the memory of the initiation.

Sage only watched, stone faced. I reached for Cara, she toward me. I felt a blow to the head, and my vision narrowed to a pinhole, and I slipped through it.

CHAPTER 44

The smell of wet dirt and fertilizer brought me back to consciousness. *How long have I been out?* My eyelids were heavy, and my limbs were like rocks. I wiggled my fingers and dug into soil underneath me. I was in the garden.

Scritch scritch. The gravelly chime of a shovel against earth echoed through my pounding head. Someone was digging a hole. I forced my eyes to open and looked up at the sky. I swung out my arm around me and craned my neck behind me. Bags of soil, stacks of small black seedling pots, bricks.

The digging stopped. I was out of time.

My arm whipped above me and grabbed a brick. I pulled it back to me and tucked it against my thigh.

Just as Lainey came into sight, I squinted my eyes so they would appear closed. A grunt; her hands underneath my armpits to pull me. I opened my eyes. Gripping the brick tight, I heaved it toward her with all my strength. I felt the brick's edge make contact and then a sharp crack as it hit bone. She screamed.

Dirt flew. I swung again. This time, a solid, sickening blow on her head. Her screaming stopped.

I rolled away, then scrambled to my knees and dropped the brick. A quick check of her pulse confirmed she was only knocked out. This was my chance. I fought through the dizziness and stumbled. The ground disappeared from under me. My body hit the bottom of the freshly dug pit with a crash; I had knocked all the air from my lungs by running straight into my grave.

I kicked and grasped at the earthen walls. *I have to get out.* It was shallow, and I had nearly climbed back to the surface when I recoiled. Something had emerged from all my disturbance of the soil.

A lily-white hand, marbled with blue veins, stuck out.

No, I thought, *Please don't be Cara. No, no, no, no.* I grabbed the hand and dug furiously around it. It wasn't Cara's face that I wiped the dirt from. "Oh, Robyn." I sobbed. Robyn was relatively fresh, I observed, my stomach turning. She hadn't been there long, was the point. *How many bodies has Lainey buried here?* The acidic vomit bubbled up in my throat. I was next. The disturbing part was I knew Lainey didn't wish me harm. It was on Sage's orders, of course. Lainey, like Jenny and even Cara, was so lost in the Wares' hypnotic rhetoric. She would kill to protect them and Artemis.

The last remnants of fog lifted from my brain. I climbed out of the hole and sat to catch my breath and figure out my next move.

I remembered Lainey's words from our first day working in the garden. "Sage had us tear out the veggies in the west corner. She wanted a new bed built up but never told us to plant anything, so we put a tarp over it." An empty pile of dirt in a garden full of dirt beds would be a pretty perfect place to hide a body, now that I thought about it. Or even a few.

I grabbed the shovel Lainey had left on the ground. The tarp flew off. The bed was weedy, if undisturbed. I dug. With every shovelful of dirt, I hoped I was wrong. I hoped there was nothing, only weeds and earthworms. I didn't have to dig long to be proved wrong. The shovel struck the body with a sharp twang.

I moved the soil from the head and found the body was facedown. The decomposition was extreme, thanks to the garden bed rich with worms and insects. I could still tell it was a man. With a sick realization, I dug into where the body's feet would be. A single blue sneaker emerged from the dirt. The other foot was half rotted and bare.

I knew who it was.

Except he didn't get up. So I tried to help him up, and that's when I saw a piece of his scalp fall away, and the blood beneath.

Lainey gasped behind me. She held her head, blood sticky in her hair. "Oh my God," she wailed. "I didn't hurt him."

"I know you didn't."

Something wasn't right. The head was smooth; from the back, the skull looked intact.

I remembered Cara's words. *All the blood coming from the back of his head.* Had she misremembered? I remembered Madelyn broken in the street. I knew what position her rag doll limbs were in as they swam in a pool of her own blood. No, you didn't forget something like that.

I reached out my hands, trembling. I looked away and took a breath, trying not to dwell on the fact that I was touching a corpse. Before I lost my nerve, I gave a push to expose the side of the body. The face emerged just enough to see clearly; it was completely caved in.

Lainey retched behind me. *Cara wasn't responsible.* I had a good guess as to who was.

"Where are they?" I demanded.

Lainey glanced at me, like an afterthought. "She lied to us all." Her eyes returned to the corpse of her long-lost leader. "She did this." Her voice jagged and sharp as a handsaw as she fell to her knees.

"Lainey," I snapped. "Where are they?"

She lifted an arm toward the beach. *Shit.*

I ran.

CHAPTER 45

Sage was waist deep in the water when I reached them. She held Cara's limp body, the white spray of the surf breaking against them. I raced down the sand and screamed at Sage to come back. "Stop!" I yelled. My feet hit the water, and my muscles seized. The water, the darkness awaiting beneath the surface. My breath quickened.

They were getting into deeper water. Cara's body floated clumsily on the waves as Sage's arms pulled her ever farther. I was helpless to stop them.

Except I wasn't. Zee wasn't waiting for me out there; not anymore. Nobody was here to save us. Nobody except me.

The water hit my legs, and I drove forward. My muscles contracted involuntarily, and my insides were buzzing. Everything in my body screamed for me to stop, to turn back. I went on. I was moving too slowly. Sage and Cara were drifting farther away from me. "Don't hurt her," I called.

"I'm saving her!" Sage called back.

A panicked voice rang over the surf. "Delia, help!"

"Cara!" She'd come to. Cara pushed Sage away and fell into the water. She didn't come up. "Cara!" I dove into the water. In the swirling dark, between the push and pull of the waves, I looked, fighting through the stinging of my eyes in the salt water. *There she is.* I swam with all the strength I could conjure; then she was lost again in the foam and confusion.

I surfaced and filled my lungs before going down again. In the haze, I reached through the water, and our hands met, fingers intertwining. When we came up again, it was together. Cara gasped. "Are you okay?" I choked. She nodded, wiping the salt water from her reddened eyes. "Cara," I said. "You didn't kill Everett—"

Hands grasped my neck from behind. I stole a shallow breath before I plunged below once more. I clawed at her fingers as the pressure on my esophagus built. My feet kicked wildly against nothing. My lungs were burning; the air was running out. *This is it.* Suddenly, the weight of Sage lifted. My body leaped to the surface, and I burst through. I breathed in. Now, it was Cara hanging on to Sage. Cara pushed Sage's head under the waves; Sage's arms waved wildly.

"Cara!" I screamed, my voice ragged and hoarse. I held on to her arm and pulled her away. "Leave her! We have to get back to shore."

Cara and I dove into the water and began swimming to the shore. I kept my eyes on her by my side the entire time. We were barely off the shoreline, but when my feet hit the sand of the beach, I'd crossed an ocean. I fell onto the coastline. Cara collapsed next to me, and we lay there for far too long. "Come on," I sputtered, spitting up water. "We have to go."

Before we could rise to our feet, Sage was standing over us. How had she reached the shore so fast?

"I'm trying to help you," she snarled.

"You killed him!" I spat. "This whole time you made Cara believe she was the one, but it was you."

Cara shook her head. "No, Delia, I told you. I saw him die."

"After you pushed him? He fell on a rock and hit the back of his head?"

Cara nodded.

"I found his corpse in the garden, Cara. He didn't have any injuries to the back of his head. The front of his skull, on the other hand"—I gazed up to Sage, silently looming above us—"it was completely smashed in."

"Don't listen to her," said Sage, her voice calm.

"Shall we take a walk and look?" I threatened. "He's right there, close to Robyn."

Cara blanched. "What do you mean?"

"I mean Sage will do anything to take Artemis and keep it. Even kill her brother. Even kill her friends."

"You don't understand," Sage said, almost too quiet to hear above the waves. "He took everything from me and made me play the role of doting sister, the complicit woman, as dumb as his acolytes who threw themselves at him. And I did it all, everything he said. Even as he took Artemis and began twisting it into a dark version of itself, a thing it wasn't supposed to be. I let him have his fun. And then . . ."

She looked behind her, out to the sea, now serene. My hand found Cara's, and we both tried to find our footing, leaning against each other as our shoes sank into the dark, wet sand.

Before I could stand, the already precarious breath in me was knocked out again, and I found myself facedown in the sand. Sage was on my back, talking to nobody. Her fingers once again curled around my throat, and on dry land, I felt their sure grip. "And then he wanted her too? The only friend I have ever had, and he couldn't let me have her. He wanted to take Cara from me just to show me he could. He couldn't let me have anything. So, I realized what I had to do to get what I wanted. I had to do what Everett did all along. Take it for myself."

I turned my head, grasped behind me, but I couldn't reach her. My muscles were at their limit, and the strength was draining from my body. I inhaled and strained to find any open passages for oxygen. There were none. I was suffocating.

"He was going to take her and cut me out," she spat. Then, suddenly quiet, Sage leaned down, her lips right next to my right ear. "Hey, Delia," she said, soothing. "You went into the ocean. This is what we call a breakthrough."

A crack of bones and flesh. The pressure on my throat released, and my body convulsed for oxygen.

Sage's body rolled off and fell right next to me, her face facing my own, eyes rolled backward and her breathing stilled. I turned over to find Cara standing over me; she held a large piece of gnarled driftwood in her hands; the veins jutted from her muscled arms. She straddled Sage's unconscious body and raised the driftwood over her head for one more fatal blow. I jumped up and caught the heavy wood as it came down. It stopped inches from Sage's face.

"No," I said, my voice just above a whisper. "Enough."

She silently dropped the wood and rolled off Sage. She curled up on the wet sand; her balled fists pushed into her eyes, and she cried. With an ache in my lungs and heart, I placed a hand on her shoulder. Her mourning was my own, and I was heartbroken for what we had all of us lost on that beach.

"Come on," I said to her. "We have to keep moving."

When we passed the bodies in the garden, Cara stopped to throw up seawater and bile into a patch of herbs. My fingers found the little plastic baggie between the tomato plants right away. Who knew Sage and I would use the same hiding place for our darkest secrets.

After calling 911 from the Forum phones, we found towels and wrapped them around us. We sat on the Forum steps until the blue-and-red lights turned in from the highway. They found Lainey and Sage right where we'd left them. Sage came to at the click of the handcuffs tightening around her wrists. While the paramedic examined my esophagus, I watched Sage being led to the police car. Before her head ducked underneath the car roof, our eyes met. She looked a million miles away.

Perhaps she was contemplating her fate, what would happen next, maybe even regretting everything. More likely, I thought, she was retracing the path that had brought her to this moment, which turns in the road she had missed that might have allowed her to triumph.

CHAPTER 46

The rain hit the window above my bed. From my position in my sheets, the tops of the apartment buildings rose above me, surrounding me. It was a strange feeling, yet in those days I was safest in the city's closeness, which I used to loathe. The morning was the hardest, of course. I woke up alone and ate alone. I didn't even have the monotony of a job to distract me anymore; maybe I could have saved it by responding to long-overdue client emails and explaining away the monthslong radio silence with a medical emergency or some sort of lie. What was the point, anyway?

So, instead, I spent my days getting reacquainted with myself. I welcomed the rain now. In my mind, it gave me an excuse to not leave my apartment and not feel guilty about it. I sat with my coffee and tried to read this book or watch this show. Sometimes it even worked, and I forgot.

Then, at some point again, I remembered.

We had returned to Washington as we had left, in silence. This time we were also in mourning. For Robyn, for Artemis, and for the pieces of ourselves we'd left behind at Salthouse Place.

I dropped Cara off at her house.

"Delia, I . . ."

"There's no need to say anything. Not yet. Go home."

She nodded and got out of the car. Tom opened the front door before she reached it. They embraced, and I turned my face to the rearview mirror as I put my car in reverse. Tom rapped on my window with a knuckle.

I rolled it down. "Hey."

"I don't know what to say." Tears were in his eyes. "You brought her home, like you said you would. I'm sorry, Delia."

"What for?"

"Everything." He bit his lip, as if he wanted to say more.

"See ya, Tom. Don't lose her again, please." I waved and rolled up the window, driving away before they were even inside.

At home in Portsgrove, I slept for days, it seemed. I turned the flash drive around in my hand at the dinner table.

"What will you do with it?" asked Mom.

"I want to make them pay for what they did." I swallowed hard and closed my fingers tight around the plastic corners, as sharp as vengeance.

"It's going to be a tough road," Mom said. "Do you know anyone with the dedication to take this on?"

A specific bleeding-heart lawyer came to mind. "Yeah, I might know a certain someone."

I dropped it off at Ren's downtown office the next week, though I was too embarrassed to stay. She called me later and asked me to explain what she was looking at on the drive. I told her everything. She'd promised she would do what she can, though she would still need eyewitnesses and survivors to come forward. I got to work on a list of names. As an afterthought, I had told her to make sure her investigators checked Sage's locked desk drawers.

Even though it was a rainy day, I got dressed and left the apartment. I zipped up my raincoat, took my bag, and put the hood over my hair, bunching the strands as I tucked them behind my neck. I walked the long route to get to the café, passing by a flower shop and stopping to look at the arrangements in the window. A memory of Jenny arranging wildflowers tugged at a small hidden part of my mind; I pushed it back into the dark. A group of skyscrapers and ever-present construction cranes pierced the clouds overhead.

I reached the café and lingered outside, indulging in the muted colors and sounds of the city in the rain. I let my hood fall from my hair and allowed the cool raindrops to dance on my skin for a moment.

Inside, I found a table and placed a manila folder in front of me, smoothing it out every few minutes. Every time the bell above the café door dinged, I looked up. Downtown was bustling at this morning hour. It continued to amaze me that this was the world I had come from, grown up in and known so well, yet it was now so foreign. Sometimes I wondered if I could ever thrive in this world again. From somewhere beneath the surface, Sage's voice asked me if I had ever been thriving, or was I surviving day to day? Which prompted the question, Who would want to live like that at all?

Ding.

It still wasn't Ren coming through the door; I knew who it was all the same. Before I could turn, he saw me. Teddy's face broke into a wide, toothy grin. "Hey, Delia!" He approached my table, ignoring my thin-lipped fake smile. "Wow, it's been forever. How are you?"

"Good, good." I held my palms down on the folder. "I've been good."

"Well, that's . . . good." He gestured behind him. I hadn't even noticed the person he'd come in with. "Ah, do you remember Nicky?"

She wrapped her arms around Teddy's waist and, yes, I remembered her. "Of course, from the polar plunge. Hi."

"Hi," she replied. She looked at Teddy. "Babe, what're you having?"

"Oat milk latte," he said. She kissed him, not so subtly marking her territory. I had to keep myself from laughing. She joined the line to order.

"Congrats," I said, watching her steal small glances our way.

"For what? Oh, Nicky? Yeah, thanks, she's cool. Delia, you . . ." He paused and examined me, like he was searching for something he couldn't quite name. "You look good. Is it cheesy to say you've got a glow around you?" He chuckled. "Because you do."

"Huh, well, I have spent a lot of time at the beach recently."

Before Nicky returned with two lattes, we caught up as much as two exes can or want to. We told each other to take care; it was so nice seeing you; goodbye. A glow, he said.

In a moment of weakness, I pulled up Brayden's unanswered text. I responded and thanked him for thinking of me and my need for a pager; I'd love to have it returned.

I didn't even hear the ding before Ren appeared before me. "Jesus, it's really you." She sat in the empty chair across from me. The air was heavy with everything said and unsaid between us in the recent months. I wanted to hug her. So I did. I almost leaped over the tabletop to embrace her.

"I'm so sorry," I said. "For everything I said and did. Please forgive me."

"Of course I forgive you. All I wanted was for you to be okay. Maybe you had to do what you did to get there."

"It doesn't make it okay."

She pulled a large binder from her purse. "This might."

"Is that . . ." I paused.

She nodded. "The case I'm building. From fraud to conspiracy to sexual assault, this is everything. I'm sure you heard Madelyn's family is also bringing a wrongful death suit against the organization. I wouldn't be surprised if more lawsuits come out once this all goes public."

"So, is it really going to be over?"

She nodded. "Thanks to you. You wouldn't believe what was in those files, Delia. Did you ever look yourself?"

I hadn't been able to bring myself to. "No."

"We can bring charges against them in Seattle because of the seminars they had here. I'm working with the federal court on the rest. If Everett was alive, he would wish he weren't. Not to mention the bodies; we can bury Sage with those."

I flinched. "Those women aren't just bodies." I thought of Robyn and missed her, in all her harshness. I thought of Madelyn and the significant loss to women-led innovation in tech. And Jenny . . . God, poor Jenny. "They were there for their own reasons, but they didn't deserve to die."

"Of course." Ren softened. "Sorry, I know I can speak callously about all of it. Jesus, you lived it. You're right; we'll make sure they get justice."

"Did you find Stacey?"

"We did. She's agreed to cooperate and tell us everything she knows. She will be an invaluable source."

My hands folded over themselves. "How is *she* doing?"

"I don't know for sure. My contacts say Sage will cooperate. The warden tells me she's quite sociable and is making friends. Imagine, she's got what she's craved, an entire population to evangelize."

"A captive audience," I noted. Ren laughed out loud, and the corners of my mouth pulled outward. *This is what it's like to joke and sit with a friend in a coffee shop in the world. This is what it's like to laugh again.*

Ren looked at my folder. "For me?"

I slid it over. "All the names I could remember."

"Thank you, Delia." She slipped it into her bag. "Out of curiosity, is Cara Snyder one of the names? Stacey's testimony will be damning to Artemis Wellness as a whole, but we need someone who really knew the Wares personally. Do you think she'll work with us?"

"I hope so. I'm going to Portsgrove this weekend to speak with her. I wanted her to hear it from me first."

She nodded, then placed a folder of her own in front of me. It was thick and held closed by a rubber band. "I have something for you too."

I read the labeled tab at the edge. *Sage Ware.* I lifted the corner to see a worn binding and tattered page edges. "Is this . . . ?"

Ren raised her hands. "There were so many boxes of possible evidence we took from Sage's office." She lowered her voice and gestured toward the folder. "These weren't relevant. Things from when she was a minor, so they would be protected anyway. If anyone asks, you didn't get it from me." She tenderly pushed it toward me. "I thought her secrets would be safest with you."

"Thank you." I nodded.

"So now what?" Ren asked.

I shook my head. "How do you mean?"

"The case will take a long time, maybe years. You can't stay around here and wait for—"

"I know." I headed her off at the pass. "I'm thinking of looking at grad schools again. Maybe not law school, but something where I can become my own person, for once."

"It's good of you, Delia."

"Thanks, I'm working on it. Self-awareness and all."

She grinned. "Huh, I gotta get me some of that."

"You know, I might have a buddy code you can use."

By the time I got home, it was midafternoon. I dropped my bag and its contents on the dining table and distracted myself with laundry. When I ran out of clothes, I opened the fridge and stared inside, telling myself I would make dinner first. I uncorked a bottle of Malbec instead. Against the falling dark outside, I watched the bloodred wine flow into the glass like a tiny wave.

Finally, I undid the rubber band and opened the folder to find a black-and-white composition notebook. Sage's journal. My fingers ran along the soft pages, the papers recounting an entire life on display. I traced my fingers over her handwritten words and began to read.

CHAPTER 47

Then

Dear Diary,

When I arrived this morning, it was snowing. The white snuffed out the harsh angles of the roof and quieted the sobbing as they walked me through fluorescent-lit halls and opened a door.

I glanced in. There's someone in there, I told the nurse.

My roommate, they explained. Did you think you would get your own suite? They clucked, You're a fifteen-year-old girl and this isn't the Ritz. They called the girl Judith and introduced me.

This is Sage.

They told Judith to show me the way to group at three and didn't even wait for the door to swing closed before they were halfway down the hall again.

The girl didn't look up. The metal frame squeaked beneath the weight of my suitcase. What are you here for? she asked.

I thought you weren't supposed to ask people that. Or is that in prison?

I thought about telling her the truth: the girls at school had finally pushed me over the edge, their jeering and laughs and looks of pity just got too much. I thought about how even the principal looked ill when he finally broke up the fight. Everything was bloody, but nobody could tell what was worse—my knuckles or her face.

I gathered my hair across my forehead and it fell over my eyes. I looked down at the bruises still there on my hands. The black and blue seeped into the color of my veins through my skin. I guess Mom and Dad, when the school counselor eventually reached them, actually cried. That's what Everett said. That's not what I meant when I told you to stand up for yourself, he said. I felt bad then. Not about hitting the girl, but about disappointing Everett. I hate when he looks at me that way. In the follow-up parent-teacher conference calls, I heard words like *brain chemistry imbalance* and *residential treatment facility*. I guess they found this place to fix me.

Only Everett was there to say bye when the car came to pick me up.

I realized Judith was staring, still waiting for an answer. I gave her the line my parents used when explaining me to relatives: I have an emotional disorder. It's so much cleaner than major depressive disorder, so much nicer than severe social anxiety.

Yeah, same. Judith turned back to her book. She told me she tried to kill herself.

I didn't know how to react. I asked what she was reading.

A book about Greek mythology, she said. There's not a lot in the library, but I've checked this one out a hundred times since I've been here.

I asked her how long that's been.

She counted her fingers before replying, Eight months now. Anyway, look—she showed me a page from her book. This is Artemis, Goddess of the Hunt. She's a badass.

Eight months? I couldn't believe it. My parents said I would be here for the weekend.

Judith chuckled. Classic, she said.

I pushed my suitcase off and it hit the linoleum floor with a bang. In its place, I lay back and curled up onto the stiff mattress, clutching the pillow that scratched my cheeks. Judith narrowed her eyes at me. She asked, What's wrong with you?

I tell her Everett says I have a fragile heart; I just feel too much.

Who's that, she asked.

My older brother, I say. I add that he's my best friend, even though he's a few years older.

She rolled her eyes and turned around to face the wall with her book.

I feel so alone; this is the first time I'm by myself. Mom and Dad were always gone, of course. But how can I live here without Everett? *Eight months? I think I'll die if I'm here for even eight days.*

—⁂—

Dear Diary,
It's been a week and if I wasn't crazy already, this place is making me insane. It's just like school again; dumb assignments while the other girls hate me and call me weird. I spend all my time alone, except for at night when Judith and I are sleeping. Or when I'm trying to sleep, but Judith is always singing along to

her headphones. It's annoying, but I'm too nervous to tell her to stop.

The only thing I have to look forward to are Everett's calls every morning, even if I only have a few minutes on the community phone in the hall. He told me I'm going to be fine, that I'm just very ill and need to listen to what the counselors tell me to do.

Are Mom and Dad coming to visit soon, I asked.

He told me they're abroad again, but they told him to go ahead and pay for whatever I need. When the forms came for parental permission to raise my medication doses, he went ahead and forged their signatures, he said. He promised it will be better soon. I don't know how that could be possible.

The white clean walls are moving closer every day. Soon, they're going to crush me. I need to get out of here.

—◊—

Dear Diary,

Mom and Dad were supposed to visit, but the nurses just said they won't make it. Typical. They never showed up when I wasn't in a loony bin. So, I don't know why I ever thought it would be different now. Judith found me crying on the floor, she sat down with me and didn't say a word.

Wiping away the tears, I looked at her looking at me. They canceled again? she asked. I nodded. She leaned against me and set her chin on my shoulder. The pressure of her touch was alarming and I couldn't help but jump. She laughed. She laughed at me!

I won't bite you, she said.

They're going to some gala across the country, I explained. They're taking Everett. They love him more, I admit through the sobs. He's smart and funny and charming. My palms against my cheeks are hot and wet. He's not the crazy ugly child.

Judith snapped, No! You're not ugly. Softly, she took a lock of my hair between her fingers, sliding them down the long strands to the very end near the middle of my chest. She whispered again, You're not ugly, Sage.

I couldn't help it. So, you're saying I am crazy?

Her eyes lit up and she smiled: I didn't even know you knew what a joke was! Despite all of my efforts, I smiled too.

Reaching toward me, she felt another handful of my hair. My fingers met her own, then waved her away. Don't, I said. I hate my hair.

Why?

It's so thin. Girls at school said it was the color of piss water.

Judith burst out laughing. What? I flashed with anger.

Nothing. She covered her mouth. I mean, piss water *is* golden so . . .

I smiled again: Don't even!

Isn't it obvious? They're jealous of you, she said. They want to make sure you never feel on the inside the way you look on the outside, because then . . .

Then what?

Because then, she said. Those bitches are in real trouble.

I could have kissed her. But I've never kissed anyone before; the idea makes me woozy. We're both asleep in our own beds now and I wonder if, when we both get out, maybe Judith and I can be real friends.

—⁂—

Dear Diary,
Judith stole a pair of scissors from the front desk. She's not supposed to have them because of the whole attempted suicide thing, but that's bullshit because she used pills. Anyway, she came into the room and showed me.

Should I be worried, I asked. To be honest, the sparkle in her brown eyes was a bit concerning. What are you up to?

A makeover, she beamed.

Considering she didn't have a mirror and the scissors weren't really for haircuts, it turned out really well! My long stringy piss water hair is gone—Judith cut a neat bob. Chic, she said. When I went to the bathroom to see, I couldn't stop smiling. The shape frames my face without hiding it; the strands lift without the unhealthy ends weighing them down. Judith was so pleased with herself. Sometimes a haircut is the best therapy, she said.

It's perfect, I told her. When Everett visits, I know he'll love it too.

—⁂—

Dear Diary,
It's been three months. My quarterly assessment came back with significant improvements seen, it said. They don't let me read the whole file, of course, but the counselors said I've shown great progress. I might even

be able to go home soon. Judith and I jumped up and down and screamed with joy when I told her. Even though she said she would be sad to see me go, she was happy for me.

I asked her when she was leaving, but she changed the subject, saying something about a new Greek mythology book she wanted to read to me. We lay down side by side on the tiny twin bed and she held the book above us while reading the words.

It's not really this place that's helped me, I told her as she was halfway through a sentence. She stopped and placed the book down on her chest; it rose and fell with her breaths. It's been you, I say. You've helped me see so much about myself I never could before.

I wish there were places that could teach girls this stuff without the bleach-scented hallways and medications, I said. She closed the book and let it fall to the floor as she turned to me and kissed me.

I froze as fire shot through me, as she held me hard against her but with the softest of touches. It lasted a few seconds, but that was maybe the happiest I've been in my whole life. We talked and laughed the rest of the night. Like real friends. I can't wait to tell Everett about her.

—⁂—

Dear Diary,

Everett is coming to visit tomorrow. We just spoke yesterday on the phone and after hearing about Judith and my progress, he wants to see me right away. He's so excited for me. I can't wait to show him how well everything is going.

To look my best, Judith is going to give my hair a trim with the scissors. She's kept them under her mattress because my hair grows pretty quick. I can't wait to see Everett. Maybe he can even tell me when I get to go home.

—◊—

Dear Diary,

It's all gone wrong.

The night after Everett left, they took Judith away. She's being moved into a high-risk facility. The nurses found the hidden scissors and thought she was going to try something again. I don't know what happened.

I can't help but think that Everett might have had something to do with it? He said he hated my new hair-cut and asked who did it. I told him Judith had gotten scissors and thought a new style would suit me. I told him I loved it. He seemed shocked at how I was acting. I was too fragile to be pretending I was so strong, he said. I have to admit, it gave me a strange satisfaction to see him so annoyed. He's always so cool and calm.

Well, he doesn't have to worry about her now because she's gone.

It's empty without her annoying singing and stupid books. How can I stay here now?

—◊—

Dear Diary,

I'm home.

Everett spoke to the nurses and I was discharged as a full recovery. I'm a success story. So, why do I feel like I'm broken all over again?

—∿—

Dear Diary,

He finally confessed to me. Judith was clearly a bad influence on you, he said. I was better off at home where he could monitor my treatment. He told the nurses about the scissors. He asked she be removed before she hurt herself or me.

I threw a tantrum. I've never done that before, never been that angry at him. I've never felt rage like that before. And how confusing that the rage felt so much like the flame I felt in my ribs when kissing Judith? How could hate and love be so similar? The pain was too much and my body felt like igniting. I wished myself to turn to stone just to stop feeling.

Sitting on the floor of my trashed bedroom, I ran out of tears to cry. Everett stepped around my messy desk, my tipped-over dresser with the clothes spilled out, and sat next to me. The loss of Judith was too much; the betrayal of Everett was too deep.

But then again, maybe he was right. It was too much to feel. I was too weak.

As he held me and hushed, I knew I would forgive him. I let him feed me the small pile of colorful pills from his palm. The glass of water he tilted to my mouth soothed my throat, raw from screaming. In the still aftermath, back in his arms, I wonder that I ever doubted him.

Now I know that he will always do what's best for me and him both. He's my brother and my best friend, after all. But if he ever takes someone away from me again, like he did Judith, I don't know what I'll do. I don't know if I'll be able to extinguish the searing rage a second time.

CHAPTER 48

The Snyder house was filled with boxes. Gone was the bachelor clutter, replaced instead with half-filled moving boxes and stacks of clear storage bins, heavy with possessions wrapped carefully in newspaper or bubble pack. Cara saw me surveying the scene. "My parents are selling the house."

We sat at the Snyders' dining room table, surrounded by stacks of plates sorted by size and style. A spread of fruit and cheese sat in the middle, and we ate with plastic forks.

"Sorry," Cara explained. "I already packed all the silverware." She wore black leggings and a formfitting athletic jacket, and between the sleek outfit and her washed hair, she looked like a new woman.

"I'm glad you came," she told me, picking the leaf off a bulbous strawberry. It tore apart in her fingers.

I felt a tightening of my stomach, a pang of guilt. "I would've been here sooner. I kinda needed to have my space and find my footing for a moment."

"I understand," she said, and I believed she did. "Besides, your mom comes by every other day to deliver food or magazines. She's been like a second mom to me." She smiled at a distant memory. "Again."

"I'm glad. She's been happy to have you back and healthy." I glanced over to the countertop and saw, among the packing paper, a stack of clean Tupperware, recognizing it was from the Albio household. I could spot the orange spaghetti-sauce-stained bricks anywhere.

"It's been so strange being here. My parents are coming home next week to finalize paperwork with the real estate agents and help with the last of the packing. Is it awful I'm anxious to see them? They would have been here sooner," she explained, seeing me stiffen and bite my tongue. "My dad had to finish up his business on the East Coast."

"I'm sure," I said. "Where will you go?"

"For now, back to Phoenix with Mom and Dad. After that, I dunno. I was thinking of California again. I've been craving sunshine."

"You could go to New York with Tom. He told me he's going back soon."

She looked down, her eyes focused on something on the table. "You're not here to talk about Tom. Don't think I didn't expect this visit, eventually."

I cleared my throat. "So, I guess you know about the case against Artemis?"

"Of course."

"Now the Feds are involved—"

"The Feds?"

"It's bigger than we ever imagined. My friend had to reach out to the FBI once she determined multiple crimes were being committed across state lines."

"Jesus." She sat back and took a breath. "How were we all so blind? Except for you, that is."

"They manipulated us and everyone else. We have a chance now to make them pay."

"Not them," Cara said. "Sage."

My breath caught in my throat as I remembered reading Sage's words; for a second, I thought about telling Cara about Sage's past. As someone who had been so close to her, maybe Cara deserved to know. However, when I looked at Cara's face painted in concern, I wondered that knowing might make it harder for her to accept Sage's responsibility. I could hear her reasoning. *It wasn't her fault; look at what her brother forced her to become.* I couldn't give Cara any excuse to sympathize more than she already did.

"Sage was complicit," I said. "I've been thinking and don't know what's worse. A man who victimizes women, or a woman who watches and lets it happen to other women."

"You're going to ask me to testify against her?" Cara asked.

I nodded. "We need all the witnesses we can get."

"Can I testify against Artemis Wellness as a company? Does it have to be against her?" She laughed stiffly. "I know you think I'm wrong for wanting to protect her even now, after everything. But she was a victim of Everett's too."

I leaned back. "It's not so wrong."

"I'm sorry," she said.

"For what?"

"For not being what you wanted me to be, then or now." Her loose golden hair hung over her lake-blue eyes, and though she was looking at me, I could feel she was miles away.

"You don't have to apologize." I said. "In fact, let's promise to be friends again, yeah? Remember? We get through it together."

She ate a strawberry and chewed before her juice-stained lips broke into a bright-red crescent. "Should we go on a picnic?"

"That would be nice."

We planned it for the weekend. "Can I invite someone?" I asked her.

"Of course," she replied. "Who?"

"Someone who owes me something," I said, ignoring her cryptic stare as I texted Brayden.

Interested in a picnic by a lake?

He responded right away. I like picnics and lakes.

Smiling, I texted him the location and told him I'd keep him updated with the details.

I decided not to keep pressing Cara, and we moved on to mindless talk about town and what shows we were bingeing. Soon, I excused myself to the bathroom. Down the hall, I peeked again into Cara's room, maybe out of pure force of habit. She had been busy packing in here, as well. Most everything was cleared from the already spartan room. The walls were bare; the collages and the photos gone.

A column of taped-up boxes leaned against the wall, each with her clean handwriting on the side: *Cara's Room*.

Stepping away, I turned back toward the bathroom and nearly tripped over yet another box. It read *Hallway Frames* on the side, and true to the description, it held the framed photos formerly on the hallway walls. I moved it to the side against the wall so I could pass by more easily. Then I noticed the box I had pushed it next to, one with flaps still open, filled with photo albums. The side read *Tom and Cara Photos*.

On the very top of the albums was the photo, the one of Cara and the Wares in front of their academy. I glanced back toward the dining room, but Cara was out of sight. Had she put this here on purpose, where I was sure to see it? I picked it up and looked again at the smiling faces of Cara and Sage, and even Everett.

But there was someone else too. I moved my finger to the face next to Everett. I hadn't noticed it before. How could I, in the state I had been in after seeing Cara in the picture? But now I saw that Everett had his hand on the shoulder of the person next to him. And the person wasn't a girl student. It was a boy.

Tom Snyder.

My hand flew to my mouth, and I jumped back as Cara slowly walked around the hallway corner. I held up the photo. "Both of you?" I said. "I don't understand. This was a prep school for girls."

"He wasn't a student. He worked for Everett. My parents gave them a big donation so they would take him."

"Why?" I pleaded to hear something that made sense. "How could you not tell me?"

Cara sighed. "After Zee, my parents were worried about me. They thought the Wares could help, but they also wanted Tom to keep track of me, keep me safe. How could they know that all they did was introduce two predators to each other and then give them a school full of young girls?" Cara leaned against the wall with one hand, as if she could barely stand her own weight.

My blood ran cold. It wasn't Nicklin that was Everett's protégé. It had been Tom all along, the shadowy figure behind the scenes, finding a way to make Artemis his. The Sorority initiations that Cara and Sage were expected to participate in had been run by their two brothers. I clutched my stomach and felt the walls spin. Everything felt as if it were breaking apart inside of me.

"Cara," I said softly. "How did Everett really die?"

She put her fists to her eyes and spoke. "He was always there, but in the background. The plan was for Everett and Sage to retire and for me and Tom to take their place. But then when Everett proposed to me, he told Tom he wasn't ready to let go. Everett said Tom still wasn't senior enough. Everett and I would take over instead. Tom became livid. He said he had waited long enough and that Everett was simply being greedy for the power and money."

"After," she choked, "Tom said we had to say Everett simply left on a trip; then he threatened us that if we told anyone, he would come for us next. We were both in shock. I was so scared. I would have agreed to anything to make it down that trail alive. But when we got back to the house, I knew I couldn't do it. I left that night. I tried to get Sage to come with me, but she was in love with Tom too. She fell for his lies, just like they all did."

Cara laughed bitterly and threw her hands in the air. "Why did all you stupid bitches have to fall in love with my brother?"

I couldn't believe what I was hearing. A wave of shame washed over me, but I couldn't fault Sage for trusting Tom. I had too.

"But why did you take the blame for Everett's death? Even after I found you, even when we were with Sage. Why didn't you just tell me the truth?"

"Because you're still in love with him, Delia. I saw it as soon as his name came out of your mouth. I couldn't trust that you wouldn't go right to him and tell him where I was."

My chest sank. I couldn't tell her she was wrong. "So why not just go home?"

"I knew Sage would have to officially assume power if she wanted to introduce Tom as the new leader. People would accept Sage as an interim Everett, but very few knew Tom was his protégé. Like I said, he was mostly in the shadows. Except when he wasn't . . ."

"Like on initiation nights?" I said, barely able to sound the words.

Cara nodded. "I told you I was in contact with Sage while I was at the cabin. It wasn't Sage. Tom would leave voice mails on my phone, which I left at the Portsgrove house. But every now and then I called the voice mailbox and heard all of his threats. He said if I told anyone, he would hurt Sage. And then when you showed up . . ."

"Tom threatened to hurt me?"

"Well, you saw what they did to Madelyn . . ." Her voice was rising, and I could see her becoming agitated. "I could only hope he wasn't poisoning your mind like he did Sage. You saw her at the end. She wasn't always like that. It was Everett and Tom. God, I thought I could save her."

"Shh." I moved to her and held her. I felt as if in yet another nightmare. No, the same nightmare that wouldn't end. My stomach was sick. I hadn't rescued Cara at all; I had delivered her into the hands of the person she feared most. "You really are safe now," I told her.

"I'm not," she snapped. "We're not. You don't know him, Delia. Not really. Everett wasn't the first."

I pushed away the darkness gathering in my brain; I pushed *her* face away. Not now. I couldn't comprehend that now.

"You have to come forward and testify."

Her head snapped up with horror. "No, I can't."

"It's the only way you'll be safe," I said. Maybe the only way any of us would be safe. "If both you and Sage reveal Tom was the one who killed Everett, then Sage won't be charged for his murder."

Cara dropped down, and I sat with her on the floor. "Maybe not Everett's murder." She sighed. "But others did die because of her. God, I really thought I could save her, even at the end. But I can't, can I? No matter how much I want it to be true, Sage isn't innocent."

My head dropped onto Cara's shoulder. No, she wasn't. But who of us was?

CHAPTER 49

The hiking trail was an unpaved path following the lake from the parking lots near the beach, up along the white rugged cliffside of the far end of Blythe Lake, and back around again. It went up in elevation, and from the highest point of the ridge, all the lake was on display. I hadn't hiked the trail in over a decade.

Along with the possibility of Brayden showing up, Cara and I had invited Mom and Tom to our picnic, which took on a life of its own once Mom was involved. She planned an entire menu, so Cara volunteered to be sous-chef for the picnic turned outdoor banquet, while Tom and I would go on a hike before meeting them on the beach for our lunch.

My plan was to get Tom talking about Artemis, about Everett. I held my phone in my pocket, ready to hit record when I needed. I just hoped he wouldn't notice how I froze whenever he got too close, or how I stiffened when he placed his hand on my back.

As we walked through the old-growth forest, I ignored my thundering heart and forced myself to pretend it was just another day.

By the time we reached the high point along the cliff, I used my shirt to wipe the sweat from my forehead. We stopped at a lookout to rest. I drank from my water bottle and observed the quiet black water beneath us. This was supposed to be the deepest point of the lake, I recalled. I ventured a look over the edge and instantly stepped back, my thoughts heady with the small unwanted voice somewhere inside urging me to jump.

Tom was braver and walked closer to the edge, peering over at the water below.

"Look, we can see the beach from here." He pointed to the yellow sandy shoal sticking out from the row of evergreens. Though if they were there already, I couldn't see Cara or Mom from the distance. "Will you miss me?" Tom asked, turning.

I nodded with false sadness. "Of course."

"Come with me."

My breath hitched in my throat. "What?"

"I'm serious. Come with me to New York."

"And do what?" I laughed, shaking.

"Whatever you want. We'll find a shithole apartment and put the bed underneath the window, so we can look up at the possibilities. You mentioned grad school—there's a ton of schools in Manhattan. Come with me. We've been through too much together to say goodbye now."

Two thoughts abruptly seared through me. First, I had to keep him close, keep him talking. Second, if I refused, what would he do to me? So, I nodded. "Yes, I'll go with you."

"It's settled," he said. He slapped his thigh and smiled. "I'll miss your mom and Cara, but I can't wait to get away from this lake."

The lake.

Cara's words: *Everett wasn't the first.* The phantom on the night of Zee's memorial, the one I felt stalking me.

A thought came unburied in me, unraveling in my stomach and tearing through the happiness that had barely settled. By the time it reached my head, I knew I couldn't keep stuffing it down repeatedly. I had to know for sure, even now.

My finger hovered over the record button, but I couldn't bring myself to push it. I would ask about Zee first. Then I would ask about the Wares and record that part only. I joined him at the precipice and looked straight ahead at the gray horizon. "Tell me about Zelda."

He didn't turn his head. He didn't make a sound for a long time. "It was supposed to be a joke," he said.

"A joke? You and her?"

"No. She was playing a joke on you and Cara."

Beneath the golden sun, an icy wind ripped through my skin and reached my bones. I collected my strength, my breath, to ask, "What are you talking about?"

"Zee was the first one to reach the beach. She told me she scrambled into the trees, reaching them before Cara got to shore, then watched you both look for her. When she tired of laughing at you both, she walked up to the road through the brush. I was driving by and saw her walking along the side of the road. She had a bloody nose. I asked her what happened; she only told me my sister was a bitch."

I kicked her, Cara said. *Hard.*

"She was going to hide out for a couple of hours and scare the both of you. I suggested we go back to my house. We cleaned the blood off her face, smoked some weed, watched some TV show. I can't even remember what it was now."

Through my dread, a fresh anger flared. TV? While we called the police and were sick to our stomachs with fear and worry, Zee was getting high and watching TV?

I turned to face him. His eyes stayed unwavering across the lake, though his feet betrayed him. With the toe of his sneaker, he traced the stone beneath him. He knelt down, his knee balanced on the rock ledge.

I stepped away from him. "Can you get back from the edge?"

He didn't move but continued to speak. "I don't know how long we were down there. At some point, I started kissing her. Started trying to take off her shirt, I remember. She pushed me away. She said she wanted to go back now and asked me to drive her back. I told her I would after we had sex. She told me she didn't want to. I asked her why not, since she'd done it lots of times before. She kept telling me no, and it made me so frustrated. Why wouldn't she? It made me angry. She got up, and I pulled her onto me. She screamed. I asked her did she want my parents to find her there with me? She told me maybe she did. Maybe she was sick of me and was ready to tell everybody I started having sex with her when she was thirteen." Tom turned to me now. His eyes flashed with a sick and unfamiliar rage. A hate. With a blink it was gone, and I wondered for a moment if I was remembering Nicklin's eyes in place of Tom's.

"She wanted to get me thrown in jail. Then she started screaming again. So, I grabbed her and held her mouth. Just to get her to stop screaming, you see? Delia, believe me." He stood, stepping toward me. I backed away.

Oh, Tom. He had never been who I thought he was. That man I thought I could love didn't exist.

"It was an accident. I didn't mean to. She wouldn't stop. And I couldn't let go. Until she stopped. When you and your mom dropped Cara off that night, I listened at my door and when I knew everyone was looking for Zee, thinking she'd drowned, I knew I had to do something. Once everyone was asleep, I carried her out in a blanket and put her in the trunk of my car. I had to wait weeks for them to stop trawling the lake bed. I had to rip out the entire trunk upholstery after that, it stunk so bad."

I remembered riding home in his car the night of the memorial, and my stomach roiled. I had been so close to her. "Why didn't you tell anyone? Why are you telling me now?"

"Because you asked." He looked surprised. "You're the first one to ever ask me."

I didn't ask for this. I don't want to hear this.

"You believe me, right?" he asked. "That it was an accident?" His fingers caressed my arm.

I pulled away with disgust. "Don't touch me."

He balked. "So, that's how it is." He moved back to the edge and grabbed hold of a twisting branch jutting out over the expanse. "I still can't believe they never found her. Where is she, do you think? I wonder where she might have drifted." His toes hung over the rock edge now as he searched the lake's surface. Another icy wind blew through me and enveloped him. He let go of the branch and tightened his jacket around him, turning to face me.

His goddamn beautiful face.

I didn't listen to my fear telling myself to back away. I didn't listen to my body screaming for me to keep my hands back in cowardice, or in forgiveness, maybe. *I am stronger than what I tell myself.* I kept moving.

And pushed.

Maybe it was the angle from where I stood, but I swear the wind carried him down without a sound. Even the leaves stopped their rustling, and it was me, alone in the silence. "Tom?" My voice was shaking. Once I gained the courage to step to the edge to look down, I didn't see the body, only rocks and dark water.

I screamed. "Tom!"

A surge of sickness swept through me, and I fell against a tree. The bark scratched my palms as I gripped to keep from going over the edge myself. Through tears, I vomited; the spasms racked my body until there was nothing left in my stomach.

My shoulders quaked, and my limbs shook. I pulled myself up, crouching against the roots and brush, and sobbed. I wanted to take it back. I shouldn't have done it, I knew. Ren's lawsuit; the federal case. The Wares would be brought to justice and pay for their sins, but Tom had gotten away with assault and multiple murders. It wasn't my place, I scolded myself. But then I thought of Cara and couldn't imagine the hurt she would have to go through if Tom was charged. She would have to testify against her brother. And the Harrises? Artemis was one thing, but did the Harris family have to relive Zee's disappearance all over again?

I had saved everyone from all that pain.

My shallow breaths evened out, and I pulled myself up, arms hanging limp against my side. All my insides were purged, and I was a shell with nothing left. The walk back was quiet and lonely. Every glimpse of the water through the trees, I checked to see if he was swimming to shore or if his body had floated to the surface. There was nothing. Him, sinking; her, drifting; perhaps toward one another.

With each footstep, I breathed a little easier. The initial panic subsided. I had never hit record; there wasn't any evidence. *It's not so hard,* I thought. It wouldn't be so hard to live with this, after all; it was necessary. In fact, how could I have lived with myself if I hadn't done it?

—⬩—

I had fully formed the story in my mind by the time I reached Mom and Cara on the beach. It disappointed Mom when I broke the news. "He couldn't even wait until after we ate to leave? He didn't want to say goodbye?"

I shook my head. "I guess not. He got some call and had to leave." I noticed Cara stiffen her shoulders back and swallow.

"When will he be back?" Mom asked.

I shrugged.

Cara closed her eyes and placed her fists over them. Then she lowered her shoulders and hands and smiled. "Don't worry, Ms. Albio, he does this a lot. Tom's a rolling stone. I get deemed a missing person after a couple weeks away, but Tom could be gone for months and nobody will think twice. Delia, do you want a beer?"

I held out my hands and caught the lobbed can of Rainier. "He talked about going back to New York soon anyway, Mom."

"Exactly. Now, Ms. Albio, let me help you plate up our spread." As she handed Mom a plate, Cara glanced at me and grinned. Nothing in her eyes questioned me, not even a little. We reverted to our teenage selves, and I shot her a knowing look that said, *Don't worry, everything is okay now.* She gave the tiniest nod that said, *I believe you.*

Maybe it was how nice the day was or how good Mom's food was, or maybe a combination, but at some point, I forgot what had happened on the other side of the lake. I could see the steep grades from where we sat, a grassy patch on the sandy shore. I felt nothing when I looked at the gray face of the rock wall.

It was an accident.

It was a sacrifice.

It was necessary.

Maybe one day, soon even, the consequences would come for me, like they had for the others. Or maybe not. I didn't let myself dwell on the thought. For the first time in a long time, I was committed to the present, the here and now.

Cara made us wait ten minutes before we went swimming. I glided into the water, crystal clear on this side of the lake. I floated on my back and closed my eyes; the water embraced me like a long-lost friend. I laughed to myself at the memory of being afraid of it for all those years.

I drifted and moved backward now, back to the time a trio of girls had swum in these waters without knowing it would be the last time they would all be together, never comprehending it was a moment that would hold us captive for a decade to come.

We lazed about, soaking up those last bits of late-summer glory. I took one last dip into the water. The cool drops slid from my skin, rosy from a day spent outside.

By the time Mom called out to us to head home, the buttery golden-hour light shone through the trees, and the air had turned as crisp as a bite of a Washington apple. On the path coming from the parking lot, a figure appeared, waving tattooed arms. Brayden smiled as he approached.

I waved and smiled back.

Cara paddled over to me. "Shall we?"

I took one last look across the water and reached for her. Hand in hand, we emerged.

ACKNOWLEDGMENTS

Until very recently, I was terrified of sharing my writing with anyone. This is why I am still in disbelief that so many amazing people have come together to make this book possible. Thank you to everyone.

First and foremost, my mentor and writing mama, Lyn Liao Butler. You picked me out of an actual slush pile for Pitch Wars, and my life was never the same. Thank you for seeing something in those words of mine and for always pushing me to go further. I am forever grateful!

To my agents, Sophie Cudd and Margaret Riley King—your guidance and unwavering support means so much to me. Can't wait to see what we do next. (To quote Sophie: Here we go!)

To Danielle Marshall, you saw the vision of what this book could be—thank you for believing in me.

A huge thank-you to the entire team at Lake Union and Amazon Publishing, including Jen Bentham, Kyra Wojdyla, Adrienne Krogh, Laywan Kwan, Gabriella Dumpit, Allyson Cullinan, Kathleen Carter, and Rachael Clark. The amount of work and magic that the editors and production managers poured into this book has blown my mind.

Jami Fairleigh and Jami Sheets—my Jamigos, who read this as a zero draft and who championed me from the literal first page. You ladies are my first and best writing friends, and I couldn't ask for better critique partners. I will always be thankful for your encouragement.

To Mia Manansala and Sarah Pekkanen, for sharing your wisdom with this anxious debut author. To Crime Writers of Color, for all you do for authors.

To my early beta readers, Bethany V., Jamie Lee, Bethany H., and Jessica L.—your thoughts and ideas were invaluable. To the Waffle Squad Pitch Wars Class of 2021! Thank you to Lulu, Larkin, Kaija, and Natalie—who watched my son so I could steal quiet moments to write.

Thank you to my readers—all of this is for you, after all!

To my family, near and far—I wouldn't be here without you or your support. To Mom, Dad, and Danielle—even when you never read a word (because I wouldn't let you), you believed in me. Thank you for letting me shut myself inside with a chapter book as a child during summer vacations, while all the other normal kids were playing outside.

And finally, thank you to David, the love of my life, and to Wyatt, my source of joy.

ABOUT THE AUTHOR

© 2022 Marcella Ratsamy

Jamie Lee Sogn grew up in Olympia, Washington, in a Filipino American home. She studied anthropology and psychology at the University of Washington and received her juris doctor from the University of Oregon School of Law. She is a recovering attorney who writes contracts by day and (much more exciting) fiction by night. Though she has lived in Los Angeles, New York City, and even Eugene, Oregon, she now lives in Seattle with her husband, son, and Boston terrier.